The woman sat tied to an upright chair, her arms bound from elbow to shoulder. She no longer squirmed to get free. By now she knew that wouldn't help.

"Don't you understand?" the man said again as he paced before her. His tone was distraught, worried. "You're never getting out of here if you don't tell me what I need to know."

"I'll die first, you son of a bitch," she managed through dry, cracked lips.

"It's beginning to look like you just might," he said.

But his voice shook. She knew he was close to breaking, too.

The woman bowed her head and closed her eyes. Her neck ached from holding it stiff with fear, and her eyes burned from the too-bright light she'd been under for more than seven hours. She didn't know how much more she could take.

The man knelt in front of her and whispered in her ear, all the while stroking her knee softly, then her thigh, where a bruise darkened by the minute.

"I don't want to have to hurt you, Angel. You're a beautiful woman. Just tell me. I promise I'll let you go."

"You'll let me go?" she whispered. "Really?"

"Yes," he whispered, rubbing her thigh more seductively now. "I promise. I'll let you go. Just tell me."

In a flash, the woman jerked back her right foot, then swung it forward with incredible force. Her pointed, high-heel shoe connected with his groin.

"Go to hell!" she yelled, her face contorting. "Go to goddam hell!"

# MEG O'BRIEN

# GATHERING LIES

MIRA

ISBN 1-55166-807-6

GATHERING LIES

Copyright © 2001 by Meg O'Brien.

Visit us at www.mirabooks.com

Printed in U.S.A.

I would like to thank the following people, without whose help this book could never have been written:

My son, Greg, whose editorial skills are truly excellent, and who saved my neck during the infamous "end of the book" when nothing was making any sense.

All my children—Robin, Greg, Amy, Kevin and Kate—who put up with me when the muse takes over and I'm miserable to be around.

Cathy Landrum, who is not only an excellent research assistant, but who, along with her husband and very patient designated driver, Randy, is an adventurous traveling companion, as well.

Heather Iker, for being my expert legal reader and keeping me straight on the ins and outs of the justice system. Thanks for all the hours, Heather, and for being a great lawyer and friend.

Al Wilding, retired Seattle police officer, resident of the San Juan Islands and new friend. By some twist of fate I found him on the Net, just when I needed another expert reader. Many thanks, Al, for your advice and support throughout the past months, and to your beautiful wife, Lotte, who puts up with our constant e-mailing. Thanks, too, Lotte, for spreading the rumor around Shaw Island that Al and I were having an online affair. I can only imagine what that's done for my reputation at Our Lady of the Rock Priory!

Rick Boucher, owner of San Juan Web Talk, the Web site about the San Juan Islands—which was where I "met" Al Wilding in the first place. Thanks, Rick. Your Web site is an invaluable source of information about the islands.

Last and certainly not least, Amy Moore-Benson and Dianne Moggy, my editors at MIRA, who keep me wanting to write even when I'm ready to hie me off to a nunnery and hoe beans for the rest of my life.

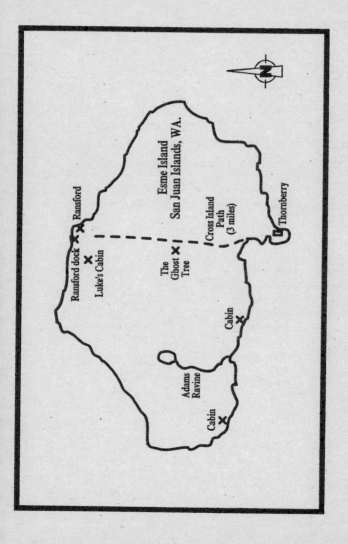

# *Prologue*

ANGEL
*April 7*

The woman sat tied to an upright chair, her arms bound from elbow to shoulder. She no longer squirmed to get free. By now, she knew that wouldn't help.

"Don't you understand?" the man said again as he paced before her. His tone was distraught, worried. "You're never getting out of here, if you don't tell me what I need to know."

"I'll die first, you son of a bitch," she managed through dry, cracked lips.

"It's beginning to look like you just might," he said.

But his voice shook. She knew he was close to breaking, too.

The woman bowed her head and closed her eyes. Her neck ached from holding it stiff with fear, and her eyes burned from the too-bright light she'd been under for more than seven hours. She didn't know how much more she could take before the inevitable happened, before words poured forth despite her will, words she had vowed never to tell him, not in a million years.

"Get it over with," she said dully, choking on a sob. "Please. Just do it now." Her eyes were red and swollen with tears, her tone begging. "If we ever meant anything to each other…"

The man knelt in front of her and whispered in her ear, all the while stroking her knee softly, then her thigh, where a bruise darkened by the minute.

"I don't want to have to hurt you, Angel. You're a beautiful woman. Just tell me. I promise I'll let you go."

"You'll let me go?" she whispered. "Really?"

"I told you I would," he said softly. "You think I like this? God, I hate it! And it could all be over. You could be home, safe and sound. All you have to do is tell me."

"You'll let me go?" she said again, looking into his eyes, the eyes she once told him were more lovely than those of any man she'd ever known.

"Yes," he whispered, rubbing her thigh more seductively now, letting his hand roam to the soft familiar flesh of the dark *V*, stroking her there as if she were a pet cat. A tingle ran through him as he realized she hadn't worn panties. That's how much she had trusted coming here this way.

"Yes," he said huskily, "I promise. I'll let you go. Just tell me."

In a flash, the woman jerked back her right foot, then swung it forward with incredible force. Her pointed, high-heel shoe connected with his groin. The man screamed, falling back.

"Go to hell!" she yelled, her face contorting. "Go to goddamn hell!"

In an automatic response to the searing pain, the man leapt to his feet and swung at the woman with his fist. It connected with the side of her head, and the chair she was tied to wobbled. Teetering precariously, it fell back, striking the cast-iron, wood-burning stove. The woman's head hit the sharp-edged corner of the stove with a resounding *crack*. Blood mushroomed from her scalp and her jaw went slack, her eyes staring. The man bent over her, still holding himself against the red-hot pain that seared through his groin.

"No!" he screamed. "Goddamn it, no!"

Kneeling again he quickly checked her pulse. It fluttered, then died. He put his ear to her mouth, but heard only the last sigh of a dying breath.

"Oh, God," he moaned. "Oh, God, you can't do this."

He fancied the woman's lips curved in a tired smile.

He sat for a long while on the floor beside her. "You were always so damn stubborn," he said softly. "Why couldn't you just have done things my way?"

He would miss her. But only a little. And now he would have to explain why he'd failed.

The man stood gingerly, still clutching himself. Light-headed, he stumbled to a telephone on the wall. Lifting the receiver, he punched in a number.

"She's gone," he said heavily, when a voice answered.

A small silence.

"No, I mean she's gone. Dead."

A tinny rumble of angry sound came through.

"No, she didn't— Look, it wasn't my—" He pressed his fist to his forehead. "Yes, I know. Yes. Right away." He dropped the receiver back onto the hook.

"Damn you, Angel!" he cried, looking at the woman's lifeless body. "All you had to do was tell me. I would have let you go."

But he knew that wasn't true. He would have had to kill her in the end.

And now he'd have to get to the other one. He'd have to make *her* give up the secret this woman had carried to her death.

If not, he'd be six feet under, along with this pile of useless flesh on his floor.

The pain in his groin ebbed, but not his anger. The man was less than gentle as he lifted the woman's body and squeezed it into a steamer trunk he kept in the closet. She was too large for the trunk, and as he pushed and shoved he heard bones break.

The lock was flimsy and didn't catch well. But that was all right. Where the trunk was going this time, it didn't need a lock. He went to the kitchen and got a towel, which he drenched in cold water. This he used to wipe the blood from the braided rug, then from his hands.

Looking around the small cabin, he debated whether to take the trunk out and bury it now, or leave it here till his job was done. Hell, he might end up with a mass grave before this mess was over.

No, he'd better do it now. The place could be broken into while he was gone.

He dragged the trunk out onto the porch and glanced around for signs of anyone nearby. Even without looking, though, he knew he was alone. That's one thing he liked about this place. It was a hideaway, for now. But in the future it could be a shelter where he could sit and think. He could picture himself a Thoreau—without, of course, the pond. It was here he might spend weekends and summer vacations, on this very porch, reading.

That is, if everything didn't go all to hell.

He looked down at the trunk, a moment of sympathy for the woman filling him with guilt and remorse. His life wasn't supposed to turn out like this. Neither was hers.

But it wasn't his fault. If she'd told him everything right off, none of this would have happened.

Dragging the trunk down the steps, he noted that the sky was an odd yellow, the air still. Hot, for April. But that was the Northwest for you. One week snow, the next a heat wave. He wondered if there would be a thunderstorm, and knew he'd have to bury the trunk deep, so the upper layer of dirt wouldn't wash away.

He got a shovel from the utility shed and went back to where he'd left the trunk, and began to dig. It was hot, tiring work, and he was still shaking from the unexpected way this had turned out. Still, he'd worked out for years, and was grateful for the hard, efficient muscles that made it possible for him to accomplish this.

When he was several feet down, he scrambled out

and used his last ounce of strength to pull the trunk over to the hole, then dumped it in. Looking down into the makeshift grave, he began to sway. Wiping his forehead, he thought, God, I feel dizzy. Must be hunger. Or this crazy weather.

But then his feet began to move, and without volition they stumbled forward. Throwing his arms out, the man tried to keep his balance, like a chicken flapping its wings. But nothing stopped the forward fall, and the man screamed out. His boots slid on the crumbling edge of the grave, and horror overtook him as the ground shook and the trunk rocked back and forth. The flimsy lock snapped open, and the lid flew back revealing the woman's bloody, broken body. The man fell on top of her, his face smacking the ooze from her skull. Dirt rained down upon them both, and like the wrath of God the ground continued to rumble and shake. Dirt choked his throat and stung his eyes. He tried to burrow an airhole, a space to keep him breathing till help arrived. But he knew, too, that help would not arrive. He was too far out, too isolated.

The next instant there appeared before him a tunnel of light. At first he thought he was dying, and he half expected to see his mother and all his dead relatives there, the way they said it happened on all those talk shows. Panic overwhelmed him. He'd read enough about near-death experiences to know they weren't always sweetness and light. One could land in hell. Then, suddenly, the sides of the tunnel burst open with a *whoosh*. Light rushed in. It took the man a moment to realize it was real light, *sky* light, a hole in the grave. The ground in its shaking had opened a path—a path he could follow, if only he could get an arm out and dig.

*"Dig, man!"* he half screamed, his fingers scrabbling in the dirt like a crazed, panicky crab. *"Dig!"* He had to survive. He'd been given a second chance, and he had to grab it.

There was only one person left, now, who knew where that evidence was. Sarah Lansing. He would get to her, make her tell him where it was. Then he would kill her. It would be easier now, after this.

# PART I

# THE SETUP

# 1

SARAH LANSING
*Seattle, WA*
*May 5*

*W*ords.

Words have consumed me, of late. They're just about all I have left, now, the only solace that remains. I sit here at my father's desk, in the house I grew up in, telling my story to a computer screen. I write, now, for no eyes but my own. Every night I obliterate what I've written, in fear of having my work confiscated by the police. Days, my fingers hover over the keyboard, ever ready to hit the delete key in the event that what passes for the law should show up at my door.

Meanwhile I gather my thoughts, putting them into words.

*Gather... Gathering... Gathered.*

I have always loved that word. It has a multitude of meanings, as in storm clouds gathering, or supplicants gathered for prayer. It can mean a woman gathering material at the waist, as my mother did, to make a skirt. One can gather one's thoughts, gather a man into oneself, gather children at one's knee.

Or—as was the case at Thornberry—it can mean a gathering of lies.

We were all lying about something that spring. And thus, having come together, having gathered for reasons none of us fully understood, we harmed ourselves, and each other, in ways we had no notion of before we began.

I will tell you this: Each of us did what we had to do. Of that, I am clear, to this day. A path opened up and we took it, not even thinking where it might lead.

It led us straight into hell.

# 2

---

It was the spring of the Great Seattle Earthquake, and life had been bad enough without the ground opening up beneath our feet. But there it is. Life has a way of taking over, of running amok, and there's not much point in fighting it—any more than there's any point in fighting it when a man leaves, betrays, lets one down.

At first you ask yourself, was it my fault? Did I wear the wrong outfit, have the wrong shade of hair? Should I go shopping for something younger, perkier?

Buy a bottle of Clairol Midnight Brown?

I remember Ian saying once that he'd been in love, at twenty, with an Italian girl whose dark brown hair fell in waves to her waist. His pet name for her had been Sophia, he told me, as in Loren. His first love, he said, the one and only true love of his life.

He said this the day he broke it off with me, and I've always wondered if it wasn't just what he told himself, to excuse the fact that he hadn't had a lasting relationship in all the years since.

Or, again, maybe it *was* me. *Am* I too blond? Too amenable? Or conversely, too argumentative?

Life also has a way of burdening one with questions that have no answers, at least none one wants to hear. Therefore, regardless of the fact that I'd been to college and was thought to be a relatively bright woman, with a career I'd been excellent at, those are the kinds of crazy-making thoughts that went tripping through my brain on the day the Big One hit.

It happened while we were at Thornberry—I and the other women. I didn't, at that point, know the real reason I'd been lured there—for that's the way it turned out, I was lured there. Nor did I know, in my mind, why I'd accepted the invitation. I only knew I was on the run: from a broken heart, a lost job, and a life that was in shambles.

The invitation to Thornberry, a writer's retreat on a tiny, private island in the San Juans, came by way of a friend at Seattle Mystery Bookshop, near the rather humble apartment I had lived in for years. When Bill Farley told me the invitation originated with Timothea Walsh, my response was immediate and positive.

"I know Timothea," I said. "I spent summers on Esme Island as a teenager. My parents and I stayed at her bed-and-breakfast."

"She's turned it into a writer's colony now," Bill told me. "I hear she likes helping beginning writers, and most of the time they have to apply. This is something new she's starting, where she invites women only, published or not, for one month out of the year. Everything's paid for, room and board. All you have to do is show up."

"But she can't have asked for me, specifically," I said, puzzled. "How did she know I was writing a book?"

"Maybe she read about it somewhere?" Bill said, a brow rising. "The papers, maybe?"

Good point, Bill. I'd been a high-profile public defender in Seattle until my arrest in January for drug possession. The local media made that hot news, splashing it all over the papers and television—which made sense, since my defense was that I'd been set up by a cabal of crooked Seattle cops. In the midst of all the media furor, someone had leaked the information that I was going for revenge by writing a book blasting the justice system, and the Seattle police in particular.

That "someone" was almost certainly my agent, Jeannie Wyatt, not that she'd admit it in a million years. Shortly after that, though, offers rolled in. From that point on, my fate as a writer—at least for a year or so if I turned out to be only a "one-book wonder"—was sealed. A bidding war began, ending forty-eight hours later in seven figures.

I'd become an overnight sensation—the Great White Hope of a New York publisher threatened with potential bankruptcy and unprepared for the advent of on-line publishing, e-books, print on demand. Rife with paranoia, they'd already dumped most of their mid-list writers, and were placing all their bets on a hot new blockbuster.

My book, someone high up had decided, would be blockbuster enough to hit the *New York Times* bestseller list.

And I hadn't yet written a word.

As for Timothea, it did not surprise me that she'd turned her B&B into a writer's colony. It was Timothea who first inspired me to write, sitting at her cherry-wood dining room table in the big white house, while everyone else was out on the beach or hiking around the island.

Tiny and remote, there was never much to do on Esme Island but swim and hike. I'd linger behind, my nose in a book, and one day Timmy—as she asked me to call her—sat me down with a pad and pencil and told me to write. She saw something in me back then, something I was too absorbed in being a teenager to see.

Later, when I took legal writing in law school, I began to recognize a few stirrings of potential in that direction. It wasn't until after the arrest last January, however, that I seriously thought of becoming a scribbler for a living.

A ludicrous thought, an oxymoron for most struggling authors—writing for a living. But once convicted and sentenced for drug possession—if that was the way it turned out at trial—there was little chance I'd ever be a lawyer again.

Some days, at least when the sun shines, I sit here in the bay window of my parents' house, at my father's desk, and look out at ships going by on Puget Sound. Before me is the Space Needle, high-rise apartment buildings, sparkling blue water and islands with lush green forests. A halcyon scene. A scene I grew up loving, with great hopes to one day be part of it, to leave my mark on it, doing nothing but good.

How then, could things have gone so wrong?

Fresh out of law school fifteen years ago, at twenty-five, I still had some of those wildly heroic ideas law students get about saving the world. Growing up, I'd watched my father defend corporate raiders and tax cheaters at Sloan and Barber. It was always expected I'd follow in his footsteps. Then, as children will, I'd opted to do the opposite with my fine new degree and become a public defender.

This was not entirely to spite my father, who had hoped I'd one day be a partner at Sloan and Barber, a daughter he could show off at the country club, since he'd never had a son. I actually considered S&B for a while, but in law school I'd begun to hear about innocent people who'd been jailed for crimes they didn't commit. Many lingered in prison ten, twenty years, while life outside the walls passed them by. Their children grew up, their wives or husbands moved on.

It was something that saddened and even frightened me. The idea that someone who had done nothing wrong could be yanked from his or her home, charged with a crime, and sent to prison for years—even life—sent chills down my spine. It smacked of Nazism, innocent people being dragged off into the night. I think this frightened me because I knew that if it could happen to one, it could happen to all.

My fear was theoretical in nature, back then. I couldn't have known that one day it would happen to me. Unless, of course, it's true that we come in "knowing" at some level what our life will be—thus explaining, for some, the kind of choices we make.

It was the advent of DNA as a means of identification in criminal cases that finally freed me of some

of those fears. DNA had been discovered in 1870 by
a chemistry student named Friederich Miescher, but
no one realized its full potential back then. It wasn't
until the 1950s that deoxyribonucleic acid was discovered to carry genetic material from one generation
to the next. Now, as everyone knows who watched
the O.J. trial, it's commonly used in criminal cases,
much like fingerprints, to prove a person guilty or not.
It can be obtained from something as simple as a
swab of fluid from inside a cheek, or a hunk of hair.

Any prison inmate who's been jailed wrongly can
afford a lock of hair. What most can't afford is a
lawyer to fight the good fight. Someone needs to get
a new trial going. Tests must be run, and DNA ex-
perts persuaded to testify pro bono—free of charge.
Sometimes agencies such as the American Civil Lib-
erties Union will help with the cost. However it's
done, it must be proved that the killer's or rapist's
DNA, found on or near the victim, in no way matches
the client's—the wrongly accused perpetrator of the
crime.

The plight of these wrongly accused became a
moral crusade for me. During my last year of law
school, I made the decision to shun the big fees my
father assured me I could be making within a few
years at Sloan and Barber. Instead—I announced with
all the exuberance of naive youth—I would defend
the poor and downtrodden.

Little did I know that within fifteen years, I'd be
one of Seattle's poor and downtrodden.

An exaggeration, of course. I tend to do that on
days like today when everything seems so black. Still,

when I was brought up on charges five months ago, I lost my job, and it looked for a while as if I'd be joining my clients on the streets. If my father hadn't died of a heart attack, leaving me a modest inheritance, and if my mother hadn't moved to Florida, leaving her house vacant, that's precisely what might have occurred.

And there again we have one of life's little tricks—it takes away the people you love, and replaces them with assets.

So what do you do? Do you say, *"Go away, Life, I don't want your filthy lucre"?* I think not. Not, at least, when the meter reader is at one's door.

So I moved into my parents' house shortly after the arrest. Then last month, in April, out on bail, I went to Thornberry along with five other women who were invited there, just like me. We were all potential but as yet unpublished authors, and I suspected from the first that each of the others was running from something—also like me.

No one admitted to that, of course. Not at first. It took the quake to make us trust each other enough to share our stories. By then, it was far too late.

Because the time sequence of the two events that changed my life this past year can become confusing, I am writing them down here in much the way I write my notes for a legal brief. Much the way, in fact, that I'm writing the notes for my upcoming trial.

It is early May now. Last January I'd taken on the case of a woman arrested for prostitution. She was middle-aged, black, not particularly attractive—in other words, a piece of meat, nothing more, to the five Neanderthal cops on duty at the jail that night.

The woman was released when the morning shift came on. Five cops from the night shift followed her into an alley and gang-raped her for more than an hour. They used everything on her—nightsticks, guns, themselves. When it was over, Lonnie Mae Brown had just enough strength left to check herself into a hospital, before falling unconscious. When she came to, she refused to report the incident to the cops.

She also refused all tests. She was afraid of retaliation—and I couldn't dismiss her fears. The rape of women in jail has been common in recent times, as has punishment for anyone who talks. Though Lonnie Mae's rape had occurred outside in an alley, public outrage about renegade cops was high on the totem pole of police reform. The stakes, for the cops, were high. For that reason, if no other, they tried to make the victim look guilty.

A young, black doctor I knew sized up the situation and called me, thinking that, as a lawyer, I might be able to tell Lonnie Mae what her options were.

Not that she had many, so far as I could see. I was there in the hospital when she woke from a sedative, and the first thing she did was shoot up straight into the air, her eyes wide and on the hunt for tormentors, hands flailing at invisible ghosts.

The most I could do for her was to be honest, since she was refusing the rape tests. I told her as gently as possible that without them, there wouldn't be enough evidence for the Prosecuting Attorney to press charges. I said if she needed to talk, though, to call me.

I fully expected never to hear from her again. But three days later, I did. She had decided to file a complaint, she said. Would I go to the station with her?

I was surprised, and I didn't think it would do her any good. But I agreed. I picked Lonnie Mae up, and stood by her side while the cop taking her complaint had a chuckle or two over her story. He clearly didn't believe it. Nor did he like the fact that I'd come in with her.

"Look, Counselor," he said sarcastically, "if this really happened, how come your client didn't get tested in the hospital?"

"She's not my client," I said sharply. "She's my *friend.* You just make sure that complaint gets into the right hands."

I was so angered by his attitude, I took Lonnie Mae home and sat with her, as she cried and wrung her hands.

"I just never thought it would do any good to have them tests," she said, over and over.

Privately, I thought she'd been in too much shock to make that decision in the hospital. But it was too late for that now, and all I could do was try to comfort her. She seemed to need to lean on me, despite the fact that she hardly knew me. I felt bad for her, and distressed that I couldn't do more for her. So I made myself available.

Lonnie Mae's apartment was comprised of two rooms, a miserable little place in the worst part of town. The halls were filled with bums, crack addicts,

pimps and rats. In the living room, on a packing crate
that had become an end table, were crumpled, un-
framed snapshots of a baby and two toddlers. She had
lost touch with them over the years, she said wearily.
"Social Services took 'em away long ago, and I ain't
seen 'em since then. I signed the papers, you know,
for adoption. I figure that's best. Ain't no kind of life,
livin' with me."

Silently, I agreed with her, but it wasn't my job to
judge her worth as a mother. Something in her defeated tone sparked my anger again, however, and
with that, I thought of something I stupidly hadn't
considered before.

"Lonnie Mae," I asked, "where are the clothes
you wore during the rape that night?"

"Oh, they's in the closet, over there," she said
tiredly. "The hospital put them in a bag."

"May I see them?"

She nodded, and I crossed over to the closet. Opening it, a whiff of cheap, heavy perfume hit my nostrils, almost gagging me. Beneath it was a scent of
sweat, a leftover, I assumed, of long nights on the
streets, hustling johns in cars and in broken-down ho-
tels.

There was gold in that closet, though. When Lonnie
Mae had been picked up for prostitution and gang-
raped, she was wearing a fake fur jacket, a red imi-
tation leather skirt, and purple fishnet stockings. It had
been three days since then, and she had already show-
ered away any sperm that might have been used as
evidence. The clothes she'd worn during the rape,
however, were right here where she'd tossed them

upon coming home from the hospital. She hadn't taken them out of the bag, or washed them—and they were loaded with sperm. In particular, the cops hadn't bothered to remove the fishnet stockings, that night in the alley. They'd torn through them, leaving them tattered around her legs, and in their macho celebration they had been sloppy, spewing DNA around like liquid confetti.

I asked Lonnie Mae if I could take the stockings. I wasn't sure what I'd do with them, but I told her I was certain they could help. She said sure, and I stuck them in the trunk of my car when I left her that day.

Later that night, Lonnie Mae's tenement burned to the ground. Dental records identified her body, which had been burned beyond recognition. The fire was thought to be "accidental," caused by a space heater that tipped over in another apartment. Four other people died that night.

Maybe it was an accidental fire. Certainly, I couldn't fault the arson investigators, who had a difficult job to do.

In my heart, however, I couldn't shake my belief that the five cops, or somebody working for them, had had a hand in it. Surely they had been told that Lonnie Mae had filed a complaint against them. They would have been questioned, even if the complaint was not believed. And the accusation, if it developed into an arrest, and then trial, could destroy them. In their minds, the next reasonable step might well be to rid themselves of their accuser. No victim, no arrest. No testimony, no trial.

Maybe they thought, too, that the murder of a prostitute would go unnoticed in a city the size of Seattle. And maybe they thought that by killing Lonnie Mae, they'd be sending a message to me: Back off from this, or we'll fix you, too.

If so, they really should have known better. Spurred on by both anger and considerable guilt over not protecting Lonnie Mae somehow, I met with a Prosecuting Attorney I had known for years. I posed a hypothetical question: If someone were to come across a piece of evidence that could put some bad cops in jail, what would be the best thing to do with it?

She gave me the party line, of course: If I were that "someone," as an officer of the court I'd be guilty of obstruction of justice if I didn't turn over evidence of a crime.

"I didn't say it was me," I told her. "What if this someone didn't trust the authorities? Or the security of the evidence lockers?"

Her name was Ivy, which sounds as if she'd be a soft touch. Ivy O'Day was no fool, however. She guessed right away that I wasn't talking hypothetically.

"This is strictly confidential, Sarah," she said. "I think I may know which cops you're talking about. We've been working with Internal Affairs, putting a case together against them for some time now. So far, it's largely circumstantial. One good, solid piece of evidence that they've actually committed a crime could help. If you've got that kind of evidence, Sarah, you're obligated to turn it over. If you're worried about evidence lockers, you can give it to me. I'll see it's kept safe."

"Still speaking hypothetically, Ivy, if I managed to find that kind of evidence, and I turned it over to you today, would you move on them? Right now?"

She hesitated and looked uneasy. "Not immediately. We're still putting our case together."

"So when would you file charges?" I pushed.

Ivy looked down at her hands, and it took her a few moments. "Maybe in a week, a month..." she said. "But, Sarah, if you have evidence..."

"I didn't say I had evidence, Ivy. Like I said, I was talking theoretically."

I asked her to keep me apprised of how their case was developing, and said I'd let her know if any such evidence came my way. But the hairs on the back of my neck had been raised in there. I wasn't all that sure, anymore, that I'd talked to the right person. The Prosecuting Attorney's office worked too closely with the cops. What if someone in the office—if not Ivy herself—had turned? Why hadn't she just said, *"Sure, Sarah, if you have solid evidence they committed a crime, we'll move on them today"?*

The fact that she hadn't did not fill me with confidence. So I hung onto Lonnie Mae's stockings, which was all that was left, now, since the fire. I had them tested secretly at a private lab in the East. Then I got a friendly DNA expert to read the results, confidentially and free of charge. There were six different kinds of DNA present, he reported, some in minuscule amounts, but more than enough to stand up in court. Five of those samples would be from the cops, I knew. The sixth would be Lonnie Mae's.

When my expert asked where he should send the

report, I told him to hold on to it for now. All that was left was to wait for Ivy to prove herself by filing those charges. Then I'd come forward with the evidence—and not until then.

Obstruction of justice be damned. I'd figure it out somehow.

The important thing was, I now knew that at some point I could get the five cops convicted of rape— and with any luck, of arson and murder, as well. *I'll get them for you, Lonnie Mae*, I promised. *You may be gone, but I swear to God, they'll never forget your name.*

It should have gone down that way. And would have gone down that way, if I'd just lain low with the evidence. But then I blew it.

The next night after work, I met with a friend, J.P. Blakely, at her office. J.P. was a Private Investigator who had helped me on several cases. I told her everything about Lonnie Mae and the cops. After talking about it for an hour or more, and considering how to proceed, both J.P. and I needed a drink. We headed for McCoy's, which was a cop hangout, and not a place we'd ordinarily frequent. It was the nearest watering hole, though, and we ran across the street from J.P.'s office in a blinding rain.

The place was nearly empty, but while we were sitting at a table out of sight of the bar, four of the five cops who had raped Lonnie Mae piled in. I knew who they were by this time, because their photos had been emblazoned across the front page of that day's *Seattle Times*. A complaint had been filed against them for rape, the caption read. The following story said the cops had issued a statement to the press denying all guilt and claiming that the prostitute in question had been out to get revenge for her arrest.

I felt a small sense of satisfaction that I'd been the one to leak the story to the *Times* in the first place. At least it was out in the open now. One step forward—and maybe, I thought, it would get Ivy off her ass. The papers had dubbed the cops the "Seattle Five," and the rest of the media had begun to follow suit. The scandal would take on a life of its own. It would not simply "blow over."

The four cops who had just come into McCoy's didn't see us, and we had an opportunity to eavesdrop. At first, they were relatively silent—gearing down from their day's work, it seemed. Then, as the drinks flowed, they became louder and louder. There was much backslapping, and I heard Mike Murty, the suspected head honcho of the Five, brag that there probably wouldn't even be a trial, now that the "black bitch whore" was dead.

They continued in that vein, while J.P. and I stared at each other, growing more and more outraged. Though we didn't hear it in so many words, there came a moment when we were both certain the Five had set that fire and murdered Lonnie Mae—not to mention the others who had died along with her.

It was then that we rose as one and strode around the divider that separated us from the bar. The bartender saw us coming, and moved away as if sensing trouble. There were no other patrons in McCoy's at that time, and maybe it should have occurred to me to be afraid. But I wasn't accustomed to drinking much, and I'd had two glasses of wine.

I grabbed Mike Murty by the arm and swung him around. "You son of a bitch!" I said. "You sick, worthless piece of crap!"

He slid off the stool and hovered over me, all six feet of him. With his thumbs in his belt and his feet planted wide, he laughed. The other three stood, too, surrounding Murty and me.

"Move along, little lady," one of them said. It was Al Garben, a weasily guy with a mustache that didn't quite hide a mean mouth.

J.P. pushed her way between them and me. Though she was only five-four, she stood toe to toe with them, her blue eyes blazing. "She's right. You always have been sick bastards."

Jake Suder laughed. "You got a problem with us, J.P.?" He stuck out a hand that was reddish and cracked, chucking J.P. under the chin. She knocked it away—but not before I remembered Lonnie Mae telling me about that hand, and the things it had done to her.

"Enjoy your drinks," I said angrily. "There won't be any where you're going."

Murty laughed again. "We're not going anywhere, bitch. Unless, of course, you're inviting us to your place?"

They all laughed, stepping forward and closing in on us. "That's right," Al said. "Maybe we'll just stop by one of these nights. You know—a routine check, to see if you're all right."

Tad Sanders, the youngest one, grinned. "Maybe

we'll find that she's more than all right. Maybe we'll find that she's real, real good.''

He leaned so close, I could smell the beer on his breath and see the peach fuzz on his chin. Not much more than twenty-two, he already had the look in his eyes of a predator.

J.P. put a palm against his chest, like a crossing guard. "Get back, asshole. All of you get back."

"You think you scare anybody?" Al Garben taunted. "Little yellow-haired thing like you?"

"You'd better be scared," I said, not even thinking as words tumbled from my wine-loosened tongue. "I have enough evidence to put every one of you away for good."

"You've got evidence, bitch?" Murty laughed. "Not by a long shot."

"Believe it," I said. "Lonnie Mae gave me all I needed before she died. And you're not getting away with it—not the rape, or her murder."

J.P. flashed me a warning. I saw it in her eyes, just before I saw the threat in Mike Murty's. J.P. grabbed my arm and pulled me away.

"Let's get out of here," she said. "C'mon, Sarah. You've had too much to drink. Let's go."

"You're right," I agreed, slurring the words a bit. "I don't know what the hell I'm talking about. Anyway, I need a shower, to wash the filth away."

We had to get our coats, and when we rounded the room divider again to go out the front door, I saw that the Five were having a serious conclave at the bar. They weren't laughing anymore.

I should have felt a small sense of victory. But even without J.P.'s warning, I knew I'd said far too much.

Late that night, I tried to throw a net of protection around myself by calling Mike Murty at home. I told him I did, in fact, have evidence that he and the others had raped Lonnie Mae. I said the evidence was safe with someone unknown to him, and that if anything happened to me, it would go directly to someone in authority outside the Seattle PD. I told him that agency would nail them for the rape, Lonnie's murder, and my death, as well. Then I closed with the argument that the Five's best chance was to throw themselves on the mercy of the court—and that they'd better make sure I stayed alive to see them there.

I thought this would stop them. At the very least, I hoped it might buy me some time.

But that's when the Seattle Five came after me.

Let me be clear. Most Seattle cops are good people, doing jobs they love and are proud of. Early in my career as a public defender, however, I'd acquired a reputation with even the good ones. To put as nice a slant as possible on it, they loathed me. I was the one who got people off after the cops worked their asses off tracking them down, taking them in, filling out paperwork, testifying in court. I didn't mind their griping about me. It got me on the nightly news, and if that could in some way help a client, I was all for it. I dressed in snappy clothes for court, and to draw even more attention, I deliberately wore my thick blond hair in a loose, flowing style I was told was sexy.

Actually, Ian's the one who told me my hair was sexy, even to the point of using it in our foreplay. One Fourth of July night we lay naked on my bed, I and Seattle's top-ranking police detective, and watched the Space Needle fireworks from my window. Almost absentmindedly, Ian stroked my hair against himself, over and over till he was fully aroused, reaching climax just as the final burst of fireworks spilled from Seattle's best-known phallic symbol. I recall getting into the spirit of things, though I never told him, during or after, how uncomfortable the position had been. In those days I'd have done anything for Ian, put myself in discomfort, even danger. I loved him with nearly my entire heart, leaving no room for anything else but the law.

Ironically, it was the law that came between us. Ian was a dedicated Seattle cop who spent long days putting evidence together to bring my clients into court. He had a hard time accepting that I had a job to do, and that I took pride in doing it.

It didn't help matters that some of the accused I managed to get off weren't innocent. That's the thing about DNA—it can be used, if one knows how to present it in court, to free the guilty as well. And a lawyer's job is to defend her client, innocent or not.

Law, I learned, has a way of wearing one's purity down.

So Ian and I would argue about my work, and at first it was fun—something we did as part of foreplay, to get us excited. Later, it became something I dreaded.

"If the jury doesn't understand DNA when the

prosecutor rams it down their throats, over and over for hours till they become benumbed, it's not my fault!'' I'd argue, my voice shaking because I wanted more than anything to get the argument over with and get back to where we were ''one.''

''*You* keep it going!'' he would shout back. ''You know exactly what you're doing, and if the jury gets bored and doesn't even listen, it's *your* fault, not the prosecutor's. You plan it that way. You weave a damned spell in the courtroom, and no one can see beyond it.''

He once went so far as to say that if I loved him, I would go do something else for a living—like mow lawns.

I couldn't believe he was serious, and perhaps he was not. Ian, a linebacker type with red hair and an Irish temper, had a way of flying off the handle and saying things he didn't mean. Later, he'd apologize, and things would go back to the way they had been. Until next time.

One night last January, however—two nights after I'd called Mike Murty and threatened him with Lonnie Mae's evidence—Ian didn't show for dinner. When I finally reached him late that night, he said he'd been busy. He didn't know when he'd have time to see me again.

The next day, three uniform cops raided my apartment while I was out. A judge I barely knew had given them a warrant based on a flimsy tip the cops said they had received. They ''found'' crack cocaine and miscellaneous drug paraphernalia in my bedroom closet.

I do not use drugs, and never have.

I was arrested coming out of a courtroom, a moment I'll never forget if I live to be older than sin. The charge was possession of illegal drugs with intent to sell, a felony, and after the usual delays and continuances, I didn't expect my trial to go forward until early December. I walked through all these procedures like a zombie, in fear and disbelief.

The next day I made bail but lost my job, and for a brief time I fell into a depression. My only comfort was that they hadn't found Lonnie Mae's evidence when they planted those drugs. I'd taken it from my trunk, after we left McCoy's, and had given it to J.P. to put in a safe place.

I was too afraid now, though, to hand it over to anyone—even Ivy O'Day. It was the DA's office, after all, that had pressed charges against me. Had Ivy told someone about my visit to her? The wrong someone? Had the cops, in fact, been searching for the evidence at the same time they planted those drugs?

Depression mingled with fear. Then, one day I woke up angry. From that morning on, my days were consumed with thoughts of how best to destroy the Seattle Five.

The next day, I walked over to Seattle Mystery Bookshop. Between talking with Bill Farley and looking through volumes on the shelves, I formulated a plan to write a book blasting the justice system in general, and crooked police in particular. Bill was all for it.

"It's a bestseller in the making," he told me, his white hair gleaming under the store's light. "Especially with you being a lawyer. It'll put you on talk shows, maybe even *Larry King Live*. You can get your story out that way.''

I wanted my story out, not just for myself, but for Lonnie Mae Brown. I still hadn't heard from Ivy O'Day, and no charges had been filed against the Seattle Five. Lonnie Mae's stockings remained in their plastic bag in a safe in the office of J.P.'s accountant, where she'd put them the night I handed them to her. After the confrontation with the Five in McCoy's, she was afraid they'd search her office, and she hid the stockings in a brown envelope with old tax forms she gave to her accountant for storage.

As for me, as the weeks went by I was growing more and more frustrated and less and less willing to depend on justice taking its course. Lonnie Mae might still have been alive if the system put monsters like those cops in jail, instead of either ignoring the complaints against them, or letting them out on bail. And Lonnie was by no means an isolated case. Time after time, over the years, I'd seen it happen—rapists, murderers, child molesters given light sentences, only to be released from prison and kill, rape and molest again.

That I had defended some of them became an issue that confused me, leaving me sleepless and worn. My faith in jurisprudence—my vision of what the rule of law required—was nearly gone by this time, a state of mind at least partially responsible for what happened later, at Thornberry.

So I bought a new laser printer and reams of paper. By this time I was living here at my parents' house, and one morning I took a cup of strong, hot Fidalgo coffee to my father's desk, sat at my computer and began. After several awkward attempts, piling up pages by the hundreds in the trash can, I found myself working twelve, fourteen, even eighteen hours a day on this, my first book, *Just Rewards*. It became more important than anything I'd ever done, and the obsessive drive that had seen me through law school carried me now into this new world of writing, with that "fire in the belly" writers talk about.

Then, in early March, six weeks after my arrest, Timothea's invitation came to spend the month of April at Thornberry. I readily agreed. Except for telling her story in my book, there seemed to be nothing more I could do for Lonnie Mae at that time. The scandal in the papers about the Five had, against all my hopes, died down to a mere dribble, and I'd grown less and less certain that the DA's office would ever charge them. A call to Ivy had confirmed that opinion. She had been clipped, impersonal. Nothing to report yet, she said. *Don't call me, I'll call you,* was implied.

So I had no one to answer to, no one to stay home for. Ian had already said goodbye, and I hadn't heard from him since. Aside from all the Sophia, first-and-only-love crap, he had said that just knowing me now could damage his career on the force. Would I do him a favor and tell everyone we knew that we were no longer involved?

Sure I would, I said. Glad to. No problem. And screw you, too.

That night I'd lit several candles of varying sizes and shapes in my bathroom, and I'd stood before the mirror with a pair of sharp scissors and ceremoniously cut my hair. I took it down to a couple of inches above the root—like Sharon Stone's, a friend said later—and with every cut, I excised Ian from my life.

It is May as I write these notes in my journal, and in the few short months since all that happened, I sometimes feel I'm growing into one of those women I've read about in books, who is older suddenly than she ever imagined she would be, and not perhaps as attractive to men as she once was. She enjoys watching romantic movies and reading sexy novels about young people, even though she knows love will probably never happen for her again. The body is going, and thus her coinage, and while that perhaps is sad, she realizes with a certain equipoise that it's much easier now to dream about a lover than to actually deal with one.

I rise from my computer and stretch my legs, thinking back on those days while I make a pot of tea, covering it with a cozy the way my mother always did. *Her cozy, her house, her pot, her tea.* It seems, some days, as if I have nothing left of my own. Not that I'm ungrateful. There are worse things than having an historic old house to live in, and enough money in the bank to get by—provided my legal fees don't eat it all up.

And isn't that a slick little trick of karma, for you— a lawyer having to worry about billable hours.

Then there's the book, if I ever finish it. How can I reveal what happened, now? With all of us sworn to silence, that leaves me with only a beginning and a middle—no end.

So I sit here at my father's desk and tell my story to myself, if only to keep things straight. My mind wants to twist the events that occurred, changing them this way and that. It wants to make what happened come out in an entirely different way.

Magical thinking, some would call it. But no matter what I do, no matter what better scene I visualize, there's no way to change things—not then, not ever.

I am under house arrest now, while the others, for the moment, at least, go free. The prosecuting attorney of San Juan County had no proof I'd committed the horror at Thornberry. Still, given the circumstances, there wasn't much he could do but have me arrested. The sheriff locked me up, and I thought at first I might spend months in a county jail. Almost immediately, however, someone—I've never known who—pulled strings to get me transferred down to Seattle.

I didn't ask for this—didn't, in fact, want it. Nor did I want the ankle cuff that lies heavy against my skin, a constant reminder that I'm not free to leave the house, even to work on my own case. One little step outside the door, and an alarm goes off at the Probation and Parole office. I can't even go to the store.

Instead, I await my fate in the home my parents raised me in, surrounded by photographs of myself as a solemn but innocent young girl, my father's arm around me, his love supporting me through all the small childhood terrors.

Funny. I thought he would always be here.

There are lace curtains at the windows, and my eyes well as I remember my mother washing and ironing them, every Saturday morning of her life. Steam would rise as she stroked with her iron, back and forth, back and forth, while into the air rose the fresh, clean scent of Niagara starch. When my mother wasn't cleaning, she was baking, and there were nights when she'd go on a tear. I would waken in the morning to find several pies, cakes and plates of cookies in the kitchen, a feast. It wasn't until I was older that I knew why she did this—to avoid sleeping with my father.

My father was a workaholic. A big, quiet man, he sweat blood from nine in the morning till six at night to keep white-collar criminals out of jail. Lies, cover-ups, deals, scams—all were an integral part of the work he performed for Sloan and Barber, one of the most elite and respected law firms in Seattle. Nights when he managed to come home in time for dinner, my father closed himself up afterward in his study, throwing himself into even more work, in a fool's attempt to forget the sins he'd committed that day.

So my father was gone, and I somehow felt my mother blamed me for that. Before she left for Florida, she'd cried. "All the hopes, all the dreams we had for you—dashed in one horrible moment!"

We barely spoke after that, and I only knew I was welcome to move into her house when a messenger arrived at my door with a key.

This, then, is some of the background I took with me to Thornberry, a background not so different from the other women, yet not so similar, either, as it turned out. Each of us brought strengths and weaknesses, skills and knowledge. This proved to be a blessing, as we would need them all before we were done.

It also proved to be a curse.

# PART II
# THE PURSUIT

# 3

On that day in April when the Great Earthquake hit, none of us at Thornberry could possibly have guessed what lay ahead, or how it would affect every one of our lives.

I stepped out of my cottage that afternoon and lingered to drink in the view. Pausing for a moment on the small porch, I looked across fir and cedar trees to the sky above the Strait of Juan de Fuca. Here in the San Juan Islands, some eighty miles north of Seattle, the sky remained light somewhat longer than in the city. Even so, I hadn't expected such an odd color of yellow at five in the afternoon. Nor had I expected the air to be so warm in April. It was the earliest spring in history, some said.

This was the first time I'd seen the sky like that, however. All week long clouds had hung over the islands, at least on those days when there wasn't fog.

For long moments I gazed at the trees, my nose twitching at their sweet, woodsy scent. Primroses had popped up among the rocks that lined my path to the farmhouse road from my cottage—which was named, after Timothea's deceased daughter, "Annie's Rose." Annie died from pneumonia when she was six, and Timmy had acquired a permit to have her buried on the property. A tiny cross marks the spot on a hill invisible from the farmhouse, but facing the sea.

There were only four homes on Esme Island, which was roughly oblong and three miles across from north to south. Ransford, the Ford house on the north side, was much grander than Thornberry, on the south shore. The other two homes were cabins, built in the 1950s and existing on Esme at the time Timothea and the Fords bought the island and built here. They lay to the west of Thornberry, along the shore, and were maintained by their original owners only as summer vacation homes.

This left Timothea quite isolated during the long winter months, which, I imagined, was why she'd set up a writer's colony when the bed-and-breakfast closed. This way, she could still have year-round visitors.

She had apparently kept it manageable, however. There were only six residents' cottages at Thornberry, each with different names and each beautifully crafted of cherry, pine, and cedar, with stained glass windows in the sleeping lofts. They dotted several acres of woodland surrounding the main house, which began as Timothea's bed-and-breakfast all those years ago. Now called simply the "farmhouse," it was a three-story white structure, similar in architecture to many of the lovely old homes in British Columbia. "What a romantic place," my mother enthused the first summer we visited. "Perhaps we'll meet our true loves here."

She said it with that light laugh that surprised me every time it came out, as my mother was more often than not rather morose. I was ten at the time, and if I thought it odd that my mother—who had been married to my father for years—still spoke of finding her true love, I refrained from saying so.

The farmhouse now served as administrative office, kitchen, and nightly meeting place for resident writers. Timothea lived in the second-floor rooms, and two office assistants remained, weeknights, in private rooms on the third floor.

As for the cottages, none could be seen by the other. In fact, once settled in, the only sign of life nearby was a now and then wisp of smoke from the woodstoves of the other five residents. We were not permitted to speak to each other or disturb each other in any way, until four in the afternoon. This, Timmy explained, was to ensure that each of us had every opportunity to write.

Arriving at Thornberry in April, I was out on bail, my trial date set for August third. The prosecution had pushed for an earlier date, but my lawyer pushed back, pleading a full schedule. In truth, she was giving me time to finish the book. I knew there would also be the usual delays and continuances, and did not expect my trial to go forward till December, at the earliest.

Which thrilled my publisher. Though I wouldn't turn the manuscript in until October, they planned to push *Just Rewards* through production virtually overnight, with a pub date of December 1. From the publisher's point of view, it was worth the unusual effort, as the trial would help to make it a bestseller. From my lawyer's point of view, I'd be getting it into the hands of the legal analysts—the talking heads on TV—right when it might do me the most good. They were known to come down hard, lately, on crooked cops. And since crooked cops were my best, and only, defense, I said sure, let's pull out all the stops.

I was ready, by then, to play any angles to bend, and if necessary, beat the judicial system.

Seeing Timmy here again after so many years, I had mixed feelings. It had been two decades since I'd last been at Thornberry, and we both had changed. Timmy, though, seemed unusually strained. I mentioned this to Dana, one of the other residents, as we walked together toward the farmhouse for dinner. I'd run into her before, coming from her cottage, and we'd found it easy to talk to each other. For the most part, we talked about the other residents and how we felt about them. Gossip, I suppose—something I seldom indulged in. But at Thornberry, after the first few days of daily isolation, we were all still wondering about each other.

This night, I shifted the basket of books I'd brought with me to return to the farmhouse library, and brought up the subject of Timothea.

"I knew her a long time ago," I said, "and she always seemed a happy person, one who knew precisely what she was doing in life. I thought she found contentment in it."

"Well, it must be difficult dealing with five different writers a month," Dana said. "Having to sit with us at dinner, listen to us jabber. Have you ever seen such a bunch of—" She hesitated.

I knew the word she was going for, and revised the first letter of it. "Witches?"

She laughed. "Except for Jane. She seems nice. I feel sorry for her, though. Grace just won't let her be."

Jane was a well-to-do young matron from Bellevue, and Grace Lopez a tough, mouthy New Yorker. Grace was thin and wiry, with short black hair, an olive complexion, and a temperament straight from the Bronx. So far, Jane hadn't been doing very well at holding her own with her. Jane was writing a romance novel, and if there was anything Grace seemed as if she'd know nothing about, it was romance.

I myself had become bored with the kind of tensions that seemed to develop over dinner every night. Aside from Jane and Grace, there was Amelia, a seventy-two-year-old curmudgeon and prize-winning poet. She and Grace would get into something volatile, and Jane would leap in to smooth things over, then get caught in the runoff.

One member of our group that I hadn't had time to form an opinion about was Kim Stratton, the Hollywood actress who'd suddenly found herself, with one hit movie, on a level with the best. Her succeeding films reportedly raked in more than the national debt, yet Kim had come to Thornberry to write her memoirs, she had told everyone on the one night she'd shown up for after-dinner coffee. The majority of the time she kept to herself in her cottage, and had acquired a reputation with the other women for being standoffish.

What kinds of memories this auburn-haired beauty

felt impelled to be writing about at age thirty, I couldn't imagine. Still, she was known as "America's Sweetheart"—at least to those not old enough to remember that Mary Pickford once held that title. Presumably, enquiring minds wanted to read everything they could about Kim Stratton.

"So you think Timothea's just bored with us all?" I asked Dana, as we continued toward the farmhouse.

She gave a shrug, and the silver-and-turquoise necklace she wore shimmered in the yellow light. Dana, from Santa Fe, was often mercifully teased by Grace for being psychic, or Santa "fey." I knew little about her life in New Mexico, as she seldom talked about it. There was a husband, I'd learned. But the kind of person he was, and what he did for a living, seemed shrouded in mystery.

"You seem to know her better than any of us," Dana answered. "What do you think?"

I wasn't certain. I no longer felt I knew my old friend, and could only ascribe this to time passing, personalities changing. I'd grown up, while Timothea Walsh had grown older. I had no idea of the forces that had moved through her life, twisting and shaping it in ways perhaps different, but just as powerfully as forces that had shaped mine.

We turned a bend in the path, and I felt myself shiver.

"You feel it, too?" Dana asked. Her dark hair moved in fine wisps over her forehead as she turned her head from one side to the other, seeming to sniff the air.

"Too?"

"This spot," she said, pulling her fringed shawl more tightly around her. "It's very strange."

She was right. The air was unseasonably warm, the sky still that strange, heavy amber. But there was something else along this one patch of trees. Every time I passed it, my legs would begin to feel weak, as if I could barely move. It was like slogging knee-deep through mud, and it lasted a few yards, then was gone.

"Old Indian ground," Dana said. "I read about it in the library here. Energies like that, you know, have a way of lingering."

My legal training had not prepared me for this kind of thinking, yet I couldn't deny that something about this spot was unnatural.

"There may even have been mass murders here," Dana continued in a low voice, "when northern tribes raided down here, killing the men and taking wives and slaves back with them."

Her words echoed something from time past. What was it? Where had I heard this before?

It took a moment, but as we continued to walk, my thoughts flashed back to the year I turned eighteen. And Luke.

Luke Ford's family owned Ransford, the larger home on Esme Island back then, and during the four summers I spent here, we had worn a path through the woods from visiting back and forth. Luke had commented more than once about the strange energies in the woods around here. How had I forgotten?

Luke had been my first love, and the exact opposite of Ian. Ian was all business, red hair cropped short, demeanor dead serious, while Luke joked, teased, flirted outrageously, and in general embraced life fully. He wore his thick, almost kinky dark hair in a ponytail that ended midway down his back. When he didn't have it contained that way, it flowed around his face, framing and softening features that were sharp and angular—more striking than handsome.

I was seventeen the last summer I spent on Esme Island, and I could not get enough of Luke. Having flirted our way through the three previous summers, lightly touching each other, then pulling back as if burned by a hot poker, we were primed that year.

We started out the first day smiling awkwardly at each other, then glancing away; our eyes, when they met, spoke too much of our feelings. One day I was walking in the woods, looking for a quiet place to write. Luke hid in a tree and nearly startled me to death, dropping to the ground in front of me. Then he whisked me into his arms with a great holler and whoop.

"Sarah! My God, I missed you this year!"

We fell to the ground together, laughing, and from there on out, I was all his. His tongue parted my lips, while a hand came between my legs to create a passage there, as well.

When it was over, my back was scratched from dry pine needles on the forest floor. The discomfort I suffered was well worth it, however. It had been my first time, and for days I was consumed by memories of Luke stroking the entire length of my body till I was nothing but a quivering mass. I sought him out, sought that feeling over and over. The woods became our trysting place, while I became Guinevere and he Lancelot, having an illicit affair behind King Arthur's back.

There was no king, of course, to cuckold. Only our parents, who thought we were still "just friends," enjoying each other's company on a lonely island every summer with few inhabitants, no television, no movies, and nothing, really, to do.

If they had known what we were up to, there would have been hell to pay. Both my parents and his were conventional, his mother almost saintly. This forbidden aspect only served to heighten our sense of danger, and therefore our lust. We experimented in ways neither of us ever had, and when we parted at the end of the summer, it was—at least for me—with a feeling of being wrenched from my soul.

It took me a long while, after that—years of law school, work and aimless dating—to fall in love again. That it was Ian I fell in love with is a mystery to me now. I never gave myself fully to him, and many's the time I felt obligated to call up memories of that summer with Luke, to convince Ian that he'd satisfied me—that I'd felt all I was obligated to feel.

After that year, I didn't see Luke again, though I heard about him a few times through my mother, who exchanged Christmas cards with his family for a time. Luke, Mrs. Ford wrote, had traveled in Europe after college, then worked in New York City. She never said exactly what he did for a living, and I remember thinking that with his lively personality he might be involved in anything from acting to simply hanging out, "following his bliss." As far as I knew, he'd never married.

I wondered if he still came to the island, and if I'd see him here. Not likely, after all these years. Still, the thought brought with it a small jolt of excitement—something I dismissed immediately as a visceral carryover from adolescence, nothing more.

"Where did you go?" Dana asked, snapping me out of my reverie.

"Hmm? Oh, sorry. I was thinking."

"Odd weather, isn't it?" she said.

We were nearing the farmhouse, with its gardens leading down to the rocky beach. She scanned the horizon with a frown. "The water seems choppy, today. Odd, since it's so warm."

"I was just thinking that myself."

Dana laughed, though the sound came out a bit hollow. "I lived in L.A. once, and we'd call this earthquake weather."

"Well, they do keep warning us that the Big One's coming," I said.

A lush scent of roasting pork and freshly cooked vegetables drifted our way from the farmhouse. We stepped up our pace, and inside the kitchen we took seats on picnic-style benches at a long table, with the other writers and Timothea Walsh. Timmy and I had talked the first day I'd arrived, but not since, except to say hello in passing. She had asked about my mother, and I'd told her Mom was living with her sister in Florida, and doing well.

''I'm so sorry about your father,'' Timmy had said.
''But I must say...''

She had paused, then shaken her head and clamped her lips shut.

''You think she's better off?'' I pressed.

She fluttered a thin, white hand at her chest. ''Well, Sarah, it's not for me to say...but your mother's life was never an easy one.''

I thought she'd meant because of my father's tendency to work such long hours, so I just nodded, and we both changed the subject.

Now I looked across the table at Timmy and wondered. She kept glancing at me when she thought I wasn't watching. I'd feel her eyes on me, and when I'd look up to meet them, she'd quickly turn away.

Lucy, the cook, was at the stove ladling out food. The daytime office staff had already left on the Friday night ferry for their homes on Whidbey. The ferry, which was privately owned and only stopped at Esme two days a week, would come again on Monday morning, bringing them back. Any other time, we couldn't get off the island if our lives depended on it.

As, of course, they soon would.

The dinner conversation droned on and on. *Another long evening,* I thought, picking at the last morsel of roast pork on my plate. Dinner, then coffee in the living room. People reading their works-in-progress to each other, critiquing each other, sometimes being careful and delicate in their comments, other times hard as nails.

Though, come to think of it, only Amelia and Dana had read aloud in the five days we'd been here. And Amelia was usually the only hard-nosed critic. Even Grace was often silent when either woman read, as if she really didn't know what to say.

The thought struck me suddenly that Grace might not be a writer. Almost immediately, I shook that off as silly. I'd been living in my mind too much of late, seeing shadows in every corner.

Still, I had thought I'd feel safer here on Esme Island than I did. There were moments, in fact, when I felt certain I was being watched.

"This warm weather is so wonderful!" Jane offered from across the table.

Jane was tiny, with short brown hair and a self-deprecating demeanor. I wondered if her size, which was not more than five foot one, caused her to feel incapable of making a mark on the world.

"I thought it would never stop raining this winter," she went on. "In fact, at one point I thought if I had to put boots and raincoats on one more child, just *one more* day, I'd go crazy."

"How many children do you have?" Timmy asked.

"Only two. It just seems like an army sometimes." Jane smiled uncertainly. "That's why it's so good to be here. My husband gave me this two-week vacation as a birthday present. He's working from home while I'm gone, so he can watch the kids."

"You're only here for two weeks?" I asked curiously. "I understood we'd all been invited for a month."

Jane's grimace was half smile, half frown. "We were, but I didn't think I could be away from home that long. As it was, I spent a full week in the kitchen before I came here, making my husband's favorite dishes and freezing them. He doesn't know how to cook."

"Some vacation," Grace muttered. She frowned and shook back her cropped black hair, then folded her arms across her chest. Grace's name did not at all fit her, as she was totally lacking in any of the graces. In fact, I had yet to hear her utter a good word about anyone.

Jane seemed to hunker more inside herself. She didn't respond.

Amelia turned to Timmy and asked where Kim Stratton was.

"She's having dinner in her cottage," Timmy answered. "She did say she might join us later for coffee."

Amelia harrumphed, then made small talk with Timmy about Thornberry, while Jane, Grace, Dana and I listened. Timmy sat every night at the head of the table, and as I'd noted to Dana, she didn't seem particularly comfortable to be there. She seldom took part in our conversation unless asked a direct question, and I recalled that she had seemed a bit shy when I was younger. I wondered silently if she'd rather have dinner alone than with a group of edgy writers.

"I abandoned the bed-and-breakfast years ago," she was saying now to Dana. Her hand went to smooth her short gray hair, a large diamond ring reflecting light from candles and sending sparkles around the table.

"It was far too much work," she continued. "Not that this isn't, but since you all do your own laundry and housekeeping, it's quite a bit easier."

A staff member—either Lucy or one of the two administrative assistants—brought lunches to the six cottages every day at noon, setting them on the porches without knocking or in any way disturbing the writers. Lunches were hearty soups or stews and homemade breads and muffins. At dinnertime, each writer brought her own basket back to the farmhouse and filled it with whatever she wanted for breakfast the next morning—eggs, bacon, muffins, fruit. Each cottage had its own small kitchen, and residents fixed their own breakfasts. There was no charge for any of this.

Thornberry, I'd been told by Bill Farley, was one of the most luxurious writer's colonies in the country now. Timothea was a former patron of the arts from Seattle, a woman who had always wanted to help other women find their place in the writing world. When she had first sat me down at her dining room table with pad and pencil all those years ago, I hadn't known this. I thought she was just being nice to the lonely kid with her nose in a book.

Now I understood the genuine kindness that lay behind Thornberry's latest incarnation. There were no "page police," no monitors of one's work. The only thing Timothea asked was that the women who came here grow in some way that might further their talent. How they did that was their own business. They might take walks in the woods, keep a journal, help out with the organic farming, or even—if they wished—simply feed the two resident goats.

The conversation this night, dominated by Grace as usual, turned to politics. Since my life in Seattle had been saturated with troublesome politics, I had difficulty participating. But Grace was young and brash. She liked to mouth off for the sake of mouthing off, reminding me of certain teenagers I'd defended over the years—though Grace was clearly in her mid- to late-twenties.

"We've got to fucking bomb them," Grace said firmly. "It's the only way."

This brought me out of my woolgathering long enough to wonder who she was talking about. Iran? The cornfields of Iowa? Anything could be turned into an enemy by this woman, I had learned.

Dana jumped in with an obvious attempt to change the subject. "Lucy, I love the way you use herbs in your cooking," she called out to the cook, who was putting cookies for dessert into the oven.

"Thanks," Lucy said. "You're writing about herbs, aren't you? We should talk one of these days."

"I'd love to," Dana said. "It's not all about herbs, but they're a large part of it. It's about using what nature gave us, to heal—something even doctors are beginning to believe in."

"Doctors!" Amelia, the poet, said scornfully. "I've never in my life gone to a doctor that I didn't end up sicker than I was in the first place. And to add insult to injury, they put you in the poorhouse doing it."

Dana smiled. "That's how I got started on my book. I was sick, and as a writer, I couldn't afford insurance. I began to study herbs and what they could do."

"I don't give much ground to herbs, either," Amelia muttered. She tapped her forehead, and her short white curls bobbed. "It's all in the mind. Doesn't matter what you take, it's in the mind."

"Oh…" Jane began uncertainly, "you mean, you could take either prescription medicine or herbs, and depending on which one you believed in—"

"Turnips!" Amelia snapped. "You could take turnips, woman! It doesn't matter what you take, it's all in the *mind.*" Grace cast a contemptuous look at both of them and went back to stabbing her pork.

Dana, who didn't eat meat, picked at her vegetables. An awkward silence filled the kitchen, and Jane stepped in again, changing the subject. Laying down her fork, she stretched and sighed.

"What a wonderful meal! You know, I can't believe I'm here. After the PTA, the constant laundry, the carpooling—this is heaven."

"Don't tell me you don't have a house full of servants," Grace taunted.

"No. No, I don't," Jane answered slowly. "I have a once-a-week housekeeper, that's all."

"But a house that's big enough for an army, I'll bet," Grace replied, zeroing in. "You people with your big houses, big cars, big everything—you're ruining the world."

"Grace!" Dana said softly. "You can't just lump everyone—"

"Don't give me that!" Grace interrupted. "It's true. The rich are responsible for most of the ecological problems in the world. Everyone knows that."

"Well, we don't have to talk about it now," Dana said mildly, casting a sympathetic glance at Jane. "Can't we, for once, just have a nice dinner?"

"And just exactly when would you recommend we talk about the way the rich ruin the world?" Grace pushed. "What *nice dinner* would you prefer to ruin?"

Jane, turning a deep shade of red, stood and carried her plate to the sink. "I think I'll turn in early," she said.

I felt sorry for her. And just as sorry for myself. There were times when I thought I couldn't stand another dinner with these women. Always fighting, arguing, picking on each other.

All but Jane, who tried, but didn't have the ongoing fortitude to stand up for herself. And Dana, who did her best to keep the peace.

The rest, excluding Timmy, reminded me of children. Women in their twenties, thirties, forties, even seventies—going on five years old. *Put a bunch of women together on an isolated island, and see what you get.*

Later, I told myself that if I'd known how bad things could really get, I might have made a point of enjoying my "final meal."

Jane would echo my thoughts. "If only I had known..." she would say numbly, over and over—though even she knew it was bad form to write that in a novel.

* * *

We were in the living room of the farmhouse when it happened—Grace, Amelia, Dana and myself. Jane had gone back to her cottage, and Kim Stratton hadn't shown up at all. Timothea and Lucy were in the kitchen, cleaning up.

As was usual after dinner, we had gathered in comfortable chairs and sofas before the huge stone fireplace. A large bouquet of freshly cut flowers filled the hollow of the fireplace rather than wood, a nod to the overly warm weather that had fallen over the San Juans this day.

All four of us were at varying stages in our writing lives. Dana was working on her nonfiction book about natural healing, Amelia on a new poetry collection, and Grace...Grace never did say. The only thing I knew at this point was that she must have had a strong reason to come to this isolated island of few inhabitants and very little communication with the outside world. Esme was owned by Timmy and two of the other home owners on the island. Electricity came by way of generators, and water by wells. There was one battery-operated radio in the Thornberry office, and one cell phone serviced through a tower on Orcas. We had been asked to leave our own cell phones behind, and Timmy believed that she and the staff should live as simple a life as the residents here.

As for weather, it could get wild here even in the spring, with gale-force winds and unending storms. No one came to Esme without a good reason.

That night, however, had started out peacefully

enough. Through French doors we could see a setting sun. A family of deer munched on grass on the lawn. Dana smiled and said, "Jane was right. This really is heaven."

Amelia snorted. "Heaven, is it? Well, if you run across God, ask him how we're supposed to keep those bloody little woodstoves going in the cottages. Someday I'd like to write an entire ten-line poem before the damn thing goes out."

Dana sent a grin to me, and I turned to Amelia. "You sound like you don't like it here."

Amelia folded her arms across ample breasts. "I didn't say that, did I?"

I smiled. "No, you didn't say that."

"Well, don't go putting words in my mouth."

Amelia stared into the fireplace as if flames flickered there.

Perhaps Dana was right, I thought. Old trauma—murders, even—must be hanging around Thornberry. Otherwise, why were so many people here in a bad temper?

Tonight was worse than ever. There was something in the air, and it was affecting everyone. Kim Stratton, I thought, knew what she was doing, hiding out at night. From now on, I vowed, I would do that, too.

"Well, I guess I'll get started," Amelia said, pulling a thin sheaf of white paper from a needlepoint briefcase.

I stifled a sigh. *Here we go again. More cutoff breasts and blood gushing from women's vaginas into male-dominated ground. God save me from the political ones.*

Amelia's latest was indeed another politically driven, and—to give it credit—probably award-winning piece. I closed my eyes and tried to pretend I was listening, while in truth I was working on my own book in my head.

I felt a jolt, and my eyes flew open.

"Did anybody else feel that?" Grace asked.

Amelia looked up from her paper and frowned. "Feel what?"

Grace rubbed the back of her neck. "I don't know...I thought I felt something."

"You did," I confirmed. "I felt it, too."

"Probably a gust of wind," Dana added. "Coming from the kitchen. Lucy's got the door open back there."

Amelia returned to her reading.

"Damn, there it goes again!" Grace jumped to her feet.

Her words were barely out before the room shook violently.

"Earthquake!" Dana cried, her mouth forming a startled *O*. She grabbed the sides of her heavy arm-chair as it slid like dollhouse furniture along the hard-wood floor, striking the fireplace and throwing Dana into the hard stone facing. She screamed. Grace stag-gered and fell several feet across the room, hitting a coffee table with her knees and falling into a book-case. Blood spurted from her nose. The bookcase pitched forward, burying her beneath it. I rose and stumbled for balance, grabbing Amelia, who looked so pale I thought she might faint. There was nowhere to go, however. Nowhere to hide.

All around us, windows shattered. Glass rained down. The tiny panes of the French doors were sharp slivers. I felt a stab on my cheek as figurines, now projectiles, flew from the fireplace mantel and shelves. Mini-blinds rattled and broke, falling to the floor with a clatter. The deep rolling motion went on and on, seemingly forever, and the piercing screech of Thornberry's house alarm filled the night.

When the rolling and pitching was over, we were all in various positions on the floor. Dana lay against the hearth, blood dripping from her arm. Grace, still buried by the bookcase, groaned, but pushed at its weight and crawled out from under. Her nose was bleeding, and Amelia, next to me, looked dazed, her mouth drooping open.

I struggled to my feet, holding onto an end table. Heading across the room to Dana, I felt the warmth of blood trickling down my cheek. The living room was cluttered with debris; plaster had fallen from the ceiling, and glass crackled under my feet as I gingerly moved first one heavy beam, then another that had fallen from the ceiling. Sliding on a pile of books that had landed in the middle of the floor, I fell to a knee and yelped as a sliver of glass cut through my skin. Red flowed through my khaki pants.

Kneeling cautiously next to Dana, I checked her injured arm. The cut was four inches long and covered with plaster dust. That helped to staunch the bleeding, but the dirt and dust of years that had fallen with it weren't good news.

''It doesn't look too bad,'' Dana said shakily, wincing at my light touch. "I think we lucked out. Sarah, your face is cut."

Grace spoke from behind us, her tone sharp. "We can't stay in here. There'll be aftershocks."

"Dana's arm has to be cleaned," I said, helping her up, then repeated, "It needs to be cleaned."

I was on automatic, operating out of shock as my mind searched frantically to remember what I'd learned in all the earthquake preparedness meetings at the Justice building. I knew we had to get out of the house, but nothing made sense at the moment except to clean Dana's wound. The fact that my own face was bleeding had no effect on me whatsoever.

"You, too, Grace," I said. "Your nose is bleeding."

Holding Dana's good arm, I began to move cautiously with her over the shattered glass toward the downstairs bathroom. The ground started to pitch again.

"Damn it, we'll be buried alive in here!" Grace yelled, grabbing Amelia and running for the front door.

Dana and I swung around toward the door, but none of us made it. The aftershock felt even more violent than the first tremor, and this time we were thrown to the floor right where we stood. A board with nails in it barely missed my chin. Dana cried out, her face twisting in pain.

Screams issued from the kitchen.

"Timmy!" Amelia cried. "She's hurt!"

The center stairway from foyer to the upstairs level came crashing down, the spokes below the banister popping free and shooting in every direction like a bundle of Lincoln Logs hurled by an angry child.

Amelia's voice rose to an hysterical pitch. "Timmy! I'm coming!" She began to crawl toward the rubble of stairs, now a huge pile that rose halfway to the second floor.

"No!" Grace yelled, pulling her back just in time to save her from a flying stair tread full of nails. "You can't get through that way!"

She gave Amelia a hard shove through the front door, which was hanging by one hinge. The woman landed on her knees in the grass, crying out.

Dana and I made it to our feet and followed. Grace was the last one out, glancing toward the blocked-off kitchen before she stumbled through the doorway. She turned and looked up, on her face an expression of horror. I followed her gaze as the two upstairs levels of the farmhouse slid toward us like the top layers of a wedding cake.

We all turned and ran. From a safe distance we watched in disbelief as the entire mass shuddered, then thundered to a heap on the ground.

When the dust had settled, we staggered numbly to the debris and stared into its mass—boards, pipes, plaster, furniture, clothes and bathroom sinks. The huge chimney had fallen, and though parts of the farmhouse living room walls remained upright, there was no longer a ceiling or a roof. Nothing was left but a pile of rubble and bricks.

It was Dana who pointed out that the ground was no longer shaking. "Do you feel that? It's stopped."

We stared at each other, a mixture of relief and fear in each face.

"It'll start again," Grace said. "When it's this big, there are hundreds of aftershocks."

"She's right," I agreed.

I didn't want to admit how frightened I was. Authorities in Seattle had been warning for years that the Big One was coming, and if this was it, there would be hundreds, perhaps thousands of aftershocks, and possibly even tidal waves, the dreaded *tsunamis*. I wondered how close the epicenter was.

My gaze swung to the kitchen wing, which was new and one-storied. It was still standing, though windows had popped out and parts of the roof had caved in.

"Listen," I said.

Grace looked in that direction, her voice sharp. "To what?"

"It's too quiet in there."

Everyone turned that way.

"Oh, my God, Timmy!" Amelia cried. She swung around to Grace. "You should have let me go to her!"

"I saved your ass, old lady," Grace shot back, hands on her hips. "You could be under that rubble with them."

Amelia flushed, her face red and tear-streaked, hands shaking. "I don't know who you think you are—"

I broke in. "Stop it, both of you! For God's sake!"

"It doesn't look all that bad," Dana said softly.

"They could be okay. But what about Jane and Kim?"

A wave of fear swept over me. Had they—had *anyone* else—survived?

"Timmy can't be all right," Amelia said querulously. "She would be here by now, checking on us. Something's happened to her, or she'd be here by now!"

We no longer had access from the front. Heading at a run around the side of the house, we made for the back kitchen door. Slowing down as we reached it, Dana held her arm to staunch the renewed bleeding, and Grace rubbed a finger beneath her nose, which only smeared the blood that had been coagulating there. My legs shook, and I could see that Amelia was none too steady. I reached out and took her arm, urging her to lean on me.

The kitchen door stuck, but we were able to force it open despite the objects that had fallen against it. Once inside, the scene stopped us in our tracks. Though parts of the roof were indeed unscathed, there were huge, gaping holes. The entire inside ceiling had fallen, as had the skylight. Glass was everywhere, on cupboards, tables, in the sink, on the floor. Copper pots, which had hung gleaming on the walls only moments before, lay in a pile. Dishes had flown from cupboards and were strewn from one end of the room to the other. The huge stainless steel refrigerator had slid and lay on its side halfway across the room from where it had stood for years. Its door lay open, and jars of home-preserved jams had fallen out and broken. Reddish-purple streams of blackberry and raspberry jam flowed like blood onto the floor.

It was this that caught my attention first. I thought it was blood, and I ran to it, then realized my mistake. At the same time, I heard a moan.

"Quiet!" I yelled at Grace, who was issuing orders to Amelia and Dana to search through the rubble. "There's somebody here."

We lifted the heavy appliance together, all four of us at one end, and pushed it out of the way. The person under the fridge was Lucy, and as her condition became clear, Amelia began to cry. "Lucy...oh, poor Lucy."

I checked her pulse, though it wasn't necessary. Lucy's neck was broken, her head twisted at an odd angle to her body. "She's dead," I said quietly.

"Poor, poor thing," Amelia whispered, rocking back and forth on her knees and touching the other woman's face as if to bring her back to life.

"For God's sake, woman!" Grace said. "It's not like she was your best friend!"

Amelia's breath caught on a sob. She looked around frantically. "Timmy? Where is Timmy?"

"I heard a moan," I said. "If it wasn't Lucy—"

We began to toss debris aside, and in a corner we finally found Timothea, semiconscious, her eyes closed.

Amelia gently touched her face. "It's all right, it's all right, all right..." she murmured over and over.

I stroked the gray hair back from Timmy's forehead, which was smeared with blood. Dana went to the sink for a wet rag. When she turned on the faucet, nothing came out.

"Damn!" She rummaged under the sink for bottled water, then in the open cupboards. Finally, she uncovered a bottle in the wreckage on the floor.

"Not too much," I warned, as Dana wet the rag. She looked at me questioningly.

"We don't know how long we'll be without, or how much more we'll find," I said. "We'd better ration it."

Dana nodded and screwed the cap back on the water bottle, handing me the dampened rag. I wiped the blood from Timmy's forehead, and she opened her eyes. They registered shock, then comprehension, then worry.

"Is everyone all right?" Her voice was shaky, but her grip on my arm was strong.

"We don't know about Jane and Kim, yet," I answered. "The rest of us are fine. How do you feel?"

"Sore. Sore all over." She tried to sit up. "Lucy? She was over—"

I pushed her gently back down. "Just rest, Timmy."

"But Lucy—"

I shook my head. "I'm sorry. We can't do anything for her."

Understanding came over Timmy's face. "Oh, no. Oh, no. Dear God." Tears welled in her pale blue eyes.

"We don't know about the cottages, yet," I said, "but the entire upstairs and parts of the living room have collapsed. I'm sorry."

Timmy squeezed her eyes shut briefly, then nodded. "I'm all right. I really am. Help me up, will you?"

"I'm not sure—"

"Just help me up!" she said angrily. Her mouth trembled, as did her entire body. "I have to take care of things!"

She put a hand on my shoulder to pull herself to a sitting position. Reluctantly, I helped her to stand, then turned to Dana and Amelia. "Will you take her outside? Stay with her?"

I turned to Grace. "Come with me and we'll check out the cottages for Jane and Kim."

Two hours later there were seven of us on the dark lawn, wrapped in blankets, with salvaged pillows and bottles of water beside us. Just that afternoon there had been ten women at Thornberry. We couldn't know the fate of the two assistants who had left for Whidbey, but here on Esme Island, one of our number was now dead.

We had wrapped Lucy's body in a blanket scrounged from the debris, and laid her to rest, temporarily, under what Timmy told us was her favorite tree. We didn't know how long that "temporary" status might last. There was no law or rescue service on the island, and neighbors in the other three houses on Esme were not usually in residence until summer.

The small battery-operated radio we'd uncovered in the office debris had lasted only a few minutes, and there were no more batteries because Timmy had forgotten to buy extras. Those few minutes, however, were long enough for us to hear that the quake had indeed been the Big One, and that Seattle was in chaos, along with surrounding cities from Olympia in the south to Victoria, B.C., to the north. The quake had been felt, in varying degrees, as far south as San Francisco, and as far north as Alaska.

It was known that the San Juan Islands had been involved, the newscaster had said, based on reports from the U.S. Geological Survey. Helicopters that would ordinarily assess damage to those outlying areas, however, were in use transporting the many wounded and dead in the cities.

As for rescue teams, they had been decimated. Workers who were at home were unable to get to their places of duty, and at any rate were involved in taking care of their own families, many of whom were missing or dead. Buildings and freeways had crumpled, much like those in the 1995 quake in Kobe, Japan. Those who had thought Seattle was prepared for such a disaster were in shock. No one had prepared for this—a 9.1, if it didn't go up from there when all the reports were in.

The last thing we heard before the radio's batteries faded was that *tsunami* warnings had been issued for the entire west coast, from the San Juans south.

I huddled in my fleece jacket and looked around at the other women. We had found Kim and Jane standing in a daze outside their cottages, which had been totaled. The farmhouse, despite its near ruin, seemed to have survived better than any other structure at Thornberry. Even the goat pen had been demolished. The goats had run off.

When the aftershocks stopped, or at least slowed

down, we would move inside and begin cleaning up. After that, we would all have to sleep and live in the kitchen until help arrived. We would have to pray it didn't rain.

Jane was sobbing, terrified for her children and husband in Seattle. She had drawn her knees up in a fetal position and refused to look at anyone. Grace had distanced herself from all of us, and Dana sat quietly, her eyes closed. She didn't talk about the husband she'd left behind in Santa Fe. Amelia was stone-faced, and in just as much shock as the rest of us, but unwilling to admit it.

I wondered why she had pretended all this time to be just like us—a guest who had been invited but didn't know anyone here. Clearly, she was closer to Timmy, and even Lucy, than she'd let on. A strange old bird, tough on the outside but with surprisingly deep feelings inside.

Kim Stratton had proven to have more gumption and selflessness than anyone would have expected. Though everything she had brought to Thornberry with her had been buried beneath the ruins of her cottage, she had helped Jane to carry her few salvaged belongings down to the farmhouse lawn. She sat silently, now, her long auburn hair pulled back into a ponytail, her face smeared with dirt and sweat.

As for me, I worried that I might not have a home to go back to now, and I worried that my mom would be going crazy without news. But that was all. I had severed ties with most friends and co-workers after the arrest. Or they had severed ties with me.

There was Ian, of course. Had he survived the quake?

And if so, did he wonder about me?

Not likely. And not that I honestly cared. There had always been something about Ian I didn't like—even when we were deep into sex, and had been together for months. In bed, I would look up into his eyes, eyes I had always thought were as lovely as a woman's—long-lashed and ice-blue—and wonder what secrets lay behind them. When he betrayed me, I felt only a small jolt of surprise.

So it was done. Over. Even my impending trial paled in comparison. All that mattered was getting out of this alive.

As I thought that, the ground began to rumble again. Jane buried her face against her knees and sobbed. I and the others hunkered miserably into our blankets, and I thought I knew what they were thinking—the same thing I'd been thinking: Had the end of the world finally arrived?

# PART III

# THE CRIME

# 4

---

The morning after the quake, a blood-red sun rose over the Sound, tinting the snowy tops of the Cascade Range. We had spent a miserable and frightening night on the lawn outside the Thornberry farmhouse. Aside from the cold and damp, there were the aftershocks, some of them almost as large as the original quake.

We stirred and began to sit up.

"I thought daylight would never come," Dana said, rubbing her arms vigorously for warmth. "This has been the longest night of my life."

I was forced to agree. I had nodded off a few times, only to have nightmares of rolling ground beneath me—nightmares that turned out to be all too real each time I woke.

I stood and shook the blanket from me, running fingers through my hair in a feeble attempt to straighten it. Since I'd cut it, it had grown out a few inches, and a natural curl made it tangle at night.

*I'd give my right arm for a shower,* I thought. *Or to wash my face.* But even though the Thornberry kitchen sink stood miraculously untouched, the water line from the well's reservoir had broken, and the pump no longer worked. Nor could we use the one toilet in the farmhouse that remained standing. Like soldiers on bivouac, we had dug holes in the ground fifty yards into the woods. Grace was responsible for this idea, as well as a large percentage of the work it took.

"I'll tell you one thing, I'm not going back inside," Jane said, "not in the farmhouse or anywhere." She gripped her blanket around her as another aftershock hit. We held our breaths till it was over, time suspended.

Afterward, Jane continued, her voice noticeably shakier. "Aren't these things supposed to get less and less strong as time goes on?"

"Yeah, and people are supposed to prepare better," Grace said pointedly to Timmy. "Why the hell didn't you put away water and emergency food rations somewhere safe? Not to mention more portable radios, batteries, light sticks, camp stoves, propane lamps—" She broke off, cussing. "Where the fucking hell was your head, anyway? One cell phone in the whole damn place? And it's under rubble now?"

Timmy blanched, but didn't answer. I thought I saw her lips tremble, but the light wasn't good so I wasn't sure. I was about to break into Grace's diatribe when Amelia did that for me.

"Timmy did her best," she said defensively. "She couldn't—"

"Couldn't what?"

"Hush, Amelia," Timmy said. "She's right. Besides, she wouldn't understand."

Amelia shot a contemptuous look at Grace and turned away.

Grace shook her head. "You bet your sweet ass I wouldn't understand. Sure, there are cans of food in the kitchen, but we can't cook it, now that the line's broken to the fuel tank. The stove is electric, and the generator's useless without fuel. Besides that, whatever was in the fridge is spoiled by now. Or soon will be."

"Well, at least there *are* plenty of cans of food," Dana said in a surprisingly irate voice. "We can damn well eat things cold! Besides, there's plenty of oysters around here. They aren't bad raw."

Grace gave a shudder. "And what do we do about water?" She held up a 12-ounce bottle of Perrier. "If these were all we could find last night, I doubt there are many more. Good God, Amelia, if Timmy had spent less on frills—"

"I suppose you have all those things in your own home," Amelia said angrily. "You're prepared for anything, no matter what."

"You're damned right, I am. It's not like we haven't had enough warnings in the past few years, even in New York. Not just about earthquakes, but blizzards, tornadoes, floods. And if you were any kind of friend to Timothea—which it seems you happen to be—or if you were a responsible person at all, you'd have made sure she stocked emergency supplies—"

"Will you two please stop!" Jane cried. She stood and flung her blanket to the ground, doubling her fists. Tears ran down her face. "My children may be dead right now! Do you realize that? While you two are harping at each other, my kids could be dead!"

"All right, that's it!" I said, standing. "First of all,

I've just about had it with you, Grace. Maybe you're right, maybe Timmy could have prepared better. But it doesn't help to stand around and rant at each other.''

I turned to Jane and put both hands on her shoulders. "Look, I know this is awful for you. But, Jane, we have to focus now on finding a way to communicate with the mainland. The sooner we do that, the sooner we may be able to reach your husband and children. At the very least, a portable radio might give us some up-to-date news. We could find out how things are going down there."

Jane fell silent, and Dana asked, "What do you have in mind?"

"I've been thinking about it all night. There are three other houses on the island. Two, as I remember, are summer cabins. Right, Timmy?"

She nodded. "They've sold a couple of times over the years, but both have been vacant quite a while."

"And the Ford house?"

"It's still there, of course. The son owns it now, but he only comes out here in the summer."

"Luke, you mean?"

She nodded again.

*So he's still around.* "Any chance he'd be there now?" I asked. "It's almost summer."

"I've never known him to be here this early," Timmy said. "And I'm pretty sure he would have let me know he was here, if he was."

"So unless someone just happens to be visiting those two cabins, we're the only people on the island, right? Then, what we need to do is check out those cabins, and Luke's house, and see if they are indeed vacant, and if they survived the quake. If so, they might have some things we can use till help arrives."

I turned to Timmy. "Two people should stay behind, just on the off chance a rescue party comes by. Do you mind? You and Amelia?"

"Leave the two old ladies behind, is that it?" Amelia said spiritedly. "Not on your life. Leave Jane. I'm as strong as she is."

"I'm sure you are," I said, though in truth I doubted it. It wasn't Amelia's age that was against her, as many women in their seventies were good hikers. But I'd seen her trembling when she thought no one was looking. It had been a difficult twelve hours, and Amelia needed rest, not the exertion of tramping through the woods. As for Timmy, she had suffered too much loss. To my eyes, she seemed close to breaking.

"I also thought maybe you and Timmy could check out the grounds here," I said. "See what kinds of vegetables are left in the gardens, like maybe some carrots still in the ground from last fall? Do you mind?"

Amelia hesitated, but looked at Timmy, who seemed very frail, suddenly. "No," she said, "of course not."

"Okay, then, let's get going," Dana said. "I'm more than ready."

We all looked at each other for signs of agreement. Kim, who hadn't yet spoken, said, "Just one thing. Does anyone here have a gun?"

Jane laughed uncertainly. "My goodness, no. Who

on earth would have thought we'd ever need one here?''

Dana shook her head, and Amelia raised her white brows and said, "That's an odd thing to ask."

"Not if you've ever been in an earthquake," Kim said. "I have."

"You mean in L.A.?"

She nodded. "The Northridge. People went nuts."

"But that was entirely different," I said. "L.A. is a big city. Here, there's no one else on the island. Only us."

Kim gave me a weighted look, then flicked her eyes to Grace.

We all followed her gaze.

Grace flushed, then said, "Oh, for God's sake! I may not be the most patient person in the world, but it's not like I'm going to kill anyone."

No one said a word.


Kim Stratton and I made our way along the shoreline to the east, while Dana, Jane and Grace headed west to check out the two cabins. Our plan was to meet at the Ford house, which was in the approximate middle of the island, on the northern shore. The more direct, cross-island path Luke and I had created all those years ago had grown over, and I hadn't been able to find it from Thornberry. Our trek would take us a bit longer than if the more direct three-mile route had been available, but we thought that if we kept a steady pace, we could be there in less than four hours.

The beach consisted of gray rock, not sand, and was lined with fir and cedar trees. At times we were forced to navigate huge logs that had washed up during storms, and in several places the shoreline came to a dead stop by boulders we had to climb to get where the beach began again.

I was grateful I'd worn my hiking boots, jeans, and a warm sweater and coat to dinner the night before. A quick check of my cottage this morning had revealed most of my belongings were buried beneath debris. There hadn't been time to see what could be salvaged—nor had I wanted to. My nerves were shot, and I felt exhausted after so little sleep.

Nor could I eat. Timmy and Amelia had put together a breakfast of fruit and found muffins. I had wrapped a muffin in a napkin and had stuck it into my coat pocket for later. Kim and I each carried a bottle of water.

Each of our two groups had an air horn that we'd found in the kitchen pantry, nearly buried by flour sacks. They were one of the few things Timmy had set aside for emergencies—not that she'd expected anything like this, I thought. More likely illness, or an invasion by bear.

*Are* there bears up here? I suddenly wondered, nervously scanning a thick stand of fir trees. Grizzlies could kill a person with one swat and eat the evidence before anyone was the wiser.

*Stop it. Better to worry about these damned aftershocks. Will they never stop?*

Unable to steady myself as another one hit, I let it take me to my knees, then flattened myself on the ground. Kim fell prone beside me.

"That one felt stronger than the others," she said,

gripping the ground with her fists. "God help us if the first one was only a foreshock."

"Don't even think it."

If I felt like I'd been through hell in Seattle before coming here, that whole business seemed more like purgatory now—the place Catholics believe you can pray yourself out of, like buying tickets to a fair. This—this not knowing what was going to happen next—was hell.

Or so I thought then, not knowing how much worse things were going to get.

I stood, brushing sharp, gravel-like sand from my knees and palms. As I did so, I felt like screaming— like running into the woods and beating on the ground. The only thing that kept me from doing that was feeling I had to keep up my spirits. If not for my sake, then for Kim's. Though she probably didn't need me for that.

On first meeting, Kim had seemed spoiled and standoffish. The two times she did show up for after-dinner coffee, she asked endless gossipy questions about our personal lives. I supposed this was what passed for conversation in Hollywood.

Still, I had to admit that Kim had been proving her mettle, ever since we'd found her outside her cottage yesterday, looking more angry than anything else.

I said to her now, as we began to walk again, "I'm amazed at how you're taking all this."

Her tone registered amusement. "Because I'm a *star* you mean?"

"Well, no…"

But that was exactly what I'd meant. "I guess you don't seem the type—" I broke off. "Sorry."

"Oh, hell, it's okay. You couldn't be expected to know that in less than two years in L.A., I went through fires, floods, riots, and the worst earthquake disaster to hit California in decades. I was in the Valley filming when the Northridge quake struck. We were all cut off from our homes for days, and the worst part was that when we got home, some of us couldn't even find our front yards beneath the rubble. Then the rains began." She gave a low laugh. "God, it was awful. I lost the first house I ever bought with my own money, when it slid down a hill onto Pacific Coast Highway."

"I'm sorry."

"Thanks. It was rough. So I guess I'd have to say that so far, this little rocker is a piece of cake."

I smiled. "I'm glad *someone* feels that way. But I jumped to conclusions about you, and I don't usually do that."

Kim rubbed a smear of dirt from her face. "If it's any consolation, you're not the first. C'mon, let's go."

This time I followed, watching the dark red pony-tail bob ahead of me. After the rosy sunset the night before, the day had turned chilly, the sky spitting rain. Kim wore only the jeans, long-sleeved sweatshirt and Saucony sports shoes she'd had on when the quake struck the day before. They were soaked clear through.

I caught up to her. "Kim, listen. I wasn't thinking

when I asked you to come with me. We should have taken more time to find you warm clothes.''

She smiled. ''Guess you've never been on location, have you?''

''No. Pretty tough?''

''Try swimming in a creek in Yellowstone when it's thirty degrees out and starting to snow.''

''Ugh. You must like your work, though, to be so successful at it. They say we thrive the most in the kind of work we love.''

''I suppose that's true, at least for some. For me, it's been a long, hard road, getting to where I am now. Some of it I don't even want to remember.'' Her face clouded over. ''What about you?''

I started to answer just as we rounded another curve on the beach—only to see another stretch of uninhabited shoreline.

''Damn,'' I said. ''Where is that house, anyway? I remembered it being closer.''

''You want to rest?'' she asked.

I shook my head. ''I do need something to eat, though.'' Pulling out the poppyseed muffin, I broke it in two and offered one half to Kim.

''Thanks. Listen, let's sit down a minute so I can take my socks off. There's so much sand lumped inside them, they're making my toes sore.''

Holding the piece of muffin in her teeth, she untied her shoes and removed her socks, stuffing them into a pocket. We both sat for a moment, eating silently.

''You're a lawyer, right?'' Kim said, as the final bite of muffin disappeared. She brushed crumbs off her jeans. ''A public defender?''

"I was."

"You were? What happened? Or shouldn't I ask?"

I gave a shrug. "It looks like we're going to be on this blasted island together for a while, so sure, you can ask. I was a public defender in Seattle. I lost my job."

"Cutbacks?"

"No. I was fired."

She looked at me sharply. "I can't imagine you doing something bad enough to get fired over."

"Really? But we hardly know each other."

"Well, it's true I haven't gotten to know you very well," Kim admitted. "And that's my fault. Believe it or not, even though I can hang loose in front of a camera, I don't feel comfortable in groups of women. I don't seem to have much in common with them, and I never know what to say. But the way you took over yesterday when the quake happened—not getting freaked out or anything—I guess I saw you as being in some sort of responsible job and never doing anything wrong."

I almost laughed. "Well, you've got some of that right. I was in a responsible job, and I didn't do anything wrong. Somebody set me up for drug possession with intent to sell, and now I've got a trial pending."

"You're kidding!"

"I wish."

"But, Sarah, doesn't being an attorney allow you more of a chance of clearing yourself? You can convince a jury you're innocent, right? Then you can go back to work?"

"Aye, and there's the rub…convincing a jury of my innocence."

Kim nodded and sighed. "I was offered a role like that—an innocent woman, behind bars. I turned it down because my agent didn't want me to play a prisoner." She rolled her eyes. "Like people don't know the difference between real life and acting these days. Laura West, who did take the part— Do you know her?"

"I know of her, of course," I said. "Julia Roberts's latest competition, right? Or so it's said. Personally, I don't think she can hold a candle to Roberts."

"I agree. Even so, she won an Oscar for the part of that inmate. I was left to look at it as the road not taken."

"Frost," I said. "'Two roads diverged in a wood, and I—'"

"'I took the one less traveled by,'" Kim finished for me, smiling. "High school. And don't look so surprised. I've got a memory like an elephant."

"I guess that comes in handy when you have to study a script."

She nodded. "It put me in demand when I was first starting out and working in low-budget flicks. Public defenders, though—they don't make much money, do they?"

"No. But I didn't go into it for that."

"Yeah, I know what you mean. I had a role in a film once as the president of a perfume company. Sylvie, her name was. She quit when she was forty to become a missionary." Kim laughed, a loud, free sound that surprised me, coming from her, and under these circumstances. "A really bad movie. Did you see it? 'Heavenly Scent'?"

I smiled at the title. "'Heavenly Scent'? I'm sorry, no. I haven't found much time over the years for movies. I usually go over briefs at night and on weekends."

"Me, too. When I'm not filming, I mean, I stay home, crash and watch TV. Of course, I usually watch movies on TV. I guess we tend to relax with the same kind of work we do."

"How true."

"So, this charge you've got against you. Is there some way you can prove your innocence? I mean, as a lawyer, you must know how to do that, right?"

I hesitated. The quake had loosened my tongue, yet I didn't feel entirely comfortable telling Kim how I planned to prove my innocence.

"Hopefully, I'll remember how to be a lawyer when we get out of this," I settled for. "Why don't we keep walking? It's beginning to look like a long day."

She wiggled into her damp shoes, and as we walked, a mist moved in over the island. I was reminded of the *tsunami* warning we'd heard over the radio, the possibility of a wave several stories high striking the shore here and engulfing us all. The one from Alaska in 1964 had reached a height of 250 feet—the approximate height of a twenty-five-story building—and had landed as far south as Crescent City, California, destroying large portions of that town. Would a *tsunami,* if it originated from a Seattle epicenter, move this way, as the newscaster on the radio had suggested? Or would it travel south?

I couldn't remember, from the earthquake preparedness sessions. We could only hope we would find a portable radio at the Ford house. Maybe even a cell phone. Though how much good that would do, if its batteries were dead, I didn't know. For that matter, would there even be service? Were nearby towers intact, or had they gone down, too?

I couldn't think about it. The worry alone was sapping my strength.

"To answer your question," I continued, as we dodged incoming ripples on the shore, "I was helping out a working woman—a prostitute. She'd been raped by cops, and they killed her to keep her from testifying. Then they came after me. Two murders would have been too much, I suppose, so they set me up with a phony drug charge to discredit me. They also hoped to scare me into shutting up about what they'd done. Well, with the victim dead, that's the way it might have gone. The story was in all the papers, as well as on the evening news, that Sarah Lansing—who'd defended criminals so 'brilliantly' over the years—was now one of them herself."

I paused to scan the line of trees, saw nothing resembling a roofline, and continued. "I already had a record as a public defender for getting the worst kinds of criminals off. That was my job, to provide a defense for anyone—guilty or not—however uncomfortable it might sometimes be. Of course, the cops hated me for it."

"They were afraid of you," Kim said firmly.

For a brief moment I felt a start, as if she somehow already knew what had happened.

But then she explained, "If this were a movie, and you were to go after them—which it sounds like you were about to do—you'd be a powerful foe. They'd have to silence you. Right?"

I paused and bent to pick up a long piece of driftwood, which I used as a staff to lean on for a moment. This talk, as well as the walk, was taking more out of me than I'd imagined it would. My knees were shaky.

"So," Kim continued, "what you would need, Sarah, is some sort of evidence the cops couldn't get to. Something to hold over their heads."

I searched her face. "What gave you that idea?"

She grinned. "I saw it in a movie. I think Brian Dennehy was the good cop, and maybe James Woods was the bad one—but I could be confusing this with another film entirely."

Her tone became serious. "All I can say, Sarah, is that you probably want to look out for yourself. These cops don't sound like they're going to be satisfied with your just being on trial. Too many things might come out, don't you think? Things that could incriminate them? Sarah, putting myself in their place, I think I'd be trying to shut you up before that time comes—and I'd do it in a way that fit the drug possession charge. Have you take an overdose, or something. In fact, I'd guess their setting you up on that charge was only a first step in a larger plan."

I stared at her. Moments passed. Finally, she

laughed, awkwardly. "Sorry. My imagination runs wild sometimes."

"That's a bit of an understatement," I said.

My eyes met Kim's, and she didn't look away, or even blink. "You're not going to let them get away with this—are you, Sarah?"

"I...no," I said. "No, I'm not."

"You have a plan?"

I realized, now, that I'd said far too much. I had allowed myself to get caught up in that syndrome of bonding with someone I'd been going through a disaster with. But who knew what Kim Stratton's motives were?

"Sarah?"

"Hmm? Sorry."

"I was asking, have you been able to get the evidence you need to prove you were set up?"

I made a wide arc with my walking stick and threw it far out over the water, watching as the swift tide carried it away. I imagined my troubles being carried off with it, disappearing round the bend—like putting all your woes into a big brown bag by your bed at night, so you could go to sleep without worrying about them.

"You know what?" I said. "I'm so tired of thinking about all this. And I'm almost sure I can see the Ford house chimney up there, through those trees."

"You're right," Kim said, looking that way. The moment of tension passed. "Thank God!" she said. "I'm getting tired of tramping around this damned island. Besides, if this were a movie, there would at least be a happy ending. I'm not so sure we're going to get one of those.''

''I'm afraid you could be right,'' I said, as Luke's house appeared before us. Things did not look good.

# 5

The Ford house—or Ransford, as it had been named after Luke's grandfather's first name, Randell, and his last, Ford—had once been even more beautiful than Thornberry. In the past twelve or so hours, however, it had taken a bad blow. One side of it looked as if a giant had come along and crunched it with his foot. The other side seemed oddly intact, like one of those inexplicable survivors standing next to a dismembered airliner, feeling guilty to still be alive.

The once broad, white portico that had fronted the house was now only a pile of lumber. The front door had fallen completely off its hinges. Tall windows beside it had shattered and now lay in glittering heaps. Kim and I made our way up a path of cobblestones that had scattered in many directions. As we reached the broken glass, I forged a path to the door, kicking shards aside with my hiking boots. Kim, in her canvas shoes, brought up the rear.

Inside, plaster had crumbled, and chairs, sofas and small tables had been strewn in every direction. The overall effect was that of a junkyard—or, I thought, Homestead, Florida, after Hurricane Andrew. A jumbled pile of wreckage.

"What a mess," Kim said.

"It sure is," I agreed, sighing. I had spent many happy hours here as a teenager, pretending to read if Luke wasn't around, listening to my dad and his talk law.

Luke's father was a judge in Seattle, and the last I'd heard, he had retired. I wondered how he'd feel if he could see this devastation. Charles Randell Ford had taken great pride in his home, as had Luke's mother, Priscilla. They were high on the social ladder, and entertained here throughout the summers, bringing in guests on private ferries that pulled up to a dock strung with tiny colored lights and Japanese lanterns. The music from the live bands they brought in could be heard all the way to Thornberry, and there were many nights when I would sneak out through my bedroom window at Thornberry and make my way through the woods to Ransford. There I would sit out of sight beneath a tree and watch people dancing on a platform erected on the lawn. I'd read *The Great Gatsby* one of those summers, and the Fords became my Gatsby—a standard for elegant living. Now and then I'd even get a glimpse of Luke— though he would more often than not be dancing with some girl I didn't know, which also, more often than not, sent me home in a bad mood.

I never knew, till that last summer when we came together, if Luke would have danced with me at his parents' parties. The one time I was invited by his parents, my own had refused to let me go. I was too young, they told me.

"But Luke's not too young, and he's the same age as me," I would argue.

I never did win one of those arguments, and came to understand how difficult it was, for a teenager, having a lawyer for a father.

"The stairs seem intact," I said, looking at the wide circular staircase that rose to the second floor. It was covered with debris, however, largely plaster and wood from the walls. The ceiling was, miraculously, still in place.

"Why don't we start downstairs?" I suggested. "Let's see if we can find a cell phone or a radio."

We began digging through the rubble with our hands, but as cuts developed, we came up with the idea of using short pieces of lumber to push things around. In the kitchen area, where the refrigerator had toppled and shattered dishes lay on the floor, we were thrilled to find a dustpan. No brush, but we used the pan to scoop trash out of the way as we sorted through it, looking for anything useful. Surprisingly, many dishes had survived intact here, and even a full set of glasses. Odd, I thought, the things that make it through an earthquake. It's like after a tornado, where one house is left standing untouched, while the one next to it is demolished.

There was little of use in the way of food, however. I would have expected the Fords to be more prepared for a disaster, as wild as the weather can get up here. There were a few canned goods—pork and beans, chicken and rice soup, creamed corn and a variety of other vegetables. Eighteen cans in all. But no radio. And no cell phone, unless it was hopelessly lost beneath rubble we couldn't lift.

I wondered where Grace, Jane and Dana were, and

what was taking them so long. We could use them to help us clear the stairs to the second level.

Exhausted, we stood with our hands on our hips and looked around, shaking our heads in discouragement.

"Reminds me of that old joke," I said.

"Joke?"

"The woman walks into her apartment with a new friend, and it's a mess. Clothes, books, tapes, food all over the place. Bureau drawers wide open in the bedroom, shoes all over the floor. The friend says, horrified, 'My God, you've been burglarized!' The woman says, 'No, I just didn't clean today.'"

Kim laughed. "Works for me."

We decided to go through the mess once more, on the theory that we might have missed something useful, focused as we'd been on finding a cell phone and radio. After another twenty minutes of scavenging through kitchen and living area, we had little to show for our efforts: the cans of food, a pair of suede gardening gloves, a screwdriver, and one huge Tweety Bird beach towel.

"Too bad we didn't bring backpacks for this stuff," I said, looking at the results of our heist. "I had two of them, but they were buried in my cottage under all the mess."

"I'm afraid I never dreamed I'd need a backpack here," Kim responded. "Talk about a babe in the woods."

I made a knapsack of the beach towel by tying the corners together, and put our cache inside.

At my insistence, Kim was already wearing the

gloves. "When we get out of this," I'd argued, "you can't be making movies with your hands all scarred up. Me? If I ever get out of this, I may just beat a few people up. I could use some calluses."

I took the knapsack and set it by the kitchen door, thinking we'd go down to the dock and look around before we left. "I guess we should tackle the second floor while we wait for the others."

Kim had been standing at the door, which, since Ransford had been built on a small peninsula, faced the opposite shoreline from where we'd come. Over the past few minutes, dark storm clouds had formed, and a brisk wind was kicking up. Kim anxiously scanned the horizon.

"What's next, do you suppose?" she said. "Hurricane? Floods? Pestilence?"

"We don't have hurricanes here," I said. Then, spotting Grace with the others on the beach, I added, "Pestilence, maybe."

Kim laughed.

We headed down the hill to meet them, but as we drew closer, Grace started to run toward the Ransford dock, which was visible from this direction. Dana and Jane began to run, too, and I strained to see what had set them off.

The dock had broken in two, with one end of it collapsed into the water. Several yards offshore, a boat lay half submerged. My gaze swung back to the dock, then fixed on a figure lying there.

"It's a man!" Kim said from behind me. "It's the body of a man."

I still couldn't see clearly, but some inner sense

told me who it was. Looking back, I guess I could say it was wishful thinking. In that instant, however, I honestly wondered if I'd conjured him up. I started running, and when I got to Luke I pushed Grace out of the way.

"Luke? Luke!" I said, taking his face between my hands. "My God!"

Blood poured from a cut on his temple, and for a moment I thought he might be dead. But then he groaned, and relief swept over me. His white shirt and jeans were soaked, however, as were his shoes. The wind was kicking up waves, and they were splashing over onto the dock, drenching us all.

I spoke his name a third time, my voice rising— and he stirred. His eyes fluttered open and fixed on mine, then widened.

"Sarah?"

I took both his hands, warming them between mine. "Hi. Yes, it's me. Are you all right?"

He looked at the five other faces staring down at him. "I... My boat. Heavy winds. It went down." He rubbed his head and began to sit up. "I must have hit something when I went overboard."

"Help me get him onto dry land," I said. Several hands supported his arms and grabbed him around his waist. We half carried him the few feet onto the beach, where he sat, gathering his strength.

I studied him, between waves of relief. Luke's hair was as curly as ever, but shorter, collar length, and tinged along the edges with gray. There were deep lines in his face, as if he'd spent a lot of time in the sun. Other than that, he seemed much the same as the last time I'd seen him, twenty-two years ago.

"God, you look good, Sarah," he said, still dazed but focusing on me.

I flushed as the other women looked curiously at us both.

"I'm over at Thornberry," I said. "We all are."

I introduced Dana, then Kim, Grace and Jane. "Luke and I are old friends, from long ago," I said.

Then, to him, "What are you doing here?"

"I was over at Orcas when the quake hit. I started out early this morning in my friend's boat, to see what kind of damage the house had taken. But it's gusty as hell out there. When I tried to get in here to dock, I got stuck on a sandbar."

He turned and looked at the wrecked boat, shaking his head. "All I remember is a flash of pain, then I was on the dock."

His gaze shifted to the house. "Oh, God. Sarah? Have you been up there?"

I nodded. "It isn't good."

"Damn. I didn't dare hope it would be, but—"

He winced as pain apparently shot through his head.

"Don't worry," I said, as rain began to fall. "Let's just get you up there. We need to find you some dry clothes and take care of that cut."

We were a miserable, wet lot, entering Ransford together. Dana and Jane made all the appropriate, sympathetic sounds, as Luke stood in the living room, looking around. Grace took a stance with her arms folded, an expression of disgust on her face as she took in the condition of the house.

"Don't start," I muttered under my breath, certain she was about to embark on a diatribe about people who didn't make sure their homes were up to code. She turned and walked off, staring through the front doorway at the rain pouring down.

"One good thing," I said to Luke, walking over to stand by his side. "You still have a roof. Most of Thornberry was demolished."

He frowned. "I'm sorry to hear that. What about Timmy? Is she all right?"

"Yes, she's fine. But Lucy, the cook..."

I let the rest of the sentence hang, and he rubbed his face wearily. Blood smeared from the cut on his temple, and I reached into my pocket and pulled out a wad of clean but damp Kleenex. Dabbing the cut, I told him to press the tissue against it for a few minutes. He did, wincing as the Kleenex began to soak up blood.

"God, Sarah, what a mess. I'm afraid I didn't know Lucy. I haven't spent a lot of time at Thornberry lately."

I wanted to ask him where he had been, and what he'd been doing all these years, but this definitely wasn't the time.

"We haven't been upstairs yet," I said. "Kim and I got here first, and we only managed to check out the downstairs. We couldn't find a cell phone or a battery-operated radio, and we thought there might be something like that in one of the bedrooms."

Luke walked over to the stairway. "It shouldn't be

too hard to clean this up. But I doubt we'll find anything. My parents stopped leaving things like phones and radios through the winter a long time ago, because the batteries only went dead.''

He shook his head. ''I'm afraid I've been doing the same, out of habit. I take everything with me when I leave here.''

''What about that boat?'' Grace said sharply.

Luke turned to her. ''What about it?'' he said, with nearly as much of an edge in his voice.

''Don't tell me you started over here from Orcas, after a major earthquake, without a cell phone or a radio.''

''All right, I won't tell you,'' Luke said testily. His lips tightened. Then, in a quieter voice to me, he said, ''What's her problem?''

''No problem,'' Grace—who had clearly heard him—said. ''I'm just a bit sick of people who don't think ahead.''

He glared at her. ''And I should care about that exactly why?''

Grace frowned and went back to staring out the doorway. I looked at Luke and just rolled my eyes. *Don't bother,* I mouthed.

''I wouldn't mind checking out the bedrooms, anyway,'' Jane said. ''Just in case you forgot and left something here.''

''I tend to agree,'' Dana said. ''Besides, you need some dry clothes. For that matter, we could all use some—if, by chance, you've got anything up there we could use? Like maybe old stuff, clothes you leave behind between summers?''

Luke hesitated, seemingly reluctant. I put this down to his still feeling rocky after having been beached.

"We women can clean off the stairs ourselves," I began, "if you—"

"No, I'm all right," he said. "I'm just certain you won't find much of any use up there. But, okay. Let's get started on these stairs."

I looked over at Grace, who still wasn't facing us. Even so, I could see from her profile that she continued to frown.

*And what the hell is that all about?* I wondered.

Original works of art and statuary lined the hallway upstairs. One statue had toppled over and broken in half; two paintings lay on the floor. Oddly enough, however, there was less damage up here than downstairs—fallen plaster, as usual, and chandeliers that hung by a single wire, looking as if they were about to fall. A glimpse into the first two bedrooms also showed some damage, but not as much as we had expected.

Luke went ahead of us, opening doors and explaining that these were guest rooms and had seldom been used in recent years. Furniture was covered with sheets, and had that kind of musty smell rooms take on when they've been closed up for a long time. At one point Luke moved ahead of us, out of sight around a corner, and Grace pulled us to a stop.

"We could move in here," she said. "Instead of the farmhouse. It's dry, and like Sarah said, it's got a roof. We'd be better off."

"I agree," Dana said. "We can go back to the

farmhouse and get Amelia and Timmy, and move back here. That's if Luke will let us.'' She turned to me. ''Do you think he will?''

''I don't see why not,'' I said, hesitating only a moment. ''I just wonder if we really would be better off, though. This house is on the northern side of the island, and if there's a major storm, it could hit a lot harder here than at Thornberry.''

''Even so,'' Kim said, ''if it storms, it storms. Thornberry couldn't be any better than this, given the condition it's in. I say we ask your friend, and if he says it's okay, we'll go back and get Timmy and Amelia.''

''No!'' Jane interrupted in a high, trembling voice.

She had been standing back from us, unusually quiet until now. We all turned, surprised at her outburst.

''They'll be looking for us at Thornberry,'' she said plaintively. ''We have to stay at Thornberry.''

''And just who do you think will be looking for us?'' Grace said impatiently.

''The rescue teams, Grace! For God's sake, use your head! They won't know where to find us if we're not there!''

''You really think there are going to be rescue teams anytime soon?'' Grace said. ''Besides, we'll leave them a note.''

''But they might not find it! What if they don't find it?'' Jane's voice rose hysterically.

I put an arm around her shoulders and said, ''Why wouldn't they find it, Jane?''

"I don't know. I don't know. I just know they won't."

Grace made an irritated sound and threw up her hands. "We'll tack it to a goddamned tree!"

Dana said, "Look, I'm sorry, Jane, but this time I agree with Grace. It would be foolish to stay at Thornberry when there's better shelter here."

Jane's mouth worked, and tears rolled down her cheeks. "Then we have to find a phone!" she cried, spinning away from me. "There's got to be one here!"

She ran down the hall and around the corner, past Luke, who was coming back our way.

"What is she doing?" he called out. "Hey! Come back! There's nothing down there!"

When she didn't respond, he went after her. We were close on his heels.

Luke stopped short before a door at the end of the hall. It was standing open, and Jane's soft cries issued from it.

"Damn!" Luke said softly. His face was rigid, his jaw clenched.

We drew up beside him and looked into a room that was nearly the size of a ballroom. It boasted a canopy bed swathed in white netting. A huge bay window looked out over the Sound, and wallpaper of red gilded roses was interspersed with floor-to-ceiling gold-framed mirrors. Several mirrors had cracked, and perfume bottles had fallen from a vanity table. Face powder had spilled from a Coty's box and dusted the floor. A big, square, Jacuzzi tub stood in the middle of the room, and one side had split open like a huge, gaping wound.

Jane was sitting on the edge of the canopy bed, jabbing at the buttons on a cell phone. As her fingers struck each time, her sobs grew louder, her voice more strident. "Jenny, Peter, where are you? Oh, my God, where are you? Answer me! Answer me, do you hear? What have I told you about not answering when I call!"

Jane shook the phone, then listened, and shook it some more. I crossed over and pried it from her white-knuckled grasp, holding it to my ear. It was completely dead. I punched the power button over and over, but no go.

"What kind is it?" Kim asked, coming up behind me. "Maybe there's a battery around here somewhere."

I shook my head. "I doubt it. It's an older model, the kind that uses a large nicad. They aren't easy to find these days. Luke?"

We looked around, but he wasn't there.

"Anyone see where Luke went?"

"He said something about finding some dry clothes for himself," Dana said.

"I'll go look for a battery," Kim offered. "Maybe in the kitchen, around the refrigerator. Some people store them there."

"Keep an eye out for Sarah's *friend* while you're down there," Grace said to her departing back. "Looks to me like he's skipped out on us."

In the bedroom, we found a walk-in closet full of women's clothes. While Grace was all for taking what we wanted and putting them on right there and then, I insisted we ask Luke first.

"Not me," Grace said, shrugging out of her jean jacket and into a green women's sweatshirt that had seen better days. "What if he never shows up again?"

"Don't be silly," I said, though I went along with her, tossing a white cable-knit fishermen's sweater to Dana. "Maybe he just remembered another phone."

"And maybe you're being naive," Grace said scornfully. "If you ask me, something bad happened in this room. He never even set foot in here. For all we know, it might even be haunted."

Dana made a sound of irritation. "Oh, for heaven's sake, Grace. What are you, a mystery writer? You can make a plot out of anything." She did wrap her arms around herself and shiver, however, and Grace laughed.

"This used to be Luke's mother's room," I said, coming across a summer dress I remembered Priscilla Ford wearing. "She died a couple of years ago. Maybe it upset him to be reminded of her."

Grace hooted. "More likely it's his wife's now, and she's left him, so it brings back things he'd rather forget."

Though I didn't let on to Grace, I had to admit that could be true. My mind had been running in circles the past few minutes. Where was Luke? And why had he been upset when Jane found this room?

*Was* he married? Did this room bring back bad memories of some sort? Or—I had a sudden thought—didn't he want Jane to find the cell phone? After all, he couldn't have known it was dead.

*Now you're really being crazy, Sarah,* I thought. *Luke is hardly part of some vast conspiracy to keep us from contacting the mainland.*

Dana had crossed over to a nightstand. Suddenly, she let out an exclamation. "Paydirt! Look!"

We crossed the room, and she held it up—a tiny but state-of-the-art portable radio. She pressed the on switch.

Nothing.

"See if it's got batteries," I said.

Dana turned the radio over and opened the battery compartment. There were four empty spaces where size AA batteries would ordinarily be.

"Wouldn't you know?" Grace muttered.

"People take them out if they're not planning to use them for a while," I noted.

Kim, who was still foraging through the kitchen, yelled out, "I've got batteries, but not for the phone."

"What kind?" I called back.

"Energizers. They were in the freezer."

Dana and I looked at each other.

"What size?" I called out.

"*C*s and double *A*s. Four each."

"God, is something going right for a change?" Grace threw up her hands. "I'll go down and get them."

"No," I said, "let's all go down. I think we've done as much as we can up here for now."

Pulling another heavy, dry sweater out of the closet for Kim, I turned to leave. It was only then I realized that Jane was still sitting on the bed, motionless, her eyes on the dead phone. She hadn't said a word in all this time.

Now she looked at me and half whispered, "They're dead, too, aren't they. Jenny and Peter."

Her voice rose. With a violent motion, she hurled the phone to the floor. *"They're as dead as this god-damned phone!"*

We got Jane downstairs with the promise of news on the radio, and found Luke in the kitchen with Kim. He had gone to his own room on the third floor, he told us, to get a dry pair of shoes he kept there, along with dry jeans and a shirt. He'd also found a bandage for the cut on his temple.

It was Kim, however, who'd found the batteries in the freezer.

"I completely forgot about those," Luke said. "I'd even forgotten about this radio."

Standing at the breakfast bar, he slipped the batteries in and pressed the on switch. Music blared forth, a Barbra Streisand rendition of "Stormy Weather." Dana looked at me, then at the windows—where a torrent of rain was streaming down—and laughed.

"Do you realize what this means, though?" she said excitedly. "If this station is coming from Seattle, things can't be as bad there as we thought."

"Maybe the early reports exaggerated the situation," Kim said. "They do that, sometimes."

"Or it's coming from Canada," Luke pointed out. No sooner had the words left his mouth than Barbra's singing ended and an announcer came on. "You're listening to CKNW, Vancouver, British Columbia."

The disappointment was palpable—especially in Jane, who had begun to show a bit of cautious hope.

The station was at its top-of-the-hour break, however, and when Barbra finished, the news began. We stood around the breakfast bar and listened to the newscaster tell of the "most devastating earthquake ever to have been recorded in Seattle, at least in recent times—the most devastating in the entire United States of America, in fact."

At 9.1, he said, it was far bigger than the 1906 quake in San Francisco, the 1989 in San Francisco, and the Northridge in L.A. It was even more devastating than the 8.3 to 8.6 quake to hit Alaska's Prince William Sound on Good Friday in March of '64. That one had sent a *tsunami* coursing hundreds of miles south to Crescent City, California, nearly demolishing that small coastal town.

"Apparently," the Canadian newscaster went on to say with an edgy tremor in his voice, "this is the long-predicted Big One."

Rescue teams from all over the world had been standing by for hours to fly to Seattle, he added, but there was so much damage at Sea-Tac and nearby smaller airports, they were on hold. In addition, train tracks had buckled, trains had been derailed, and freeways were damaged from as far south as Portland, Oregon, to as far east as Idaho. There seemed no easy way in to Seattle or surrounding towns, except by boat. And with the ferry slips and marinas damaged, it would be a while before those could be used.

Looting was rampant, the newscaster continued, and throughout the night people had been shot for food and water. There was talk that the National Guard might make an attempt to land on the Seattle waterfront, from amphibians. This was only a rumor, however. The newscaster pointed out that details were scarce, since the usual lines of communication into and out of Seattle, including telephone service, were down. Even cell phones were useless in some areas, because towers had collapsed. Amateur radio operators, "hams," were manning their radios from their homes—those who still had homes—and getting information out as quickly as possible. Some of the CBC's information came from ham radios in Seattle, some from private parties and some from the city's earthquake preparedness center.

"Oddly enough," the newscaster continued, "we here on the mainland, in Vancouver, have been relatively untouched by the quake. However, the city of Victoria has suffered extensive damage." He went on to describe the damage to Victoria, on Vancouver Island, B.C. "Victoria lies on a peninsula that juts south toward Puget Sound, and this, geologists believe, is why it was especially hard hit."

He finished with "For the most part, this quake—now being called the Great Seattle Quake—seems to have affected Washington State, Victoria, B.C., and points south, while leaving mainland Canada relatively unscathed."

There was no mention of the San Juan Islands.

"It can't be good for us that Victoria got hit," I said, when the broadcast was over. "They're the closest city to us, but they'll be busy with their own rescue efforts. It'll be a while before they expand those efforts out here to the San Juans—if at all."

"But they will do a search and rescue, won't they?" Dana said. "I mean, I know they're Canadian, not U.S., but they're so close. And they've got ferries that come over here all the time."

"With tourists," Grace pointed out, "and to the bigger islands, not to these little private ones. As for a search and rescue, with more than one hundred seventy islands to cover..."

She shrugged, and Jane made a sound of despair.

"Still," I added quickly, "there may be hope from Vancouver."

Grace shook her head. "They'll be sending their people to Victoria."

"Well," Luke said brusquely, flipping the radio off, "we'll just have to pull together and start helping ourselves."

"Does that mean you're sticking around?" Grace said.

"I don't exactly have a way off the island," he answered irritably.

He and Grace were definitely not hitting it off.

Dana put an arm around Jane, who was dry-eyed but shaky. "Things aren't so bad, now," she murmured soothingly. "We've got this place, and it's a roof over our heads—" She looked questioningly at Luke. "It's all right if we stay here, right? I mean, with Thornberry in such bad shape..."

Luke nodded. "Of course. In fact, let me see if I can find some rain gear for us to wear on the trip back to Thornberry. I've always kept some in the outside pantry."

He went through the back door, closing it tight as a gust of wind nearly ripped it from his hand.

"See, Jane?" Dana went on. "We'll be warm at night. We'll bring as many supplies as we can find from Thornberry, and I'm sure we'll be all right till help arrives."

"But—"

"No 'buts.' We have to believe your children have shelter and food, too. We have to *know* they're all right. Do you understand?"

Jane didn't respond. Dana looked up, sighing.

"Meanwhile, Grace, I have to agree with Sarah. Your lousy comments, not to mention your vulgar use of one particular four-letter word, are making things worse. I really wish you'd shut the hell up."

"Fine." Grace's mouth formed a thin, hard line. She turned to Kim, her pose defiant, hands on her hips. "I suppose *you* have an opinion you'd like to share, too?"

"Only that I've had co-stars who are *almost* as bad as you. Just not quite," Kim said.

Grace turned on her heel and stalked off in the direction of the living room. "To hell with you all."

Before she was out of sight, another aftershock hit. Old pros now, Dana, Kim, Jane and I hit the floor. We were in open space in the kitchen, where anything that could fall from shelves had already done so. Still, the floor was covered with debris, and my knee, where I'd cut it earlier on broken glass at Thornberry, struck something sharp. I stifled a cry.

Grace had stopped short in the doorway, bracing herself against it on either side.

When the aftershock was over, we got to our feet again. Kim brushed off her hands and said in a helpful tone, "Standing in doorways isn't always the best way, Grace. We found that out in the Northridge. If the wall hadn't been braced right, it and the doorway could have collapsed on you."

"Well, it didn't," Grace responded ungraciously. "And isn't that just too bad? I could be dead now, and you'd all be happy with that, I'm sure."

Ignoring her, I winced as pain ran through my knee. My own nerves weren't all that good, and I hated to think what all these aftershocks were doing to Thornberry.

"I wonder how Timmy and Amelia are holding up," I said. "I'll feel better once we get them back here."

"Just one thing," Kim said in a cautionary tone. "We were lucky this time. Sometimes aftershocks can bring down a house that was undamaged, or seemingly undamaged, in the first tremor."

"My, aren't we the little expert now," Grace said, folding her arms. "And just where did you go to earthquake school?"

"In L.A.," Kim snapped. "And if you and I were the only people here, I wouldn't even bother to try and save your miserable ass!"

This was the most outspoken Kim had been with any of the women, and Grace's mouth dropped open.

"Lady," she said when she'd recovered, "you don't even want to think of taking me on."

Kim snorted, shaking her head. "I could whip you faster than a rum cream pie. *If* I cared to—which I don't."

*"Enough,"* I said, groaning, *"please,* will you both stop? I suggest we get going—the sooner, the better. And when we get back here, let's assemble some furniture in the living room to dive under, just in case the walls do come down."

Jane's chin went up. "If you insist we stay here, then I'm not making that walk back to Thornberry. Not in this storm, and with trees coming down all around."

Dana's arm had begun to bleed again, and she held it close to her chest while saying gently, "How do you know there are trees coming down, Jane? We didn't see anything like that. Besides, look—the rain has almost stopped."

"No, it'll start again. And there's more wind now than ever," Jane insisted, her voice rising to a near-frantic pitch. "Just listen to it! When the earth is unstable and the winds are this high, that's what happens. Especially when it's been raining. The trees come down."

Grace seemed about to make a snide comment, but looked at me and Kim, and apparently thought better of it.

"I'll go find Sarah's disappearing *friend,"* she said, "if, in fact, he is out there getting us rain gear and hasn't just run off somewhere. Then I'm out of here.

Anybody who wants to come can come, but I'm leaving.''

Kim, Dana and I agreed that we should all take advantage of this lull—minor though it was—and leave for Thornberry immediately. Though the hard rain had stopped and there was now only a steady light downpour, we knew all too well that things could get worse.

Nothing we said, however, could convince Jane to come with us, and she was obviously in such bad shape we didn't feel right pressuring her further. We finally helped her to settle into the living room with blankets from the upstairs closets, a flashlight and a bottle of water. Luke came in moments later with two packages of crackers he'd found in the outside pantry, and a small kerosene lamp filled with oil.

''There's some other stuff,'' he said. ''Cornmeal, cookies, that sort of thing—but rats got into them. That's why we stopped keeping stuff out here.''

Grace followed him in. ''Rats the size of a cat,'' she said with an uncharacteristic shudder. ''We were almost attacked by one.''

I couldn't help smiling. ''You don't like rats?''

Grace tossed me a yellow slicker and didn't answer.

''I checked the generator out back,'' Luke said as he took one last look around. ''I was pretty certain I used up all the fuel before leaving last fall, though, and I'm afraid I was right.''

He did find enough slickers and weatherproof jackets, however, for all of us. We suited up, saying goodbye to Jane and leaving the radio with her. She agreed not to turn it on more than once, at the top of each hour, to hear the news. We could only hope she would stick to that agreement. Once the batteries in that radio were gone, our connection to the outside world would be gone, as well.

"If anything happens," I said, "even a small tremor, take the radio and get under that table over there. Okay?" I pointed to a long, high table behind a sofa. Both had slid across the room into the dining area.

There was no response. "Jane…you'll do that, won't you?"

A bare nod. She was sitting cross-legged on the ivory carpet in the midst of rubble, looking forlorn. Beside her was the kerosene lamp Luke had found in the pantry. It would ward off the dark until we got back.

I looked at the others, shook my head and shrugged. We left Jane that way, though no one felt good about it.

"Jane's probably safer staying there," Kim said, as the five of us reached the shoreline, with Luke in the lead. "But I'm worried about her state of mind. I saw this after the Northridge quake—that shocked, stunned look, the fear of moving in any direction. It's worrisome."

Grace repeated, "Worrisome? I'm warning you, you let somebody like that get out of hand, and she's a danger to everyone."

"Someone 'like that'?" I said.

"She's nuts, Sarah! Totally gone. Can't you see that?"

"I can see she's panicked about her children. Most mothers would be."

"I don't suppose you have any," Dana said to Grace.

"Any?"

"Children," Dana said.

"No," Grace answered. "I've never had that so-called thrill."

"Well, aren't they the lucky little kids," Dana replied sharply, "not to have to live with you."

Remarkably, Grace held her tongue, and I was grateful. If even Dana was losing her patient, peace-keeping nature, God only knew what things would be like by tomorrow.

We were returning to Thornberry from the opposite direction Kim and I had come. This way was a bit shorter, Luke had told us. It had only taken Dana, Grace and Jane longer because they had stopped to check out the two cabins along the way.

As we passed those cabins, I realized that with all that was happening, we hadn't asked them what they had found.

"Not much," Dana answered. "Like Timmy said, they're obviously summer places, pretty much empty except for furniture. We can come back again and look, if you want. There might be something we can use."

"Both of them were in bad shape," Grace added, "from the earthquake. Broken windows, fallen beams. Like Thornberry and Ransford, both had generators. According to the fuel gauges at both cabins, though, one was empty, the other less than a quarter full. And the lines to both were broken, just like at Thornberry.''

"Toward the end of the summer," Luke said, "most of us only order enough fuel to get by till we leave. Traditionally, we've all agreed that it's best not to have too much fuel on the island when we aren't here. That tends to discourage squatters, since winters can get pretty bad here without heat."

"How does fuel get delivered here?" I asked.

"There's a private company that brings it to us in fifty-gallon drums. We order it as we need it, and they usually come out several times a year. Not much chance of them getting here now, of course."

"Somehow, I thought the twentieth century might have caught up with Esme Island," I said. "I should have realized there wouldn't be power lines, much less phones, but the thought never occurred to me."

"Well," Luke said, "there are some benefits to being self-sufficient. In the cities, if the power goes out, things fall apart pretty quickly. Here, we at least know not to depend on modern amenities. We get by pretty well."

"Unless there just happens to be a nine-point-one quake," Grace muttered.

"Yes. Unless there's a nine-point-one quake."

Luke strode ahead of us again, and we were all silent the rest of the way back to Thornberry. With time to think, I couldn't help wondering what was going on in Luke's head. When he'd first regained consciousness, he'd seemed glad to see me. Since then, however, he had seemed polite but distant. Not at all what I might have expected from someone I'd once spent a summer making wild, passionate love with—even if it had been twenty-two years ago.

What had come between us, since that moment when we first met again on the dock?

We arrived back at the farmhouse just before dinner, and Dana and Kim took Luke directly into the living room to survey the damage there. Grace and I found that Timmy and Amelia had managed to clean most of the debris out of the kitchen. They had even unearthed the long wooden table, and the picnic-style benches were back in place on either side. In the middle of the table was a small bunch of daffodils from the garden, a bright, touching reminder that some things had survived. Candles flanked it.

"We got the generator out of the rubble, too," Timmy said, clearly proud of the job they'd done while we were gone.

"We haven't been able to get it working, though," Amelia said. "It seems full of fuel, so it must be damaged, somehow."

She pushed back her gray hair, which was matted to her forehead from perspiration; her arms were black with soot. Both women looked dusty and disheveled. Even so, they seemed energized by their day's work.

"We thought we could at least use the fuel," Amelia continued, "but we can't get it out. There's some sort of theft-proof device to prevent that."

"You had your fuel locked up so nobody could

steal it?'' Grace said to Timmy, shaking her head. ''Out *here?*''

Timothea opened her mouth, but Amelia answered defensively, ''She didn't know it was on there! It's not like she ordered the tank that way.''

''Then, why didn't she have the damned thing taken off?'' Grace threw up her hands. ''Oh, never mind. Nothing makes sense around this place.''

''Not everyone has the kind of money you apparently do to hire help—'' Amelia began.

Timmy interrupted. ''Hush! It's none of her business.''

''You've got that, lady,'' Grace said, and stomped away.

''Timmy?'' I turned to her. ''Are you in some sort of trouble?''

She, Amelia and I were the only ones left in the kitchen; Grace had joined Dana, Kim and Luke in the living room. My question to Timmy was only out of concern for a friend—I didn't mean to pry.

Still, she clamped her mouth shut and walked away.

I turned to Amelia, who was sitting at the table passing a weary hand over her eyes. Since the quake, it seemed her sharp retorts had been softening a bit. We all, in fact, except for Grace, had been losing our initial irritability with each other. There were far too many other things to worry about now.

''What's going on?'' I asked.

''Timmy's nearly broke,'' Amelia answered heavily. ''She'll hate me for telling you that, but it's true, and she needs to face up to it.''

"I don't understand," I said, sitting down across from her.

"This place hasn't made a profit in years. For a while, she was able to get by on her savings, and then there was the insurance money after John died. But that only lasted so long." Amelia blinked back tears. "You have no idea the things she's been forced to do, the way she's had to live."

"I never would have guessed," I said. "The way she dresses, the diamond rings..."

"The clothes are classic, they never go out of style. The rings? Fake. She sold off all her jewelry months ago."

"But this place—the free room and board, all the luxurious touches."

One new improvement since I'd been here in my teens was the bathhouse nestled in the woods, made of cedar and fir, with stained-glass windows and sea-blue tile. Though we had commodes and sinks in our cottages, the bathhouse, with its showers and claw-foot bathtubs, was available to all of us. It was in shambles now, like the cottages—but before the quake we could shower surrounded by trees, birds and even deer. No expense had been spared to make the residents at Thornberry feel welcome and comfortable.

"It hasn't been entirely free up until now," Amelia said. "Residents usually pay a fee. The fees don't cover everything, though, and I've been helping Timmy out a bit with expenses." She shook her head. "Don't get me wrong, I don't mind. Timmy and I have been friends forever. But I'm about at the end of my own resources. The truth is, she's going to have to shut down. And that's what she won't face up to.''

"I'm so sorry. I had no idea.''

"Well, she won't even believe it herself, dammit! I thought I had her convinced to close down last month. Then all of a sudden she's inviting people right and left and getting all excited about it, like nothing's wrong and never was.''

"Inviting people. You mean us?''

"Well, yes. I mean no offense, but how she'll pay the bills for expenses this month is beyond me. I told her I couldn't help this time, and she said it was all right, she'd found an investor.''

"An investor? Who?''

Amelia shook her head. "That's what worries me. She's shutting down on me these days, not confiding in me as much.''

"I should talk to her," I said. "Maybe I can help, somehow. Do you know how she got into this mess?''

"Spending too much, like everybody else," Amelia said. "Timmy has too much heart. She loves running this place, loves helping new writers.''

"I know, she always did. But couldn't she cut down on expenses, even charge more for room and board? She doesn't have to do it all alone.''

"That's just it," Amelia said. "Timmy thinks she does. She would die rather than admit she's not making it on her own.''

"But she's not—not if she's taking help from you.''

Amelia shrugged. "That's different. Timmy and I have been friends forever, and I'm probably the only

person she trusts anymore—though sometimes I wonder if that's even true.''

Luke, Dana, Grace and Kim came back into the
kitchen, and a few minutes later Timmy joined us.
Both she and Amelia were relieved to hear we had
found Ransford with its roof still intact, and Timmy
was especially glad to see Luke. She and he talked
for a few minutes privately, off to one side.

We gathered around the table, and Amelia wiped
her hands on the apron she'd dredged out of the debris. ''I really wanted to surprise all of you with a hot
dinner,'' she said apologetically. ''I hated to think of
you out in that storm and coming home to canned
peas and raw carrots—that's all we could find for
now.''

She put plates of cold vegetables before us. The
''plates'' were napkins that she'd shaken the dust out
of. Every single one of the dishes, she told us, was
broken. Only a few heavy mugs had survived.

''I never would have believed we'd end up with
such a mess. China and crockery, the best and the
oldest, all in tiny pieces.''

''Not to worry,'' I said. ''As soon as we revive
ourselves, we'll all go back to Ransford. We'll have
to carry over whatever we've salvaged here, but we
can do that. And Luke's here to help.''

I looked at him, and he nodded.

''Let me take a look at that generator, too,'' he
said. ''Maybe I can figure out how to get that anti-
theft lock off, and we can siphon some fuel out to
use in the generator at my house.''

"I'll help," Dana offered. "I'm sort of mechanical. I fixed my toaster once at home."

"I can change the spark plugs on a VW," Kim said. "Unfortunately, that's *all* I know anything about, and our cars are where we left them, by the ferry dock in Seattle. Probably under rubble now."

"You should worry," Grace said testily, keeping to form. "They'll probably send a chopper after you."

"And see if I give *you* a ride if they do," Kim retorted.

Amelia looked at me. "Have they been doing this all day?"

"Bonded at the hip," I replied.

"Come to think of it, where is Jane?" Timmy asked, looking around. "I don't know where my mind is! I just realized she isn't here."

"We had to leave her at Ransford," I said. "She was afraid to walk back here, what with the aftershocks, and the storm."

"How is she doing?"

"She's worried sick about her children. I think she'll be all right once we get some word that they're safe."

Timmy looked doubtful. "Provided that word ever comes. I hate to think—" She broke off, seeing our faces. "I'm sorry. We must endeavor to keep our spirits up…no matter what."

She laughed then, a short, nervous laugh, while patting her frizzy white hair with one hand. The diamond ring flashed and glittered, as if it were real.

We finished dinner at six, and, since the rain had

let up, decided to use the remaining daylight to go through our cottages once more. We still hoped to find personal items—toothbrushes, in particular, and warm clothes and sturdy shoes.

It was agreed we would meet back at the farmhouse in an hour, and then set off for Ransford together. If the hour passed and not everyone had returned, Amelia would signal those still missing with one of the air horns she'd found in the remains of the Thornberry office. That way, we could all leave together, at the same time. Meanwhile, Luke would work alone on the generator. Thanking Dana and Kim for their offers of help, he told them with a smile that he was relatively certain he wouldn't run across any toasters or spark plugs out there.

While the rest of us had been over at Ransford, Timmy and Amelia had handled one more difficult task, that of burying Lucy. No one spoke about the small mound in the yard, though it could be seen through the hole in the wall that once was a kitchen window.

"We weren't able to go very deep," Timmy had said apologetically. "We simply hadn't the strength."

Amelia had patted her arm. "It will do for now," she'd reassured her.

The two women had found early wildflowers in the woods and had placed them on Lucy's grave. Timmy had also fashioned a tiny cross out of twigs. "Lucy wasn't particularly religious," she said, her eyes tearing, "but she had a good heart. I don't suppose a cross and a bit of a prayer could hurt."

I agreed, and on the way to my cottage I stopped

by the dirt mound to say a small prayer. Dana and
Kim followed me and stood by my side. Grace stood
a few yards off, watching us, but made none of her
usual snide comments.

I was glad when we all went our separate ways, to
our cottages. I hadn't had a moment to myself since
before dinner the night before, and my nerves were
raw. Hurrying down the path to my cottage, I tried
not to think about Dana's theory that spirits of dead
Native Americans inhabited the grounds of Thornberry.

At any rate, there was more to worry about now
than spirits. In particular, I had to find the slender
metal box I'd brought with me to Thornberry. Only
eight inches long by five wide, and an inch thick, it
resembled an oversized powder compact. I'd brought
it here with me in my purse, then taped it to the bottom of a desk drawer. This morning I'd panicked
when I couldn't find it. It had been like looking for
a needle in a haystack amidst all the debris.

*It has to be here,* I told myself over and over now.
*It must have fallen free, and it's buried beneath the
heavy items I wasn't able to lift this morning.*

This time I did lift them, running on the same kind
of adrenaline one hears that a mother has when her
child is trapped under a car. Tossing overstuffed
chairs and end tables aside as if they were mere feath-
ers, I scrabbled in the rubble of my cottage, rushing
to beat the encroaching dark.

*These past three months can't have been for noth-
ing. If I've lost that evidence, I'm lost, too.*

The small metal case held Lonnie Mae's fishnet

stockings. In the beginning, I'd given them to my friend, J.P. Then I'd hired J.P.—Judith Patrice, a name she loathed and never used—to investigate the backgrounds of the Seattle Five for something that could be used against them in court. Other rapes, perhaps. Anything that might tarnish their reputations.

My thinking was that unless the fire investigators came up with something suspicious about that fire in Lonnie Mae's building—something leading them to the Seattle Five as the murderers of Lonnie Mae and the others in the building that night—I didn't stand much of a chance of nailing the cops for anything but rape. And knowing the light sentences they might get for raping a black woman, especially one who was no longer alive to speak for herself, I wanted more on them. I wanted the bastards crushed. Annihilated. Put down for all time.

So I hired J.P., and just to make sure the stockings were protected, she had hidden them in her accountant's office with those tax papers. The Seattle Five, we hoped, would never in a million years think to search for them there.

Holding a prime piece of evidence back from the courts was hardly the best way to go, and I was certain I'd be in very hot water when all this was over. Still, with any luck, I wouldn't be dead.

Then, several days before coming to Thornberry, I had opened a plain brown envelope in my mail, to find the stockings inside it. There was no return address, and no note of explanation. I tried to reach J.P., but calls to her office turned up only the information that she was "away." I left messages, but none were returned.

J.P. wasn't the kind to ignore a client, or a friend, without some explanation. I began to worry, and tried to reassure myself that she had simply gone off somewhere to follow a lead. She hadn't had time to write a note, but had sent me the stockings thinking I might need them before she returned. Certainly, I wouldn't have been able to just waltz into her accountant's office and ask for them, so that made sense.

I decided finally to sit tight. Anything I said to the police at this point might only complicate matters for her. J.P. was smart. She was tough. She could take care of herself.

Not that anyone would have known it. At five foot four, with long honey-colored hair and sky-blue eyes, J.P. looked like an angel. She was, in fact, often called "Angel" by co-workers and friends. I had met her for the first time four years ago when she worked on a case for a client I'd defended. There was little money to investigate the alleged crimes of those in need of public defenders, but J.P. had donated her time—something she did on a regular basis. J.P.'s mother had once been convicted of shoplifting, and without the kind of money needed to prove her innocence had gone to jail for ninety days. J.P. was twelve at the time, and she swore that when she grew up she'd do some kind of work that would help those who were innocent, like her mother.

Angel...a woman who was, indeed, one of those "angels amongst us."

Given that, I knew she wouldn't have gone off like

that without a good reason. Even so, when she sent those fishnet stockings back to me, I felt a swift, sickening sensation. Something told me I had to put them where no one could find them—and quickly.

I'd found the metal case in my father's office. It was something he had used to carry a few cigars in, when he traveled, and it was right there where he always kept it, in his desk drawer. Solid silver, it had been engraved in gold on its lid with just one word, *Allegra*, and when I had asked him years ago what that meant, he said he didn't know. He'd found the case in an antique store. Intrigued by its unknown history, which I thought mysterious, I had called it the *Allegra* case after that, making up stories in my head in which it had belonged either to a rich man's mistress or a royal courtesan.

That day I had squeezed the stockings into it, still in their plastic bag. Then I slipped the *Allegra* case beneath a corner of loose carpeting in my father's study, and tacked it down. I'd have done that in the first place, if I hadn't been afraid something would happen to me despite my threat to Mike Murty. If I were to be murdered, or die in an "accident," the entire house might be searched by the authorities, and Lonnie Mae's evidence found and taken into custody. After that, it could all too easily disappear.

I know how that sounds—like paranoia. But it was the way I'd come to think. Finally, I had brought the *Allegra* case with me to Thornberry, just in case the Five broke into my parents' house and searched it while I was gone. I had taped the case beneath that drawer of my desk. Not the sharpest of hiding places—but then, why, I reasoned, would anyone on this remote little island be looking for it? I wasn't so far gone as truly to suspect anyone here.

Continuing my search through the wreckage of my cottage, however, I was no longer so sure. Even my manuscript pages seemed to have disappeared.

I hadn't thought to look for my manuscript, at first. There had been all kinds of papers scattered on the floor that morning, and I'd assumed it would be a simple matter of picking them up and putting them in order when I had more time. Now I saw that the fallen pages were blank—fresh new bond, not printed on yet.

For weeks my manuscript had piled up alongside my computer at home. Then, this past week, it had piled up in a box beside my laptop here at Thornberry. Every day the stack became a bit higher, and with every rising inch my spirits rose. I was coming closer and closer to getting my story out—to nailing not only the Seattle Five, but crooked cops from NYC, to L.A., to Chicago and beyond. My research had uncovered more than I'd bargained for: new details about the problems in L.A.'s Rampart Division, the shooting of unarmed blacks by police in NYC, and similar abuses of police authority all across the country.

My inability to find even one of the pages of my manuscript now, and the *Allegra* case, heightened my level of panic. The script had been in a box five inches deep. On top, I had placed a heavy, lichen-covered rock I'd picked up in the forest for a paperweight. "Brain," I had called the rock, because the gray lichen reminded me of the weblike connections in a brain. I'd hoped it might inspire me.

And here it was—Brain—lying up against a baseboard, alongside my fallen laptop. The laptop was beneath a two-by-four, broken; the screen was in several pieces.

No manuscript pages, however. And no box.

It was then I remembered my backup disk. That, too, I had always placed on top of my manuscript at the end of a day's work. JUST REWARDS, I'd written on it in thick black ink, next to a Mickey Mouse logo. The box of disks had been the kind they make for kids, the cheapest I could find at the time. *Thank God I always back up,* I thought.

But the disk was nowhere in sight. I looked everywhere it might possibly be, and ended up cursing myself for not hiding it somewhere safe. That sickening sensation hit me again. Who was here? Who at Thornberry would do this?

*No, stop it. There's no one here. No one knows you, or knows anything about you.*

There was Timmy, of course. I had told her, briefly, about my arrest, before I'd accepted her invitation. I thought she should know, and wasn't sure if she would still want me here. But Timmy had been understanding about my troubles, expressing only sympathy. She had urged me, strongly, to forget all that and come here for a month of relaxation.

Besides, Timmy would have no reason to take anything from my cottage. Especially not those particular things.

She had been here all day, of course, while we were

gone. She could have come to my cottage alone. She could have—

*For God's sake, Sarah! You're getting as bad as Grace.*

I was tired, strung out. There had been too much happening in the past twenty-four hours, and I was seeing shadows under the bed—or the pile of junk that used to be my bed.

One possibility remained. The cottage's small kitchen range was now halfway across the room, on its side by the desk. I couldn't lift it alone, and would need help. But the disk, and the manuscript, might have been tossed there by the quake, the stove then landing on top of them. The *Allegra* case might be there, as well.

I was grasping at straws, I knew. But anything was better than believing that one of the women at Thornberry had come here to get her hands on Lonnie Mae's evidence—and my work. That was just me, thinking crazy thoughts.

And not for the first time. In Seattle, there had been a night in February when I'd thought I heard someone in the house, downstairs. I'd become so paranoid, I'd even thought seriously of buying a gun for protection. But then the noise proved to be trees scratching a window, and I never heard it again.

I sat on an overturned bookcase now and surveyed the mess in my cottage. I couldn't be sure those items weren't here somewhere. There was far too much debris; it would be an all-day job to go through it thoroughly.

So my worries were needless—weren't they?

What's more, they were ridiculous. I would go to Ransford with the others tonight, and come back in the morning to search some more. I might even get Luke to come with me, and help me get that stove off the floor.

On my return to the farmhouse, I learned that Dana had uncovered two backpacks in her cottage, as well as assorted vitamins and herbs. Grace had dug up an extra pair of hiking boots that fit Kim, and Kim had found a pair of sweatpants almost identical to the ones she'd been wearing since the day before. Amelia's offering was a large bottle of aloe hand lotion, which at first seemed frivolous, but turned out to be a blessing: everyone's hands were raw and inflamed from scavenging through wreckage for the past twenty-four hours.

I added my own salvaged items to the mix—two pens, a yellow legal pad, a backpack and a copy of a book titled, *How To Survive Life's Little Challenges.*

Everyone laughed at that, which had been my reason for bringing it. Kim, however, latched onto it and said she'd enjoy some good bedtime reading.

Looking at our "insignificant" little finds on the kitchen table, we all had to agree there was a time when we might have turned our noses up at them— especially since everything was wet from the rain. Now we glommed on to them as if they were gold. Everything would dry out, even shoes.

When reminded by Grace that Ransford was fully furnished with linens, Amelia argued that with no heat throughout the night, they might need extra blan-

kets. She was all for searching through the debris outside, from Thornberry's upper floors. Luke said don't
bother, they would have heat at Ransford, after all.
He had managed to get the anti-theft lock off Thornberry's fuel tank, and had siphoned some fuel to take
with us.

Everyone had her own opinion about what we
should take from Thornberry to Ransford, and Timmy
showed signs of breaking when she said tearfully, "I
can't leave my things behind. I just can't."

"Well, you can't take them with you," Grace argued. "What do you think we've got here, for God's
sake, a covered wagon?"

The walk back to Ransford, she argued, was too
long to be carrying all the sentimental odds and ends
Timmy refused to leave behind. The two of them argued back and forth until I thought I would scream.
I restrained myself from telling them both to shut up,
but did wonder aloud why I couldn't have been invited to someplace comparatively peaceful to write
my book, like a third world country on the brink of
war. That had some small effect—enough, anyway,
that Timmy compromised on what she brought with
her. Grace gathered her own contributions together,
declaring that she, at least—if no one else—was prepared to hit the road.

Timmy had found an old map of the island showing
a three-mile-long utility road through the forest to the
other side. The map was so old however, she couldn't
be sure the road was still there, or if it was, that it
wasn't overgrown. We took a vote and agreed to try

it, hoping to save time. Before we left, we nailed a note to a tree for potential rescuers.

Luke and I hadn't had a moment to talk alone, and again I wondered if I only imagined that he was avoiding me. He led the way along the narrow, half-overgrown trail, brushing fir and cedar branches aside with a large walking stick, and warning us of potholes. In his other hand he carried a gasoline can full of diesel fuel. Grace and I each carried cans, as well. We had found them, old and rusty but usable, in a storage shed on the Thornberry property. A miracle, we called it, as these would be better than the plastic gallon milk bottles we had been planning to use.

Grace, Dana and I followed Luke in a single line at intervals of a few feet, while Kim, Timmy and Amelia brought up the rear. Each of us carried either backpacks or lunch baskets, filled with whatever supplies we'd thought might be helpful over the next few days. Three of us carried flashlights, which gave only minimal illumination in the darkness of the woods. Overhead, the wind whistled through the tall trees like the cries of demons mocking our stupidity in thinking we might actually survive all this.

Once, Grace drew up alongside Luke and said something I couldn't hear. I saw him shake his head angrily and stomp on ahead of her.

As Grace dropped back, Dana moved up to her and said, "What was that all about?"

"Nothing," Grace said scornfully. "He's an idiot. Like all men."

Dana fell back next to me. Hefting her lunch basket

full of supplies, she said, "I feel like Little Red Riding Hood."

"Well, watch out for Grace," I muttered. "My bet's on her as the Big Bad Wolf."

Dana laughed softly. "Amelia could be Grandmother, right?"

I smiled. "Only if I can be Goldilocks. I could use a bowl of nice hot porridge right now."

"But that's a whole other fairy tale," Dana protested.

"Hah. You think this is a fairy tale? More like a nightmare. And while we're at it, where the hell is that bread-crumb trail?"

Dana giggled. "Are we almost there yet, Mom?" she called ahead to Grace.

Grace ignored her and continued to follow Luke, the two of them stomping through branches and limbs of trees like angry giants crashing through a forest of Pick Up Sticks.

We must have walked close to two miles before Luke stopped, sniffing the air. Grace did the same.

"What is it?" I called out.

"I smell something," Luke said, as we all drew up alongside them.

"I smell it, too," Grace said. "It's like...like a fireplace. Wood smoke."

"Maybe Jane managed to build a fire?" Dana said hopefully.

Luke's gaze swung to the north, to the line of trees ahead of us. The sky was tinged with a rosy glow.

"What the hell is that?" Grace said.

"Northern lights?" Kim suggested, following her gaze.

"I don't think so," Timmy answered nervously. "They aren't usually red. More green, or blue. Besides, it's…the light is flickering."

"Oh, my God," Luke said softly. "Shit!" He began running.

I could smell the fire now, and a fine ash had begun to fall on my face and hair.

"It's Luke's house!" Dana cried. "Jane's in that house!"

We crashed through the underbrush behind Luke, all of us running as quickly as we could along the tangled path. Vines reached up to grab my ankles, slowing me down and nearly sending me headlong into a tree. My breath became labored, and a pain shot through my chest. At one point I was forced to slow down and take a breath. Timmy stopped beside me, doing the same, but Amelia raced by us.

Before my arrest, I had run every day, but since then I'd become too sedentary, spending long hours at the computer working on the book. Now my lungs ached so much, I thought they might explode. But as the others pulled ahead, we began to lose their light. I grabbed Timmy's hand and half dragged her along with me. Shoving my way through snarled weeds, I thrust aside low-lying branches, skirting rocks and potholes, my flashlight showing the way only dimly. Ruts became traps, and trees slapped my face, tearing at my eyes like claws.

I knew we were almost at the house before I could see it. The flames reached above the tree line now, licking at the night sky with a thunderous roar. I felt the heat, and, looking down, I saw that a gray coating of ash had covered my sleeves.

Within moments, Timmy and I caught up to the other women, who stood in the trees on the periphery of the Ransford front lawn, staring at the house. It was engulfed in flames, and the women were like ghosts in the dim light, bathed in ash, their eyes blazing reflected red from the fire's glow.

The smoke and ash filled our lungs, and we began to cough. "Cover your mouths!" Timmy cried, taking her silk scarf and wrapping it around her mouth, tying it in the back. "Use whatever you can!"

I had already pulled my jacket collar up around my mouth. Peering above it, I didn't see Luke anywhere.

"Where did Luke go?" I yelled, as the roar and pop of the fire nearly drowned out my words.

Dana and Kim pointed to the house. I took off, covering the last few yards to the front lawn within seconds, praying he had already found Jane safe. The closer I got, however, the more intense the heat became. Huge chunks of cinder flew up into the night sky, then spread out to the surrounding trees.

The conflagration was total; it was clear we were too late to save Ransford, even if we had the water to do it, which we did not. All three stories were engulfed in flames.

For one long, desperate moment, I thought that Jane couldn't possibly have escaped. But then I spotted her, no closer to the house than I was, but off to the right, at the forest's edge. Jane was watching the fire consume Luke's house, her face crimson and bathed in sweat.

I ran to her, reaching out my arms. "Thank God! Oh, thank God, you're all right."

She slowly turned and looked at me. Her eyes were vacant, but a small smile curved her lips. The effect was so eerie, I shivered, despite the fire's heat. My arms fell to my side.

"You said they wouldn't come," Jane said in a monotone.

"What?" Confused, I shook my head.

"You said they wouldn't know we were here."

"I don't... You mean the rescue teams?"

"You said they wouldn't know we were here," she said in that same flat voice. "Well, now they will."

My eyes widened in horror as I realized what she meant. I turned to the other women, who had come up and were standing behind me. There were stunned expressions on their faces, as well.

"Jane...oh, Jane, you didn't," Dana cried softly.

"You idiot!" Grace yelled, grabbing Jane by the shoulders and shaking her. "What have you done? *Do you know what you've done?*"

"Stop it!" I yelled, pulling Grace back. "Leave her alone!"

Grace turned and swung at me, hitting me on the shoulder. "She set the goddamned fire! She's destroyed the only place on this freaking island with enough shelter to help us survive!"

"It was the only way," Jane said in a low, reasonable voice, as if explaining something obvious to a child. "Don't you see? We didn't have any flares, or any way to call for help, so I had to make one. A flare, I mean. I had to do something they would see for miles and miles. So I poured out the kerosene from the lamp, and I made a torch, and I set the curtains on fire in the downstairs rooms. When I was sure they had all caught, I ran out.'' Again, that eerie smile. ''I've been waiting for them to come.''

''Are you *insane?*'' Grace shouted, reaching a hand out as if to strike her, then letting it fall to her side. ''This won't tell them there are people here! They'll just think the earthquake did something to set it off!''

''No, you're wrong,'' Jane insisted, though her voice began to show signs of doubt. ''They'll come because this house belongs to somebody important. They always take care of the important people first, don't they? You said that, Grace, you said the rich run the world.''

Grace opened her mouth, as if aghast. But for once, she seemed to have no answer. Dana put an arm around Jane and began to whisper soft, soothing words. Timmy and Amelia joined her, and Kim stood a few paces away, hands jammed into her pockets, staring at the fire.

Grace drew me aside. ''You know what this means, don't you? Somebody's got to watch her every minute from now on.''

''I know,'' I agreed wearily, rubbing ash from around my eyes. ''What she did was crazy. But you know—to play devil's advocate—Jane may be making some sick kind of sense. Orcas Island is close enough for a fire that size to cast a glow from here, and someone should at least report it. Especially if they know about Thornberry being here. It's not like this is one of the uninhabited islands."

"And what if they do report it? You heard what they said on the radio. Everyone's busy in the city now. It could be days before rescue helicopters or even boats make it up this far. Shit, for all we know, it could be weeks."

"Well, I for one refuse to think that way," I said irritably. "And I've got to believe that among the seven of us—eight, now, with Luke—we've got enough smarts and guts to get ourselves through this."

Grace gave me a disgusted look. "You don't get it, do you? We are in serious trouble—"

She broke off and swiveled around as Kim said, "Where is Luke?"

No one seemed to know. His house was burning down, and the only clue we had was that Amelia had seen him disappear into the woods on the east side of the house.

Grace threw up her hands and stalked off. Walking closer to the fire than I would have thought safe, she stood with her hands on her hips, as if defying it to burn her.

Kim appeared beside me and said, "If you ask me, she's the one who needs to be watched."

"What do you mean?"

She covered her mouth and coughed to clear her throat of smoke. "I mean, I think she's more interested in your old boyfriend than she lets on."

"Grace? Interested in Luke?" I rubbed my irritated

eyes. "It looked to me like they loathe each other. Besides, I think she's afraid."

"Afraid? Are you kidding? That woman doesn't have a skittish bone in her body."

"You wouldn't think so, would you. But she's way too edgy, and I have a feeling that's not her normal self."

"And you base this on...what?" Kim said.

"I don't know—instinct, maybe. I think that when Grace is her usual self, she can do anything she sets her mind to. In fact, I see her as one of those people who goes on outreach trips, climbs mountains, survives on twigs and skins deer for dinner."

"Good God." Kim shuddered. "If that's true, then it's worse than I thought. I have to admit, though, that I sort of agree. No offense, but of all of us, I thought she might be the one to take charge after the earthquake. Instead, it was you. There are times when Grace—"

"—seems far too concerned about how we're going to make it until help arrives?" I finished for her.

"That's it. Most of the time she acts like she's just fed up with being around all of us. Then, the next minute, I get the feeling she's got something else entirely on her mind."

"Something we don't know anything about," I agreed. "And it's got her more spooked than even the quake. You know, I hate to think this, but you may be right. Maybe we do have two people to keep an eye on, not just one."

Kim said thoughtfully, "You don't think she'd really hurt one of us, do you?"

I looked at her, surprised. "Grace? No, actually, I wasn't thinking that at all. I was thinking more of what Jane did, and whether Grace might let her temper get the better of her and do something equally as damaging. It's the anger that worries me, the fact that it's always there."

"Shh," Kim warned. "Here she comes."

We watched Grace stride down the lawn in our direction. Her hands were deep in the pockets of her anorak, her hiking boots kicking red-hot cinders aside. For the first time, I thought she looked tired and defeated.

"I'm surprised those trees aren't on fire by now," she said heavily.

Kim agreed. "I've seen a few fires in Malibu, and I would have thought the whole island would be in flames by now."

"L.A. is a tinderbox compared to Esme," Timmy said, coming up to us. "It rained buckets here all winter, and the trees are still green. It's also lucky Luke's family had the foresight to keep so large a clearing around the house."

I began to walk toward Dana and Jane, who stood several yards from us. Amelia was still with them, standing a bit apart.

As I approached, Dana said worriedly, "You don't think the fire will spread over the whole island, do you?"

"I don't know. We're about three miles from Thornberry here, which could help if the wind doesn't come up again. Timmy seems to think we'll be okay."

I looked at Jane, who wouldn't meet my eyes. "You know what you've done, don't you?" I couldn't help saying, as if reprimanding a delinquent child.

Jane turned away, and I didn't push. Part of me wanted to shake her, the way Grace had, to make her accept responsibility for the situation we were in now. The other part felt compassion and understood the stress she'd been under, worrying about her children.

Though, as I thought of it, Jane had never really seemed quite stable. Even before the quake, there had been signs that she might break, if only under Grace's bullying. I wondered what was going on in her life that might have contributed to this—this insanity.

"I feel so sorry for Luke," Dana said softly. "Where is he, by the way?"

"We don't know. He seems to have disappeared. Again."

We stood helplessly and watched, as the home Luke and his parents had lived in every summer of his life burned to the ground.

When Luke returned shortly after that, he said only that he hadn't been able to face the loss. He'd gone into the woods to be alone for a while.

He seemed devastated, and we all told him there was no need to apologize. We could certainly understand how he felt.

# 6

Falling asleep in Thornberry's kitchen that night proved to be difficult. We had decided to trust the remaining structure to hold against the constant aftershocks, as hard rain had begun again. Even inside, however, we were only partially safe from the elements. Arranging ourselves as far away from the holes in the roof as possible, we wrapped ourselves in the same blankets we'd used the night before. Because of the weather, they hadn't been able to dry, and were still damp. Timmy, Amelia, Jane, Dana and Kim lay near the old potbellied stove in the kitchen. Luke said he was too warm-blooded; he'd sleep near the back door.

"One thing—" Dana said, "there's plenty of wood for the stove now, with all this debris. We're actually pretty lucky that way."

This gave us all a few doleful laughs, which was better than none.

I sat with my back against the wall a few feet from Luke, uncomfortable with being so close to a stove after the fire at his house. Ridiculous, but there it was. The warmth of the old potbelly brought back terrible pictures of flames licking hungrily at wood, the terrible roar, and finally, the thunderous boom as Ransford collapsed in on itself. Luke's home—gone so quickly in a huge plume of cinders and flame.

*My* home, as I had one day hoped—in my most secret of dreams—it would be. Sitting under that tree in the woods and watching Luke's family host their parties on the lawn, I'd envisioned one day living at Ransford myself. Not because I envied the house and the parties, but because I wanted to be with Luke.

*One day I'll marry the boy I love.* One of those romantic dreams that most girls have at seventeen. We write his last name down after ours, over and over. We haunt jewelry stores in the mall with our girlfriends, picking out the ring we imagine he'll give us, and we sort through the bridal magazines for the wedding gown we cannot wait to wear.

Adolescent dreams—but dreams, nevertheless. They sit in the background of our minds until one day another, better, dream supersedes them.

At forty, I had to admit that I hadn't yet found that better dream. Nor did I even have the one about Luke anymore. Somewhere along the way, I must have lost my capacity for dreaming. Still, I had hated to see Ransford destroyed that way.

Shivering inside my parka, I turned to the present, wondering if we would ever get off this island alive. We were not the most proficient band of campers, nor were we, by nature, hunters and gatherers. Almost anyone could have found more useful items in our cottages or the farmhouse to salvage. We had not done well.

This I attributed only partly to a lack of skill in that direction, however. Since the quake had occurred,

most of us had been walking around in shock—
seemingly back up to speed, yet doing and saying
things that were at best stupid, at worst damaging,
either to ourselves or others. No one seemed precisely
themselves, or at least the selves I imagined them to
be. I kept seeing things in some of the women's ac-
tions that appeared to be suspicious, though I hadn't
a clue why.

As for Luke, the fact that he'd appeared on our
doorstep seemed a good omen. I guessed that, privately, everyone was relieved to have a man aboard.
Even Grace seemed to be warming up to him since
his house had burned down.

Maybe it was something genetic, going back to
caveman days. There seems to be something about
having a man around, at least a good one, that gives
most women a sense of security. We've "brought
home the bacon, fried it up in a pan." We've proven
we can raise children alone, make a decent living, and
do without hearts and flowers on Valentine's Day.
Now and then, however, we can still admit that it
feels good to let a man drag home the brontosaurus
loin.

We had left Ransford when the rain had begun to
pick up. The fire was still smoldering, and though we
thought the rain would keep it from flaring up again,
we agreed that someone should remain awake at all
times throughout the night, keeping watch. If a glow
in the sky began to be seen from here, we would get
up and start moving our small store of supplies to the
shoreline.

I took the first shift because I felt I'd never sleep.

Better that the others get some rest. If help didn't arrive in the morning, we would have our work cut out for us, making Thornberry more livable.

The rain turned to a downpour around midnight, bringing more gale-force winds. They howled through the openings in the farmhouse and blew debris around in the living room. I could hear paper skittering about in there...Amelia's manuscript, no doubt, from the night before, the one she'd been reading when the earthquake hit. She must have forgotten it was even there. The newspapers that came by ferry each week were likely being tossed about, and books, too.

As the hours wore on, I began to get sleepy—so sleepy, I was afraid I'd nod off during my watch. Several times I got up and walked to the windows, just to stay awake. There was still no glow in the sky, and I assumed that the downpour had done its job and put the fire out.

It was close to dawn when, despite all efforts to the contrary, I must have fallen asleep. I don't know how long it was before a sound jerked me awake. *Footsteps,* I thought groggily. *Footsteps outside.*

Motionless, I strained to hear above the howling winds. I was no longer so sure, suddenly, of footsteps. Rather, I thought a shutter somewhere might be flapping back and forth.

But as the sounds grew louder, and I became more awake, I knew that my first assessment was right— someone was walking across the flagstone terrace outside the back door.

We had not locked the door; it had seemed a ludicrous idea, given that in places we had no walls.

Furthermore, there was no one else on the island, so far as we knew, but us.

Now I wished we had locked up. The footsteps grew louder, and I was pretty sure this wasn't a rescue party. The night sky, beyond the windows, was pitch-black, and a rescue party would have had lights. They wouldn't be walking around in the dark.

I turned to wake Luke. Only then did I realize that while I'd nodded off, he'd gone.

Jumping to my feet, I tossed the blanket off. My gaze flew from one window to the next as a dim figure appeared, no more than a dark, moving outline, but coming closer and closer to the back door.

I ran to the door, where Lucy had kept a thick walking stick she'd picked up along the shore. Grabbing it, I raised it and stood off to the side of the door.

"Luke?" I called out. "Is that you?"

No answer.

"Luke?" I called again, more loudly.

Still no answer.

A moment later the door opened, and in a split second I saw that it wasn't Luke, but a total stranger. Raising the walking stick, I struck with every bit of force I could summon, hitting the intruder's middle. His eyes widened in shock, then closed as he crumpled to the floor.

# 7

Everyone was up now, and gathered around the man, who was conscious but still sitting, winded, on the floor. His jeans and flannel shirt were soaked clear through, as was the camouflage jacket he wore over them. Dark hair was plastered against his forehead, above eyes that seemed just as dark. It was hard to tell in the dim illumination from the stove and my fading flashlight.

My first impression was, *a mercenary, a looter.*

But then he grinned and rubbed his stomach, saying, "Damn, woman, but you've got a heck of a swing."

"Who are you?" I demanded.

"And where the hell did you come from?" Grace said, appearing beside me. "How did you get on the island?"

"I didn't 'get on' here, I live here," he managed to say, grimacing in pain as he pushed himself to his feet.

"Where?" I said doubtfully, still holding the walking stick at the ready. "We checked all the other houses on the island and none of them were inhabited."

"I live—or should I say, *did* live—in one of the

cabins over on the west side. I'm Gabe Rossi. Now, if you don't mind, who are you lovely but rather dangerous ladies?''

"You're the owner of one of those cabins?'' I asked, ignoring his question as well as the attempt at charm.

"I am,'' he said, rubbing his stomach again, ''or I was, till it got creamed in the earthquake last night. No, let me see...two nights ago now, isn't it? I seem to have lost all track of time.''

"You weren't around the cabin when we checked it out yesterday,'' Grace said, her tone clipped and patently suspicious. ''Where were you then?''

He shrugged. ''I'm sure I don't know. I might have been out in the woods when you came by. I lost my well water, and had to build a latrine.''

We each knew that made sense; we'd had to do the same thing ourselves.

"There weren't any supplies in either of the cabins,'' Grace continued in that same tone. ''No food, no flashlights, no water. Both those cabins were empty. They looked abandoned.''

"Well, I just bought the cabin a couple of months ago. Apparently, it was vacant and on the market for years. I hadn't had a chance to stock up, and I came in on the ferry late Friday afternoon, just before the quake. I thought I'd look around, see what I needed, and go back on Monday for supplies.''

"So you figured you'd go without food a whole weekend?'' Grace said, raising a brow.

"Well, no, I brought a few things, but—'' He broke off. ''Look, I feel like I'm getting the third degree or something. How long do I have to stand here and defend myself? It's been a rough night.''

Dana stepped forward and said, ''He's right. If anybody had treated us like this yesterday, when we were looking for some kind of help—''

She pulled out one of the kitchen chairs. ''Here, sit down. Are you hungry? We don't have much, but we can share.''

She went to a low cupboard where we'd stored our supplies, taking out cans.

The newcomer took a seat. I looked at Kim, who, I thought, had probably been through this sort of thing before: strangers looking for shelter after a quake. She gave a shrug, as if to say, *Could be.*

After a moment I took a seat across the table from him. ''Did you see someone else outside?'' I asked. ''Another man?''

''No, no one at all. I was shocked to find even you here.''

Grace sat at the end of the table and continued to look on suspiciously. Throughout, Timmy had been silent, hanging back behind the others. She did not join us at the table.

''Timmy,'' I said, ''do you know this man?''

She shook her head, but didn't meet my eye. ''No...no, I don't.''

''I'm sorry, I've never had a chance to meet any of my neighbors,'' he said to her. ''I just bought the Arnold place. Do you know Dave Arnold?''

Timmy nodded slightly. ''Yes...yes, I know Dave.''

''Did you know he sold his cabin?'' I asked her.

Timmy shook her head. "I'm not sure. I don't remember." She walked away, holding her hands over the potbellied stove as if to warm them.

I stared after her, then back at the man who had introduced himself as Gabe Rossi.

"What are you doing wandering around the island at this hour?" I said.

"Well, I saw a fire over on the north side, and went to check it out. It was smoldering by the time I got there, so it was too late to do anything. Damn mess, though—must have been a pretty big house."

"It was. It belonged to a friend of mine."

He reached into his pocket. "Well, then, maybe your friend would like to have this. I found it on the ground nearby."

He held his hand out, and in his palm was a gold, heart-shaped locket. I took it.

"Look inside," he said.

I didn't have to do that to know what was in the locket. I'd seen it around Jane's neck every day since she'd come here. One evening on the way to dinner she had shown me the photographs inside—a little girl on the left, a boy on the right.

I looked around for Jane, but she had gone outside—to the latrine, Grace said. "Dana went with her."

I slipped the necklace into my shirt pocket, thinking I'd give it to her later.

Amelia came to sit at the table, and asked Gabe Rossi if he had a radio. The one that we'd left at Ransford with Jane—our one source of information from the outside world—had gone up in flames with the house.

"I brought a Walkman radio with me on Friday," Gabe said, "because I like listening to music on the ferry. It was still on my belt when the quake hit, so I didn't lose it then, but I set it on my porch railing earlier this evening while I was chopping some firewood. A stupid move. It fell off the railing, and a ton of wood just collapsed right on it. Smashed it to pieces."

"You had it till just a few hours ago, though?" Jane asked, coming inside and sitting beside him. It was the first thing she'd said to anyone since we'd arrived back at Thornberry, but she clung now to Rossi's every word.

"I did," he said, "and I hate to be the bearer of bad tidings, but from what I heard last night, we're better off here. Things are a mess in Seattle. Not only in the city, but for miles around. There's looting in the streets, and people are being shot." He shook his head. "Godawful shame. Seattle, I'm afraid, just wasn't prepared for this."

"Did you bring a cell phone with you?" Jane asked eagerly, her fingers going around his arm.

"I did," he said. "But I'm afraid that's gone, too. It was on a table in my cabin at the time of the earthquake, and half my ceiling fell on it."

At the sight of her crestfallen expression, he added, "But you know, I've been through earthquakes before. In fact, I was in Japan when the quake hit Kobe. I may be able to be of some help to you."

"Or another mouth to feed," Grace muttered.

"True," he admitted, smiling. "But it seems you could use an extra hand around here. I can help repair things, and it looks like you don't have enough heat."

"The hoses from the fuel tank to the house got crushed," I said. "And the fireplace is gone. We've been using the woodstove, but it's too big a room, and there are far too many openings for the wind to come through."

"Well," he said, the grin coming back again, "it just so happens, I can fix hoses to fuel tanks. I can fix all kinds of things."

"Swell. We ask for a rescue team and get Tim the Toolman," Grace muttered.

"Pardon me?" Rossi said, giving her a sharp look.

"Nothing." She folded her arms and turned away. One thing about Grace, she seldom swerved from the role she seemed determined to play—that of a boor, a lout, a churl.

Though, on second thought, she did seem to be listening to Gabe Rossi's every word.

"We accept your offer of help," Jane said, brightening for the first time since the quake. She touched Rossi's hand with her own. "We accept all the help you can give us. It's lucky you're here."

"Fortunate, indeed," Amelia added.

I wondered if they were right. Had we lucked out in having Gabe Rossi show up at our door? Or would he, as Grace seemed to think, turn out to be a burden?

Already, Dana was feeding him, even though we had little to spare. And Jane was looking at him as if he'd arrived amidst a blare of trumpets announcing the Second Coming—despite the fact that he had no radio, no telephone, and nothing much to offer except perhaps a few skills as a handyman.

I had an eerie feeling about the way this man had landed on our doorstep, and how easily the women, except for Grace and myself, seemed to welcome him. Amelia tittered as Rossi told her how much he loved her poetry. He'd read several books of her verses, he said, and quoted a few lines from one. She actually blushed.

As Rossi turned to me, I thought I saw something in his eyes, some slight hesitation. "My guess," he said, "is that you're the one in charge here."

"I don't know that anyone's in charge," I responded. "We're all just pulling together."

"Oh, don't be shy," Dana interjected, smiling. "Sarah's a lawyer. She thinks more logically than some of us. That's why we put her in charge."

"Really, a lawyer?" Rossi said. "Where do you practice?"

I stretched and gave a yawn, ignoring the question. "You know, it's almost dawn. Why don't we see if we can get some more sleep before the sun comes up? We can talk later."

"Good idea," Grace said, giving me a look. "I'll take my shift now."

"Shift?" Rossi asked.

"Lookout," Grace said pointedly. "In case someone else just happens to wander on by."

"Oh, I don't think that's very likely," Rossi said, smiling, "but I guess it couldn't hurt. Why don't you let me take that shift for you?"

"No, thanks. I'm awake now."

"But you must have had a difficult day," he insisted. "Let me help out, while you rest."

"*No*," Grace said emphatically. She turned to me. "Where the hell is Luke, anyway?"

"I don't know," I said. "I've been wondering that myself." Where would he go in the middle of the night? And why hadn't he returned?

"Maybe we should look for him," Grace said.

In part, I agreed with her. He'd been gone far too long. On the other hand, I was pretty sure Luke could look after himself. And since when had Grace taken to worrying about him?

"He might have gone back to his house, to check it out," I said. "In fact, the more I think of that, the more it makes sense. Let's give him till dawn. If he's not here when the sun comes up, we can go looking for him."

"Luke?" Gabe Rossi asked. "Is that another member of your group here?"

"He's a friend of Sarah's," Dana explained. "He washed up on shore yesterday. It was his house that burned down."

"*Dana,*" Grace said.

"What?"

"You don't have to blab all our affairs to an absolute stranger like that."

"But I'm not! I was just telling Gabe—"

"And may I point out that you don't even *know* Gabe."

"Well, you don't, either, Grace," Dana said.

"I know about men," Grace retorted.

"Grace!" Amelia said.

"I'm just being honest," she answered. "We don't know a thing about this person. He *says* he's the owner of that cabin. He *says* he came in Friday night on the ferry."

"You don't believe him?" I asked, as the newcomer sat watching us argue about him. "What makes you think he's not telling the truth?"

"Nothing but my tailbone," Grace snapped, "which always aches when there's some animal around that could bite me in the back."

Gabe Rossi grinned. "I promise not to bite you in the back, Grace. Though I must say, it is a lovely back."

Amazingly, Grace's face turned a deep shade of pink. Stunned, we all turned to look at her. Never for a moment had any of us considered Grace's back— or that it might be attractive in any way, let alone "lovely."

"All right," I said firmly, "this is what we'll do. Grace will keep watch—not because of you, Mr. Rossi, but—"

"Please, call me Gabe. You make me sound ancient."

"As I was saying...Gabe, Grace will keep watch, because that's the way we set it up. There's no reason to change that now. Meanwhile, you should get some sleep so you'll be up to all those repairs you talked about."

He nodded. "I guess that makes sense. Just show me where I sleep."

I thought of putting him in the kitchen with us, but

didn't feel comfortable with that. If Luke had been there…

But Luke *wasn't* there.

I took Gabe Rossi into the hallway, where Timmy and Amelia had cleared a rough but serviceable path through the wreckage of the stairs. I led him to a corner of the hall, where I gave him one of my own blankets, and held my flashlight on him so that he could see to make a "bed" for himself on the floor.

"I'm afraid this won't be very comfortable," I said, "but you are dressed warmly. I think you'll be all right."

"Actually," he said, pulling off his jacket, then unbuttoning his shirt, "my clothes are soaked clear through. I wonder if you'd mind—"

Before I could say anything, he had peeled down to skin. Standing there bare-chested, he looked like someone who spent twenty-four hours a day working out at a gym. I couldn't take my eyes off him, and for several moments I simply stared. He was, I thought, the handsomest man I'd seen in a long time. Certainly the most naked.

When he reached for the zipper on his jeans, I blinked, coming out of my daze.

"Would you mind?" he said, grinning.

"Mind?"

"Turning around? I'm a bit shy."

I blushed. "No, no, of course not, I can—I mean, no, I was just leaving."

"You were?" The grin widened. "I thought you were waiting."

"Waiting?"

"For my clothes." He held the wet shirts up. "I thought you might put them over a chair for me, near the woodstove. So they can dry?"

I was deeply embarrassed now. And he knew it.

Taking the shirts, I turned my back while he removed his jeans. First, there was the sound of the zipper, then Rossi jumping on one leg, then the other, as he pulled them off. Trying not to envision what all this looked like, I admitted to myself that for these few moments, at least, I'd felt less like a jaded forty-year-old, and more like the woman I used to be.

By the time he told me it was all right to look, I had myself under control again. I turned and saw that he'd wrapped my blanket around him. Taking the jeans, I said, "Sleep well," and headed for the door.

"I'm sure I will," he said. "And I very much appreciate your taking me in like this. Especially since I'm clearly a desperado."

"I don't know about that," I said, turning. "I do know we're all very tired and on edge, so if you aren't on the up and up, I suggest you don't try anything."

"Yes, ma'am!" He grinned. "To be continued in the morning, then?"

Not knowing how to answer that, I turned and walked away.

Laying Rossi's clothes over two chairs, I set them near the fire. Grace was standing at the back door, pacing back and forth, clearly agitated.

"What's wrong?" I asked.

"Nothing. I just don't like all these strangers showing up."

"I think this guy's probably okay," I said.

"You do, do you? You have an instinct? Well, I don't trust your instincts. Not where men are concerned."

I wondered why she would say that. Grace didn't even know me—or about my relationships with men. Did she?

When Luke still hadn't come back a half hour after the sun rose, we decided to go out looking for him. Not that we were seriously worried. However, anything could have happened, we reasoned, between the constant aftershocks and the storm.

Timmy decided to stay behind at Thornberry, to oversee whatever repairs Gabe Rossi was able to make. He had gotten up before the rest of us, and was already dressed in his dry clothes and working on the fuel tank when we opened our eyes.

"I couldn't sleep," he explained. "Too many distractions."

His tone and the twinkle in his eyes implied that we were the distractions, and that we weren't unwelcome ones. I was irritated at first by this, but when no one else seemed to mind, I decided I might be overreacting.

Grace, who had kept watch while we slept, had figured out a way to make coffee. She'd built a small fire pit behind the kitchen terrace, and boiled water over it, in a saucepan. Then she poured the hot water over a sieve full of Folger's, using a paper towel as a filter.

Three days ago, any one of us might have turned up our noses at the thick, cloudy brew this made, but we gulped it down thirstily now, grateful for its warmth, its aroma, and the surefire hit on our nervous systems.

Armed with artificial energy, we set out to look for Luke—Jane, Dana, Kim, Grace and I. Amelia stayed behind with Timmy again, and I couldn't help but wonder if she was doing this to help Timmy, or to spend more time with our newcomer. Gabe Rossi's charm was fast working its way with her—and even the other women, before venturing out, had said a few words of encouragement to him, wishing him luck with the fuel tank hoses. What's more, I'd seen Dana fussing with her hair—something she hadn't done since the original quake.

I managed to keep busy cleaning up before we left, which didn't leave much time to say anything to Rossi. If that made me seem less than hospitable, I didn't much care. There was nothing about this man that made me trust him, despite his charm. I would bide my time. See how things turned out.

Jane had insisted on coming with us. "I can't stand just sitting around thinking," she said. Dana agreed to keep a close eye on her, and the rest of us finally agreed to take her along, but with reservations. No one trusted Jane anymore.

She seemed normal enough, however, as she and Dana set out along the shore to the west, while Grace and Kim went around the island to the east, the way Kim and I had gone the time before. I took the middle track, alone, assuring them that with my renewed memories of the island I'd be all right.

Besides, I added, we needed to go in at least three

directions, to save time. We could all meet again at
Ransford, where we would undoubtedly find Luke
sifting through the ashes from the fire. And if we
didn't find him there, we could at least reassure ourselves that the fire was out and no longer a danger.

In truth, I wanted desperately to be alone. There
had been far too much togetherness the past few days,
and I'd lived alone all my adult life. Never having
had siblings, I was accustomed to this, and didn't
mind it. In fact, even under the best of circumstances,
I craved isolation.

I also didn't honestly believe anything had happened to Luke. Whatever he was up to, he wasn't in
danger, I thought, or I'd have sensed it. I'd have felt
that aching in my collarbone—the one that signified
Luke was in trouble.

It had been that way with us, all those years ago.
Once, when we were both fifteen, Luke had been
swept off a rock and had fallen into the water at high
tide, a mile or two from his house. I'd been sitting in
the Ransford library, reading, waiting for him to come
home. He'd gone for a walk, his mother had said, and
should be back any moment.

Luke, too, liked being alone. He would go off on
these solitary walks at the drop of a hat, and we all
knew he'd come back when he was ready. He'd done
that, his mother said, from the time he was eight.

That particular day, though, I couldn't stop thinking that something was wrong. It was nothing I'd logically put together. The day was much like all the
others. A good, hot, summer afternoon—no rain, no

wind, no trouble. Just this aching along my collarbone, a feeling that Luke was in danger.

I'd put my book down and gone to the window, looking out. Then I'd begun pacing. After a while, I'd gone outside to stand on the path, in hopes I might see him from there. Before I knew it, I was on the beach, walking toward a natural seawall he'd taken me to a few times. I knew he loved standing alone on that jetty, loved the waves coming in and licking at his bare feet. I also knew his parents had warned him to stay off the jetty at high tide, because he could all too easily be swept into the water.

When I got there, I didn't see him at first. Then I did. He was indeed in the water, trying to grab hold of a rock. His hands kept slipping. He'd just get to the rock, and the waves would drive him back out. He'd "ride" one in again, and the same thing would happen. I ran along the breakwater, not even thinking about the waves as they lashed at my legs, threatening to pull me in as well. All I could think was, *I've got to get to Luke.* If I could just get to him, somehow it would be all right.

When I reached him, I held out both hands to try to catch him, not realizing at first how foolish that was. The rubber soles of my tennis shoes slipped on the rocks, and I could see now that this was why Luke's hands had slipped each time. The rocks were covered here with inches-thick algae. I nearly went in along with him.

"Get back!" he yelled. "Go back, Sarah! Get help!"

I wanted to. I was so deep-down afraid, my entire

body felt like a steel rod, painful and unbending. My teeth chattered, and my hands shook. But I couldn't do it. I couldn't leave him there.

I found a rock that was smaller, and clean compared to the others. Wrenching off my T-shirt, I tore the armhole as much as necessary to loop it around the rock. Then I used the rest of the shirt to hang onto as I stretched farther and farther out, reaching for Luke.

"Here!" I yelled. "Here, this way!"

He saw what I was doing, and when the next wave brought him in, he grabbed for my hand.

And missed.

It took three tries, but at last we connected. Once I had his hand in mine I gave one mighty tug. With the help of the incoming wave, I got him halfway up on the rocks. He began to slide, but now that I had him, I wasn't letting go. I could feel the T-shirt stretching and, above the noise of the waves I heard it tearing. I knew it was about to come free.

Letting go with both hands, I grabbed Luke by his shoulders, dragging him farther up to safety, even as my own feet slid from beneath me on the wet granite. The receding wave began to pull me with it, but by this time Luke had a good grip on the rocks, and he hauled me up against him, holding tight.

It was only then that I realized that in using my T-shirt, I'd left myself naked from the waist up. My breasts were pressing hard against Luke's bare chest.

For several seconds, I don't think either of us thought of the danger we were still in. My eyes met

Luke's, and I could see there the passion that would finally be played out two summers later.

Coming back to our senses, we scrambled up onto the jetty "path" and ran along it, with Luke in the lead, till we reached dry ground. There, Luke ran to a bush, where he'd hung his shirt on some branches. Beneath the bush were his shoes.

"Here, put this on," he said, handing me the shirt and not looking at me. He bent down and put on his shoes, making a great deal of tying the laces, and taking forever to do it.

At the time, I thought he was embarrassed that he'd had to be saved by me. Later, I learned he had been feeling too many things, and didn't trust himself to see me naked again.

I didn't see Luke for three days after that. When we did see each other, we didn't talk about that moment. Instead, we laughed about our "close call," as if it had all been a lark, a day in the park. Luke did thank me, once, for "saving his life," but even that was done in a humorous tone, which was fine with me. I don't think either one of us wanted to explore how close we'd come that day. Close to dying—but also, in a strange way, to living.

What would it have been like, I wondered now, if we'd made love that day at fifteen? Would I have ended up pregnant? Would he have hated me in the morning?

Again, the road not taken. I would never know how my life might have turned out, had Luke and I done things differently. I might have lived out that adolescent dream and become Mrs. Luke Ford. I might have lived at Ransford, and been a housewife and mother instead of a lawyer.

Hell, I might have gone nuts, like Jane.

Sighing, I thought now about how much my head hurt, and how tired I was. Coming to a small clearing in the woods, I decided to sit a few minutes and rest. Ransford could wait.

Propping my back against the trunk of a tall fir tree, I listened to the singing of birds. They had gone somewhere since the quake, and for a long while the skies had been silent. It seemed a good omen that they'd come back. Perhaps, like the dove after the Great Flood, they brought good news—in this case, that help was on the way.

I touched my collarbone. It was all right, I thought, to take my time. I didn't have that aching now. Luke was all right, I was sure.

A few minutes later, my eyes still closed, I stretched. A psychotherapist I'd seen shortly after my arrest had taught me to release tension by deep breathing. I'd forgotten about that, and did it now, taking in long deep breaths from the diaphragm and letting them out, taking them in and letting them out. Now and then I felt a small aftershock, followed by one that was larger than the others. They seemed to be diminishing in strength overall, however, and most barely shook the ground. Rather, they were like an old, arthritic man, grumbling and complaining as he crawled out of bed in the morning. The fault's sleep had been disturbed. It needed time, now, to get back to normal.

"You've changed, Sarah."

My eyes flew open. Luke was standing a few feet away. His jeans and shirt were black with soot. So were his hands, and there was a smudge on his cheek.

I sat up. "Been at the house, I see."

He nodded.

"We're all looking for you," I said.

He smiled, taking in my messed-up hair, sleepy eyes and the shirt pulling out of my jeans. "It must be hard to find someone when you're sound asleep."

"True. I figured you were all right, though."

"Psychic, now, are we?"

"No, Dana's the psychic one here. I just thought I might have some sense of trouble, if there was any."

He sat heavily on the trunk of a fallen tree, across from me. "Ah. The collarbones. I remember."

I smiled. "It seems they still work."

"Well," he said, "I couldn't sleep, and I went over to Ransford, looking for things. Photographs, old letters...whatever."

"Did you find anything?"

"Not much. When I got there, it was still dark, and the ashes were still smoldering despite the rain. The fire hadn't spread into the forest, though. Thank God for 'the greenest hills you've ever seen.'"

I smiled at the reference to the old song. "Don't tell me you remember how crazy I was about Bobby Sherman."

"I remember a lot of things about you," he said. "And what I didn't remember is all coming back."

Our eyes met for a moment. Luke glanced away first, looking down and picking at his hand as if to remove a splinter. "Damn! There's broken glass all over the place. Anyway, I was more tired than I thought. I fell asleep on the beach, near the dock. When I woke up, the sun was shining, and I looked up at the house, forgetting at first that it wasn't there anymore."

He rubbed his face, looking weary and defeated. "I'm afraid your friend Jane did a good job on it."

"I'm so sorry, Luke," I said. "Jane's been crazy, literally, since the quake. She's worried about her children."

"I can understand the worry," he said with an edge. "What I can't understand is why she had to set an entire house on fire. My God, she could have built a bonfire on the shoreline! Why on earth—" He broke off, shaking his head.

I realized now that last night, when the fire first happened, he'd been in shock. The shock was wearing off, however, and anger had begun to set in.

"Luke, she lost it," I said. "I can't explain why. I didn't know Jane before I came here, and it's only been a week since we all arrived. I do think something was wrong before she ever got here, though. Something in her marriage, maybe."

"Where is she now?"

"She and Dana are checking out the shoreline, looking for you. Grace and Kim, too, but they went in the opposite direction."

A strained smile appeared in Luke's eyes. "You needed to be alone. That's why you were sitting here when I found you, right? You'd gone off on one of those trips you take."

"Trips?"

"Into the past. The future. Wherever it is you go."

"I guess. In this case, the past."

"You really do seem to have changed, Sarah. What's happened to you?"

"Since we last saw each other, you mean?"

"Well, since you started looking as wary as you do now."

"I don't know, Luke. Maybe I've just grown up."

"I think it's more than growing up. You seem hard."

I gave a shrug. "I prefer to see it as cautious."

"Don't do that. Don't play games, not with me. Sarah, what's happened to you?"

"I don't know. My father, maybe." Better to go there than to tell him the whole stupid story of Ian.

"Your father?" Luke said. "My dad told me that James had died of a heart attack, but he didn't say much more than that. What did he do?"

"Turned on me, when I got arrested. Wrote me off."

"Really? That's hard to believe."

"You weren't there."

"No, but it's still hard to believe. You were always the apple of your father's eye."

"Yeah, well, before he died he told me I was a huge disappointment to him."

"He actually said that?"

"On his deathbed, no less. Funny thing is, I've never been sure if he was disappointed in me because—according to the cops, at least—I'd broken the law, or because I got caught."

Luke smiled. "Knowing your father, I'd guess it was the latter. Either way, Sarah, I'm sure he didn't mean what he said. He loved you very much."

"Maybe he shouldn't have," I said. "Loving people too much can lead to an early death."

"Sarah, you did not cause your father's heart attack," Luke said firmly. "That's not the way it works."

"Sure it does. Where do you think the term 'broken heart' came from? My father died two weeks after I was arrested. Two weeks to the day."

He hesitated, as if wondering how to respond. Finally he said, "If James Lansing had a broken heart, Sarah, it wasn't because of you."

I narrowed my eyes. "Oh? What does that mean?"

Again, he seemed to hesitate. "You really don't know?"

"No, I do not know. What are you talking about?"

"Sarah, your father's heart was broken years ago—back when you and I were kids. Look, I'm sorry, but I thought you knew."

I went cold all over, and drew my knees up, wrapping my arms around my legs for warmth. "Knew what? For God's sake, Luke, spit it out."

"Your mother, Sarah. She was in love with someone else. For years."

I drew back, half laughing. "That's ridiculous! Where did you hear such a thing?"

"From my mother—a long time ago. And it's not ridiculous, Sarah. It's the truth."

My mouth went dry. I licked my lips and fought back in defense of my parent, though something in me whispered that Luke was not lying. "Well, I don't know why your mother would say such a thing," I said, my voice uncertain. "My mother and father were...well, maybe not always the happiest couple. But there certainly was never anyone else."

Luke shook his head. "I can't believe you never saw it."

"Saw what? Dammit, Luke!"

"Your mother, Sarah. Your mother...and my father."

"My moth—" This was the last thing I'd expected, and shock left me speechless.

But with Luke's words, a memory flashed back: My mother bathing nude in a cove near here, and being caught by Luke's father. Luke and I came upon them just after Luke's father had surprised my mother. At least, that's what I thought—that he'd surprised her. I remembered that she was blushing and grabbing for her towel, and when she saw us she became even more nervous, pulling on her clothes behind a bush—but not before we'd seen that her skin was pink and her lips full and puffy, as if...as if, I thought now with a shock, bruised by the same kind of lovemaking that Luke and I had discovered by then.

Never had this occurred to me before. My mother...and Luke's father?

Of course. How stupid of me. *Of course it was true.* There had been signs—the way they looked at each other, the way they danced together. But I'd either refused to see them, or as a teenager I'd just never thought of my parents having love lives.

Had my mother found her "true love," as she'd put it that day she described Thornberry as "romantic," a place where we might find our "true loves"? Or was her fling with Luke's father only a summer romance, just as mine turned out to be with Luke?

Dazed, I shook my head.

"What?" Luke said.

"I just wonder if I was born stupid, or if I somehow got this way."

"You aren't stupid, Sarah. You just like to believe in people. You're shocked when you find you can't, and even more shocked when people don't believe in *you*."

I looked at him sharply. "How come you know so much about me, when we haven't even seen each other for years?"

"Despite what I said about you earlier, people don't change all that much. Maybe they become more of what they once were. Or a little bit less. Basically, they stay the same, though. That's how I knew you weren't guilty of that drug charge, the moment I heard about it."

"You did?"

"Of course I did. But, Sarah, I can see why you weren't believed. I've got a friend on the NYPD, and we've talked about this recent rash of accusations against cops. There are a lot of people trying to nail cops these days, especially since that scandal blew up in L.A.'s Rampart Division. Most of the people who were arrested falsely were released from jail or prison when it came out that they were innocent. And that was right—they should have been released. But the extensive media coverage brought out a whole slew of real criminals claiming they, too, were set up. And a lot of good cops in other cities are being brought up on charges, when all they were doing was their jobs.''

"The ones who set me up were not good cops," I said with an edge.

"No, and I'm not saying that—just that sometimes cops need to be given the benefit of the doubt."

I laughed scornfully. "Sounds like you've changed, too."

"In what way?"

"I don't remember you being all that conservative."

"I've just grown up enough to look at all sides now, Sarah. As a lawyer, you do the same thing. To get at the truth in a case, you have to."

"Not me," I said bitterly. "My job is to get my clients off. The truth rarely matters."

"Well, then, maybe this charge against you is your karma coming back to bite you."

"My karma? God, now you sound like Dana."

"I just think it's true, that what goes around comes around."

"And if you were a lawyer, you'd do what? Not try to get your guilty clients off?"

"No. I just wouldn't be a lawyer in the first place."

I bridled, staring at him for a moment. Then I laughed, breaking the tension. He did, too.

"Seems like old times, us arguing like this," he said.

"Except that you would have been on my side back then."

"I'm still on your side, Sarah. I'd like to help you."

"Great. You have a magic wand?"

"No, but I might, if I knew what you had. What's your defense, Sarah? Have you got any evidence? Something that could prove those cops did what you say they did to that woman, then set you up? Do you have anything like that?"

I hesitated, on the alert suddenly. "Come to think of it, how do you know so much about my case?"

"Well, from my father, I suppose. At least partly. Your case hasn't exactly been low profile, Sarah. When it first came out it was all over the news."

That was true enough. But I was remembering that Luke's father, as a judge, had a lot of contacts with the Seattle police department—friendly contacts that went way back. Even if Luke were innocent of trying to trap me, did his father, for some darker reason, send him here to pry information from me? Was Luke perhaps on his way from Seattle—not Orcas—when he washed up at the Ransford dock?

He seemed to read my mind. "Tell me you aren't suspecting my father of being corrupt."

"Not corrupt, precisely. I'm just wondering who else he might be talking to. The judicial world is a small one."

"Sarah, look, forget my father. You can either trust me or not. If you do, I might be able to help you. Just tell me if you've got any evidence to back up those rape charges."

I thought a moment, and realized that I really wasn't certain whether I could fully trust Luke. I also realized that my lack of trust wasn't based on anything I knew about him, but rather on what had been done to me by other people.

Finally I said, "I do have something."

His eyes widened briefly. "You do? That's great. What is it?"

"I...I'm not prepared to say."

He frowned. "Not even to me?"

"No. I'm sorry, but not even to you."

He made an exasperated sound. "Have you turned this evidence over to the cops?"

"You're joking. Who the hell am I supposed to trust in the department? It used to be evidence went into an evidence room and was kept safe there. Now it gets stolen. Or tainted."

"Sarah, for God's sake, you're letting paranoia take over. For every bad cop in the Seattle PD, I'm sure there are a hundred good ones."

"Maybe so. But they don't wear signs, so who can tell?"

"Trust *me,* then. Tell me where this evidence is, and I'll keep it safe for you."

"I...no. I can't," I said.

"You aren't willing to trust me with it?"

"No."

At his pained look, I added, "Not you, specifically. I just can't trust anyone. Not anymore."

"So that's what it is," he said.

"What?"

"That hardness I've been seeing in you. You've built up some mighty strong bastions, Sarah."

"Well, if I have, it's with good reason. And I don't see that as hardness—just an intelligent use of my brain power."

"How intelligent is it," he said, "withholding evidence? You could be disbarred for that. You could go to prison."

"I'll get around it somehow. Or not. Right now, the only thing that matters is protecting myself."

"You've got a trial coming up, haven't you? You've got an attorney? If you've got evidence that could incriminate someone else, your attorney can get you off."

"Maybe. Or we could both end up dead."

"Dead? Have you been threatened?"

"Not directly. But it didn't take much to figure out that if they killed to shut their victim up, I was next on the list. You don't think they were really going to stop at just having me arrested, do you? Blackening my name? Hell, no. Their next step would have been to drown me in the Sound and make it look like a suicide. People would believe that, after all. They'd think I couldn't take the scandal."

"That doesn't make sense, Sarah. You're not dead, you're very much alive. If they wanted to kill you, why haven't they done it by now?"

I just looked at him.

"Sarah?"

"The reason they haven't killed me is because I told them what I've got on them. And it's enough to put them away for good."

His eyes widened. "You *told* them? The Seattle Five? And they haven't come after it? They haven't killed you already, to stop you from using it?"

"Luke, don't be naive! I told them it was in a safe place where they'd never find it, and if anything happened to me it would go to someone capable of putting them behind bars."

"Who?" Luke said softly, leaning forward. "Who has the evidence, Sarah?"

I laughed, but shortly. "What do I look like, an idiot? I tell you, you slip and tell your father, he tells the wrong person—deliberately or not—and it's all over for me."

I was becoming more and more angry, and I thought for a moment Luke would continue pressing and we'd end up in a real argument. It wouldn't be our first—though as teenagers, we'd argued more as an exercise, not about anything like this.

But he eased back. Smiling, he said, "Look, this is not something we should be at odds over. Not after all the years we've been friends. What do you say we call a truce? Okay? Just promise me you'll come to me if you need help?"

I felt a small aftershock run along the ground. It reminded me how close I'd come to never seeing Luke—or anyone—again.

"Truce," I said, softening. "And yes, I'll think about it. Luke, I don't mean to sound as if I don't trust you. I've just learned to be wary these days. Can you understand that?"

"I guess I can. Though, with me—" He broke off as he saw me stiffen. "Never mind. God knows, we've got enough to handle here. I can't even imagine what we'll find when we get off this island and back to Seattle.''

We both settled back, while I, for my part, wondered what my mother was thinking and feeling, having heard the news of the quake. Was she worried about me at all? I had told her I was coming to Esme, and that the house would be vacant for a month. Since she'd turned it over to me to live in, I had thought it best to make her aware that I'd be away for that long.

Luke was silent, too. Was he wondering how his father was? I had somehow assumed he and his father had talked since the quake, because he didn't seem worried.

''What about the judge?'' I asked. ''Have you talked to him? Is he all right?''

''I think so. He managed to get word to me through a friend with a ham radio, a few hours after the quake. We couldn't talk long. All the ham radios available were needed for the rescue efforts. But he said he was all right. Seattle, though, is a mess.''

''We heard that. It's good that you know your father's all right, though.''

''Yes.''

''Is there, uh, anyone else you're worried about?''

He grinned. ''You mean a wife?''

''Or whatever.''

''Not at the moment. I was married, but that was over long ago.''

''What happened?''

''We just weren't compatible, I guess. I was still a kid, just out of college. We got married in London, and she had a career there. I wanted to come back to the States and she didn't. After a while we parted— amicably, or as amicably as that can get.''

"Are you still in touch?''

"Not for years.''

"What are you doing now? Where are you living?''

Luke smiled. "You'll never believe it.''

"Sure I would. Let's see…you mentioned a friend in New York. You're living there? You're an actor on Broadway? Or a star of stage and screen?''

He laughed. "Have you seen me on stage or screen?''

"No, but all those little plays you put on as a kid…what else would you be?''

"Actually, I'm a detective, of sorts.''

"A *detective?*''

He laughed again. "I sort of like to think of myself that way. I work for a consulting company called KMK. They send me out to consult with other companies around the world. This last several months I've been on an island in the Bahamas. My job was to find the safest place to put docks for new ferries connecting the surrounding islands, and then tell my clients how they could put them there at a reasonable cost, but without impacting the environment in a negative way. Three months from now I could be working in Ottawa. Or Paris. I never really know.''

"Well, that fits,'' I said.

"In what way?''

"That you travel a lot. After that year that we were, uh, together, I heard you were wandering about Europe. Going to college there. Dana says Sagittarius men can't sit still. They love to travel.''

"Oh?" He grinned. "And you were talking to Dana about me?"

"No." I looked away. "Just talking about signs in general. That made me think of you."

"Well, did Dana also tell you that Sagittarius men are very loyal?"

"No, as a matter of fact, she said they were off loping after a new woman every other week. They need a fresh face, is what she said. Just like they need a fresh view. They aren't very dependable as lovers, either. They might even disappear for years at a time, she said, then turn up as if nothing had changed at all."

"Ouch."

"Yeah. That's pretty much what I said."

"Well, maybe I'm on the cusp or something."

"Ha."

"Sarah...I really am sorry we've been out of touch for so long. It's wonderful, seeing you again like this."

"Funny, you haven't really been acting that way."

"Well, I didn't know what you expected. I thought I should keep my distance for a while."

"But not from Grace, right?"

"Grace?" He looked perplexed. "What about Grace? I don't get along with her at all."

"Oh, please. Since when hasn't that been an indication of some sort of sexual tension?"

"*Sexual?*" He laughed. "Well, I must admit I do find Grace rather...different."

"Different?"

"Sarah…who's being naive now? Don't you think maybe Grace likes women, rather than men?"

At this, I laughed. "You think she's a lesbian? Why—because she doesn't let anybody give her any grief? Or maybe it's because she's tough and knows how to take care of herself."

"Not that, no. You should know me better than that, Sarah. I just thought…well, she doesn't seem turned on by men."

I let out a hoot. "You mean by *you,* don't you? Grace hasn't given you a tumble, so you just naturally assume she's a lesbian, because what woman would *not* be turned on by you?" I ran a hand through my hair, laughing. "Oh, God, it's been so long since I've been around a man, I must have forgotten how the male ego works."

He had enough goodwill to laugh at that. "Admittedly, I have always thought of myself as being able to charm birds—and women—out of trees."

"That's you, all right, Luke. A real charmer." I sobered. "Until, that is, you lost interest and went loping off, as Dana says, after the next fresh face."

He frowned. "You're deliberately twisting things. At eighteen, we just naturally went our separate ways. Why are you making it sound as if I walked out on you?"

I stood and brushed leaves and twigs from my behind. "Oh, I don't know. Maybe so I can be sure to see you in a clear light now, and not through some romanticized haze from twenty-two years ago."

He stood, too, holding his arms open. "Here I am,

Sarah. It's me. Just me, no matter what light you choose. You'll still get the same thing.''

''We'll see,'' I said, crawling behind my protective wall again.

The soft singing of distant birds suddenly became a loud cry, a cawing. Shading my eyes, I scanned the sky. ''Something's wrong with them. What do you think it is?''

''Either they've spotted an intruder bird, or are warning each other that there's a hungry animal out there.''

As we watched, turkey vultures began to wheel and circle. I felt a chill. ''You're probably right. Maybe they found a dead animal.''

In the next moment, however, I heard my name being called. Kim's and Dana's panicky cries carried over the air.

Luke and I turned in the direction they seemed to come from, and ran through the brush. I could hear the cries getting closer, and as I passed old tree stumps I remembered them as landmarks from years before. We were running toward Adams Ravine, a deep gorge created in the island by an ancient quake. As children, Luke and I had pretended there was a bridge over the ravine, and called it the Bridge of San Luis Rey. We imagined tiptoeing across it and looking down the two hundred feet to the bottom, the rope bridge swaying and threatening to topple us into the yawning chasm.

This was nothing like those early imaginary exploits, however. Dana, Kim and Grace were standing on the edge of Adams Ravine, looking down. The expression on Dana's face was one of horror.

Running to stand beside them, I looked to where Dana pointed, her hand shaking. Halfway down the ravine, on a shelf perhaps four feet wide, lay a body. The jean shorts and pink shirt were all too familiar.

"Jane," I breathed. "Oh, God, no."

She had fallen atop a long, thin, broken tree trunk, perhaps five feet high. Its ragged top had pierced her completely through, and blood lay in pools around her. The vultures were circling, impatiently biding their time until the human intruders left. Their hungry screeching was what Luke and I had heard.

It seemed clear, even from this far away, that Jane was dead. "I'll go down," Luke said. "If she's still breathing…"

He let the words hang, and we all knew that even if Jane were breathing there would be little we could do. With so much blood loss, she would need transfusions. Surgery. Neither of those was available to us.

He began to lower himself down, hand over hand on the outcroppings of bushes and roots. Here and there he would dig the toes of his boots into the dirt, but it was still wet from the rain, and slick. That, and the aftershocks, made it slow going. He would get to a certain level, then have to stop and hang on. Once, I thought for sure the trembling ground would shake him loose and tumble him into the ravine.

I had wanted to go down to Jane, and Grace had offered, too. Luke had insisted it would be safer if he went alone. I could see, now, that this was true. Most of the surrounding ravine was bare of trees and shrubs. There was one natural path of roots, however, that bulged out from the sides of the cliff. This led from where we stood to where Jane lay, in a more or less direct line. If we were to follow Luke and fall, we would take him down with us. And vice versa, if Luke were to follow one of us.

I turned to Dana, who was clinging to my arm and crying. "What happened?" I said, taking her by the shoulders. She was shaking so much, I tightened my grip automatically, as if to keep her from flying apart. "Dana! Tell me what happened!"

Tears filled her eyes. "I...I lost her. I'm so sorry. I don't know how she got here."

"You lost her?"

"I mean, I don't know what happened! She went into one of those cabins, the one we thought Gabe Rossi might own. She said she thought we should check it out again. God, I don't know why she did that! Why did she have to do that?"

Dana's eyes fixed on me, wet and haunted. "After she went into that cabin, I had a sudden, terrible feeling she was going to burn it down, like she did Luke's house. But that didn't occur to me at first. I just thought she was curious."

I shook my head, hardly able to believe what I was hearing. "You let her go up to this cabin alone, after what happened at Ransford? Dana, you were not supposed to let her out of your sight!"

"I told you, I'm *sorry!* You just don't know—" She gulped, and caught her breath, speaking more quietly. "Sarah, I stayed down by the shore because I'd tripped and twisted my ankle, and the path up to that cabin was so steep, I didn't think I should try it. But when Jane didn't come back, I finally went up there to get her." Dana shook her head, her expression dazed and disbelieving. "She just wasn't anywhere around. It was like she disappeared into thin air."

I looked down at Dana's ankle, at the same time noting something, peripherally, about the ground on the edge of the ravine. Grace interrupted, however, distracting me from my train of thought.

"Where did you look?" she demanded of Dana. Then, to me, she said, "Kim and I ran into Dana at Luke's house."

"At Luke's house?"

"I had a feeling," Dana explained quietly, in an obvious attempt to calm her voice, "that Jane went back there to see if the fire had attracted a rescue team. It was the only thing that made sense—except, why didn't she just come back down from the cabin and go with me?"

She began to cry again. "I am such an idiot. I keep thinking I *know* things, and the truth is, I don't know a goddamned thing anymore! If I did, maybe I could have found her in time to save her."

Kim, who had been staring down into the gorge, turned to me. "I don't know what her reasons were for disappearing on Dana, but obviously Jane wasn't at Luke's house. We started to look in the woods, and we found a path from the house, mostly overgrown. It brought us here."

Kim's eyes blurred with tears. "Grace spotted Jane

first. She started to go down there, but we talked her out of it.''

''We didn't think there was anything we could do,'' Dana said, her chin still trembling. ''And we were afraid Grace would fall and we'd lose her, too. We started calling for you, Sarah, to let you know what had happened so you'd come here instead of the house.''

She looked at me, drying her eyes on the back of her hand. ''Actually, I thought of you walking through the woods all by yourself, and I...I was worried something might have happened to you, too.''

It seemed to me that Dana was trying to tell me something. Was it that she didn't think Jane's death had been an accident? And why did that thought even occur to me?

I started to ask her if that was, indeed, what she'd meant. But Luke had reached Jane's body and was feeling for a pulse, first in her wrist, then her neck. I saw him lean down and put an ear close to her mouth. Finally he looked up at us, shaking his head.

I felt tears sting my eyes. For the first time, I almost hoped that Jane's children hadn't survived the quake. At least, that way, they would be together now. Jane could stop worrying, at last.

# 8

Even if we'd all been rested and up to it physically, it would have been difficult to bring Jane up from the ravine. Now, with the constant aftershocks, and with all of us exhausted from lack of sleep and not enough food, it was impossible. Luke suggested we leave Jane where she had fallen, offering to cover her over with rocks from the hillside until the rescue teams came.

Placing the rocks—necessary because of the predator birds—took what seemed to be forever. I watched Luke inch along the sheer side of the ravine, gathering them one by one and gently placing them over Jane's body until every inch was covered—every inch, that is, but the terrible hole made by the spear that had penetrated her chest. He moved heavily, revealing an exhaustion that was reflected in his ashen face. We all wanted to help, but again he was adamant that we stay above.

"If any of you fell…" he called up, shaking his head. "I don't think I could do this again."

We linked hands and watched silently, as Jane—a woman we hardly knew yet already missed—disappeared beneath one rock and then another. Dana prayed aloud, and I think this was the first moment when we knew, not in theory, but beyond a shadow of a doubt, that this could have been any one of us.

We'd been luckier than the people who'd died in the quake—thousands of them, probably. We were luckier than Lucy or Jane. But we were living on borrowed time. How long could it last?

Afterward, we sat at the kitchen table at Thornberry, looking at each other silently, everyone reluctant to be the first to speak. I had taken Timmy aside when we arrived, and told her about Jane. She had paled and gone outside. Ever since, she had been sitting beside Lucy's grave, bent over as if in grief, her mouth moving in what I took to be prayer.

Gabe Rossi, the newcomer, was outside fixing the goat pen, in case the goats returned. We had come in through the front, and hadn't spoken to him yet.

I finally put into words what I'd been thinking from the moment we'd found Jane. "We have to at least consider," I said, "that Jane's fall wasn't an accident."

I counted the startled eyes that turned my way, looking for at least one pair that seemed less startled than the others. There were none, however. Not that I could detect.

"But that's—that's crazy, isn't it?" Dana said. "Who would want to hurt Jane?"

"I don't know. But over the years as a lawyer, I've been at a lot of crime scenes. I've learned to look for certain things."

"And?" Luke said.

"And there was something at the edge of the ravine that struck a familiar chord in me, something I'd come across in a criminal case years ago. I just didn't have time to process it while we were there."

"What was it?" Kim asked.

"The ground at the edge of the ravine. It was torn up, as if there had been some sort of scuffle. If Jane had simply fallen over—let's say she lost her balance during an aftershock—the earth wouldn't have looked that way."

"But several of us were there before you and Luke got there," Dana pointed out. "Me, Grace and Kim. We probably did that by looking over the edge to see Jane."

"I don't think so. The edge was sort of rounded, not a flat shelf. If you'd kicked up that much dirt so close to it, you would probably have slipped and gone over, too. No...for the ground to have been stirred up that much so close to the edge, there must have been a scuffle."

"She's right," Kim said. "I remember standing back from the edge because it was rounded that way. I could see that if I wasn't careful, I could easily just slide right off."

Timmy's voice, thin and unsteady, came from the open kitchen door. "Are you saying you think Jane was pushed over? By someone here?"

That gave me a start, as I hadn't seriously considered that someone at this table might have murdered Jane.

"I...no," I said. "I guess I was thinking that there must be someone else on the island."

"Ten little Indians," Kim murmured.

"What?"

"The Agatha Christie book, *And Then There Were None*. Except that here, it's the reverse. Instead of disappearing, people keep showing up."

"It's more like some goddamned nursery rhyme," Grace said. "'London Bridge is Falling Down,' or something. Which one is it where people hold hands and it's all very chummy, all these kids dancing around in a circle—until some poor slob gets picked to be 'out'?"

"I'll bet you were the one who was always out," Kim said, though her tone was more gently teasing than insulting.

Grace didn't snap back, and for the first time since the ravine, Dana actually smiled. "Have you ever noticed how many of those nursery rhymes are about food? 'Jack Sprat could eat no fat'...'Old Mother Hubbard went to her cupboard'...'Little Jack Horner sat in a corner, eating his Christmas pie'..."

"Not to mention Little Miss Muffet with her curds and whey," Kim said. "And of course, 'Peter, Peter, Pumpkin Eater.'"

Dana buried her face in her hands. "Oh, God! I would kill for a taco right now!"

For some reason, we all found that funny—even Grace, who burst into laughter with the rest of us. I suppose we must have been on the point of hysteria by then. It did help to release some of the grief and tension we'd carried home with us from the ravine.

"All right," I said, when we finally settled down. "The first thing we've got to ask ourselves is, 'Who was not with someone when this happened?' 'Who was somewhere alone?'"

"I was," Luke offered. "For a while, anyway."

"I was, too," I added. "For a while." We looked at each other.

Grace fixed her sharp gaze on us. "So you two met each other in the woods? Like, just by coincidence?"

"Yes, by *coincidence*," I said. I was in no mood for her barbs right now.

"Gabe Rossi was alone out there for a while," Kim said.

"Who's Gabe Rossi?" Luke asked.

"I forgot," I said, "you haven't met him. He showed up last night after you went out. He owns one of the cabins along the shore."

"And you don't know where he was at the time Jane must have fallen into the ravine?"

"Amelia told me he left here to go back to his cabin and get something. Right?"

Amelia, who was guiding Dana's sprained ankle into a pan of warm water that she'd heated herself over the outside fire, nodded.

"He went to his cabin to get some tools."

"I thought there wasn't anything at his cabin," I said. "He told us he didn't keep anything there over the winter."

"Well, to be fair," Dana answered, "I think he meant food and other kinds of supplies like that. I don't remember seeing any tools there, but we were hurrying to meet you and Kim at Ransford that day. We didn't look in all the drawers, just the ones we thought might have food, or flashlights or radios. And maybe he had an outside storage room we didn't see, like at Luke's house."

"I hate to say this…" Kim began, then fell silent.

"What?"

"Well, if Gabe was gone for a while, that left Timmy and Amelia alone. Did either of you… Did either of you leave the other by herself?"

Neither woman answered at first, and I think the rest of us were stunned, the idea was so absurd.

"You aren't really suggesting that either Timmy or Amelia might have killed Jane?" I finally said.

Kim shook her head. "No, I'm not. Not really. But as you say, we have to consider everyone—not leave anyone out."

I was not comfortable with making either of these women suspects. I didn't know if it was because of their ages, or because I honestly liked them both. Still, I had to admit that it wouldn't be fair, or even smart, to rule either of them out.

Looking over at Timmy, I said, "I know this is ridiculous. But *did* either of you leave the other alone this afternoon?"

"Only to go outside in the garden," Timmy said.

"We never left the property," Amelia added quickly.

*Too quickly?* Amelia's answer raised doubts, but I decided to let them pass for now.

"Well, then, what time was it, about, that Gabe Rossi left to go to his cabin?"

Amelia looked at Timmy, who shook her head and turned away. "It was shortly after you all left," Amelia said. "He came back a while before you did."

"So he could have done it," Grace said. "He could have taken some back trail and been at his cabin when

Jane went up there to check it out. He could have taken her out behind the house, where Dana couldn't see, then led her to the ravine and pushed her over.''

"But *why?*" Dana said. "Why on earth would he have killed Jane? I can't even imagine her being a threat to anybody."

"Maybe she saw something she shouldn't have," I said.

There was a small silence.

"And maybe Gabe Rossi isn't who he says he is," Grace offered.

"You're right, ladies," he said from the door. "I'm not at all who I say I am. I'm a killer. A cold-blooded killer."

He had been holding one hand behind his back, and as he swept it forward, I think we all jumped a mile, thinking it must be a gun. But in Gabe's hand was a huge, radiant bunch of lilacs, and on his face was a wide grin.

"Before I off you, however, I intend to bury you in flowers. How's that for a switch?"

He plunked them down on the table, and their sweet, life-affirming scent filled the room. Looking up at the grin, the twinkle in the eyes, I don't think any of us could have considered this man to be a cold-blooded killer.

"And you must be Luke," he said, reaching into his shirt pocket. "Timmy's been telling me all about you." His hand came out of the pocket and opened up to reveal a perfect, sky-blue bird's egg, no bigger than a quarter.

*"Por moi?"* Luke raised a brow and looked at it, and then glanced sharply at Gabe Rossi. "Why?"

"Well, the ladies seem to have chosen you as their protector," Gabe said. "So I figure you're just the man to save this little bird's life."

Luke shook his head as if bemused, but took the egg Rossi handed to him. Holding it in his own palm, he blew on it a bit with his warm breath, and I remembered something I'd forgotten over the years: Luke with a baby bird in a shoe box, feeding it from a medicine dropper, the way kids will. He was thirteen at the time, and wanted to be a vet when he grew up. Eventually, the baby bird reached the point where it could fly, and Luke and I had a ceremony, releasing it to the skies.

Rossi and Luke met each other's eyes. There was something between them, some challenge. Maybe it was just that age-old thing of two dogs pissing on a fire hydrant—two male egos butting up against each other in the midst of all this estrogen.

I noted that Dana and Kim, and even Grace, were looking at Luke as if he were some kind of savior. Give a woman a man who's nice to animals—or birds—and they lap him up like cream.

Not that I blamed them. Luke had certainly proved himself to us, between burying Jane and helping us in so many other ways, since he'd arrived on the island. Aside from that, he had the kind of personality that endeared him to women. He was quiet but kind, firm but open to listening to another person's viewpoint.

Not as classically good-looking as Gabe Rossi,

though—and I would have bet my last penny that the other women would have fallen more for Gabe's openness and charm.

"When you came in," I explained to Gabe, "we were talking about possibilities—wondering which one of us might be a killer, ludicrous as it seems. We couldn't rule you out, any more than we ruled out Timmy and Amelia."

He took off his jacket and sat across from Grace, Kim and me. "But, ladies, I don't even know what you're talking about. Who am I supposed to have killed? Who's died?"

I remembered then that no one had told him about Jane.

"One of the women," I said. "Her name was Jane Parrish. We found her in a ravine, dead."

"And you think I pushed her over? Good God, ladies! Why on earth would I do a thing like that? I didn't even know the woman!"

"You met her last night," Grace pointed out.

"Well, yes, but if you don't mind me saying so, I was a bit out of it last night. Somebody, you may remember, whomped me with a walking stick."

He gave me a worried look. "And now you think I've done in your friend? Pushed her into this ravine, is it?"

"As I was saying," I told him, "we've been going over the possibilities. You were only one of them. Nothing personal."

"Oh, glory be! Nothin' personal, is it? I'm bettin' ye'll all be sleepin' with yer walkin' sticks t'night!"

He lapsed into the Irish brogue so quickly, it startled me.

"You know, we never did ask you what you do," I said thoughtfully. "When you're on the mainland, that is. What kind of work do you do?"

He grinned and dropped the brogue. "You might say I'm one of those YETI's you hear about. Young Entrepreneurial Techies. I suppose I don't qualify for the 'young' part anymore, since I hit thirty-five. But the kids who work for me do. I own a software company."

"Really?" Kim said. "Which one?"

"Dark Kingdom. You've probably never heard of it. We came out with something similar to Loom, but with better graphics. It hit big, and now I do the voices in some of our games, just for fun. One of our biggest successes had an Irish locale. I called it Bloody Mist."

Dana shuddered. "Sounds gruesome. I'm sorry, but I wouldn't want my kids playing some of those games."

"Do you have children?" Rossi asked.

"No—I just know I wouldn't want their minds growing up that way. Jane felt that way, too. We were just talking about it the other—"

She stopped, looking down at her hands.

"Gabe," I said, "Jane went up to check your cabin this afternoon. Apparently, you were there, too. Did you see her?"

"I'm afraid I didn't, no," he said. "And just for the record, I'm very sorry about your friend. You don't really think someone pushed her, though, do you? I mean, if she was out in the woods walking alone, she probably just slipped and fell. The ground is treacherous after the quake and all these rains."

"It would help if someone had *seen* her slip and fall," Grace pointed out.

He shrugged. "I'm afraid I can't help you. I didn't see your friend. On the other hand—" He paused, looking at Luke. "I did see you."

Luke stared. "You saw me? Then you must have been at Ransford. What were you doing there?"

"I was actually nowhere near Ransford. I was walking from my cabin back to Thornberry, through the woods. I saw you—and you were standing at the edge of a ravine, looking down into it."

I turned my eyes to Rossi, confused. "You must have seen us all at the ravine. We were all there with Luke."

"Not when I saw him, you weren't. He was alone."

Luke pushed back his chair, jerking to his feet. "You're lying! What the hell's going on here?"

"I am not lying," Gabe said calmly. "I saw you standing at the edge of a crevasse, looking into it. Your hands were full of mud and you were wiping them on your jeans and staring at something. I watched you for several moments."

Luke paled and looked at us all, shaking his head. "He's lying. I went directly from Ransford along a path that wasn't anywhere near that ravine. I ran into Sarah in the woods, and we didn't leave that spot until we heard the rest of you call. There is no way I could have been at that ravine when Jane fell."

"Then what were you doing there?" Rossi persisted. "Because you were there. I saw you with my own eyes."

"That's crazy!" I said. "Luke would never have hurt Jane. He wouldn't hurt anyone."

"Sarah—" Grace began.

"No, I'm telling you, it's crazy! I've known Luke for years."

"May I point out that you haven't seen him in years?" she said reasonably. "May I also point out that your *friend* has done quite a bit of disappearing since we met up with him? And who knows what he's been up to?"

I turned on her angrily. "I can't believe you would buy any of this, after all Luke has done to help us. For God's sake, Grace, why would you take the word of a man who just showed up here in the middle of the night, and who none of us even knows?"

"What reason would Gabe have to lie?" Grace argued.

"I don't know. But if Luke says Gabe is lying, then he is. Besides, I already told you—Luke and I were together in the woods."

"Well, all I can say is, it's awfully damn lucky the two of you have each other as alibis. Real convenient, him running into you in the woods. And you into him."

"So now you think it was *me* who killed Jane?"

She folded her arms. "What about the two of you together?"

"For God's sake, Grace!"

"All I'm saying, Sarah, is how do we know? None

of us knows anybody else here. We don't even know *why* we're here—not really."

"She's right," Dana said tentatively. "I've been thinking about that. I mean, I'm not published or anything, and nobody's ever even heard of me." She looked at Timmy. "No offense, but I have been wondering why you invited me here."

Timmy seemed at a loss for words, and Amelia filled in for her. "In the first place, it's not true that no one has ever heard of you, Dana. Many people have read your articles in *Prevention*, and someone recommended you."

"Really? I was recommended? By whom?"

"I don't quite remember now, but Timmy and I went through a file of recommendations, and you came out with some of the highest points."

"I don't get it," Dana said. "Who wrote these recommendations?"

Amelia gave a slight shrug. "People who have been associated with Thornberry over the years."

"You mean alumni?"

"Some are alumni, and some are simply people who supported Timmy when she turned the bed-and-breakfast into a writer's colony. Most were old friends."

Kim spoke up. "What about the rest of us?"

"You were all chosen in the same way," Amelia said. "We were very meticulous in our process, weeding out names until we ended up with the best. Timmy wanted women with the greatest potential, who were writing about women's issues in some way, and who had some experience in life, so that they knew firsthand what they were writing about. Women of conviction, who stood by their beliefs.''

Amelia went on in this vein, explaining the selection process at length—and at some point I began to doubt her explanation. I was reminded of the old saying that when one is going to lie about something, it's best to be brief. Inept liars often go into too much detail, feeling they have to explain themselves too much in order for the lie to be accepted. Amelia, I thought, had gone too far, perhaps, with that business about our "great potential."

In all modesty, I was ready to concede that Timmy might have looked upon me that way because she had been in on my beginnings as a writer. In fact, she'd been responsible for them. I could also see her thinking that way about Kim. As a film star, Kim had a certain status in the world that could carry her book to success. Presumably, she'd also had some sort of life experience that was worth reading about—even if none of us knew, yet, what that was.

But Grace? How could Amelia describe her as someone with "great potential"? I'd never seen any proof whatsoever that Grace was even writing a book. I'd almost decided, for that matter, that she was here under false pretenses—one of those people who talks a good talk, but never seems to get around to the walk. Grace had told us she was a graduate student, who lived on grants and went from one writer's colony to another all year long. I knew there were many young, would-be writers who lived that way—professional students, in a sense. They were often the literary types, who spent so much time applying for grants, they often had little time or energy left over to pour into a book.

And then there was Jane. She had claimed to write romance novels, yet no one had ever seen a manuscript or heard her read from one. We had all attributed this to shyness, yet I'd wondered if she were serious enough about writing to devote herself to it, with all her concerns about family.

Not that I had a problem with that. But from what I'd learned about writing in the past few months, I understood it now to be a full-time job, something that required tunnel vision. Writers, I'd learned from reading the bios of the famous ones—the ones who made it—were not necessarily "nice" people, by most accepted standards. They tended to be people who neglected their families, shut themselves up in a room for hours on end, and often didn't bother to wash.

This was definitely not Jane.

Doubting that poor woman, however, was probably my low point that evening. If this went on, I thought, we'd all be at each other's throats before long.

Amelia put my thoughts into words. "I think we all need to pull ourselves together, now," she said firmly. "This is not the time to start accusing each other. We must stand as one until help arrives. And no offense, Sarah, but isn't it possible that the earth on the edge of that ravine was disturbed some other way? Perhaps from Jane trying to stop herself from slipping down the side?"

I hadn't thought of that, and admitted it was possible.

"But if Gabe is telling the truth about seeing Luke at the ravine—" Dana began, casting an uneasy glance at Luke.

"If he is," Amelia interjected, "we will know, sooner or later. Meanwhile, it does no good to be at each other this way."

*"Meanwhile,"* Grace argued, "we do need to watch each other's backs, just in case. I suggest we don't allow anyone to go wandering off alone from now on."

For the past few minutes Luke had sat silently, listening to the speculation that he might be a killer. Now he spoke in a reasonable tone. "I agree with Grace. None of us really knows each other here— except, of course, that Sarah and I know each other, and both of us know Timmy. In this instance, however, we need to treat everyone in the same way. So I'll tell you what—I'll pair off with you, Grace, since you seem the most suspicious of me. Aside from Gabe, that is, and quite frankly I don't trust myself with him right now."

Gabe shrugged. "I'd certainly prefer not to be paired off with a killer."

Luke's mouth tightened, and Amelia spoke up. "I'll pair off with Gabe."

Luke shook his head. "I don't think—"

"Don't even bother to argue," Amelia said. "I assure you, I'm more than able to protect myself."

Luke argued the point a bit more, but Amelia finally won out.

"All right, then," he said reluctantly. "Dana—you and Kim seem compatible enough. Which leaves

Timmy and Sarah. How do you two ladies feel about spending some quality time together?''

I wasn't so sure about that, at first. Being partnered with Timmy would keep me here at Thornberry, when I might have preferred the freedom to roam the island.

On the other hand, it might give me more time to search among the debris of my cottage for the *Allegra* case. If I had to pair off with Timmy, she would be the best of all possible worlds. There was no reason, after all, to suspect my old friend of foul play.

# 9

That first night after finding Jane dead was the most difficult, I think, since the quake. I couldn't get her out of my mind enough to sleep, and the other women tossed and turned all night, as well. I kept seeing poor Jane on that ledge, covered with rocks. She should at least have been buried like Lucy. She should have flowers on her grave.

She should still be alive.

That she wasn't was too ugly, too unthinkable. What if her husband and children had survived and were looking for her? What if they came here with the rescue teams that would surely, eventually, arrive? Who would tell them? How could anyone face those two beautiful children and tell them their mother was dead?

I thought of Jane's locket, realizing that I had forgotten to give it to her after Gabe had turned it over to me. She had died without it. A treasured locket with fresh, young faces inside. To grow up without a mother, their lives indelibly changed...who would want to be the bearer of such tidings?

I lay in my blanket on the kitchen floor and stared at the opening in the ceiling. The rain that would inevitably return was holding off, and stars twinkled brightly as if they hadn't a care in the world. I supposed that since they had all been dead for millions of years, and only their reflected light was left to be seen, they actually *didn't* have a care. Not anymore.

I wondered if we'd all end up that way—a piece of reflected light in the sky. Was that the only way we, and whatever light we'd managed to create in our lives, would survive?

Dark thoughts for a dark time. And now that I had moments alone to think, I had to ask myself: Did I really believe what I'd said about signs of foul play at the ravine? Or was that only the old paranoia kicking in?

Yes, the ground had been torn up, and it was probably true that if Jane had simply fallen over during an aftershock, that wouldn't have occurred. Could Amelia be right—that Jane, having begun to slip down the ravine, had clawed frantically at the edge, tearing mounds of dirt from the surface as she slid to her death?

Or could the others have kicked up the dirt that way, in sheer panic, when they first found Jane? Surely that was the simplest explanation—and if I were to stick to the rule of Ockham's razor, as taught in law school, the simplest of the two theories would be the preferred one. To quote the old monk, "It is vain to do with more what can be done with less."

Or to put it another way, the fact that bad things had happened in Seattle, and to me, didn't mean they were happening here, and to Jane. That someone here on Esme Island might have murdered Jane was too complicated a theory.

But say that's what happened. Then, why? Jane was too ordinary, too innocent, to have been connected in any way to the same people who'd been out to get me in Seattle. Jane, and the Seattle Five?

I couldn't see it.

But it didn't have to be about me. It was my own fear—and perhaps the fact that Lonnie Mae's evidence seemed to be missing—that had made me come up with that scenario. Perhaps Jane had brought her own secrets with her from Bellevue, something that had nothing to do with me at all.

Alternatively, had she, as I'd suggested earlier, seen something she shouldn't have?

That opened up even more difficult questions: What did she see, and whom? Who on this island—who at Thornberry, right now—would murder a woman like Jane in cold blood? And why?

So much for Ockham's razor. The old monk had a good idea, but maybe life was less complicated in the fourteenth century. None of my theories was simple, and each one led to a question more complicated than the last.

The only thing I knew for certain was that I'd have to make a thorough search, now, for the *Allegra* case. If I found it under the debris in my cottage, fine. If not, then someone here had taken it.

*Ergo*, someone here posed a danger to me.

And that same person might have killed Jane.

By ten the next morning, only Timmy and I were left inside the farmhouse. Everyone else had gone off in pairs, to carry out chores that ranged from searching the horizon for passing boats—in which case, a fire would be built on the edge of the shore—to fishing or gathering clams and oysters off surrounding rocks.

Contrary to Luke's plan, I left Timmy alone in the kitchen for what I hoped would not be more than an hour, while I went in search of Luke and Grace. I needed Luke, or someone strong, to help me lift that range in my cottage. Grace might be as strong as Luke, but I felt I could trust him more. If the evidence case was there, I didn't want anyone else knowing about it—especially Grace. There was something about her I just didn't like, and I would have to think of some way to get Luke away from her, if only for a few minutes.

I spotted them through the trees, as I was walking along a path in the forest near Thornberry. A tangle of six-foot blackberry vines lined the path, and I scanned the trees beyond through a break in the vines.

They were standing by a thick, hollow tree stump with ferns growing from inside it. Grace stood with her back to Luke, running a frond between her fingers in a slow, thoughtful way. Luke said something to her, and I quickened my pace and opened my mouth to call out.

What happened next stopped me dead in my tracks. Luke took Grace by a shoulder and whirled her around, pulling her into his arms. They stood that way for several moments. Astonishingly, Grace looked frail and helpless, as if she were melting in Luke's embrace. All I could do was watch, unable to move in any direction.

When my wits finally returned, I took a step back, more out of shock than a thought to run. My foot landed on a twig, which snapped with a loud *craaack*. Luke dropped his arms and jerked around, and the look on his face was one I'd never seen before. His facial skin stretched tight, like a cat instantly on the alert for danger. His eyes were sharp as they searched the stand of trees.

"Who's there?" he called out.

I was so shocked, I didn't answer at first. Then I debated trying to disappear behind the wall of blackberry vines, and running back to Thornberry along the path.

But when Luke called out again, I couldn't do it. I stepped forward.

"It's me," I said, shading my eyes and squinting as if it were difficult to see that far. "Who's that? Oh, Luke. And Grace. I didn't see you there."

"What are you doing out here?" Luke said, his voice still tight. "You're supposed to be with Timmy."

"She, uh, sent me out to look for thistle. She says it's healing to drink when it's been boiled, and she thought we could all use some, if only to strengthen our immune systems—at least that's what Dana says, it helps to keep people from getting sick..."

I was babbling, saying too much, just as I'd thought Amelia had done earlier, in explaining how we all came to be invited here.

"Anyway," I finished lamely, "I've only been gone a few minutes. I'm sure she's all right."

"That's not the point, Sarah," Luke said angrily,

running a hand through his hair. "We need to keep an eye on her, same as everyone else. You never should have left her."

I folded my arms and bristled. "Well, I'm sorry if I can't quite see Timmy as a serial killer, but if you want to, that's your prerogative, I suppose. Anyway, what about you? And Grace?"

He hesitated, giving me a sharp look. "What about us?"

"What are you two doing that's so helpful today? Aren't you supposed to be down by the shore? I thought your job was to hunt for oysters and clams—whatever you could find that was edible."

"We're on our way there," he said irritably.

"Oh, and you were going to carry all these oysters and clams in what exactly? Your pockets?"

His face darkened. "What the hell are you talking about?"

"I'm just saying I don't see any buckets."

Luke stared at me, opened his mouth, then shut it. He turned with a frown to Grace. "She's right," he said. "You didn't bring the buckets?"

Her chin went up. "No, I did not bring the buckets. I thought that was your job."

"Grace, I'm sure I told you to bring the buckets."

"Well, I didn't hear you say to bring any buckets." She planted her hands on her hips.

"So what did you think we'd do without buckets?" Luke said.

"I guess I fucking thought we'd carry those crappy little things home in our crappy little pockets!"

There was a moment of silence as the two of them

stood nose to nose, like two fighting cocks. Then all of a sudden, Luke laughed. Grace, to my amazement, broke into laughter, too. They laughed so hard, they both doubled over, tears running down their cheeks.

I watched them for a minute, and when they didn't stop, I began to feel more and more like an outsider. Luke—one of my oldest friends, and my first love— had for some reason connected with the one person in our group I'd never been able to stand.

What's more, they had connected as a man to a woman. Apparently, Luke had lied about his feelings for Grace.

Disgusted, I turned and left, heading for my cottage.

On the way to my cottage I thought about what I'd seen. Luke's initial anger toward me, I supposed, might have been just a reaction to having been caught at whatever he and Grace were doing.

But why? Neither one was married or otherwise involved, as far as I knew.

Of course, I didn't know. And that was the thing. Since the quake, the other women and I hadn't asked many questions of one another. Survival had seemed the prime directive. I did know Grace had claimed to be single when we first talked after arriving at Thornberry.

But what about Luke? Except for our talk in the woods earlier, in which he had said he'd been married but wasn't anymore, I didn't know much about his current life.

Putting logic to work—and being as honest with

myself as possible—I asked myself why seeing him there like that with Grace had upset me so much. After all, hadn't I been telling myself for months that I didn't want to be involved again with a man? That I didn't have time for it, and didn't trust it?

I was feeling shaken, I reasoned, only because Luke had stirred up old feelings from a younger, more innocent time. And who wouldn't want to go back to those times, if only in memory? Who wouldn't be swayed by them?

I didn't know why I used the word "swayed." It came naturally to my mind, and from there I had to wonder if Luke had been deliberately trying to sway me into caring about him again—and not for romantic reasons. Had he been manipulating me? And if so, for what purpose?

Entering my cottage, or rather its rubble, I still had no answers. I only knew I would lift that damned range by myself, if it killed me.

It almost did.

The range had fallen facedown. I had found a short two-by-four, and managed to slide it underneath in a two-step process. First, I used a thin but semi-sturdy stick, sliding it past the burner knobs and lifting the range just enough to create a space of a few inches. Then, quickly, before the stick could break, I shoved the two-by-four under. By wiggling it back and forth, and pushing it at the same time, I eventually managed to work it halfway under the stove.

This took far longer than I'd imagined it would, and when I was done I was tired and sweaty. My limbs shook, which I attributed to a lack of protein in my diet over the past few days. I hoped Gabe and Amelia would have some luck fishing today. Amelia had declared herself an old hand at backpacking, and it was clear now that her "tough old bird" act was more than that. She was proving to be strong physically as well as mentally, now that the initial shock of the quake had worn off. I had no doubt that if Gabe Rossi tried anything with her, she'd flatten him.

Wiping my brow on the tail of my shirt, I got on the floor, lying prone to see under the stove. There was debris under there, some scrap papers from my desk—but no manuscript and no disk. Something glinted way in the back, however. I tried to use a long piece of debris as a stick to slide whatever it was toward me, but it was wedged too tightly under the stove. To retrieve it I would have to try lifting the stove even higher.

It was old, and heavier, even, than I had thought it would be. I wondered if it was made of cast iron inside. At home, I'd been able to move my range out from the wall for spring cleaning. It was not a job I liked, but I could physically do it. This range, though it was smaller, weighed a ton.

By a lengthy process—similar to the building of the pyramids, at least according to some—I managed to wedge increasingly larger objects under the top edge of the stove. Finally, I was able to fit the two-by-four under it, propping the stove up high enough at this end to see under it completely.

Relief swept over me as I recognized the *Allegra*

case. *Thank God. Something is going right.* I reached back carefully and pulled the case out.

Quickly, I opened it to see if it still held its treasure inside. It did. Lonnie Mae's fishnet stockings lay there in the sealed plastic baggie, still intact.

My release was so great, I nearly fainted. My vision went dark, then came back. My hands shook uncontrollably. Closing the case, I held it to my chest, breathing in and out, trying to regain my strength.

Behind me, I heard a footstep, and shoving the case quickly inside my shirt, I began to turn around, expecting to see Timmy. She must, I thought, be looking for me by now.

Something landed on my head, heavy and crushing. Pain split me in two, and everything went black. I felt my bones go slack, and my body slid the rest of the way onto the floor. Then I was conscious of the fact that I was moving—moving over rubble and dirt, though I couldn't see who was dragging me.

After that, nothing.

# 10

When I came to, I was in the farmhouse kitchen, lying on the big dining table. Grace and Luke were standing over me, and there was something soft pillowing my head. Someone had thrown a blanket over me, and Timmy was at the kitchen sink, rinsing blood from a rag. The pain in my skull told me the blood must be mine.

"What happened?" I said, groaning as the effort of speaking shot daggers through me.

"We found you unconscious on the path to the farmhouse," Luke said, stroking my forehead. "You must have crawled there. Do you know what happened?"

"I know I didn't crawl there. Somebody dragged me."

"Dragged you?" He and Grace looked at each other. "Why would anyone do that?"

"Why would anyone clobber me over the head?" I snapped, groaning again.

Timmy spoke worriedly from across the room. "I don't like this. I don't like it at all. It just gets worse and worse...."

I looked at Luke. "She means," he said, "that now

that someone's attacked you, it's more likely than ever that Jane was attacked, too.''

Suddenly, I remembered the *Allegra* case. I put a hand over my chest to see if I could feel it inside my shirt. It wasn't there.

Panicked, I tried to sit up, but Luke pushed me back down. ''Wait. Give yourself time.''

''You don't understand. I lost something. It must have fallen out, and—''

''*You* don't understand,'' Grace said. ''Sarah, you've got quite a lump there, and whatever was used to hit you, it cut through your scalp.''

I lifted a hand and felt for the wound, which was on the back of my head and about two inches long. My fingers came away bloody. Timmy came and put a clean, damp rag over it, pushing me gently back down to hold it in place. In her eyes were sorrow and concern. She fussed over me, trying to get me to drink water, but I choked on it and pushed it away.

''You didn't see who hit you?'' Luke said. ''Nothing at all?''

''You must have seen something,'' Grace said.

''I told you, I didn't!''

And why were they so relentless about this?

That scene in the woods came back to me. There was something going on between Grace and Luke, that much was clear. But did it have anything to do with whoever clobbered me?

''Please, Sarah, try to drink some of this,'' Timmy urged, holding the water bottle to my lips again. She lifted my head, carefully avoiding the cut. ''I'm so, so sorry, my dear.''

I took a few sips, then sat and swung my legs to the floor, wincing as pain shot through my entire body. "I have to get up," I said. "I need to look for something."

"You're not going anywhere," Luke said, standing squarely in my way.

"Tell us what you've lost," Grace said. "We'll look for it."

"No. No...I can't."

I didn't know what else to say. Even when Luke and I had talked earlier, I hadn't thought it a good idea to tell him about the evidence I had against the Five, or the fact that I'd brought it here with me. Now that it was missing—unless it had simply fallen from my shirt and was still lying back there—I didn't feel safe telling anyone. Even if I could trust Luke, he would almost certainly tell Grace about it, now that they were getting close.

No, I couldn't risk it.

"I want to go myself," I said. "I need to walk and get my strength back."

"You need to *lie down* and get your strength back," Luke argued.

"What the hell is so important?" Grace said. "Just tell us what it looks like. We'll find it."

I wasn't going to win this one. And if I pushed the argument much more, I'd be giving too much away.

"It's Jane's locket," I lied, remembering that it must still be in the pocket of my other shirt. "Gabe found it at your house after the fire, Luke. I'd like to give it to her children, if I can find them when this is over."

"That's all?" He raised a brow. "Sarah, don't you realize that whoever struck you down could still be out there? The locket can wait until we figure out who did this to you."

"No. No, it can't wait. You don't understand."

Grace's manner changed, suddenly. "You know what? She's right, it can't wait. Let's go look for the damned thing, Luke. She won't give us a moment's peace till we do."

"I agree with them," Timmy put in. "I'll make you some hot tea, Sarah. I found a wonderful old thermos jug, and I saved hot water in it from the fire Amelia made out back this morning. I even found an old can of crackers, the English kind, that come in a tin. I think they must be from way back when I had the bed-and-breakfast, but believe it or not, they're still good."

I couldn't stop Timmy from wanting to take care of me, and I couldn't stop Luke and Grace from leaving. I finally had to let them go on their fool's errand—looking for Jane's locket—and pray they wouldn't find the *Allegra* case in the process.

Or that if they did find it, they wouldn't understand what it was.

Momentarily, I considered following them, thinking I might find it first—but when I stood up I realized how weak and rubbery my legs were.

Timmy helped me outside to a lounge chair in the sun, then brought me the hot tea, and crackers wrapped in a white linen napkin with the Thornberry Bed-and-Breakfast logo on it in an elegant, satin script—TB&B. Those napkins were memories of better times for Timmy, and I wondered how she was finding the strength to keep going through all this. If, as Amelia had said, Timmy had been close to bankruptcy, finding an investor must have seemed like a last-minute miracle. I could only imagine how thrilled and relieved she must have been. And now, to have lost Thornberry this way… Would she ever recover from the loss?

She tucked a blanket around me and left me there, saying she had chores to do in the kitchen. I wanted to talk to her, ask her how she was feeling, but she seemed closed down, turning away when I tried to make contact. This, I thought, is how she's dealing with it. Shutting reality out as much as possible.

I settled for thanking her, then sipped the tea, slowly feeling my spirits revive. I couldn't choke down the crackers, though. Instead, I stared at Lucy's grave, and thought of Jane. Two down. Almost three, with me? Lucy, of course, had been an accident. But we still didn't know about Jane.

And if someone wanted to kill me, wouldn't they have done more than hit me over the head?

Of course, they might have been dragging me into the woods to do just that, when Luke and Grace came along. Whoever it was might have dropped me when he or she heard them coming, then hidden in the woods, watching to see if Luke and Grace would find me or go in another direction.

But it would have to be two someone's, wouldn't it, if everyone had stayed in pairs the way they were supposed to?

Two killers? On one small island?

It didn't seem likely. But if so—who?

I told myself the very idea was absurd, but more and more I kept leaning toward Luke and Grace. Grace was the one amongst us who had never seemed to fit. And now Luke had apparently joined forces with her.

If he had, this wasn't the Luke I knew. Or thought I'd known. My thoughts moved back over the years, and I remembered a hot August day, that year when Luke and I were seventeen. We'd been sitting on the Ransford lawn under a blue-and-white canvas gazebo his parents had erected for entertaining guests during the cocktail hour. Luke and I faced the Sound in white wooden lawn chairs, sipping lemonade, while his father and mother, and mine, talked at a round patio table. Luke's father said something about needing a stronger police force in Seattle, and that ever since the Vietnam riots people had been getting out of hand. There was too much disrespect for the law, he said.

My father argued that the police were getting out of hand, and that a lot of the arrests they made during those years were phony. Most of those people were released without charges, he said, and besides being immoral, arresting innocent people was a complete waste of the police department's time.

It's funny I hadn't remembered that, till now. My father, a liberal?

Well, what other kind of lawyer would—right or wrong—defend white-collar criminals as if they were angels? That I'd never thought of him as a liberal before was due, most likely, to my having been his child, and the fact that children seldom see their parents clearly.

Luke, to my surprise, had taken his father's side that day. Not that we shared in the adult conversation, but we had begun making snide remarks, in undertones, about nearly everything they said.

Luke had snickered at my father's comment. "Your father," he said, "could make Hitler look good."

I had bridled at that. "Your father would jail Jesus if he showed up today."

"My father would at least put Judas where he belonged," he replied.

"And my father would get him out!"

When I realized the absurdity of my argument, I burst into giggles, and Luke laughed along with me.

Luke's mother called to us. "What are you two children doing over there?"

*Children.* We were seventeen.

I turned, and saw that she was patting her neck and face with a handkerchief, blotting the perspiration away. She wore a long, flowered dress that day, and a floppy sun hat. I seemed to recall that she even wore white gloves, and I wondered why she always had to put on a show. My own parents had dressed in shorts and shirts, the same way they did at home on weekends.

"We're just talking, Mother," Luke replied.

"It sounds to me like more than talk," his mother said coyly, and by this time everyone was looking over and snickering at us—the two teenagers who had nothing to do but spend their time giggling and horsing around.

Luke stood up and grabbed my hand. His eyes met mine with an unspoken message. "Let's take a walk," he said.

"Where are you going?" his mother called out.

"For a walk," he answered, his hand nearly burning mine with its urgency.

"Well, don't be gone long. It's nearly dark."

"We won't," I said, already wet with anticipation. "Don't worry."

It was after midnight when Luke took me home to Thornberry. By then, my parents were wild with worry. We couldn't have cared less. I had already brushed the leaves and twigs from my hair, but my lips still felt bruised from Luke's. It wasn't a painful bruising—more like that of grapes when their sweetness is released into an elixir; a heady, intoxicating, balm.

Now, sitting here all these years later, I had to admit to myself that it was way past time to take a good hard look at the kind of men I'd been attracted to over the years. Luke was not bad, but he was a "bad boy" type—the kind most young girls, and many women, are attracted to. He seldom followed the rules, seldom listened to his parents or did as he was told. If there was something Luke could do that was averse to convention, he did it.

And when it came to women, he was fickle, at best. Back when his parents were having those lawn parties that I wasn't allowed to attend, he always had a different girl to dance with, always someone new hanging on his arm.

Until he and I got together that last summer. After that, I didn't see him with other girls, and I thought he'd finally found The One. Me.

Maybe he had. Or thought he had. *Summer loves.* Why do we always think they'll last forever? And why are they so exceptionally sweet?

Well, Luke seemed to have reverted to the old ways now. Grace in his arms in less than seventy-two hours? For all I knew, that might not even be a record for Luke, the grown man.

I closed my eyes and leaned my head back, letting the thin, white April sun warm my face. There was so much more to think about than Luke, or any man. *"Sufficient unto the day is the evil thereof."* The past three months had brought with them more than enough of that—my arrest, my father's death, my mother's move to Florida.

I didn't understand my mother—never had, though there were many poignant memories of her, like the one of her starching and ironing her lace curtains every Saturday. I had thought her very rigid, to be so particular about whether her curtains were spotless all the time.

Apparently, she wasn't all that rigid. Under the surface lived a married woman who had taken Luke's father, a married man, as her lover.

I must have dozed off for a while. When I opened my eyes again, the sun had dropped low in the sky, and Amelia and Gabe Rossi were back. The pungent scent of fish cooking over an open fire reached my nostrils. I assumed Gabe Rossi was behind the kitchen cooking it, as Amelia's and Timmy's voices drifted through the broken window behind my head.

"He's pretty handy to have around," Amelia was saying. "I wonder what his real story is, though."

"Real story?" Timmy asked.

"If you ask me, there's something odd about the way he showed up here."

"I don't know if it's all that odd," Timmy remarked. "The first thing *we* did was check out the other houses on the island for either people or supplies."

"That's true. Maybe it's something else about him, then…"

Amelia's voice trailed off, as other voices came from the path leading from the cottages. *Luke and Grace.* I knew they couldn't have found Jane's locket, because I still had it in my other shirt.

But had Luke and Grace found the *Allegra* case?

My stomach tightened as they came into view. Part of me wanted them to have found it, while another part hoped it was well hidden somewhere in the bushes. The alternative was that a third, unknown person had knocked me unconscious and taken the case for his or her own purpose.

Luke and Grace were both empty-handed. Grace was looking at Luke and smiling—until she saw me sitting there. Then the smile faded. She shoved her hands into her pockets and walked over to me with the usual swagger.

"Not a sign of that locket," she said. "Sorry. We looked everywhere."

"She's right," Luke said. "We looked everywhere it could have fallen—if you'd been dragged from the cottage. Sarah? I'm confused. We didn't see any sign that somebody dragged you. The dirt on the path didn't look as if it had been disturbed."

"Maybe whoever attacked me smoothed it out," I said.

"I suppose that's possible. But are you certain you're remembering correctly? Might you just have staggered out onto the path?"

"No. I distinctly remember being dragged."

"Maybe you're remembering wrong because of the knock on the head," Grace said.

"I am not remembering *wrong,* Grace."

"All right, all right! You don't have to get testy about it. Anyway, we didn't find it. Maybe a blackbird took it."

"A blackbird?" I squinted up at her.

"Well, you know how they like shiny things."

"I thought that was magpies."

"Same difference. Is that fish I smell? Thank God." She turned and went toward the back of the kitchen, sniffing.

I looked after her. "For a city girl, Grace seems to know a lot about the country," I remarked to Luke.

"Oh?" He sat cross-legged in front of me, on the ground.

"Well, rats, blackbirds, magpies..."

"I think they've got all those in New York City," Luke said mildly.

"So she told you she was from New York?"

"I guess she mentioned it. Why?"

"Oh, just that you two seem to be hitting it off. I haven't seen Grace actually nice to anyone since we arrived here."

He grinned. "Are you jealous?"

"Me? Jealous of Grace? Don't be silly."

"Aw, come on now. Say it. You still have feelings for me."

"Sure I do—and we're on a Hawaiian island right now, with hula dancers and a pig in a pit. Dream on."

"I didn't say I *wanted* you still to have feelings for me. I just said that you do."

"Ha. You'd love it. Then you'd have two of us fawning all over you."

"Fawning? You think that's what Grace is doing?"

"Of course, that's what she's doing. Jeez, you men! You know exactly what's going on. You just never want to admit it, because then you'd have to do something about it."

"I admitted it that summer with you," he said softly. "I did something about it, too."

I looked away, unable to stop the heat that rose to my face. "That was a long time ago."

"And we've both changed. I know that, Sarah. But tell me you didn't feel something when you saw me half dead on that dock."

"Of course, I felt something. I was scared to death you *were* dead. We were friends. Why wouldn't I be worried?"

"Friends?" He ran a finger beneath my pant leg to the hollow behind my knee.

I jerked my leg back. "Stop that."

"Aha! You felt something."

"You're right. I felt a snake run up my jeans."

He grinned again. "You know, speaking of being attracted to someone, I thought I saw you giving old Gabe the eye last night."

"Gabe Rossi? You've got to be kidding."

"Why? He's good-looking, friendly...even charming, some might say."

"Too damned charming, if you ask me."

"You think so?"

"I know so. I've had my fill of charming men."

"Including me?"

"I hadn't noticed you being all that charming lately. But yes, for the moment, including you."

"Does that mean that in another moment you might change your mind?"

Inside the kitchen, Timmy was ringing a small bell to let us know dinner was on.

"In another moment," I said, "I'll be eating a decent meal for the first time in three days. I won't even remember you."

"I remember a time when you were hungrier for me than for a decent meal," he countered.

"Teenagers. They'll eat anything."

I realized what I'd said, and the heat rose higher. I could feel it in my scalp.

He stood and held out his hand.

"What's that for?" I said.

"To help you up. Damn, woman, you sure are mean today. Must've been that knock on the head."

"I'm mean all the time now," I said. "And getting meaner by the day. You'll see."

We dragged chairs out onto the terrace and ate around the fire, with the food on napkins in our laps. The fish tasted like the finest ever served in a five-star restaurant, and there were more than enough oysters to go around.

The kitchen faced the woods, and the setting sun glinted off the tops of the trees. Beneath them the shade was a grayish purple, fading into black. As the night began to encroach and shadows deepened, I fancied I could see the ghosts of those old marauding Indians, watching us. Now and then I thought I saw one move.

Would this island ever be free of its sad past? I wondered. Or would it always be burdened by the weight of those tragic events? And were the deeds of the early settlers finally catching up—but with us? Were we the ones to pay?

That was the way it felt, that we'd all been brought here by some cosmic force, to pay for some unknown deed.

Or was it a current deed, known to only a few?

Whichever, Esme Island was no longer the paradise of my childhood, and the differences went beyond Timmy, Luke and me. There was something afoot here, something moving in and out of us like a dark cloud.

But could it change people all that much? Could the Luke I'd known—unconventional, yes, but good—

become a killer here? Or had that happened sometime during the years we'd been apart?

I didn't know. And I hadn't turned out to be all that good about judging men lately. In fact, since Luke had flirted with me a while ago, I'd been less and less inclined to see him in any clear light at all.

The thought occurred to me that for all I knew, that might have been the purpose of his flirting—a deliberate act, designed to blur my emotional vision.

I looked around at our little group and tried to come up with alternatives. The most obvious was Gabe Rossi. He was the one who had somehow been on the island without showing his face, all the while we'd been out there looking for survivors.

"Gabe," I said, wiping my hands on my napkin and setting it on the ground, "when you're not here on Esme, who are you? I mean, I know you said you owned a software company. But are you married? Do you have children? Where do you live?"

He gulped down a piece of fish and smiled, then swallowed some water. "Well, let's see…first of all, I live south of Seattle. Gig Harbor, actually. I'm not married, and I don't have children. I've been too busy setting up my company and getting it off the ground, I'm afraid. One day I suppose I'll have to see about getting married, though."

"Isn't there someone you're worried about? A mother or father? A brother?"

"My family is all living in the East," he said. "I guess right about now they're more worried about me. That's why I was so bummed when the cell phone broke. I tried to reach them right after the quake, but

I guess the towers around here were down. I thought if I just kept trying, sooner or later I might connect. What about the rest of you?''

Amelia and Timmy both said they had, sadly, outlived their families, and Kim said her agent and her studio were probably going nuts in L.A. Dana was oddly silent about her husband in Santa Fe. And Grace didn't bother to answer.

Nor, I noticed, did Luke. In fact, he had been watching Gabe closely throughout the meal, while at the same not giving an inch to Gabe's attempts at conversation.

"What about you, Sarah?" Gabe asked. "Any family?"

"My mother. She lives in another state," I said.

"Anywhere nearby?"

"Not really. Why?"

"I just wondered," he said offhandedly, "if she might be affected in some way by the quake. Before my radio went out, I heard it was felt all the way to Montana and as far south as San Francisco."

"Just how did your radio go out?" Luke asked. "I don't remember being around when you mentioned that."

Gabe met his suspicious tone without flinching. "That's right, you weren't here when I first arrived. Well, like I told the ladies, I brought a Walkman with me when I came over on the ferry. When that first shock hit, I must have dropped it somewhere. Didn't even realize it was gone until later."

"That's too bad," Luke said. "We really could have used a radio—"

"Wait a minute," Grace and I said, almost simultaneously.

I looked at her, and we both knew we'd caught the same thing. I was the first to speak. "The night you arrived here," I said to Gabe, "you told us you were out chopping firewood when an aftershock hit. You said the radio fell off your railing and got smashed by falling wood."

Luke looked sharply back at Gabe. Gabe kept his eyes on me, the ready smile never leaving his face. "Really? I said that? Well, shoot, if I did, it must be true. I guess my memory hasn't been too keen since all this happened. Shock, I suppose. That'll do it."

His eyes met Luke's. "Like you not remembering you were at that ravine by yourself, right? Shock. That's all it is."

Luke didn't answer for a moment. Then he said, "Right. I guess that's what it is."

The tension in the air was so thick, it gave me chills. Suddenly Grace, of all people, jumped up and said brightly, "I've got an idea. Let's do something fun. I'm so damned sick of these long, cold nights and trying to sleep through them."

"Fun?" I said, curiously. "What did you have in mind?"

"I don't know. Play games? Tell ghost stories? *Something.*"

"I know how to drum," Dana offered. "We could dance around the campfire. Maybe it would bring in some good spirits."

Grace let out a groan.

"No, really," Dana said. "We've got those big,

old, empty spring water bottles inside, the ones Timmy had water brought over in for people who didn't like the well water. If you turn them upside down, they make perfectly good drums. Wastebaskets, too.''

"I like the idea," Kim said. "I was an Indian in a movie once, and—"

Grace broke in. "You were an *Indian?* What did you do, dye that red hair?"

"Well, sure. I can play all kinds of roles. My agent calls me a chameleon."

"A chameleon..." Grace said thoughtfully. "Meaning you can fit in anywhere, and be anything, with no one being the wiser?"

Kim met her challenge. "Yes, I can do that. And somehow, I suspect you can, too, Grace."

There was a silence as the two women stared each other down. Then Dana jumped up and grabbed Luke's hand, and Kim's. "C'mon, let's go get us some drums."

There were other protests, but for the first time Dana stood her ground, unwilling to play the part this time of the amenable one. "You'll see," she said. "It'll be fun."

It turned out to be both more and less than fun. It started with Timmy, Gabe and I following Dana's direction with simple drumbeats. Timmy sat on a straight chair brought out from the kitchen, complaining that her arthritis was kicking up since we hadn't had heat or warm baths. I had noticed her limping earlier, and wondered. Gabe and I sat on the ground

with the upside-down five-gallon water bottles between our legs, beating on them with our palms.

"Once you get into the rhythm, it's hypnotic,"
Dana said. "It can even take you into another space."

"She's right," Kim added. "Think tropic isle,
palm trees, reggae."

"Think a nice soft bed," Amelia groused. "Forget
palm trees."

She was squatting by the fire, teasing the dinner
coals into flames. Once Amelia got it going, Dana
took her hand and led her, along with Kim and Luke,
into forming a circle around the campfire. At first, no
one touched, but left a few feet between themselves
and each other. As we began to drum faster, however—something that seemed to take us over almost
without our volition—they took each other's hands.
Kim made Hollywood-type Indian sounds like "Hey-
yahh, Ho-yahh," and danced like someone out of an
old fifties' Geronimo movie. At first I thought that
she hadn't, apparently, seen the more authentic
*Dances with Wolves.* But then it became clear she was
simply having fun, trying to make us laugh. In that,
she succeeded.

Luke, after a rather restrained beginning, fell in line
and did the same. After a while he had me in stitches,
and I remembered from long ago how he could always make me laugh.

Then I saw his hand reach out to Grace, and their
fingertips touch. The look on his face was one I
couldn't fathom. It was intimate in some way that
seemed old, as if they'd known each other forever.

My smile faded, and the aching in my head that I'd almost forgotten, increased.

Luke leaned over and whispered into Grace's ear, and she smiled and nodded.

Dana was watching them, too, and her eyes met mine. The message passed between us: *What's this all about?* I shook my head. *You're guess is as good as mine.*

This went on for a few more minutes. Then Luke and Grace parted. Luke came over and grabbed my hand, and Grace took Gabe's, both of them urging us to get up and dance. That left Timmy alone, but Dana sat with her and took over my drum. Amelia complained that she was out of shape and out of breath. She sat on an upturned tree stump, outside the circle of dancing.

Now that Dana was drumming, the beat took on a slow, contemporary rhythm, like that of a forties' dance band. I glanced over at her in surprise, and saw that she had her eyes closed and was swaying sensually back and forth.

Luke began to draw me closer, and before I knew it we were slow dancing, as if in a ballroom or at a prom. The drumming slowed even more, and over Luke's shoulder I saw that Grace and Gabe were close now, as well. Grace was more clingy than I'd ever seen her, an arm draped over Gabe's shoulder, her hand at the back of his neck, teasing his hair. Gabe laughed softly and nuzzled her neck. It occurred to me that catastrophe, like politics, makes strange bedfellows.

We two couples were the only ones remaining on

the "dance floor," and the others, including Kim, were silent, watching us. I began to feel that Luke and I were alone on a cloud, that the past three days hadn't happened, and that, in fact, the past twenty-two years hadn't, either. It felt like old times, Luke and I dancing in the forest at seventeen, with the music from his parents' party drifting through the trees. The "old-timers," as we had loftily called them, were stuck with a wooden dance floor and bright lights, noise, and far too many drunken people. We were the lucky ones—alone in the world, with soft tufts of grass tickling our bare toes and the smell of pine all around.

As Luke drew me closer, I could feel his heart beat the way it always had against mine, and I could almost hear the familiar pulse in his neck throb as he began to grow hard, pressing into me, his arm tightening around my lower back. His lips at my ear were warm, his breath even warmer. My legs grew weak, and I leaned into him, wanting to feel him the way I always had, wanting never to leave him, and for this night never to end.

It was almost as if we were kids again, and when Luke's hand slid up between us to feel my breast, I began to shake. I was so aroused I had to hang onto him, for fear I'd lose control in front of everyone. But a quick glance around showed that Grace and Gabe had disappeared, the drumming had stopped, and everyone else had gone inside. I saw their shadows moving in the candlelit kitchen, heard their voices as they carried over the air.

Luke whispered, "Let's go into the woods," and

nothing could have stopped me then. It was just as if we'd been carried back to those years, and none of the terrible things of the last few months, nor of any time in our lives had occurred. Hand in hand we ran into the woods, with only the moonlight guiding us.

"Here," Luke said in a soft, urgent voice, then, "no, it's softer over here."

He had found a carpet of grass to cushion us, just as he always had. My white knight, I'd called him, always seeking to protect me, and not only from the uncomfortable ground. Not that the grass helped all that much. Our lovemaking had always been so passionate, we had come out of it scratched and sometimes even bleeding. Our backs, shoulders, legs and arms would tell the tale, and for days we would have to wear clothes that covered them so that our parents wouldn't know.

It was no different now. We had each other's clothes off within seconds, and when my skin touched his again after all those years, it flamed, just as it used to. "You feel so good," I whispered, and he whispered back, "You, too. Where have we been all these years?"

"I don't know," I answered.

"I missed you," he said. "I didn't realize till now how much I've missed you."

We had no use for foreplay, and when he came inside me I knew that feeling again, that sense of being with the only one, the one I'd been "created for." I knew it was silly and romantic, but the words from the Frank Sinatra song "That Old Black Magic" came to mind, and that's what it felt like. Magic. All the years wiped away, and all the tears gone with them. I was with Luke, and that's all that mattered. The world was a better place, and anything could happen now. Seattle would be rebuilt, I would win my trial, I would come out of it all right. Luke and I were together again.

I was so busy concocting this dream, this fantasy, I didn't even remember that I hadn't thought about the *Allegra* case since it disappeared that afternoon. Nor had I wondered again who took it. All that was distant, now, afloat in the far away future. Nothing to worry about here.

"Oh, there you are!"

We had fallen asleep, and I looked up to see Grace staring down at us. We were still naked, and I grabbed for my clothes, holding them against me. My head began to throb again.

"Sorry," Grace said, though she looked more angry than regretful. "We were worried when you didn't come back."

I felt more naked in front of Grace's scornful eyes than I'd ever felt with Luke or any man, and I managed to get to my feet and duck behind some bushes, yanking my clothes on. As I was pulling my T-shirt over my head I heard her say in a low voice, "What the hell are you doing? You're going to ruin everything! We'll never find—"

I emerged from the bushes, and Luke made a sound. Grace turned to see me standing there, and broke off in midsentence.

"Find what?" I said. "What is it you'll never find?"

They were both silent, and Luke looked away.

Finally Grace said, "A way off this damned island, if nobody here can control themselves!"

"I thought that included you," I said. "Didn't I see you go off with Gabe Rossi?"

Her mouth hardened. "We were talking," she said. "That's all."

"Must have been some talk. There are twigs in your hair."

Quickly, her hand went to her hair, as if belatedly to hide the evidence. There were no twigs, however. I'd been faking her out—something I often did in court with a reluctant witness: *"You say you saw my client that night, Mr. Smith? Were you wearing your glasses?"*

If a hand went automatically to the eyes, I knew the witness ordinarily did wear glasses, but not always, since he hadn't worn them to court. He also possibly was not wearing them the night he allegedly saw my client rob a liquor store. It was enough to create a small doubt in the minds of the jurors. *"So you do wear glasses, Mr. Smith. Why aren't you wearing them now? Why weren't you wearing them the night of October eighth?"*

Grace had fallen for my trick, which surprised me. I would have thought she'd be sharper than that. Maybe she was still in the throes of passion, and therefore mind-muddled.

"You know," she said waspishly, "I've been trying to like you."

"Well, that's more than I can say," I told her.

With that, I left the two of them alone in the woods. Obviously, they had things to talk about. Like what they had to "find."

A small metal case with fishnet stockings in it? I wondered.

And there I'd gone again—falling for the wrong man.

I knew, now, that I would have to be doubly on the alert. It was not a pleasant thought, that I would have to be wary of Luke, but I hadn't become a total idiot there in the woods. Only half a one. He and Grace had banded together for some reason I didn't know, but I couldn't disregard the fact that Jane was dead and someone on this island had attacked me. It was certainly a possibility that either Luke, Grace, or both, had had something to do with that.

Which still left questions. Had they come to Esme separately and unbeknownst to each other, only deciding to become a team after meeting here? Or did they plan it from the first?

As for the others, I was about ready to rule out Dana, Amelia and Timmy as villains of any kind. Though there were things about each of them that raised issues in my mind, I didn't sense anything sinister there.

Kim was another matter. She had questioned me quite a bit about my evidence against the Five, when we walked together to Ransford the first day. That could, of course, have been only out of friendship. One woman's concern for another. But it wasn't something I should just put in the back of my mind and forget.

Grace, of course, was a whole other matter. I couldn't even begin to figure out whether she was what she claimed to be. Did she have genuine feelings for Luke? And if not—then, what?

Finally, of course, there was Jane. Poor Jane, who had died either accidentally or on purpose.

Gabe said he had seen Luke at the ravine, at about the same time Jane must have either fallen or been pushed. Was he telling the truth or lying? And if he was lying, why?

Jane had gone up to Gabe's cabin alone, while Dana waited on the shore. Had she run into Gabe? Had she overheard or seen something that would have made her a danger to him? Or was someone else there?

The problem was the quake. Under other circumstances, Jane's death would be under investigation by now. She wouldn't still be lying under a bed of stones. But the quake and its aftershocks had left us all depleted of reserves. Tonight had been the first night we'd actually relaxed, and even then there was an undercurrent. We each knew that someone amongst us could be a killer. I think that deep down, however, we didn't really believe it. Rather, we didn't *want* to believe it.

After all, if there was a killer walking the grounds of Thornberry, what could we do about it?

What *would* we do about it—if we found such a thing to be true?

That was the question running through my mind that night. As I later discovered, it had been running through the minds of everyone else, as well.

# *11*

Things went crazy after that. Tensions were heightened in a way they hadn't been before, and I wondered if the sensuality of the dance had done it, reminding people that they had lives, and even possibly loves, in another place.

Everyone showed uneasiness differently, however. Amelia and Timmy snapped at each other, Grace snapped at everyone, and Dana flirted outrageously with Gabe. He didn't seem to mind, and flirted back, all grins and "Aw, shucks," and twinkling eyes. On the surface, at least, he reminded me of a leprechaun, a huge Italian leprechaun that had woken up the other night in the forest and made his way to our door. Now that I was getting used to him, I tended to like him more, and though it surprised me when Dana flirted with him, it did not at all surprise me when Kim did.

I saw her heading down the path to her cottage, where she was going, she said, to look for more of her personal belongings. Gabe followed shortly after, leaving the backyard and his work on the fuel tank hoses behind. So far, his efforts at fixing the fuel tank had been blocked by a missing part. He'd been trying one thing after another to "Mickey Mouse" it, but nothing was holding.

I wondered if he was bored, and had more interesting things than a fuel tank in mind with Kim.

Another outcome of the night of dancing was that we were beginning to let down our guards with each other. We were no longer pairing off, watching each other's every move—and no one seemed to worry about it or even mention it.

I know that in retrospect this seems foolish. We were all still in varying phases of shock, however. None of us was thinking as clearly as we might otherwise have been.

Luke and I barely looked at each other at breakfast, after that night in the woods. We poked away at oysters and fish, which came to be our standard meal. Luke and Grace said they had actually seen a doe run through the forest the day before, so they knew the deer were back. But neither of them had the heart to kill her—even if they'd had the means, which they didn't. There was some scattered kidding about making bows and arrows, and that if we got hungry enough it might come to that.

In our hearts, we all hoped that rescuers would show up soon so we wouldn't have to face the more painful tasks of survival. At this point we were getting beyond the first stages of disbelief, then fear, and were entering into a more desperate state: the "What if this is the last day of our lives? Shouldn't we live while we've got the chance to?" state.

That, at least, is the only explanation I can come up with for what happened next.

The women began to squabble more seriously amongst themselves. They began to fight over everything—and especially the men. Everyone wanted the men's attention, their help, their companionship. Even Amelia and Timmy vied for Luke's and Gabe's affections, and their interest in the two men was not at all maternal. Timmy took to using the bottom of a shiny pot as a mirror and fussing with her hair, the fake diamond rings flashing in the sunlight. Amelia approached things on a more intellectual level, discussing her poetry with Gabe, and the mechanics of building ferry docks with Luke.

Kim and Grace, especially, were at each other's throats. Grace became more abrasive, butting in on any woman she saw with either Luke *or* Gabe. Kim had already set her sights on Gabe, or so it seemed, and the two women were constantly snarling at each other. As the "fairest one of all" in our group, I'd have expected Kim to be the more self-confident. Instead, she appeared to grow increasingly pale and unhappy as the days wore on.

As for Gabe, he spread his attentions equally amongst everyone, even me. He found me one day crawling over the debris of Thornberry's living room, and offered his assistance. I had given up looking for the *Allegra* case, or my manuscript and disk. By this time I knew I would not find them. I also knew someone had deliberately taken them.

I just didn't know who.

And until I did, I had decided, I would be like Gabe—treating everyone the same way, giving no more regard to one than another. And that included Luke.

Sooner or later, with any luck, the truth would rise, like cream, to the top. I only had to survive till it did.

The day Gabe helped me with the rubble in the living room, I was feeling particularly vulnerable. I'd remembered that when the earthquake struck, I'd been holding a pencil with a large rubber eraser on it in the shape of an orange tabby cat. Ian had given it to me one night when we were in bed, a kind of joke. "You're like a cat," he had said. "I don't know how you do it, but you always land on your feet."

This was long before the Seattle Five and our breakup. Ian had been commenting on my ability to win a case, no matter how difficult it got or how much the odds were stacked against me. I had used the pencil with that eraser often after that, because it reminded me even on the darkest days when things weren't going well, that I *was* good—and that even if I never made much money as a public defender I would leave a good legacy behind.

Who I would leave it to was anybody's guess, as it didn't look, at that point, as if I'd ever have children. Ian didn't want them, and there was certainly no one else in sight. There might have been, if I'd had the energy or time to look around. Ian was never what I would have called the "man of my dreams," and I frequently thought that I should be with someone else, someone who loved me more and wanted more for me. Someone who respected my work.

Instead, I settled for Ian, who at least gave a good neck-and-shoulder massage. Ian—who had made it clear he had seen too much, and that this was not the kind of world to bring a child into.

My options had been few and not pleasant: I would be single forever. Or, I'd marry Ian one day, and be childless.

Therefore, that day at Thornberry when I took it into my head to go looking for the cat eraser, it wasn't out of longing for Ian MacDonald. It was solely because I needed something to hang on to, something from the old life that reminded me I'd done well; that even if I didn't have anyone to leave a legacy to, I had at least risen to certain challenges in life.

The living room had been only half buried by the two upper stories, and I made my way gingerly through the other half. There were so many books scattered on the floor, it seemed it would be a mammoth task to find anything as small as a pencil and eraser. I sighed, already tired and out of sorts, and began.

Gabe appeared as I was trying to lift a heavy oak bookcase off the floor. I saw him, at first, outlined by a rare bright sun in the doorway—a misnomer actually, since there wasn't a doorway anymore, but rather a huge, gaping hole to the outside. For a moment, I thought he looked like an angel. The sunlight had surrounded him with a fiery halo. When he moved out of it he looked more like the leprechaun, with a grin on its face.

"Wait," he said. "Let me help you with that."

I had the bookcase partway up, but was standing there bracing it against my shoulder, waiting for my energy to return so I could push it the rest of the way. Gabe was by my side in an instant.

"This is one heavy sucker," he said, grabbing the other side and helping me get it to an upright position against the wall. "Why didn't you ask for help?"

"You mean like everyone else around here?" I said caustically. "Can't do a thing without the help of a big strong man?"

I was beginning to sound like Grace, and I bit my lip. "Sorry."

But Gabe only laughed. "I think I know what you mean. But really, it's not all that unusual for women to turn to a man in these circumstances. That's what we were made for, after all—to do the donkeywork. They send us out to fight the wars, build the bridges, dig the ditches..."

"Plenty of women do that now," I pointed out.

"Sure, but not nearly as many women as men. Not yet, anyway. And just think of it—if we didn't have our muscles, what good would we be? Women are having babies without men now, and they're working and supporting themselves. Having a bit of hard physical labor to do gives a man a feeling of importance."

"Ah, so that's what you're feeling, with all these women fawning all over you," I said. "Important."

He gave me a look so intense, it raised goose bumps along my arms. "Don't tell me you're jealous," he said.

"Not for a moment." I turned to the pile of books on the floor and began to pick them up, hoping the eraser would be under them so I could get out of there. But I knew my face was flushing.

"Are you looking for something special?" Gabe asked, bending down to help me.

"No," I lied, "and I don't think you should put those books back on the shelf that way. This thing will probably come down again in the next aftershock."

"Good thinking." He started his own pile against the wall, as I was doing. "See? That's what I was talking about. Women—they figure out the best way to do things. We men—we just lift and carry, shovel and sweep."

"'Tote that barge, lift that bale'?" I laughed. "Give me a break. That leaves out a hell of a lot of scientists, philosophers, architects, mathematicians… and, come to think of it, yourself. Writing software is not exactly a 'tote that barge' kind of skill."

"That's true," he admitted. "I guess I was just trying to—"

"Set me at ease? Make me like you? Sucker me in?" I sat back on my heels and faced him. "Look, I don't mean to offend. I just don't go for this Prince Charming approach. The last time I fell for a prince, he turned out to be the troll under the bridge."

This time Gabe didn't laugh. "I'm very sorry to hear that," he said. "Sarah, you are far too lovely to be set upon by a troll. What happened? Can you tell me?"

"I could," I said. "But I won't. It's personal."

"Of course it is, and I don't mean to intrude. It's only that sometimes I wonder if we'll ever…"

He sighed and looked tired. Surprised, I finished

the thought for him. "Ever get off this island? I wonder that, too."

"And what will we find out there, when we do?" he said.

I noted that there were fine lines of strain around his eyes, lines that had been covered up till now by the way his skin crinkled when he smiled.

"I'm not that different from all of you," he said. "I wonder if my home is still standing. And my business. For all I know, all of Gig Harbor could be under water. Sarah, individual secrets don't seem to matter that much out here. In fact, you know what? I'll tell you mine, if you'll tell me yours. Maybe just talking about things would help."

"But I don't have any secrets," I said.

"Sure you do. We all do. Haven't you noticed? Everyone here has something they're carrying around, like some terrible heavy pack on their shoulders."

"You think so?" I didn't tell him that I, too, had thought that.

"I don't just think so. It's obvious. Everyone's afraid of something, and it's not just the quake."

"I guess you would know," I said pointedly, "as close as you've been getting to everyone."

He gave me that intense look again, and despite myself I felt a small tug at my groin.

"You know how to get under a woman's skin, don't you," I said thoughtfully.

"Not yours, apparently," he said, and the grin was back. "But you can't blame me for trying."

"I don't blame you at all. I just don't know whether to believe you."

He began to stack books again. "That's okay. I like to think I'm sort of like God—I exist, even if you don't believe in me. Anyway, I guess I was forgetting that you already have someone to tell your secrets to."

"Oh?"

"Luke, of course. You and he are old friends, aren't you?"

"Yes, but that doesn't mean I feel close enough to him now to tell him any secrets—if I even had any in the first place."

"Are you saying that you and he haven't shared *everything*," he teased, "now that you're back together again?"

"We are not back together, not in the sense you're implying. We're just friends."

"Hmm. Come to think of it, I have seen him with the inscrutable Grace quite a bit."

I busied myself with the books. "I wouldn't know about that."

"Sure you wouldn't."

I sat back on my heels again, dusting my palms off. "Look, Gabe, thanks for helping with the bookcase, really. But I don't need any more help right now. I'd actually prefer to be alone for a while."

He hesitated, then stood, brushing his own dusty hands on his jeans. "I understand entirely," he said. "I'm feeling a need to be off by myself, too. But, Sarah—"

I looked up at him.

"Promise me you'll come to me if you do need help? Of any kind?"

I hesitated. Who was Gabe Rossi to go to for help? What did I know of him? And what kind of help was he talking about?

Finally I said, "Sure. I'll send up smoke signals."

He groaned. "Given that fire over at Luke's house, smoke signals might not be too appropriate here. Just give me a whistle, okay? I'll be around."

Somehow, I was sure he would be.

It was while I was looking under a pile of magazines and papers from an antique desk that I found the photo album. It was the older kind, with gold leaf letters on a worn brown cover. The cover and the inside black-paper pages were held together by a black cord. The photographs were yellowed, some of them cracked or with broken corners.

Curious, I sat on the floor and began to leaf through it. The first few held photographs of Thornberry when Timmy and her husband had first opened it, the kind they probably took to send to friends. *This is our wonderful new home. Those are the gardens on the left, and the next photograph shows the Sound, which is almost at our front door.*

Then the snapshots of guests began, and I was startled to find my ten-year-old self staring back at me. There I was, in an ugly one-piece bathing suit I wouldn't have been caught dead in three years later. My hair hadn't yet begun to frizz, and it was cut straight, Joan of Arc style, with bangs.

I'd forgotten how plain I looked, and all of a sudden I remembered hearing some of the boys in school talking about me. *"She's a pudding face,"* one said.

*"Thinks she's hot and she's not,"* another added in a singsong voice. *"Sarah's a tubby, Sarah's a tubby."*

I was not a "tubby," and this photograph proved it. But those words made me feel that way—for years.

*Dear God.* The things that hurt us in childhood, and that we forget. But how much of our adult selves do they affect in some way we're never even aware of?

Suddenly I knew why, when I was still practicing law, I'd had a mania for makeup. I always had to make sure I looked thin and stylish on television when I was in the middle of a trial. God forbid any of those ten-year-old boys, now grown, should see me on the evening news and still think of me as a "tubby." Even better if they now saw me as "hot."

I laughed softly, but with a touch of dismay at the lengths I must have gone to over the years to be accepted by men. What had I done to turn myself inside out for Luke? And then for Ian? And how had that affected my relationships with them? Had I come across as not quite real? Or worse—someone with vulnerabilities that could be used? Exploited, even?

It was too new a thought, and I felt uncomfortable with it. Laying it aside for the moment, I looked instead at the next photo, one of my mother and father. They were sitting side by side on a fallen log in the woods, their arms around each other's shoulders. They looked happy enough. My mother was in shorts and a T-shirt, her arms thin and strong from the gardening she did at home. Her toes peeked out of white sandals, and she had rested her chin on her palm. Her blond hair was naturally curly, like mine became later, and she wore it short.

My father was graying even then, and a bit more stiff about having his picture taken. I could tell this by the way he sat, his back straight, not relaxing on the prickly wooden log. It must have dug into his bare thighs, I thought, smiling. He never really did like wearing shorts, but rather gave in to my mother, who would tease him into it by telling him he had good legs. I often wondered if she just didn't like having to wash and iron his long pants.

Their names were below the photo—Anne and James Lansing—and beneath that was the date. The photo had been taken around the same time as the one of me at ten.

I wondered what had happened between my mother and father between that time, and the year I was seventeen and my mother was having the affair with Luke's father. Did she come to feel too alone, with my father returning home from work every night and shutting himself in his study to work? What kind of life could they have had? And how had Luke's father filled the gaps?

I skimmed through the pictures of other guests, and the ones of Timmy and her husband planting organic vegetables, then posing, with smiles on their faces, in front of the fireplace. Timmy had bunches of wildflowers in her arms, and wore a bright scarf with an East Indian design.

Poor Timmy, I thought, not for the first time. What a loss she'd suffered—first her husband, then Thornberry. What would she do now?

Finally I came to a snapshot of Luke's father and mother one night when they'd come to dinner at Thornberry. Timmy had often had neighbors in to meet her bed-and-breakfast guests, giving them a bit of social life on what was then just as isolated an island. Luke's parents, I knew, had come over more than once.

I stared at the image of Charles Randell Ford, and tried to picture him making love to my mother. He was quite handsome, though in truth, as her daughter, I couldn't picture *anyone* making love to my mother—not even my father. Was Luke's father tender with her? I wondered. Did he talk to her about things that amused her?

He was, I remembered, more attentive than my father. Much like Luke in that way. On those long summer days when I would sit in the background and listen to him and my father talk, Charles Ford would include me now and then. He was already on the bench at that time, and I felt flattered that this well-known and highly respected Seattle judge would think that I, at fourteen, fifteen, might have an opinion worth hearing. But he did, and would even challenge me at times, making me stand up for myself and my opinions. After a while I learned to do this without hesitation, and it was probably Charles Ford who molded me into the lawyer I became, even more so than my father.

I had even thought, briefly, of approaching Judge Ford when I was arrested in January, to see if he could help me in some way. The only reason I hadn't was that I knew he might possibly end up hearing my case. And if I spoke to him about it beforehand, he might have to recuse himself and turn the case over to someone else.

I didn't want that to happen. Though I hadn't talked to Luke's father on a personal basis in years, I'd gone before him with cases now and then, and I knew him to be a fair judge. Tough, but fair. Having him assigned to hear my case could be a blessing.

I leafed through more photographs, and it struck me suddenly that all four of our parents must have been, at that time, still in their thirties and early forties. Luke's father was the oldest, I knew, but he couldn't have been a day over forty-two then, since he was now in his mid-sixties. As for my mother, I had never thought of her as being this young when I was a teenager. Younger than I was now.

Seeing my parents and Luke's in this way opened up a whole new world of understanding to me.

I closed the photograph album and sat there thinking. Luke's mother and my father were now gone. Would my mother and his father get together again, the way high school sweethearts sometimes did, after thirty or forty years and other loves had passed?

It was too soon, probably, for my mother to think of that. My father had died only three months ago, and one doesn't easily get over the loss of a spouse one has lived with for that many years. I had seen my mother in mourning, and I knew that whatever had happened in the past, the loss she felt was real.

It had shocked me when, shortly after my arrest, my mother had abruptly moved to Florida, with little explanation. She needed to get away, she said one night, and would be visiting her sister, my Aunt Rinna. The next morning, she was gone. A messenger brought me the small brown envelope, with only the key to my old home and a note: *Feel free to house-sit. Love, Mother.*

At first I was too angry and hurt to even consider doing that. I had lost my father, too, and was still in mourning. How could she leave like that? Why couldn't we have helped each other through our pain?

But then Lonnie Mae was murdered, and I threw myself into her case. I hid the evidence with Angel, and then, to be on the safe side, moved into my parents' house, which at least had the comfort of a security system.

So my mother had given me that: a safe haven, for a while. And when the invitation to Thornberry had arrived, the island had seemed to me an even safer place to hide out for a month—from the Five, from reporters, from life.

I sighed. Life, unfortunately, has a way of finding one, no matter how far one runs.

Getting up, I brushed plaster dust from my pants and put the album on the low stack of books I'd started. For a moment I considered showing it to Luke, but quickly discarded the idea. Too many memories, too many moments that could never be recaptured. Like the tattered edges of the yellowed photographs, they had seen their day.

Later that afternoon, while I was picking early lettuce in the garden, Angel suddenly came to mind again. I hadn't heard from J.P. Blakely since the day she sent the *Allegra* case back to me, and as my hands went into the dark, moist earth, her face seemed to appear before me. Not anything as mystic as an apparition; just a brief, sharp flash of memory.

Angel was one of the best PIs I'd ever met, and in my line of work I'd had occasion to meet a lot of them. When the *Allegra* case first came back from her with no note attached, I'd assumed she was in a hurry to get somewhere. For whatever reason, she must have thought the evidence would be best off in my hands while she was gone. It could have been a case that had taken her out of town. Or the new boyfriend she'd told me about—the one she'd said she met at McCoy's one night. Either one of those possibilities made sense to me at first.

But now I wondered, would she have been out of the office that long without any word to me? Calls to her secretary, up until the day I left for Esme, had continued to elicit the information that Angel was "away" and would call me when she returned.

Every night before she'd left town, I'd waited with my cell phone at eight o'clock, J.P.'s usual time to call. Sometimes she'd have new information to report; other times we just talked as friends. Angel was the most supportive person in my life at that time, and I looked forward to talking with her every night. More than anything, I missed Angel as a friend. The nightly calls had become like anchors for me, holding me steady in rough seas. Was she back in Seattle, I wondered, when the quake hit? Was she still alive? Would I ever see her again?

The thought had occurred to me, of course, that the

Five had gotten to her somehow. That she'd been hurt—or worse. But I remembered Angel saying to me one night, "Don't worry if you don't hear from me now and then. I may have to go out of town for a bit."

Angel's secretary was the only person I'd left a forwarding number with when I came to Thornberry. Since we were asked not to bring cell phones here, I had left Thornberry's office number, with instructions for Angel to call me as soon as possible. She didn't, though. Not once in the week I'd been here before the quake.

*Something was wrong.* Every fiber of my being told me that something was terribly wrong. The green leaves of the lettuce crinkled in my palm, bringing me back. I'd been making a fist, bruising my crop. Timmy would have a fit. But there were so many emotions welling up in me, and I wanted more than anything to run into the woods and scream. Get it all out. All the fears, loss and betrayal, beginning with my arrest in January and leading up to the quake. There had been no real time alone since then to let down, no time when I hadn't been trying to be strong for everyone else.

It would have been easier without Luke and Gabe here, I thought. I was a competent, independent woman, given to running my own life and solving my own problems. Now, suddenly, I wanted to lean on any man—just point one in my direction. It was stupid, I knew, but the impulse persisted. I wanted to tell Luke, in particular, what had been going on with me, answer all his questions. I wanted to tell him about my evidence against the Seattle Five and about Angel. More than anything, I wanted to solicit his help in finding the *Allegra* case and keeping it safe. And I wanted him to help me find out who had taken my manuscript and disk.

The fact that I didn't trust him enough to open myself to him left me feeling more alone than if he'd never shown up.

As for Gabe, what woman here wouldn't want to fall for his charming ways? What woman wouldn't like to accept all the help he had to offer, and let herself lean for a while? We had all been through a terrifying, exhausting experience, and none of us was as sure of herself or as confident about life as she had once been.

We were all suffering from that syndrome survivors of earthquakes get: we were hypervigilant, constantly on the lookout for the next danger. The minute the ground would start to shudder again in an aftershock, even the smallest one, we'd leap to our feet and look for the nearest table to crawl under. At night, we found it difficult to sleep. We told ourselves and each other that we had to stay alert in case the quake had only been a foreshock and there was still a bigger one to come.

In short, our nerves were a mess, and the rescuers we had hoped for were only a distant dream. We knew, now, that we might have to survive here—with each other—for several more days. Possibly even weeks.

If there had been any news from the outside, any at all, it might not have been so bad. With only each other to talk to, however, and to toss ideas around with, we tended just to bring each other down. That was another aftereffect of the quake: a deep depression set in. We had passed the initial shock stage and moved into anger. Now, faced with helplessness against the situation, we lost our spirit.

This, more than anything, I think, is what led to the terrible thing we did.

# *12*

As I've said, it started with that night of dancing and the emotions that were aroused. The backbiting amongst the other women accelerated as one day passed and then another, with no sign of rescue. Soon they were openly fighting, and it was all I could do to keep them apart.

Why I didn't end up that way myself, I cannot honestly say. The thought has occurred that I had Ian to thank for it, because I simply wasn't all that interested in the men. Oh, I had feelings just like the rest. Especially for Luke—and now and again for Gabe, as well. But my intellect had clamped down on those feelings, and I was able to remind myself that I'd been hurt, and all too recently. This was not the time to get involved again. This was the time to be cautious. To protect myself. And somehow, I managed to stick to that.

It didn't help anyone that there wasn't much to do after the first few days. Though it was true that fishing, clamming and prying oysters off rocks took up time, that was actually easier and quicker to do than driving to a modern supermarket, filling up a cart, driving home and having to put it all away.

As for laundry, we all learned to wear our clothes

a couple of days in a row. When we couldn't stand ourselves any longer we'd go down to the beach and wash one outfit at a time, hanging it to dry on bushes. When it rained, we brought our clothes inside, hanging them on a line that Luke had strung up in the hallway.

Our earlier plans for beginning to clean up the mess around Thornberry and our cottages soon faded as hunger and weakness became a major part of our days. We did do some work of that nature, but not nearly as much as we'd originally envisioned. Going without the ''necessities'' of life proved to be more difficult than we had thought, and a lot of that was surely the mind-body connection scientists talk about. Once depression set in, we could no longer talk ourselves into feeling good when we clearly didn't. We were not on an adventurous camping trip, with a comfortable bed and a full fridge awaiting us at home. We might even—as Grace one evening pointed out—actually die on Esme Island.

It was because of the backbiting and arguing on the other women's parts that I left the farmhouse on the fifth night and went off in the woods to be alone. Everyone else was in the kitchen, including Luke and Gabe, playing a game that Dana had made up with stones she had gathered from the gravel driveway. Dana, at least, was trying.

But as the players began to fight over who had the most stones and whether someone had cheated, even Dana lost it, jumping to her feet and sweeping all the stones from table to floor. ''Will you people, for God's sake, act like *adults?*'' she yelled.

There was only a moment's silence before everyone began shouting that *she* was acting like a three-year-old, and where the hell did she think she got off, knocking all their stones on the floor?

It was at this point that I threw up my hands and excused myself, saying I'd be back in a few minutes. I took a flashlight, and hoped that if anyone noticed they would assume I'd gone out to the latrine. Not that they were likely to miss me, with all that bickering going on.

I wandered along the shore, glad for the full moon and a rain-free sky. The water rippled gently, sometimes reaching the toes of my boots. There had been no sign of a *tsunami,* for which we'd all been grateful, and the aftershocks had done no more damage since the first few days. At least, none that we were aware of.

I lost track of time, and was surprised when I came to the Ransford dock. Looking up at the house, I was even more startled to see that only a bare shell had been left by the fire. This was the first time I'd been here since that night, and I hadn't pressed Luke for specifics.

What a terrible shame, I thought. That beautiful house, gone now for all time. I was relatively certain Luke wouldn't rebuild. Not if he traveled that much. More likely he'd put up a small cabin here, as a weekend getaway for those times when he worked out of Seattle. Luke had always liked the idea of having a getaway, and had at times quoted Thoreau: *"Simplify, simplify, simplify."* He had admired Thoreau and the way the author had gone to jail rather than pay taxes to a country that, as Thoreau saw it, was committing a holocaust on its own ground against the Native Americans. Luke had pictured himself in a small cabin one day, not the luxurious kind of home his parents had always had. His cabin, he had said, would have just enough room to read and contemplate.

I'd always been intrigued by men who set up lifestyles of this sort that didn't include a woman in them, and then wondered why they didn't have a woman.

I took the path up to the house and stood on the edge of the fire's rubble, trying to picture Jane here, setting that fire. I tried to feel her desperation at wanting to be rescued, at being reunited with her children.

Nothing would come. I hadn't known Jane well enough, and I didn't know her children or husband at all. I didn't even know what it felt like to be afraid for a child. There had never been one in my life.

I did have a dog when I was ten. She was part Bichon Frise, white and fluffy. Her name had been Tufts, because of the way her hair stood up on end by her ears. Tufts had been my constant companion for at least a year, and had lived up to the promise of the woman who had raised her; she was affectionate and fun. Tufts, in fact, gave out more affection than I'd had from either of my parents, though they did their best. They did try.

Tufts got out of the house one day and was struck by a car. I remembered kneeling over her, seeing the extent of her injuries, which were many. I listened to her strangled breaths and knew she could last only another minute or two. I couldn't bear the pain she must have been feeling, and I leaned close to her ear and whispered, *"Let go, Tufts. Just let go."*

As if she knew what I was saying, Tufts died in my arms, and that was my first lesson about death. When it was inevitable, the only thing left was to let go. That was true for the dying and the one who survived, as well, and I had done my best. There were still moments, however, when I longed for another dog in my life. Just as there were moments when I longed for another man.

I don't know what made me go around the Ransford house and into the woods, in the direction Luke had gone that night of the fire. I found a path there, however, at the edge of the back lawn. It was nearly hidden by two huge boulders and a thick stand of shrubbery. Curious, I followed it for no reason other than to see where it led, and to keep walking—to clear the cobwebs from my brain.

The path was narrow, with twists and turns. It led into a part of the forest I'd never explored, and the trees kept getting thicker, the night darker where the moon couldn't get through to guide my way. I used my flashlight to see where I was stepping, as the path was overgrown. There were gnarled tree roots poking out of the ground, and old dead tree stumps appeared right in the middle of the path. Even with the flashlight it was an obstacle course, and I had to be careful not to trip and fall. This was becoming more like work and less like fun, and I considered turning around and going back the way I'd come. Just a few more yards, I told myself. Let's see what lies ahead.

I'd been on the path for perhaps ten minutes when

the sound of snapping twigs came from behind me. Several times I turned around to look. Had someone followed me over from Thornberry? Were they looking for me, after all?

I pointed the beam of my flashlight back down the path, but could see no one.

"Hello?" I called out. "Who's there?"

No answer.

Was I hearing only deer, perhaps, startled by my presence? They must have run into places like this to hide after the quake, areas most people didn't inhabit.

I knew, however, that the Thornberry deer usually went still when faced with an intruder. Since hunting had never been allowed on Esme, they had no reason to fear man, and would stand motionless for moments assessing the situation. If the intruder approached them, they would seem to tiptoe silently backward, as if hoping not to be seen, till they were hidden by brush.

This noise was more stealthy than that of the deer. It would stop when I stopped, and begin again when I took another step. For the first time in my life, I began to feel afraid of the Esme Island woods. After all the years of considering the tall trees and shady groves my friends—my companions in both loneliness and love—I now felt surrounded by danger.

I began to walk faster, thinking that this path must surely lead to the shore, that it must have been an old path used for carrying in supplies from the ferry. On an island there are few places one can go, and all paths lead eventually to the water.

Irrationally, I thought that once at the water, I'd be

safe. Why I thought that, I didn't know, because the truth was I'd be trapped. But as I picked up speed, the sounds behind me did, too, and I knew for certain, suddenly, that I was being followed.

I no longer stopped to look back. If Luke had followed me out here, I reasoned, or even Gabe, they would have called out to me. They wouldn't be trying to hide their presence.

Or would they? Images of Jane on the ledge of that ravine rose to my mind, making my breath short and my legs wooden from fright. *I shouldn't have come out here alone—we should have stuck to the pairs plan. What was I thinking of?*

I looked for a side path, somewhere to duck in and hide. Whoever was following me had picked up their pace to match mine, but if they couldn't see me around a bend, if I could duck into an offshoot without them being aware of it, they might think I'd run straight ahead. I might even be able to see them as they passed.

There was no offshoot, no place to hide. The firs and bushes on either side combined to make a thick wall. I turned off my flashlight and began to run. The sounds behind me told me that the other person was running, too, no longer attempting to hide the fact. Branches whipped at my face, and I stumbled several times over fallen trees. I knew that if I fell, if I didn't get up immediately, he would be here. He'd have me.

I ran faster and faster, and somehow managed to almost fly over the brambles in my path. It seemed as if the path would never end, and I realized suddenly that I must have been running parallel to the shore, not toward it. I was inland, running to the east or south, not the north. There was nothing this way, nothing for a long way but more woods.

I was so certain of this, it came as a shock when the path came to a fork. The one to the left was so well hidden, I almost passed it. At the last moment I swung onto it, hoping the noise I was making in the underbrush would seem to be coming from the path on the right. My shock was even greater when within moments there appeared before me a clearing. The full moon illuminated the clearing, and I could see that in the middle was a small cabin. It was built of wood that looked relatively new, and appeared quite different from the other two cabins on the island. There was a window on either side of the door. No light came through from inside.

I had never known the cabin was there, and I was stunned.

As I drew up short, I realized that the sounds behind me had stopped after I'd taken this fork. Still, I couldn't trust that my pursuer wouldn't double back and come this way. I ran silently over the grass toward the cabin, thinking that if I could get inside I might be able to lock the door behind me. There might even be something in there I could use to defend myself. Eventually, someone at Thornberry would realize I had been gone too long and come looking for me.

At the door I touched the knob, then hesitated, wondering if someone actually might be inside. As far as we knew, there was no one else on the island, but what *did* we know? Luke had turned up, then

Gabe. Was there someone else out here who hadn't bothered to find his way to our door? Or someone who was deliberately hiding here?

At this point, it hardly mattered. I needed a place to hide for a while, to think. I turned the knob and pushed the door open, stepping inside. Everything was dark, and I realized there was no moon shining in. I reached behind me for an inside lock and couldn't find one. Panicked, I knew I would have to shove something up against the door. But what? I didn't dare risk using my flashlight and letting whoever had been following me know I was here.

I stood for a moment listening for sounds from the outside. Nothing. No footsteps running across the grass, no sound other than that of my own breath, labored and heavy. I reached into the dark for something, anything, to prop against the door.

My hand touched living flesh. Fingers wrapped around my wrist. It was then I knew the breathing I heard was not only my own.

He had somehow gotten here before me.

I opened my mouth to scream, but not in time. A hand clamped down to cover it, bruising and hard.

# 13

"Be quiet."

I heard the voice in my ear, muffled, an undertone.

"I'm taking my hand away now. Don't make a sound, Sarah."

I knew then who it was, and as the hand came away I whirled around and swung at Luke's face. My eyes were growing accustomed to the dark, and I could almost see the handprint after I'd connected. Though I tried to keep my voice low, anger boiled up, astounding me with its ferocity.

"What the hell do you think you're doing? What the hell is going on?"

Luke's own hand went up to touch the smarting skin. Even in the dim light, I could see that his eyes were blazing.

"I'm trying to keep you out of trouble, dammit!"

"Oh, really? And just how are you doing that? How did you even get here? I left the farmhouse before you did."

"You went around the shore. I took the shortcut through the middle."

"Like hell you did. You were following me."

"I was *not* following you, Sarah. I've been here a good ten minutes."

"Well, *someone* was following me. Who else—"

"I don't know who else, dammit! But from the way you're acting, you've gone and led someone here!"

He turned his back to me, and I heard him light a match. The glow from a candle cast a dim illumination around the room. I saw now that the windows were covered with black tar paper. It was nailed around the frames so that no light could escape. Along one wall was a cot with a sleeping bag on it. Beside it was a bottle of water.

Then my gaze fell on a long table. Some loose manila folders lay on it, next to a pen and a white lined tablet. Beside the tablet were two stacks of bond paper, one shorter than the other, indicating that someone had been reading and then laying the already-read pages down next to the main stack. A few inches away was a computer disk with a Disney label. On it, in thick black ink, were the words JUST RE-WARDS.

"That's my book," I said, feeling numb. "You're the one who stole my book."

Luke didn't answer, and as I looked at him I could see the thoughts behind his eyes, scurrying around like so many disturbed mice. *I should have hidden the manuscript and disk,* the eyes said. *I should have locked the door.*

But he'd forgotten. Or he'd been too sure he'd never be discovered way out here.

"What's going on?" I said, my throat so dry the words cracked.

"It's not what you think," he said, crossing over

belatedly to lock the door. The lock was there, higher than I had thought it would be.

"Oh? What exactly am I thinking, Luke?"

He pulled out a chair in front of the table. "Sarah, sit down. I can explain."

I almost did sit down. But then I noticed a small propane tank in a corner. From the tank ran a line, and that line went into a small generator; plugged into the generator was an AC power supply.

There wasn't much else in the room, and very few signs of damage. My gaze traveled to a flannel shirt on the table, next to my manuscript. I lifted it up. Beneath it was a cell phone. A green light blinked, the same kind of light that blinked on mine when it was "on" and waiting for calls. Or for calls to be made.

"You've had this all along?" I asked, my throat still dry.

I was certain of the answer. But I wanted to hear it from Luke's mouth—that he'd had a working cell phone all along and had betrayed each and every one of us by keeping it to himself.

"I…yes," he said. "I keep it here all the time."

"All the time?"

"I, uh, built this cabin ten years ago. I use it sometimes rather than heat up the big house."

"And the phone. It works?"

"It works," he admitted.

"The towers are back up?"

"Some."

"From the first?"

"Almost from the first."

It felt as if all the air went out of me. My knees were weak, and I sat on the chair positioned in front of my manuscript. Anger mixed with confusion, and I didn't know what to think.

"You've been in touch with the mainland? With Seattle?"

"A couple of times. It hasn't been easy to get through. But, yes."

"Have you called for help? Are there rescue teams coming? The Red Cross? Anyone?"

"I… People know we're here," he said, not meeting my eyes.

"Are they coming to rescue us?"

He hesitated. "Not right now."

"For God's sake, Luke!"

"They have their hands full, Sarah! It's a mess out there!"

"Well, you could have informed us of that, at least. Why haven't you?"

"I had my reasons."

"What reasons? All this time we've been worrying about the people back home, about how we'd ever get off this island, whether we'd even live, in fact— and you have a cell phone?"

He stood with his arms folded, distanced from me in every way. "I'm sorry, but everyone would want to use it, and the battery wouldn't last long enough for that."

I shook my head, still dazed. "Forget that—for the moment. You said you'd explain."

"About the book? I took it to keep it safe, Sarah."

"*Safe?* It's in the hands of someone who's betrayed us all—'' I stopped, my heart missing a beat. ''You're working for the Seattle Five,'' I said. ''They sent you here to get the book and—''

I clamped my mouth shut on the words *the evidence.*

''And what?'' Luke said softly. ''What, Sarah?''

''And the disk,'' I recovered. ''They wanted you to find out how much I know.''

''Oh, come on. Listen to yourself. I'm an engineer and I live in New York. What possible connection could I have to a bunch of renegade cops in Seattle?''

''I don't know…I don't know. But there's *something,* and dammit, Luke, I'll figure it out.''

He stood at one of the tar-papered windows, as if looking out.

''Why did you think someone was following you?'' he asked, after a minute.

''Because I heard them.''

''It could have been a deer.''

''Sure, I get stalked by deer all the time.''

He gave me an irritable frown. ''Was it someone from Thornberry, then? Did you see anyone follow you from there?''

''I wasn't looking. I left all of you—I thought—playing that stupid game.'' I studied his face. ''Why wouldn't it be someone from Thornberry? Is there somebody else on the island? Someone we still don't know about?''

''No. At least, I don't think so.''

''Dammit, Luke!'' I flew to my feet. ''You've got to give me something. *Anything.* If you don't, I'm going back to Thornberry right now and I'm telling everyone about this cell phone and the fact that you haven't, apparently, been using it to help us in any way."

His voice turned hard. "You can't do that, Sarah. You absolutely cannot tell anyone."

"Oh, really? Well, that's where you're wrong. I can do anything I damn well please." An unpleasant thought occurred to me. "Unless, of course, you're planning to stop me somehow."

He rubbed a hand over his face. "Hell, Sarah, I don't know what to do with you now. I have to think."

"Well, while you're thinking about 'what to do with me,' I'm leaving," I said, turning to the door.

"I wouldn't do that if I were you."

I reached for the lock. Before I could blink, he was at my side, his hand stopping mine.

"You can't go out there again, not alone. Whoever was following you may still be there."

"And what would he—or she—want from me, Luke?" My head was beginning to clear, and I could think of only one answer to that: Lonnie Mae's evidence.

Which brought to mind the missing *Allegra* case. "Is this manuscript all you stole from me? Or was there something else?"

I watched his eyes as he formed an answer, and thought I saw a brief flicker when he said, "What else are you talking about?"

"Anything," I said. "I don't really know."

I went over and touched the top page of my manuscript, which looked as if it had been barely touched by the quake. The pages were still clean and white, barely rumpled.

"I see you're on page seventy-three," I said. "How's it looking, so far?"

"I'm not an editor," Luke answered, "but I think you're doing an okay job."

"Well, gee, thanks. I'm afraid you won't be reading the ending, though. I haven't figured that out yet."

I picked up the manuscript and disk. "In fact, you won't be reading any more of this at all."

The cell phone began to ring, a low, muted sound.

Luke took a step toward it, making a motion as if to answer it—but then stopped himself.

"Go ahead," I said. "Take it."

"It can wait."

"Maybe so, but I can't. I can't wait to hear who's calling and what they have to say."

With that, I grabbed up the phone and held it to my ear.

A shockingly familiar voice said, "Luke? Luke, is that you?"

*"Mother?"* I said, stunned.

With a click the phone went silent, and Luke grabbed it away from me.

Suddenly I was afraid again. *What had he done to my mother?*

I no longer knew this man. I couldn't even imagine what secrets lay hidden within him—or what he might be willing to do to preserve them.

"Don't come any closer," I said, backing off.

He reached out a hand, and I whacked it away. "Don't!" I said.

He frowned. "Sarah, relax. I wouldn't hurt you."

"I don't give a damn about me! What have you done to my mother?"

"Nothing! Absolutely nothing. She's all right. I promise you."

"I don't want your damn promises! I don't even know who you are anymore."

"I'm the same person I always was, Sarah."

"No. That person would have confided in me, told me what he was up to here. Luke—" My voice shook. "Why was my mother calling you? What in the name of God have you done?"

"I'm telling you—nothing. She got in touch with my father because she was worried about you after the quake. He gave her the number here, so she could call me and I could reassure her you were all right."

"Then why did she hang up when she heard my voice?"

"Sarah, for God's sake! She probably lost the connection. That's been happening all the time since the quake. Don't make some sort of conspiracy out of it."

I stared at him. Was he right? Was that all it was?

"I want to call her back," I said.

He shoved the phone into his back pocket. "No. It's a waste of power, and I need to preserve that as much as possible, till we're rescued."

Luke stood facing me, his face rigid. A gulf the size of an ocean lay between us.

"Did you kill Jane?" I said, my voice low as the telephone's ring had been.

His eyes narrowed. "Kill Jane? Now you're sounding crazy, Sarah. You think I could do something like that?"

"I don't know. Maybe. And what about me? Are you the one who attacked me at my cottage?"

Luke shook his head as if dealing with a six-year-old child whose fantasies had run amok. I wouldn't have been at all surprised to hear him say, *tsk, tsk.*

"Sarah, be reasonable. Grace and I found you on the path. We didn't go near your cottage. Besides, we were together. We're each other's alibi."

"Interesting word, Luke—*alibi.* You and Grace need alibis?"

"That's not what I meant," he said. "I just want you to reason this through, see it logically. Where has that legalistic mind of yours gone?"

"Screw my legalistic mind," I said, my voice shaking with anger. "You know what really bothers me about all this? You knew Jane. You met her before she burned Ransford down, and you must have seen what she was like, how afraid she was. How could you not tell her you had a working cell phone? Why didn't you help her get in touch with her children? Dammit, Luke, if you had, Jane might never have burned your house down!"

"I told you," he said angrily, "the cell phone's battery won't last forever. Besides, most of the phone system in the city is down. I probably wouldn't have found out anything, anyway. It would have been a useless waste to try."

My tears turned to anger. "That's not good enough, dammit. Why have you been keeping this place a secret? You're working us, Luke. You're conning all of us."

"I'm sorry you feel that way," he said coolly. "Maybe it is time for you to leave. Go back to Thornberry, Sarah."

He leaned back against the table, his arms folded, waiting for me to leave. A heavy silence filled the room.

"So all of a sudden it's safe out there?" I said. "There's no one out there stalking me?"

"What the hell," Luke said. "You've always preferred taking care of yourself. I'm sure you'll be all right."

I was so taken aback by his coldness, I wanted to slap him again. Not out of anger but to shake it out of him. I felt that the only way I might find the old Luke again was somehow to break through that stony barrier.

At the same time, I knew that no matter what I did, it wouldn't make a difference. Luke had never been easy that way. When he made up his mind on something, he stuck to it, no matter what. If you were his friend, that meant dogged loyalty. If not—

I unlocked the door and walked out. In my arms, I held my manuscript and disk. Behind me, I left any number of dreams—dreams I'd only half known I had. Luke had brought them all back—and now he'd crushed them for all time. I would never again feel I knew him.

I would, however, find out what was going on with my mother.

"How's that for a promise, Luke?" I said softly, looking back once from the edge of the forest to say goodbye.

*"The woods are lovely, dark and deep,"* I remembered from the Frost poem. Too dark, and not at all lovely that night. I virtually flew back to the main path, the way I'd remembered running in dreams—as if my feet barely touched the ground. If someone followed, I didn't know it, because I didn't stop once to listen. I just kept running, and if anyone had tried to grab me, I would have swung at them so hard it might easily have killed them. That's how high my adrenaline was.

When I got back to Ransford, I took the middle, shorter path to Thornberry and ran even faster now that I was more sure of the way. Halfway there a huge figure loomed before me, arms outstretched. My heart leapt into my throat and my limbs went weak. I heard a howl and felt a breath on my cheek.

The breath was only a breeze, the "howl" an owl's hoot, and the figure turned out to be a tree. I'd forgotten about the Ghost Tree, as Luke and I had called it years before. The full moon illuminated it just as the darkness had hidden it the other night when I was here. Its outstretched limbs seemed to reach for me, and I almost saw it as a sign...a sign that something on this island, at least, was trying to protect me.

I was so out of breath that my lungs hurt, and I stopped for a moment to rest in the hollow of the

Ghost Tree—an opening the shape of a triangle in the trunk, and just large enough to squeeze into.

It was then I heard the sound. It came from that part of the path I'd already traversed, and it was definite, now—the snapping of twigs that told of a footfall. I crouched farther back into the tree and tried to still my breath. As the footsteps grew closer, I wondered if I would be seen. My clothing, a gray T-shirt and jeans, was drab; the red-and-black lumberman's jacket I'd been wearing in bad weather had been left behind this night. But the moon was so full, it might, if the shadows weren't just right, reveal me.

A comic book I'd read as a kid came to mind—the hero closing his eyes when he hid so that he wouldn't be seen. It was an old myth, and some say a true one: if you look at your enemy, he'll just naturally, by some strange energy, be drawn to look at you.

I squeezed my eyes shut and covered my face. But when the footsteps sounded just before me and stopped, I couldn't help risking a peek. My eyes focused first on hiking boots, then upward at jeans, and finally the shirt and the face.

It was Grace. I saw her features clearly in the moonlight. For a moment her head turned toward me, and I was certain she saw me, as well. But then Grace murmured, "Damn tree! Scared the wits out of me!" She took a smack at it with her fist and moved on.

I felt my nerves and muscles collapse, and couldn't have gotten up out of the tree's hollow then if my life depended on it. I stayed there a good fifteen minutes after that, long after I heard Grace's footsteps move farther and farther away through the woods toward

Thornberry. When I could trust myself to move without making too much noise, I crawled out onto the path again. Standing there a minute, I thought about the manuscript and disk I was holding, and turned around, going back to the tree. Shoving them into the far recesses of the hollow, I covered them with piles of dry leaves from around the base of the tree.

Satisfied they were hidden as well as they could possibly be—certainly better than in any hiding place I might find at Thornberry—I walked the rest of the way back to the farmhouse.

I hadn't the strength to run, and if anyone had wanted me, they could have had me that night. I was easy prey.

The rest of my trip back to Thornberry, however, proved uneventful, and when I walked into the farmhouse I saw that everyone was there, except for Luke. Grace sat at the table with her arms crossed, listening to the others talk. The stones had been put away, and in as normal a voice as possible I asked who had won.

"Timmy did," Dana said. "Where did you go, Sarah? We were worried about you."

"I just felt like walking. There's a wonderful full moon. Have any of you seen it?"

I waited for Grace to say she'd been out walking, too, but she said nothing.

"Are you kidding?" Dana said. "All you have to do is look up."

I did, and there it was, shining through the opening in the roof. The full moon—a friend again.

"We don't even need lamps tonight, hardly," Dana said.

Amelia, who had found knitting needles and yarn somewhere, was hard at work on something long and green that looked like a scarf. She agreed. "It's warm enough to go without a fire, too, don't you think?"

"It might be a good idea to do that, anyway," Dana said. "In case there's another quake."

"Well, don't wish that on us," Amelia said. *"Knit one, purl two,"* she murmured.

"Don't worry, I won't," Dana answered. "But statistically, there are more quakes around the time of the full moon. And some full moons are worse than others that way."

"Oh?" Kim said. "Why?"

"I don't remember. I just know they are."

"What about this one?" Amelia asked

"I'm not sure. I just think we should be prepared. In case."

Grace didn't say anything, but I did catch her looking at me now and then. I stared her down finally, and she looked away.

"Where's Luke?" I asked of no one in particular, though I was curious to hear Grace's answer.

"He went for a walk, too," Timmy said. "I'm surprised you didn't run into him out there."

"Well, it's a big island." My glance at Grace told me she was no longer looking at me, and apparently not going to answer.

"We thought maybe you two had planned to go out for a walk at the same time," Dana said.

"Not at all," I answered.

"Now, come on," she teased. "Weren't you and Luke more than friends when you knew each other before?"

This did elicit a quick glance from Grace. So quick it was barely noticeable. "Oh, just teenage stuff," I said, brushing off Dana's comment. "It's been a long time since then."

"This place has a way of bringing out strange emotions, though," Kim said.

I looked at her and wondered if she was talking about herself and Gabe. I realized suddenly that Gabe wasn't here. I hadn't been accustomed to including him in the group, and hadn't noticed his absence till then.

"What about Gabe?" I asked. "Where is he?"

"He went to bed early," Kim answered. "Said he wanted to read for a while."

"He's out in the hallway?"

"With a lantern." Dana grinned. "Just like John Boy."

"Oh, I don't know," Amelia said wryly, "if I'd ever compare Gabe Rossi to John Boy."

"More like *Peck's Bad Boy*," Kim agreed.

"Who's that?" Dana asked.

"It was an old movie with Jackie Coogan," Kim answered. "'Peck's Bad Boy' became a label for someone who was an embarrassment or an annoyance. A rascal, some might say."

"It was a book, first, by George Wilbur Peck," Amelia added. "*Peck's Bad Boy and his Pa*. And believe it or not, it was even before *my* time. I'm surprised you know about that movie, Kim."

"Well, I did go to film school," Kim said.

"Really?" Amelia looked at her, I thought, with a blend of surprise and new respect. Then, flushing, she said, "I'm sorry, I guess I assumed you had just—" She stopped, bit her lip and went silent.

"Just what?" Dana asked, still in a teasing mode. "Sprung from a film canister full-blown?"

Amelia shook her head. "Not exactly."

Kim looked uneasy, and busied herself with folding napkins that we'd washed earlier and hung on a line.

"So you won the game, Timmy?" I said, changing the subject.

"Oh, it wasn't anything," she answered, shrugging it off. "I'm an old hand at games, remember? When you and your parents came here, we always played games at night after dinner. There wasn't much else to do."

"That's right, I'd forgotten that. You always won at Scrabble and Monopoly, too. In fact, as I remember, Ms. Timothea Walsh, you were always the smartest of us all."

She blushed at the compliment and patted her hair. "Well, I don't know about smart. But after all those summer nights, year after year, I would hope I had developed some skill, at least, for board games."

Timmy was being self-deprecating, but now that my memory had been jogged, I recalled that I had always thought of her as a pretty sharp cookie. In fact, I remembered my mother saying as much.

"You can't slip anything over on Timothea," she said one day when I'd accidentally dropped a cut-crystal glass here in this very room, and broken it.

My mother caught me trying to hide the evidence in the trash, and told me I'd be better off 'fessing up. "Timothea is one person you don't want to play games with—not in any way. She will always find you out somehow."

Until I remembered that, I had been thinking of Timmy as a bit of an airhead—a woman who'd always had it easy, always had more than enough money, at least until recently, and didn't make very good use of her seemingly good brain. It occurred to me now that this was an impression she gave, with the fluttery voice, the nicely coiffed hair, the diamonds and the overall wispy personality.

But was that only an impression? A carefully constructed image?

If my mother had been right about Timmy, if she really was all that sharp, how had she allowed herself to fall upon hard times?

And once fallen, wouldn't she get right back up and fight? In any way she could—and to whatever lengths necessary?

I thought back on Amelia's story about Timmy's potential bankruptcy and the way she had found an investor. An investor she wouldn't talk to Amelia—her best friend—about.

I also thought of the way I had been invited here, through Bill Farley at Seattle Mystery Bookshop. Certainly he'd always been friendly enough, supportive, always finding just the right books for my research.

But had I told him more than I really should have by letting him in on the topics I was researching?

My mind was running a mile a minute, and part of

me believed what I was thinking while the other part told me I was simply grasping at straws. Surely there wasn't any sinister connection between Timmy and Bill Farley, or—assuming Bill knew nothing about any of this, and had been used by someone with a hidden agenda—between Timmy and the Seattle Five.

But Thornberry had always been Timmy's first love. Even when her husband was alive, Thornberry had consumed her every waking moment. She loved her home, loved the guests, loved even the work involved. She had been a small tornado dashing around the place, keeping things in order, seeing to everyone's needs.

She must have done the same when Thornberry became a writer's colony. In fact, the first week we were here, I'd seen her acting much like the old Timmy, adding all those extra touches such as flowers and candles on the table, and not stinting on the food or other luxury items. The bathhouse always had fresh linens and scented lotions and, for anyone who wanted to bathe at night, a multitude of scented candles. There were even rose petals to scatter in our baths, and fresh rosemary, as well.

All these things cost money—even the ones that came from the Thornberry gardens. Timmy must have found herself a very well-to-do investor.

But what interest was he charging for his loan? What did Timmy have to do to repay the debt?

"Where did you walk to?" I heard Dana ask.

"Hmm? Oh, sorry. Just around the woods, taking in the night sounds and the moon. I think I might have heard some deer."

"But you didn't run into Luke? I wonder what he's up to."

She didn't mean it as anything more than casual interest, I was sure. But I wondered why I couldn't bring myself to tell anyone what I'd discovered about Luke. Surely they had every right to know that he had a cell phone, and every right to know, as well, that help wasn't coming anytime soon.

It wasn't so much a loathing to reveal his betrayal, I told myself, as not wanting anyone here to know I was on to Luke till I knew what he was really up to. After all, he had let me go. He hadn't done me any harm, when he easily might have. I felt safe keeping my suspicions to myself for a while longer. And this way I had the upper hand. I could blow his cover any time.

It didn't turn out that way, of course. Things seldom turn out precisely as we plan. Seldom, however, do they turn out quite so badly.

Kim and I remained at the table after everyone else turned in. We spoke softly so as not to disturb the others, who were sleeping on the floor around the stove as they did every night.

"Kim," I said, "why did you call Gabe 'Peck's Bad Boy'? I thought you liked him."

"I do," she said. "It's just that he's impossible."

"You said he was an annoyance."

"I meant that as a joke. Just when I think I've hauled him in, he wiggles off the line."

"Are you serious about him, then?" I asked.

"Oh…probably not. It's just real easy to get bored

here." Laughing softly, she added, "I thought I was starting to hate L.A. Now I miss it so much..." She gave a shrug.

"Look," I said, "I don't mean to be hurtful, honestly. But doesn't it occur to you that Gabe is playing all of us?"

"Sure," Kim said. "In fact, he reminds me of any one of a number of young men I know in Hollywood—conning and scamming to get close to someone they want something from. But so far, I haven't figured out what it is Gabe wants."

"Well, he's a man," I said, smiling.

"True. I just thought..."

"That he actually cared about you and not the others?"

"I guess. That's the way he's been acting—at least, when he's with me."

"And don't they all," I said.

Kim shook her head. "Girl, you sure have been bitten by some venomous snake. Who did that to you?"

"A rattler," I said. "The kind that coils itself up and waits for just the right moment to strike."

Her eyes widened. "Are you talking about Luke?"

I shrugged. "If you'd asked me that yesterday, I'd have said no. My snake in the grass was in Seattle. Now, I'm not so sure they aren't all over the place."

"Well, that guy in Seattle sure did a number on you. Is it over?"

"Dead, cold and buried," I said without thinking. But as the words left my mouth, feelings rose up that surprised me. Was Ian dead? Was he buried beneath tons of concrete in Seattle?

At the thought that I might never see him again, I felt a deep, painful loss. We can leave a lover, it seems, and even be apart, with no contact for years. But he's always there. Always someone who might show up again, someone we might run into on the street, someone at the other end of a telephone line. We always know we can pick up that phone and find him there—even if it's different and there's nothing left of the old relationship at all. At least the person we've put so much energy and time into loving is still there.

With Ian, I might not know for weeks. And a world without him seemed less, somehow. Not a world I looked forward to going back to as much as I might have if he were there.

I pulled on my jacket and went outside to stand by Lucy's grave. The moon had dipped lower in the sky, and clouds hovered over the horizon to the west. A breeze had come up, whipping my hair in every direction, and I shivered, wrapping my arms about myself.

*I should have told them,* I thought. I should have told everyone what I found in the woods and what I suspected about Jane. If she was murdered because of something she knew, something she might have run across by accident…that meant anyone here could do the same, and be in just as much danger.

Luke's cabin, for instance. Had Jane found that? And his cell phone? That would have seemed like a miracle to her, one she wouldn't give up on easily. She would demand to use the phone to call her children.

And if Luke had denied her access to the phone, as he had me? What might she have done?

Put up a fight, certainly. And Jane, in the state she was in, would have been a formidable foe.

Was Luke unable to fend her off? Would he have gone so far as to kill her, if he couldn't dissuade her?

He could easily have done that at the cabin, then carried her to the ravine to make it look as if she'd had an accident. Gabe said he had seen Luke brushing dirt from his hands. And if Jane was already dead when she fell—

*That would explain why no one heard her scream.*

This was something none of us had thought of, or at least discussed. If Jane fell, or was pushed, into the gorge, why didn't anyone hear her scream?

Still deep in thought, I heard the scrape of a foot behind me. Every nerve went on alert, and I almost swung around to defend myself against whoever it was. That's how on edge I felt.

"Hey, hey," Gabe said, as I raised my arm. "Easy, now! It's only me."

I relaxed only a little. "That doesn't necessarily reassure me," I said.

"Oh, glory be," he said, grinning. "Sounds like I'm falling under that famous 'umbrella of suspicion' I've heard so much about in the news over the past few years."

"Everyone's under suspicion here," I said, "since Jane died."

"I guess I can understand that." He stood with his face toward the descending moon, and I saw that the grin had faded a bit.

"I just thought you might be able to use some company," he said. "Okay if I share *your* umbrella?"

"Mine?"

"Well, sure. You don't think you're immune to being suspect, do you?"

"I hadn't thought about that," I said. "But, gee, thanks for giving me something else to worry about. Has someone been talking about me?"

"Oh, everyone's been talking about everyone. If those ladies in there don't kill each other before they ever get rescued, I'll be surprised."

"What do you mean?"

"Well, first off, they were at each other's throats over that silly stone game. Then they all came up with reasons to pick at each other—who left the dinner fire burning, who jockeys for the closest place to sleep by the stove, who drank too much water today, who..." He sighed, a deep chuckling sound. "Saints preserve us from quarreling women in the middle of an earthquake."

I had to smile. "To tell the truth, they were pretty much like that even before the quake."

He turned to me. "You don't say? How did you ever last a week like that?"

"I almost didn't. I was planning to hide out in my cottage for the rest of the month—when all of a sudden I didn't have a cottage."

He laughed. "And now you're all living on top of each other, with everybody thinking the person closest to them killed poor Jane. Sounds like one of those old mystery novels. *Ten Little Indians,* wasn't it?''

Kim had mentioned that book, too. A coincidence?

"Speaking of which," Gabe went on, "it seems astonishing now, but that book of Christie's first came out as *Ten Little Niggers.* Did you know? I suppose in the U.K. that was still acceptable in the forties. When it came out over here it was titled *And Then There Were None,* and only later, *Ten Little Indians*—'' He broke off. "Which isn't all that politically correct now, either, come to think of it."

My stomach had done a tiny flip-flop at the use of the *N* word, which had become so volatile in recent years, especially in courtrooms. Now, since Lonnie Mae, it actually made me cringe.

"No, I didn't know that about Christie's book," I said. "But could you see it being called *Ten Little North American Natives?* I doubt any New York publisher would let that happen."

"True. It's more than two words, isn't it? Marketing would never go for it."

I looked at him, surprised. "You sound like you know something about publishing."

"Not book publishing, as such, but I do have to come up with just the right titles for my software, or it never sells. Just sits there on the shelf growing a beard." He smiled. "But to get back to Christie, she wasn't alone in being politically incorrect in that era. Here's something I came across in my own research for titles. Do you remember the song, 'Up a Lazy River'?"

"'...by the old mill run'? Sure. I remember my mother singing it around the house.''

"Well," he said, "the title originally was 'Up a Lazy Nigger.'"

"I don't believe that," I said even more uneasy now. "I'm sure it's a myth."

"Not at all. Would you like to hear the story behind it?"

"Not especially." I folded my arms. "I'm sure I wouldn't believe a word of it."

"Well, trust me," Gabe said, "you can believe it. According to my research, Hoagy Carmichael—you know who he was? Wrote 'Stardust,' and 'Georgia on My Mind'?"

"One of my favorite songwriters," I said. "Long before my time, but his music is timeless, as they say." Where was this leading?

"Right. Well, back in the late thirties, Hoagy was visiting a jazz club where a well-known clarinetist named Sidney Arodin, Jr., was playing. Hoagy was impressed with the music to a song Sidney had written, called 'Up a Lazy Nigger.' He told Sidney he loved the music and wanted to have the song published, but that he'd have to change the lyrics. Sidney said fine, and the rest is history."

"That's...truly bizarre," I said. "Are you sure it's true?"

"Absolutely. The old sheet music even lists the two of them on it. But before you castigate poor old Sidney as a racist, there's something you need to know. Sidney Arodin was well-known in scholarly jazz circles as the first person to record interracially, with blacks and whites. Apparently, despite his lyrics, he was not at all racist. It just wasn't uncommon to refer to blacks by the *N* word back then.''

"I see. And your point in telling me all this, is?"

"That racist behavior, or what is perceived as racist behavior, is not always what it seems. That may be something to keep in mind when you're working at nabbing those cops you're after."

Red flags went up. "Wait a minute. What do you know about that?"

"About your arrest? And the rape of that black woman? Sarah, it was in all the Seattle papers for weeks. And now you're writing a book about it, right?"

"You are a virtual fount of information," I said.

"Come now, Sarah, you are here at a *writer's* colony," he said patiently, as if to a child.

"So? Maybe I write poetry."

"Hardly. No, we'll leave that to Amelia. The fact is, Sarah, the people I work for ran a thorough investigation on you after your arrest. There isn't much we don't know about you—and we didn't need to read about any of it in the newspapers, or *Publisher's Weekly*. Though I must say, they do have you being offered, and accepting, quite a deal. We didn't know that until recently."

I stared at Gabe Rossi, my knees going weak and spots forming before my eyes. My flesh turned cold, and when I could speak my voice was no more than a whisper.

"Who the hell are you?" I said.

"I'm somebody who can help you," Gabe answered. "If you let me."

"Help me." I continued to stare. "I don't— Who *are* you?"

"Well, I'm not a software developer," he said, "except by hobby. I'm a cop, Sarah. And I'm Ian MacDonald's new partner. I was sent here to protect you."

# 14

I was speechless. Stunned. Before I could recover, a dark figure moved toward us from the farmhouse. I wasn't sure, at first, who it was, as the approach seemed almost stealthy. When the figure came close, it stopped short, as if surprised to see us there.

That's when I saw it was Grace. She called out, "Sarah? Is that you?"

"Watch your step with her," Gabe said in an undertone. "She is not your friend."

As Grace came up to us, I saw that she fixed Gabe with a stare. He didn't give an inch, but continued to stand close to me, almost hovering.

"Timmy was worried about you," Grace said to me. "I told her I'd come out and see where you were."

I found my voice. "Well, here I am, Grace."

"Are you, uh…are you coming in?" She shot a glance at Gabe.

"Yes, I'm coming in. When I'm ready. Is that all right with you?"

She frowned and turned back to the farmhouse, stomping all the way. *"Why I even bother…"* I heard her mutter.

"Charming lady," Gabe said. "And don't you

think it's interesting that she and Luke are chumming around so much?''

I just looked at him, and Gabe shook his head. ''Sarah, Sarah, Sarah…I had hoped I'd be able to ease into this. But you've got to open your eyes. Luke and Grace are in this together, and they are both a danger to you.''

I couldn't take my gaze from his mouth, as if by its shape and movement I could detect whether what he said was a lie. ''Ease me? Into what?'' I managed to say.

He sighed. ''All right. Let's cut to the chase. Luke Ford is keeping all of us on this island. He's also keeping us out of touch with the mainland. You and I both know why he's doing that.''

My words came out in a jerky counterpoint to what was in my head. ''No. I don't know why. Why Luke would do that. If he is.''

Taking a step back, I said, ''Funny, I don't recall Ian having a partner. Not in recent years.''

''We started working together a month ago,'' Gabe said. ''And I've been undercover. You wouldn't have heard of me.''

I was still half in shock and not inclined to buy anything he told me. But I was getting my legs back as well as my voice, and I wanted to hear it all. ''Tell me why you think Luke is keeping us here.''

''Isn't it obvious, Sarah? He's waiting for you to tell him where the evidence is.''

I kept my expression carefully blank. ''Evidence?''

''Why do you think he turned up here so conveniently right after the quake? Why do you think he killed Jane?''

I couldn't answer.

Gabe took me by the shoulders. ''I saw him at the ravine, Sarah. Open your eyes. I can understand that you wouldn't want to believe it, but you've got to. Until you do, you're leaving yourself open to danger.''

''And you're suggesting that I do...what?''

''Turn that evidence over to me for safekeeping, Sarah. Let me help you put the Seattle Five away— for good.''

I tried to lick my lips but there was no saliva. ''I don't know what evidence you're talking about. And even if I did, why should I trust you rather than Luke?''

''Because a man who keeps five women captive on an island when all he has to do is use a cell phone to call for help is not to be trusted.''

''You think Luke has a cell phone?'' I said, still not quite willing to give Luke up.

''I don't think it, I know it. He's been using it to stay in touch with the people who are after you, Sarah. That's what he's here for—to get you.''

My emotions were so mixed, I was shaking. I started to walk back closer to the farmhouse, and safety. But Gabe grabbed me by the arm, pulling me onto a bench. I could have fought him, but something in me still wanted to hear what he had to say. We were within thirty feet of the kitchen door. If he tried anything, I could yell for help.

"Sarah," he said, sitting beside me, "Ian sent me to help you. You have no idea how much he wanted to come himself. He's been frantic with worry about you."

"Oh, has he, now? That's pretty interesting, Gabe. Especially as Ian hasn't even spoken to me since I was arrested in January. I guess you didn't know that."

"Actually, I do know that. And there was a reason for it. The only way Ian could help you was to keep his distance. If the department thought he was taking sides, he'd have been yanked off the case. As it is, he still can't appear to be helping you. The Seattle Five have people in power behind them. They have a whole damn committee, in fact—and Judge Ford, Luke's father, is at the head of it."

"Luke's father. Judge Ford. He's the head of a committee that put the Five in power? But that's crazy! Judge Ford would never—"

"Sarah, it's not just him. There are others—people who on the surface seem like nice, ordinary, law-abiding folks. They just happen to believe that bad cops are doing a job that needs to be done when they 'rid the world of scum,' as they see it. And you know, Seattle's not alone in that. In every big city where cops have been arrested for abuse of their badges, there's someone at the top who at some point, whether their motivation was good or bad, gave them permission to 'go out and do what needs to be done.'"

There was something to what he said. In researching my book I'd learned that in many people's minds, the mayor of New York City had created an atmosphere for abuse with his "get tough on crime" policy. No one was saying he intended cops to take that edict and turn it into wrongful shootings or arrests based on ethnicity. But in many cities, cops were being hired too quickly. They weren't investigated thoroughly enough, and some were known spousal abusers, while others were macho types who just wanted to get out there and act like the vigilante cops they'd seen on TV and in films. The kind of cops who only wanted to serve and protect were being infiltrated by the other kind—and though the good guys are still in the majority, there are enough of the renegades to do a good deal of harm.

But—actual committees who backed the vigilantes? Sent them out to arrest people who might be innocent, with no regard for the rule of law?

And Judge Ford as head of such a committee? It was unthinkable.

But then I remembered that scene, again, from years before. Luke's father and mine on opposite sides, with Luke's father arguing that Seattle needed a stronger police force, that there was too much disrespect for the law. My father countering that the police were getting out of hand and that arresting innocent people, besides being immoral, was a complete waste of the police department's time.

I remembered saying to Luke, "Your father would convict Jesus," and Luke countering, "Yours would get him off."

Had Judge Ford, my childhood mentor, gone beyond the law to enforce respect for it? Was that possible?

And had Luke followed in his footsteps?

"What about Luke?" I asked Gabe. "You said he was sent here to 'get me.' What did you mean by that?"

"Luke's father, Judge Ford," he said, "sent both Luke and Grace here to find out what evidence you have against the Five, and to get it away from you. Ford's committee doesn't want the Five going to jail. The Five are the best people they've got."

"The Five are rapists and murderers, for God's sake! You're saying they're the *best* they've got?"

"You've just made my point, Sarah."

I shook my head, trying to clear it. "I can't believe Luke and Grace would be party to such a thing."

"Believe it," Gabe said. "As far as I know, they've only worked together this one time, because of Luke's connection to you. It was thought he'd have the best chance of getting the evidence away from you."

"What made this committee think I even had any evidence?" I asked.

"Sarah, think. You talked about it openly in McCoy's bar to one of the Five—Mike Murty. He reported this to Judge Ford, and orders went out from Ford to get that evidence at any cost."

"Any cost?"

"Sarah, for God's sake, will you listen to what I'm telling you? Your life is in danger here."

"And you were sent here by Ian, you say, to protect me."

"Exactly."

"Then will you please explain how I got bashed over the head? Where were you then? Off fishing with Amelia, right? And how come..." I stopped myself from saying it: *How come the evidence is missing?*

"I've had to stay undercover," Gabe said. "I didn't know whether someone else here might be in on it with Luke and Grace, so I've been spreading myself thin—too thin, at the time you were attacked. But I've been trying to get to know everyone, find out who might be here under false pretenses."

"You're thinking there's a whole bunch of people here, just waiting to get their hands on that evidence?" I gave a low laugh. "And I thought *I* was paranoid."

"Not when you think of what's at stake—the lives, possibly, of five Seattle cops. Not to mention months of ongoing bad publicity for the force."

"All right, look. Assuming I'm buying any of this," I said, "who the hell is Grace? What is she doing here?"

He shrugged. "To be honest, I don't know who she is, just that she's in on it with Luke. It's obvious they know each other, and if that's true, doesn't it seem unlikely she'd just *happen* to be here?"

"But how could Judge Ford arrange to have her invited here? If she's not even a writer—"

Then I got it. *Timmy.*

Timmy, who needed money to keep Thornberry alive. Timmy, who had found an investor, just in the nick of time. Timmy—who had invited all of us here.

Judge Ford and our hostess were old, old friends.

Would she do anything for him? Or for pay? *Had* she done anything—including betraying me?

"Does Timmy know about all this?" I asked. "Does she know why she was asked to invite Grace? And about Luke's involvement?"

"We're not sure how much she knows," Gabe said. "But you remember when Luke was pairing people off the other day? Didn't you think it was odd that he paired you with Timmy? You're one of the most capable people here—and he virtually confined you to the farmhouse that day."

Gabe was right. That same day I caught Luke and Grace in the woods, in each other's arms. And shortly after that, I was attacked at my cottage and the *Allegra* case disappeared. Moreover, it was Luke and Grace who "found" me.

It all fit—and to continue to deny it would put me in further danger. It wasn't as though Gabe was telling me something I didn't, in my heart, already know—that I couldn't trust Luke and Grace. I'd known that from the moment I'd seen them in the woods, holding each other. I knew it when they broke into laughter together, shutting me out. I knew it when Luke came on to me only a few hours later, as I was sitting outside in the lawn chair. And later, when we danced.

*He was working me.*

But another thought occurred to me. "It seemed to me," I said, "that Grace was rather hot and heavy after you the other night, when you were dancing."

"She was. She wanted to know who I 'really' was, where I'd 'really' come from. Not that she was all that obvious in her questions, but I knew she and Luke were suspicious of me.''

"What did you tell her?''

"Same thing I'd said before—that I owned a software company, lived in Gig Harbor. Nothing mysterious.''

I sat silently, thinking about what he had told me. In the farmhouse kitchen, candles and lamps had been put out. It was getting late. And dark.

"Sarah,'' Gabe said, "I saw your book in that cabin Luke has, back in the woods. The same day I found his cell phone there. I read some of it, and it's pretty powerful stuff. But that brings to mind a question—why do you think Luke took your manuscript?''

"I'm not sure. To find out how much I know, I suppose.''

"And possibly to find out where you've hidden your evidence against the Five?''

"But I didn't put that in my book. I've never told anyone.''

"He couldn't have known that, though. Not until he read your manuscript. Sarah, I can't stress enough how careful you have to be until we get off this island. I'll do my best to protect you, but as you've seen, I can't be everywhere at once. And I'd never forgive myself—nor would Ian forgive me—if anything happened to you.''

"Ian.'' I laughed shortly. "You know, this really doesn't sound like the Ian MacDonald who dumped me unceremoniously three months ago. How do you and he fit into this?''

"Ian and I learned about Judge Ford's committee, and we managed to infiltrate it. There are three other members of the committee, besides Ian and me. We meet secretly and underground—literally—in a room they call the Whale Room, several stories down in a private building in Seattle. Ian and I have only been to a few meetings, but this committee has been in existence for quite a while. Months, really."

"But surely they know Ian and you are cops?"

"Of course, they do. And that's the beauty of it. They think we've turned. That's what I was saying, Sarah. We couldn't have done that if he hadn't dropped you like a hot potato the minute you so publicly announced your intention to go after the Five. Ian and I have pretended to go along with all of Ford's orders to find you, get our hands on the evidence and then silence you. Our real intent, of course, has been to protect you. I'll be honest, Sarah. We aren't doing this simply for humanitarian reasons. You're a major part of the case we're putting together against the Seattle Five. In fact your evidence against the Five is the first real break we've had. God knows, that infamous Blue Wall of Silence hasn't helped. But you, Sarah—you could help put them and their bosses away for a very long time."

"How do you figure on getting to the bosses?"

"What we hope is that as long as you—or we— have control of the evidence, and it's safe, one or more of the Five just might cop a plea and talk."

I got up and walked to the path, looking back at the farmhouse. I remembered how good it had felt, the first day I arrived, to be here again. How safe.

"Have you been in contact with Ian since the quake?" I asked.

"I was for a day or so right after the quake. Before my phone went out."

"How is he?"

"Unfortunately, he and Judge Ford's other committee members were stuck underground in their meeting room, waiting for rescue. Ian said they'd heard reports that there was looting in the streets. Not only that, but killings—cold-blooded, senseless killings. People are being shot in the streets, Sarah, for no reason at all. It's tragic, Ian said, to see what's going on. Seattle is like a country at war, and Ian and the rest of the department will have their hands full for weeks, once this is over."

"And, you—you were here on the island already, when the quake hit? You came over on Friday, just as you said?"

"Yes. The only thing I left out is the fact that it was Ian who sent me. Once we learned that you had come here to Esme, he was anxious that I get over here somehow and look after you. It was a last-minute plan, and I hopped on the ferry without thinking about provisions, clothes, anything."

"How did you find out where I was?"

"I'd been asking ferry operators and passengers for days, and finally I ran across the captain of the private ferry that comes out here. He remembered bringing you here." Gabe smiled. "The guy told me he remembered you because you were especially attractive. Like Sharon Stone, he said. Short blond hair, great figure…"

I ignored the compliment and fell silent, mulling it

over. While my logical mind tended to believe him, my gut was having fits. Finally I said, "There's only one problem, so far as I can see."

"And that is?"

"I don't have that evidence with me, Gabe. It's back in Seattle. And by now, it could well be lost forever under a pile of rubble."

I watched his face, hoping to see something telltale in his expression. But in the dim light I saw nothing but a flicker of disappointment.

"Christ, Sarah. That's something we never considered. We were so sure you would have brought whatever it was with you—that you wouldn't have left it at home for an entire month, where the Five might get their hands on it. But if it's been lost in the quake…"

"Well, of course, there's always the chance it survived. I'll have to see, when I get back."

He took my hands. "Sarah, let me help. Tell me where it is, and I'll call Ian and tell him to check it out."

"But Ian's stuck underground. Isn't that what you said?"

"He was, but they were rescued after the first couple of days."

"You talked to him when he got out, then? He's all right?"

"Yes. He's fine."

"Is he coming here?"

"I'm not sure, Sarah. He's got his hands full, but he said he was doing his best to get a rescue team out here to us."

"Well, that's wonderful. It shouldn't be long, then. The evidence can wait till we get back. Right?"

He dropped my hands and ran one of his own through his hair. "Sarah, look. I don't know how to say this without it coming out wrong. But what if something should happen to you between now and then? What if Luke or Grace should get to you? Hurt you? I mean…oh, hell. Tell me what the evidence is, please, Sarah, so I can see it gets into the right hands. Tell me where to find it."

"Gabe, I wish I could. Honestly. But I gave it to a friend for safekeeping, and I don't know what she did with it. I don't even know if she's still alive."

I saw frustration cross his face, and almost hated myself for lying. Everything Gabe had said made sense. And it wasn't entirely that I didn't trust *him*. It was myself I didn't trust—to make the right decision for all concerned.

One thing was clear, now: Gabe hadn't stolen the *Allegra* case. That left six other people who might have done it. And my bet was on Luke. Or Grace.

"I know it's hard for you to accept what I'm saying," Gabe said. "But, Sarah, please at least do one thing for me? Be careful. Watch your back every moment of the time we have left on this island. Don't trust anyone."

"What about you?" I said. "Shouldn't I trust you?"

He grinned, and Gabe the Charmer came back. "If you did, then I'd be *really* worried. But yes, Sarah. I hope one day you'll come to trust me."

# 15

Gabe asked me not to tell anyone that Ian was sending help. "We don't want to force anyone's hand," he said. "Let's just wait until it happens."

From the moment he and I had that talk, I knew what I had to do. Based on what he had told me, and how much sense it made, I decided to heed Gabe's advice—and my own instinct—and not trust anyone.

Still, I couldn't just stand around and wait to see who on Esme Island might actually be after me. Maybe it was Luke and Grace, as he'd said. And maybe there was someone else. The point being, I could no longer wait for the *Allegra* case to turn up. I had foolishly thought that given enough time, the person who took it would show himself—or herself— in some way. I had also foolishly thought I had all the time in the world to resolve this here on Esme.

Now, with help on the way, the never-ending days seemed impossibly short. What if we were rescued before I found the *Allegra* case? Before it was back in my hands? Everyone here would go his and her own separate way. In the blink of an eye, I could lose for all time my one opportunity to put the Five behind bars.

For that matter—what if I'd waited too long already? What if the person who took it had destroyed it? Had taken the stockings out and dumped them in the Sound?

And who aside from Luke and Grace would be motivated to do that?

I thought of Timmy with her potential bankruptcy; and even Kim, who had seemed on the brink of saying something about her life, at times, then stopping. I thought of Dana, who didn't want to talk about her life at home.

She's the one I began with, the morning after my talk with Gabe.

"You never say much about yourself," I commented, while we were washing clothes in the Sound.

"Don't I?" she said. "No, I guess not."

When she didn't continue, I added, "Is there some trouble back home? I don't mean to be nosy, but we are all in such a mess here, Dana. And tempers are rising from so much stress. Maybe it would help if we could talk to each other."

Dana sighed and sat back on her heels. Her pant legs, as mine, were rolled up to the knee, but still they'd gotten wet as we squatted in the water, scrubbing our clothes with a bar of soap. She began to rinse and wring out a T-shirt.

"The truth is, Sarah, I'm leaving my husband. I'm not going back to Santa Fe when this is over."

This wasn't anything I'd expected to hear, and I sat back on a low rock and gave her my full attention. "Really?" I said. "You planned this all along?"

She nodded. "I'm in love with someone else, and we're meeting in Vancouver—" She broke off. "That is, we were supposed to meet in Vancouver. Who knows, now?''

Her face was drawn, and the sadness that filled it made me reach out to her. That she was a ''runaway wife'' had never in a million years occurred to me.

''Do you want to talk about it?'' I asked.

''I suppose, the way things are now, it wouldn't hurt. The truth is, my husband—well, he started being abusive right after we were married, two years ago. I stayed with him because he threatened to kill me if I left, but a few months ago I finally screwed up my courage and decided to walk.''

She wiped sweat from her brow with a soapy hand. ''I wasn't sure how I'd do it, but when the invitation came from Thornberry, I jumped at it. I wasn't going to stay the whole month, Sarah. That was just what I told my husband. I was going to take the ferry back to Seattle one day, rent a car and drive to Vancouver. I'm walking out—leaving my clothes, credit cards, everything I own behind in Santa Fe. I'm hoping he won't be able to track me down.''

''My God, Dana. I had no idea.''

''Well, at first I didn't trust anyone here with the truth. And now—'' She shrugged. ''If there was anyone I'd trust, it'd be you, Sarah. Please don't tell anyone else, though. If I do make it to Vancouver, and my husband manages to find me…''

''Don't worry, I won't say a word. But you said you're meeting someone? A lover?''

She gave me a weak smile. ''I don't know how that'll work out. But I fell in love with John—that's his name, John—at a powwow that was held in Santa

Fe last year. He's part Cherokee, and he's sweet and kind. We found we had a lot in common, and one thing led to another..." She dipped her hands into the cold water again.

"Is John from Vancouver?" I asked.

"Actually, from a little town outside the city. He should have made it through the quake just fine, considering what little damage Vancouver suffered. That's the one thing that's kept me sane here."

"He must be going crazy, though, wondering how you are," I said.

"I know. That's why—" She broke off.

"What, Dana?"

"Oh, I'm just being silly. But if only there was a way to get a message to him."

I fell silent.

"What about you, Sarah?" Dana asked.

"What about me?"

"Well, you and Luke. The way he looks at you sometimes..." She rolled her eyes.

"I'm sure you're wrong about that," I said, frowning. "Luke and I were friends a long time ago. But like you and your husband, we don't really have much in common anymore."

"What about Gabe, then? Grace said you two were having a very intense talk on the path last night."

"She did, did she? She told all of you this?"

"No, I just happened to overhear her talking to Luke. I figured she was warning him that he'd better get out there and stop you or he'd lose his newly found girlfriend again."

"She didn't actually say that, did she?"

"I didn't hear everything. Just her saying, 'You'd better get out there and put a stop to that—right now.'"

So Grace didn't want me talking to Gabe. But why? Was she afraid he'd tell me exactly what he did tell me about her and Luke?

"I hate to say it, but I still don't like Grace very much," Dana continued. "I'll bet that woman has a live shell for a heart."

"A live shell?"

"Just waiting to go off at the slightest touch," Dana said. "You know—a hard case. In fact, if Kim hadn't been with her at the time, I wouldn't have been surprised if Grace had killed Jane."

"But why would she?" I asked.

"Who knows? Maybe because Jane looked cross-eyed at her one day."

*Or maybe something else,* I was thinking. Gabe's belief was that Luke had killed Jane, since he'd seen him at the ravine. I didn't want to believe that at first, but it was seeming more and more possible that Gabe was telling the truth.

So—what if Jane found out why Luke and Grace were on the island? What if she overheard them talking, or saw something between them, the same way I had? It could have been anything, and it could have occurred at Gabe's cabin just as easily as anywhere else. Luke could have been there with Grace, and if Jane walked in on them…

Kim and Grace had supposedly been walking along the shore together at the time Jane died. But had

Grace left Kim for any length of time? And if so, why hadn't Kim mentioned that?

I would have to talk to her next.

"You know," Dana said, "this place is beginning to feel damned spooky. Do you get the feeling there are things going on here that we don't know anything at all about?"

"I do," I said. "I most definitely do."

Over the next few days, Gabe continued to work the women, and now and then he would slide a glance at me as if telling me, *This is only a job. Hang on. Help will arrive soon.*

So I watched as he flirted and smiled, getting close to each woman to find out who and what they were. My feelings were mixed about this. I hoped he would succeed and discover if anyone here, aside from Luke and Grace, posed a danger to me. At the same time, I prayed he would find that there was no one else.

As for my initial suspicions about Gabe, I was beginning to set them aside. As I watched him help first one woman, then another build a fire, gather food or search through their cottage rubble for something lost since the night of the quake, I even felt a twinge of jealousy now and then. Gabe's style of helping was never a "take charge" one, as if the person he helped were less competent than he. Rather, he offered his services as a friend, and he was never overtly sexual toward any of the women. We all came to relax around him, assured that he was not going to expect "payment" of that sort when all was said and done. At least, not if that payment was unwanted.

Luke, on the contrary, was growing ever more distant toward all of us, except Grace. They spent long hours away from the farmhouse together, and no one knew where they were or what they were doing. Each time they would come back with fish or oysters, and that would be their excuse. They had been out "scouting" for food.

Luke took me aside once in the midst of all this and asked me point-blank if I would confide in him finally, tell him where I'd hidden the evidence against the Five.

"If anything should happen to you, Sarah—" he began.

"What could happen to me?" I countered, with a flicker of fear. *What do you have planned for me?* was the thought that ran through my mind.

"I don't know," he said, "and that's just it. You felt that aftershock last night."

"Yes." We had all felt it and been frightened by it. It was worse than any since the original quake.

"Sarah, my father says the U.S. Geological Survey believes it was actually a new quake from a previously undiscovered fault. If that's true, there could be others. And they could get worse. All I know is, if anything happens to you, I'd want to be able to get that evidence to the right people and finish the job for you. I'd do whatever I had to do to clear your name."

"That's very kind of you, Luke," I said carefully. "But aren't you assuming a lot—that something might happen to me, rather than you? What if it's the other way around?"

"Well, of course, that could be the case," he

agreed, frowning. "Anything could happen to any-body here, and we should be thinking of what to do in that event. We should all make lists of family and friends to be notified afterward, and—" He hesitated. "I hate to say this, but we should ask everyone if they have any last requests."

I was forced to agree that we should, indeed, do all that. I led him away from any idea of my telling him where Lonnie Mae's evidence was, however, by saying, "And that reminds me. Is it okay now if I call my mom from your phone? After all, if things are as serious as you say they are—"

He smiled. "No need. I asked my father to call and tell her you were all right. She knows, Sarah. In fact, she sends her love."

"Really?" I raised a brow. "When did you do that?"

"Just last night," he said. "You were asleep when I came in."

"You mean, when you and Grace came in."

He looked away.

"Still," I said, "I'd like to talk to my mom, my-self."

"Well, actually, she isn't in Miami now. She and your aunt are on a short trip to Bermuda. They left this morning, early."

"You're kidding."

"No. I guess your aunt thought your mom could use a short vacation."

For some reason, I didn't believe that for a minute. What I did believe was that Luke didn't want me calling my mother.

"My agent, then," I said. "I'd like her to know I'm all right."

"I told you last night, Sarah, we can't use what little cell power we have left just to let people know we're all right. Don't you think everyone here would like to do that? Including me? I'm sorry, but you can't call anyone until the rescue team arrives."

I was beginning to get angry. "And just what does your father say about a rescue?"

"Like I said, it's a matter of coordinating the different teams and seeing who can be spared, and when. He'll let us know."

It was a few hours later that I made my way through the woods to Luke's cabin, thinking I'd help myself to that cell phone, despite him. When I got there, I found the door had been padlocked. The lock was old, rusty and heavy-duty. I doubted it could be broken through without a very strong tool.

I tried the two front windows, which were the only ones in the cabin. The other three sides were made of solid logs. That's when I discovered that the windows were now boarded up from the inside with plywood.

Bitterly disappointed, I also felt afraid. From the moment I'd seen that Luke had a cell phone, I'd been hopeful in a way I hadn't been before. Some communication with the outside world—any communication—was better than none. Now, Luke had effectively prevented everyone but himself from having that contact with the outside world.

This made me even more certain that Gabe had been telling the truth.

* * *

Over the next few days, the tensions amongst us grew to a fever pitch. Our early attempts to cooperate and work together to survive became more a test of our ability to survive alone. We grew farther and farther apart, and the backbiting was fierce. I do not exclude myself from this. My nerves grew thin, and I saw shadows everywhere. My life in Seattle, bad as it might have become, seemed like Utopia now, compared to being on Esme Island with these people.

In particular, I could no longer face Luke comfortably, after the things Gabe had told me about him. Every instinct cried out that to trust Luke could be the most dangerous mistake I'd ever made where men were concerned. If he hadn't gone to such great lengths to keep us from contacting anyone, I might have felt differently. But that, and his seemingly unholy alliance with Grace, sealed his fate, as far as I was concerned.

And then there was Kim. She and I barely spoke anymore. This wasn't personal, as I still liked her more than anyone else at Thornberry, except perhaps for Dana. Dana and I were still getting along reasonably well, but none of us was communicating anymore on a very clear level. We had all drawn in on ourselves, as if to protect what little of our ''selves'' we had left.

It was while we were eating dinner one night that another quake occurred. It shook the farmhouse as if it were a child's toy, and the remaining ceiling came crashing down on us. We all dived under the table, and when we crawled back out, no one was seriously hurt.

Dana did have dust in her eyes from the flying debris. She hadn't been able to not look, she said. "If this was going to be the last minute of my life, I wanted to see everything there was to see."

Later, she told me privately, "I think it was my guilt making me think I was going to die."

"Guilt?" I asked.

"I...well, about leaving my husband, running off that way," she said. "In fact, this whole damn mess has felt like karma to me. It's like my sins are all coming back to get me, in one fell swoop."

"Dana, I don't think it's a sin to leave an abusive husband," I said reasonably. "You need to protect yourself. And if it is karma, it must be for all our sins. Otherwise, why are we here in it with you?"

"You might not be, you know," she said. "There was an old TV show—I think it was *The Twilight Zone.* I remember watching reruns of it when I was a kid. Anyway, the point of it was that you only exist for me because I'm here. If I weren't here, you wouldn't exist—at least for me and in this time and space—at all."

"Then where would I be?" I asked, amused.

She shook her head. "I'm not sure I understand it, really. In a parallel universe, maybe, having a good time?"

"Well, gee, thanks a lot, then," I said.

She grinned. "If I could, I'd *whoosh* you away from this awful place with my thoughts, Sarah. But like I said, I've never been sure how that really works."

After we checked each other out for injuries, we

all began the cleanup, which was almost automatic by now. Gabe had been gone since before dinner, and we all expressed worry about him. We were shaken and tired, but agreed that if he wasn't back by the time we finished the cleanup, we would go looking for him, in case he'd been hurt in the quake.

Kim went outside to check for any exterior damage to the farmhouse and Dana picked up fallen silverware and other odds and ends. When I'd finished my chore—sweeping up shards from any glassware we'd been foolish enough not to nail down the last time we used it—I looked around and noticed that Gabe still hadn't returned.

"This doesn't feel right," Dana said. "I think we should go now and find him."

She was noticeably shaking from exhaustion, however, and, looking around, I saw that Timmy and Amelia were both quite pale. Luke and Grace were outside checking the fuel tank for further damage, on the chance that it could become a fire hazard. They weren't part of the discussion.

"I'll go," I said. "There's no sense in all of us traipsing around the woods in the dark."

"But you can't go alone," Timmy protested in a surprisingly strong voice. "Someone should go with you."

"No, really, it's all right," I argued. "I'm in better shape right now than anyone here."

She continued to look doubtful, saying, "I'm sure Gabe must be fine. After all, everyone's safer outside than inside during a quake. Isn't that right?"

I agreed that this was right for the most part, but said that it hadn't been true for Jane—had it?

Timmy looked away, as if unable to meet my eye. "I just thought it would be best if we were all careful, now," she said in a low voice. "I don't want anything else happening to anyone."

"Well, I don't think anything will happen to me. Do you, Timmy?" I watched her expression carefully.

She shook her head, but still didn't look me in the eye. I thought she looked very old in that moment. Timmy's initial spunk after the first quake had left her; she'd become shrunken in both appearance and spirit. Even the diamonds no longer had their dazzle, and I felt pity for her even as I wondered what she was really thinking.

I left by the front door to avoid Luke and Grace, and took with me a battery-operated lamp and a small flashlight that I stuck in my belt. At the last minute Dana insisted I also take an air horn.

"Just in case," she said, giving my arm a squeeze. Her eyes were red-rimmed and her voice shook.

I didn't fear the quakes so much anymore, but the woods and the dark were something else. I'd had the misfortune of seeing that low-budget movie a few years ago, where the young people are alone in the woods and being chased by—

Well, the whole problem was, I'd seen it alone, in the dark, in my apartment, and at night. I hadn't slept for a week. In fact, that movie left a lasting impression on my nerve centers, and as I made my way along the beach this night, sticking to the outside edge of the forest because of the high tide, I was sure there were all kinds of demons lurking just inches away in the trees.

The memory of my experience in the woods after leaving Luke's cabin the other night was impossible to shake, as well. Skirting the tree line to avoid stepping into the water on the shore, I kept looking over my shoulder to make sure Grace wasn't following me, this time armed with a hatchet. After a while, when no one popped out to hack me to bits or push me over a cliff, I began to calm down.

I had a specific destination in mind—Gabe's cabin. I'd found him there the day before, looking through the damage to see what needed to be done to rebuild. I thought that if he'd been at the cabin when tonight's quake occurred, he might well have been hurt.

As I rounded the bend from where the cabin stood on its low hill, I could see the dim light of a lantern or flashlight through the windows. Stepping up my pace, I began climbing the path to the front porch. This was the path Dana hadn't wanted to take with Jane, when she'd twisted her ankle.

It suddenly occurred to me that I hadn't seen Dana limping since that day, and that her ankle had healed rather quickly. Which was not necessarily a cause for suspicion. In fact, under other circumstances, it would have been cause for celebration.

*You've got to get a grip, Sarah. Keep thinking of everyone here as a possible killer and you'll find yourself totally alone.*

To the side of the rough path, I noted that a tree had fallen, its giant roots sticking up like ancient fingers, as if clawing the air. The roots were coated with mud, and I remembered that the tree had been standing yesterday. Apparently, the quake had dislodged it.

I shivered and hurried on. As I neared the cabin, I called out, "Gabe? Gabe, are you there?"

I knew he had to be, and wondered if he'd heard me. My voice had been soft, forced as it was through tightened lungs, an effect of the nervousness that had rattled me on the shore. I watched the door to see if it would open.

It didn't.

My eyes scanned the windows—two on either side of the door. This was a much larger cabin than Luke's.

I called out again, more softly this time. "Gabe?"

When he still didn't answer, I paused on the bottom step. *He's on his way back to the farmhouse. He just forgot to take the lamp. Maybe after this latest shock, he wasn't thinking.*

But then why hadn't I run into him along the way?

I forced myself to take the three steps onto the porch. But the cold taste of fear was on my tongue, and a chill climbed up my back.

With one hand on the doorknob, I raised the other to knock. Then I stopped, hearing an odd sound inside. It was muffled, like the sob of a woman. Several deep breaths followed, then a groan. The hair on my arms and the back of my neck prickled, and at that moment I could not have moved to save my life.

I heard a man's voice, in harsh tones, saying, "Do what I say. Just do it."

Involuntarily, my hand twisted the knob, and I thrust open the door.

There, on a brass bed in the one-room cabin, were Gabe—and Kim. They were both naked, and neither one had noticed my presence. Kim was on her knees over Gabe, with tears running down her cheeks. He had grasped her head on either side and was pulling her down to him. Her auburn hair made a curtain that brushed his abdomen, and as it did he thrust himself up to her, at the same time pushing up and down in violent strokes. With each stroke he groaned, and Kim let out a strangled sob.

Nausea rose in my throat, and my stomach clenched so hard I nearly doubled over. In the next instant I was on them both, yanking Kim back and yelling, "What the hell do you think you're doing!"

Gabe's eyes had been closed, and when he opened them they were glazed over, as if he was having trouble focusing. Then they cleared, and he saw who I was. Startled, he pushed Kim away and jerked up to a sitting position.

"This wasn't my idea, Sarah! I swear. She came on to me—"

"Shut the hell up!" I said.

Kim remained silent, kneeling on the bed, her face in her hands.

"Kim?" My voice shook so much I could hardly speak.

"Go away, Sarah," she cried. "Please, just go away."

"Are you telling me this is what you want? I don't believe it! Why are you crying?"

"This is none of your business!" she said angrily, raising her tear-filled eyes to meet mine. Her face was flushed and damp with perspiration. "Go back to the farmhouse! Stop butting into things that are none of your business."

I didn't know what about all of this upset me more: seeing Gabe and Kim like this—or Kim's tortured face.

But she was right. It wasn't my business.

I turned on my heel and ran back through the doorway, down the steps and onto the path. In my shock, I had dropped my lantern, and I didn't think about using the flash, but just ran—anywhere, to get away from there.

Somehow I stumbled off the path and into an open area. There was no moon, and I became disoriented. I didn't know if I was heading toward the shore or deeper into the woods.

My boot struck something, and I tripped. Hurtling face downward I thought I'd never stop. It was as if I were falling into a pit. My hands went out and grasped something long and hard—yet not hard. My fingers scurried over it to see what it was, and it felt like flesh. Like skin, but rigid underneath.

There was hair. And a terrible, sickening stench.

*A carcass. The carcass of a dead animal. Oh, God.*

I pulled my flashlight from my belt and flicked it on. Shining it toward the thing, I nearly fainted when I saw a foot. Then a leg. My flash followed the carcass up until it hit upon a face. A woman's face, covered with dirt and worms. A bare wisp of blond hair showed through.

Oh, God, no. Oh, God, *please,* no!

I rubbed the dirt away, hoping I was wrong. It couldn't be who I thought it was, there was no way—

But I wasn't wrong. It was Angel—J.P. Blakely, my friend and PI.

I began to scream. Somehow I remembered the air horn. I scrambled around for it, found it and pressed the button. The horn blasted through the woods, a demon shriek. The sound was so fierce, it might have burst my eardrums.

But I couldn't tell if it had. I was screaming too hard.

# 16

Neither Gabe nor Kim came in answer to my call for help. Luke, Grace, Dana and Amelia reached me first, pulling me out; my limbs were so weak, I was unable to climb out alone. Timmy trailed behind, clutching her chest.

"Who is she?" Luke said tensely, flashing a light onto Angel's face as he jumped down into the grave. "Who the hell is she?"

"I've never seen her before," Dana answered, covering her mouth and nose against the rising stench.

"She wasn't part of our group," Amelia said.

Timmy stared into the grave, a horrified expression on her face. Words tumbled from her mouth, so low we couldn't hear them. Once, she gagged.

They had brought flashlights, and we'd set them around the makeshift grave. They did not shine down enough, but they did illuminate our faces, which were white and strained.

"I knew her," I managed to say through chattering teeth.

Luke looked up at me. "You knew this woman?"

"She was a PI. I hired her to help me...with my court case."

He shook his head as if confused. "I don't understand. What the hell is she doing here?"

"I have no idea. The last I heard from Angel—" My voice caught. "It was several weeks ago."

"That's her name? Angel?"

"J.P. Blakely, but everyone called her Angel." Despite my efforts not to, I began to cry. My remorse and grief were overwhelming. If she hadn't been working for me...

"Why would anyone have done this to her?" Grace demanded.

I could only shake my head.

Dana put an arm around me. "I'm so sorry," she whispered. Flinging her other arm out, she looked to the sky and cried, "God! What next?"

Timmy began to whimper. "I never meant for anything like this..." Her words trailed off.

We all turned to stare at her.

"What did you never mean?" Grace asked sharply.

"I..." Timmy looked dazed. "I don't know. What did I say?"

Amelia drew her close and patted her shoulder. "She just means that she never meant for anything like this to happen when she invited you all here. She thought it would be a wonderful month for you."

Luke climbed out of the grave. "It looks like she was struck on the head by something. I'm not an expert at these things, but I'd say she hasn't been here very long. Days, maybe."

"But she couldn't have gotten to the island after the quake," I said.

"No. I think she must already have been here."

Luke swept his flashlight around the grave. "This hole is really shallow. And you see that steamer trunk? She's still half in it, and it looks to me like somebody put her in it, then covered it over with dirt. This last quake must have dislodged everything."

"Which could explain why we never saw it before," Dana said, looking up at Gabe's cabin through the trees. "It's funny Gabe never saw anything going on here, though."

"That reminds me. Where is he?" Luke said.

"And Kim?" Dana added. "Did you find them, Sarah?"

I couldn't answer.

"You came out here looking for Gabe, didn't you?" Luke said to me.

I nodded.

"Was he here?"

Again, I was mute. All my thoughts were of Angel. I wondered what she'd been doing here, and how long she'd been here. Since the time she sent back the *Allegra* case and had gone "away"? Since even before I'd come to Thornberry?

And if so, why?

What lead could possibly have brought her here?

And who had murdered and buried her here?

A feeling of enormous loss swept over me. Not only had Angel been a friend for years, but someone I'd counted on to help me out of this mess with the Seattle Five. There was really no one else I'd turned to after my arrest. Angel had been my only confidante. Now she was gone—and it was all because of me.

"Sarah?" I heard Luke say.

I looked away from Angel's face, to him.

"I asked you a question," he said. "Did you find Gabe here? And have you seen anything of Kim?"

I'd have given up Gabe in a second. But not Kim. It wasn't passion I'd seen on her face, but fear. And pain.

Until I knew what that was about, I couldn't tell them about her.

"No," I lied. "I just found this—"

I looked away from Angel, and walked toward the tree line, no longer able to bear the sight of her in that monstrous pit.

Several minutes later, I was surprised to find that only Luke remained. The others were gone.

"They went to look for Kim and Gabe," Luke explained. "I told them I'd wait here with you, and that we should go back to staying in pairs, especially after..." His voice trailed off. "Hopefully they'll find Kim and Gabe together. Back at the farmhouse, maybe."

Not likely, I thought. And in cold, hard point of fact, I was worried sick about Kim. I hoped that wherever she was, she was not with Gabe.

# 17

"So, what the hell happened here?" Luke asked me, after a moment.

"I told you, I don't know. I didn't even know Angel was here."

"Not that. What were you doing out here in the woods? Timmy said you were checking out Gabe's cabin."

"I did."

"Then, I repeat—what were you doing out here? This was the wrong direction to go in if you were heading back to Thornberry."

"I don't want to talk about it!" I snapped. "Not right now. For God's sake, Luke, Angel was my friend. I still can't even believe that's her down there."

"Well, then, let's think about it. Maybe she came here because she wanted to talk to you?"

"No. She could have called me. At least, before the quake."

"Maybe what she had to say to you was too important to say over the phone."

"I guess that's possible. If her own phone was tapped, maybe, or—"

"Or what?"

"If she suspected the Thornberry phone might be tapped."

I looked at Luke. Why should I figure this out with him? Why should I trust him any more now than I had before all this happened?

*Because you saw Gabe that way with Kim. And you can't trust him, now. You can't even trust what he told you about Luke.*

The whole world was at a tilt. Angel was lying in a cold, damp grave on Esme Island, and I didn't know where to turn next. Or who it was safe to turn to. I wanted to exonerate myself from the guilt I felt over her death, but couldn't.

"I need to get her buried," I said. "I don't want her there in the open, like...like Jane."

With that, I couldn't help it. I burst into tears.

Luke said, "Oh, God, Sarah," and put his arms around me. "I'm so sorry." He held me until I regained some control, then patted my shoulders and wiped my tears away with his thumb.

"C'mon, let's get started," he said. "It won't take long."

Kneeling, we shoveled the loose dirt back onto Angel with our bare hands. This, I believe, is the moment when I lost all hope. Tears streamed down my cheeks, and though I tried to murmur prayers, I no longer believed they would be answered. There was an evil on this island, a madman—or woman—walking amongst us, and nothing made sense anymore.

Halfway through, I sat back on my heels and faced Luke. "Did you do this?" I asked, my voice harsh and unnatural, my hands hanging loosely at my sides.

"If you did, you have to tell me. Just *tell* me, for God's sake! Don't leave me wondering. And if I'm next, get it over with. You can bury me right here, bury me with Angel—"

Tears filled my eyes again, and I let them run down my face unchecked. There had been too much. Too many deaths, too many quakes and aftershocks—so many that all the shocks, both physical and emotional, seemed to blend together now.

Luke's eyes met mine, and I did my best to see if he lied, but found nothing but sympathy there.

"I swear to you, Sarah, I did not kill your friend. And I didn't kill Jane. I don't know how to make you believe that."

"Well, I do," I said angrily. "Tell me what you and Grace have been up to. If you won't tell me, how can I believe anything you say? Look, I know you're here because of me. That's obvious. All those questions about what evidence I've got against the Five, the fact that your father is involved—"

I stopped myself midsentence, wondering belatedly if I'd said too much.

Luke sighed. "Okay, Sarah. You've figured us out. And you're absolutely right. My father did send us here. Further, I wish to hell it didn't, but the truth is—this has everything to do with you."

"We thought we were protecting you," he said as we sat on the ground over Angel's grave—he on one side, I on the other. "I'm sorry, Sarah. We thought we were doing the right thing."

"You and your father. And Grace. You were all

doing the right thing. For me.'' If there was skepticism in my tone, it was nearly overwhelmed with exhaustion. I no longer had the energy to do much except listen, and it was a measure of the state I was in that I didn't care what happened at that point.

Angel was dead. One of the best friends I'd ever had was dead.

The many times I hadn't made the effort to see her or talk with her ran through my head. The Friday night she'd called me a few months ago, and pleaded with me to make the rounds of a few bars with her. She was lonely, she said, and hoping to meet a man. ''It's this damn work of mine, Sarah. It doesn't leave me any time to do all those things they tell single women to do. Like join a church, you know? Anyway, who'd want *me* in their church?''

She was wrong about that. Oh, Angel was unconventional. She liked to drink at the end of a job, and she was tough and gritty beneath that blond, blue-eyed exterior. In appropriate moments she would cuss, raise hell and, in general, let everyone within hearing know she was around. But her heart was good, and everyone who took the time to know her, loved her. They'd have been happy to have Angel in their church.

The problem was Angel herself. She would never have been happy with the kind of man she might meet in a church, and she knew it. Her thought processes would simply never work the same way as his.

So I could have been more of a friend. I could have gone with her that night. But I didn't like bars—I saw them as dead ends where meeting men was concerned. Not only that, but it was dangerous to leave a bar with a man these days.

_Oh, Sarah. It was more than that. Admit it._

So, okay. The truth is, I was too involved with Ian at the time. And Ian didn't like me having friends. He wanted me all to himself.

I was reminded of a book by Merle Shain. She wrote that she would never give up her friends again for a man, and the next time she married she'd take her friends along with her as a dowry.

_Why didn't I give Angel more time? I hired her, I took the best efforts she had to offer. She was always there, ready to help. Where was I?_

I knew Luke was talking to me but I had trouble connecting. Finally his words began to filter through.

"...This thing is much larger than my father, me or Grace," he was saying. "Sarah, we've reached a point in this country where something has to be done. Everywhere you look, there's so much rage. Road rage, on-the-job rage, people going into a rage over standing in line—whether it's the Department of Motor Vehicles, the supermarket, the banks or college registration lines. People in the cities, at least a lot I've known, have come to dread going out to run errands. They know there will be lines and traffic everywhere, and they won't be home for hours. Not only that, but you can't get through to real people on the phone. You have to punch numbers for this, numbers for that. God, Sarah, I've experienced that kind of anger myself. I nearly broke my phone once, throwing it across the room."

"What does this have to do with anything?" I said,

not really caring except to wonder, *Why are you telling me this? What are you trying to convince me of?*

"I'm just saying that in a world where there are violent athletes, violent entertainers and violent rock musicians—in a world where people are hitting other people on the streets for no reason at all and children are shooting each other in schools—it's just not surprising that there are cops who aren't much different. There was a show on *60 Minutes* that said forty percent of all police officers are guilty of violence in their own homes. Part of the problem is that applicants aren't always screened well enough, especially when there's a push to beef up a department with more men. Remember what happened when the World Trade Organization met in Seattle? All hell broke loose."

He reached down to pick up a small rock, absently brushing wet mud from it as we talked. "Don't get me wrong, there are plenty of police who are not violent at home or on the street. Most of them live good lives. But the rest have been worming their way into the departments, and they're the ones who are scary. They're the ones we have to try to stop."

He looked at me. "Sarah, the bad ones, no matter where they are, come out of the same milieu as the Seattle Five. They're hired to stop crime, and they decide for themselves that it's not important *how* they stop it. They make up evidence that wasn't there, and they cover up evidence that was there. The thing is, the city leaders want the streets cleaned up, and in some cases the cops are given silent authority to do that, in whatever way they can."

"I wasn't a criminal," I said angrily. "They had no right to plant those drugs in my house."

"You think I don't know that? It's because of you, and people like you, Sarah, that my father's trying to do something about it. He and the FBI have been working together to root out problem cops for several months now. So when you were set up—and he never for a minute believed you hadn't been set up—it was only natural he'd want to help you."

This was beginning to sound all too familiar. Wasn't it basically the same story line Gabe had fed me?

Except that in his version, he and Ian had been the white hats, and Luke, his father and Grace were on the black hat side.

"I seem to remember your father being tough on crime," I said. "Seems to me he'd be on the cops' side, Luke—not mine."

"Not when those cops are committing crimes," he argued.

"And as a matter of fact," I went on, "Gabe told me *he* was working against the Five. He said he was a Seattle cop and that *he* was sent here to protect me. He also told me that you and your father were on the criminal side."

Luke shook his head. "And why doesn't that surprise me? Don't you see, Sarah? Gabe must be one of *them*. He's stuck closely enough to the truth to be convincing, but the fact is, if he was who he said he was, I'd know about it. My father would have told me. Sarah, Gabe must be tied in with the Seattle Five somehow, and I'm willing to bet that from the moment he showed up at Thornberry, he's been out to get his hands on your evidence against them.''

I almost laughed. ''And you, Luke? You haven't been doing the same?''

''Dammit, it's different with me! My father was certain the Five set you up, and he wasted no time asking me to fly out here to help.''

''You and Grace, you mean.''

''Yes, me and Grace. But not Grace, at first. He asked me to come keep an eye on you, but I couldn't come right away. I was in the Bahamas wrapping up that job I told you about. If I had known you were in this much danger, I would have left, anyway, but at the time I didn't know it was this serious.''

He sighed. ''All right, look. I'll tell you the whole thing. Grace and I knew each other in New York. We…dated, but only for a while. She and her brother were both on the NYPD, and one night a few months ago Grace's brother was out on patrol with another cop. The other cop shot a black man in Harlem, claiming he thought the guy was pulling a gun. When the victim turned out to be unarmed, the cop planted a gun on him to make it look like self-defense.''

''I think I remember that.''

''You probably heard of something similar on the news. But, Sarah, these things happen more than the public is aware of. Not all of them make the news. In this case, Grace's brother knew the other cop had lied. In fact, he'd tried to stop him but couldn't. Ramon—Grace's brother—finally threatened to testify against the guy if he didn't turn himself in, and the next day Ramon was murdered. It was made to look like a street shooting, and Grace couldn't prove Ramon's partner had murdered either him or the Harlem victim. But Ramon had told her the way the Harlem shooting had gone down, and she believed him. She kept digging around, trying to prove her brother's innocence, and the rest of the department started harassing her for it. Eventually, when she was unsuccessful at proving anything, she quit out of disgust.''

''Well, if that's true, I feel bad for her. But it doesn't explain why she's here.''

''She's here because my father asked her to come. My father had met Grace in New York, back when we were still dating. They had numerous conversations about the NYPD and what had happened to her brother. He knew she had quit the force and needed money. He also thought it would be helpful to have someone near you that nobody knew. Someone he could trust to help look after you. When Grace heard about what had happened to you, she was more than ready. It was too much like what had happened to her brother. She couldn't turn him down.''

''Funny, I haven't exactly seen Grace Lopez as being my guardian angel.''

''Yeah, well, it's true Grace has been mean as hell lately. But trust me, she's only been that way since she lost her brother. Also, it was part of her cover here to not act too friendly with anyone.''

''Well, I must say, she certainly succeeded at that. But how did your father get Timmy to go along with this?''

''My father's very wealthy, as you know. He's always liked Timmy and respected what she's been try-

ing to do here. In fact, when he learned recently that
finances were getting thin for her, he gave her enough
to keep things going. He's never asked for anything
in return, until this past month. He told her you were
in danger, and explained that Grace was an undercover policewoman he wanted her to invite here, to
keep an eye on you and ensure your safety. Timmy
wasn't crazy about the idea. She had to cancel an
invitation to a writer she was looking forward to
meeting—but she felt obligated to go along with it.''

No wonder Timmy had been so irritable. I couldn't
imagine her letting someone else tell her who should
stay, or not stay, at her beloved retreat. She must have
severely regretted her decision to invite me, and the
trouble I had brought along.

"So you and Grace came here to *protect* me," I
said.

"That's right."

"You, your father, and a former New York City
policewoman—who also happens to be your very
young ex-girlfriend—all came here to help little old
me."

"Yes. And it's true she was my girlfriend, but that
was over a long time ago." Luke shifted uneasily.
"After her brother was killed, she didn't have any
interest in romance."

"She dumped you?"

"It...was mutual," he said. "I travel a lot. I
couldn't give her the support she needed—not that
she asked for it. Truth is, although I consider our relationship a thing of the past, I'm hoping it will help
her come to terms with her brother's death, her help-

ing us put the Seattle Five behind bars. In any event, she's highly motivated to see this through. Grace might not be the most cordial person in the world right now, but she's probably the best friend you have.'' He met my eyes. ''Other than me, that is.''

''Well, that's a fine story, Luke. It all fits together nicely. But—out with the rest of it.''

He sighed and threw up his hands. ''Why do I keep forgetting I'm dealing with a lawyer? Okay, look, my father wasn't making much progress in Seattle until the Seattle Five went after you. When that happened, he saw that he could use your trouble to throw a net around them.''

''So the truth is, he's been using me. You, too.''

''If you want to look at it that way. Personally, I thought we were helping you.''

''I'd have been okay on my own,'' I said, though I frankly doubted that. Something in me just had to say it. I didn't much like things going on behind my back, even if people were well-meaning.

''You might have been okay on your own,'' Luke said. ''But the truth is, I wanted to help you.''

''Why?'' I asked, standing.

''Can't you guess?''

''No, I can't.''

He stood, too, and we both brushed our hands off on our pants.

''Sarah,'' he said irritably, ''you are an obstinate wench. You always were.''

''I am not a wench.''

''Sure you are, and what's more, you used to be *my* wench.''

"Yeah, well, I used to not have any molars, either. We all grow up, Luke."

"I really do care about you, though," he said.

"You do, huh?"

He gripped my shoulders. "You don't believe me? Even now?"

The truth was, I did believe him. After all that had happened, he was the only person on Esme Island I did believe. And I wanted it back—that feeling from the old days, when he and I were the only people in the world, when we were all that mattered.

There was still a missing link somewhere, though.

"There are a few things that don't fit," I said. "How did your father know I had some sort of evidence I was holding over the Five's heads?"

Gabe had told me Mike Murty reported my threats to Judge Ford. Orders went out from Luke's father, Gabe had said, to get that evidence—at any cost.

"My father had Mike Murty's phone tapped," Luke said, "long before Lonnie Mae Brown's rape. He'd suspected the Five of other crimes, but hadn't been able to get anything solid on them. Unfortunately, they were careful enough not to say anything incriminating on their home phones—until the night you called Mike Murty, that is."

"So he heard me threaten Murty with a piece of evidence, and sent you here looking for it? To do what with it, Luke?"

"To keep someone like Gabe Rossi from getting his hands on it, in the first place. And then to bring it, and you, back to Seattle safely, so it could be used in court against them."

"Why didn't you just tell me why you were here, then?"

"Well...we were afraid you'd tell the wrong person."

"Meaning Gabe?"

"And anyone he might be in contact with."

I fell silent, thinking. At last I said, "Do you know who Gabe really is?"

"We think he could be some sort of corrupt cop hired by the Five. Or maybe he's just a criminal they have something on and he's doing this to keep out of jail. It could be anything. I asked my father to check him out, but he hasn't come up with anything yet."

"Your father would know, though, if he really was Ian MacDonald's partner?"

"Your former lover's partner?" Luke softened it with a smile.

"Whatever." Luke and his father certainly had been delving into my life.

"Well, no one's found a connection yet between Gabe and MacDonald. If he told you he was Ian MacDonald's partner, he probably lied."

"One more question, then. Why were you so reluctant to let me call back my mother?"

He shook his head. "There are some things you've just got to trust me on."

"Like hell, I will. What's going on with my mother? Is she involved in this mess somehow?"

"Not really. That is—" He broke off. "She wasn't."

"But she is now?"

"Look—"

I grabbed him by the front of his jacket. "If you and your father have gotten my mom into trouble somehow, I swear to God, Luke, I'll kill you both!"

"She's not in trouble," he said, grabbing my wrists. "Not now."

"But she was? Tell me, or I swear—"

"All right, dammit! Yes, she was in trouble—for a while. After you called Mike Murty that night, he and his friends paid a little visit to your mother. They threatened her life if she didn't get you to back off. She was supposed to tell you that, so you'd drop the case against them."

I was aghast. "But she never said a word!"

"I know. She talked to my father, instead."

"She talked to your father—instead of me?"

"Sarah, I told you how close they'd been when they were young. Your mother didn't want to trouble you with the Five's threats because she thought you had enough to worry about. So she talked to my dad."

"And then what?"

"Then he had her whisked off to Florida in the middle of the night. He put both her and your aunt— so your mom would have company—in a safe house in Tampa, far away from Miami. That's where they are now."

"Not in Bermuda? In *Tampa?*" I pulled away from Luke and rubbed my temple. "Why the hell didn't you tell me that? Never mind, I know. You didn't trust me with the truth because I might have told Gabe. My God."

I couldn't believe this had happened to my mother,

and that she hadn't even told me. She'd turned to someone else, instead.

"I know what you're thinking," Luke said gently. "But she loved you too much to come to you. You'd already been arrested and you'd lost your job. How could she lay that burden on you? She's your mother, Sarah."

A mother I'd been thinking I hardly knew. And I guess that was true, because I never in a million years dreamed she would do something like that to protect me.

But could I trust that she was all right, even now? That would mean trusting Luke—and his father. Not just with a story this time, but with my mother's life.

I had to get off the fence.

"I want to talk to my mother," I said. "Now."

Luke tried to argue the low remaining juice in the cell phone's batteries again, but I wouldn't hear it.

"No more putting me off," I said firmly. "You want that evidence? Hell, I'll give it to you. It's all yours, Luke. After you let me talk to my mom."


When we came to the middle, cross-island path, we veered off in the direction of Ransford and Luke's cabin. I have to admit I felt a certain amount of fear, walking by his side through the dark forest. If I'd been wrong yet again about a man—if Luke had in fact been lying to me—he could have killed me right then and there. But he didn't, and when we came to the cabin he took a key from the pocket of his jeans and opened the padlock. Inside, he closed the door and locked it again before lighting the candle.

He had hidden the cell phone this time, and pulled it out from under a loose floorboard under the cot by the wall.

"If anybody managed to get in here," he explained, "I didn't want them to find it."

I didn't tell him Gabe knew about the cabin, and the phone. First I'd call my mother.

He trusted me to dial the number myself, standing beside me and feeding it to me as I punched it in. This reassured me somewhat, but I socked that number away in my memory banks for future use, just in case.

A man's voice answered. I held the phone out a bit so Luke could hear, and gave him a questioning look.

"FBI," he said in an undertone. "He's guarding them. Tell him who you are."

"I...this is Sarah Lansing," I said. "I want to talk to my mom."

He asked me for a code name. Again, I looked at Luke.

"Tell him, 'Bluebird.'"

"Bluebird," I said, feeling a bit foolish.

"One moment," he answered.

My mother came to the phone immediately. "Sarah? Oh, honey, it's so good to hear your voice! I've been worried about you."

"Mom, are you all right?"

"Yes, I'm fine. Is everything all right there?"

"Yes," I said, "it's fine. Are you sure you're okay?"

"Honey, I haven't been better. Randell found us this wonderful little house, right on the bay. And we've got the nicest FBI men staying with us. Two of them, and they watch the house like hawks. I...oh—'' she said uncertainly, "I suppose you must know by now what happened."

"Someone threatened you, right, Mom?"

"Yes, dear. I'm sorry, I didn't want you to know. Who told you?"

"Luke," I said. "He told me you didn't want to burden me with it. I wish you hadn't felt that way, Mom. I'd have taken care of you."

But as much as I might have wanted to, could I have? I frankly doubted it. If they'd gotten to Angel, they could just as easily have gotten to Mom.

"Well, you don't have to worry about me, dear. I'm here with your aunt Rinna, and we're safe as two peas in a pod."

I smiled. "Isn't it 'close' as two peas in a pod?"

"That, too." She laughed.

My mom had always gotten her sayings a bit twisted. It reassured me to hear her do this now.

"And what about you, dear? And Luke?"

"I told you, we're fine."

"I'm sure you are," she said, "but that isn't what I meant. You are on Esme Island together. Have you finally found the man of your dreams?"

I smiled. "Look, if you're sure you're all right, Mom, I'm signing off now."

"So you're not going to answer that one," she said. "Well, take care, then. Sarah...I'll be so glad when all this is over with. I really do worry about you. But I know if Luke is with you, you'll be just fine. Randell says Luke would never let anything happen to you.''

I hung up and looked at the man in question. "She sounds okay. Actually, she sounds pretty good."

"So do you believe me now?"

"I...yes. I believe you now. Unfortunately, there's just one problem. *You* shouldn't have believed *me*."

He frowned. "What does that mean?"

"Luke, I'm sorry, but I lied. About giving you the evidence, that is. I don't know where it is."

His face cleared, and he smiled. "Oh, that. Not to worry. I've already got it."

He knelt and pried up another floorboard, sticking in a hand, then holding up the *Allegra* case. "I found this on the path the other day, when you sent Grace and me on that wild-goose chase looking for Jane's locket."

My eyes widened. "You had this all the time? And you never told me?"

He stood and faced me. "I was going to, but like I said, you seemed to be getting pretty close to Gabe. I was already suspicious of him, and I was afraid that if he convinced you to trust him you might tell him where this was."

"For God's sake, Luke! And you? What exactly did you plan to do with it?"

He grinned. "I planned, my suspicious little wench, to give it to you—when the moment was right."

He put the *Allegra* case in my hands. "I guess that would be now," he said.

# *18*

We got back to Thornberry an hour or so later, and Kim had returned. She was mute, huddled by the stove in a blanket as if trying to get warm. Salt streaked her face from tears that had dried there. Timmy and Amelia sat at the table, talking softly and looking worried. Grace sat silently across from them, watching Kim.

Luke went to join Grace, speaking in a soft voice that didn't carry.

"I'm really worried about Kim," Dana said in an aside to me. "She won't even look at us. I don't know what happened to her."

"I think I do," I said.

I went over to Kim and said gently, "Come outside with me. Let's talk."

She didn't move or respond.

I tugged lightly at her arm. "Kim? We have to talk about this. I'm going after Gabe. I'll get him for you—and I'll get him for me, too."

She stirred. Turning her pale face to me, she said in a voice just above a whisper, "Can you do that?"

"Yes," I said. "I can, and I will."

If Gabe was working with the Five, that meant he was responsible for the threat on my mother's life. I was just as sure, now, that he was responsible for Angel's death, too, and for attacking me at my cottage.

With my help, Kim managed to get to her feet. It was as if she'd become old and arthritic, or as if her spirit had flown so far away, it was no longer there to help her move.

Outside, I built up the fire from coals that still burned from dinner. After heating water in a pot, I fixed us each a cup of hot tea.

"Here, drink this—" I said, pulling her blanket around her. Her teeth were chattering, her lips blue, as if she were chilled clear through. We both sat on tree stumps, close to the fire.

Kim wrapped her hands around the heavy mug, one of the few that had survived the quakes. Holding it to her lips, she didn't drink. Instead, she seemed to be letting the rising steam warm her.

I sipped from my own mug, then said, "You didn't look all that happy back there in the cabin. What happened?"

Tears filled her eyes, and she wiped them away. "What the hell," she said, her voice coming out between rough, indrawn sobs. "He's going to tell everyone, anyway."

"Tell them what?" I urged. "Kim, we may not have much time."

"About my past." She flicked a glance at me. "Oh, it's not all that new a story. Struggling young actress, broke, making porn movies out in the Valley to pay the rent. You know how many of us there were at the time? I could name you names—all working actors now in the legitimate sector. But I wouldn't. We all know how that could damage our careers now.''

"But, Kim, you're right, it's not a new story. Look at Marilyn Monroe with the nude calendar photos— pretty shocking back in those days. That didn't hurt *her* career.''

She laughed, a bitter, caustic sound. "We're not talking nude calendars here, Sarah. We're talking hard-core porn. With men, with women, with…'' She gave a shudder. "With animals. God, I can't believe some of the things I did.''

I couldn't help it. A sound of shock escaped my lips. *America's new Sweetheart?* With a past like that? She was right. Even in a so-called enlightened age, something like this could destroy her career.

"What about denying it?'' I said, though without much hope.

"He knows too much,'' she said, confirming my worst fears. "I guess he's got contacts on the LAPD. Sarah, some of those videos can still be found, if you know where to look. He wouldn't even have to have the tapes—he could just tell the tabloids the names of them and anyone could dig them up. Not only that, he's going to put stills from them on the Internet. That's what he said. Unless—''

"Unless what?''

"Unless I help him get something he wants from you,'' Kim said softly, not meeting my eyes.

"Ahh.'' The pieces were coming together.

She ran her fingers through her hair, and as the blanket slipped from her shoulders, I saw bruises on her pale skin: an imprint of Gabe's hands. My anger rose.

"God, Sarah," she said, "he seemed so nice at first. There aren't a lot of guys like that left. Most of them are into their own careers, and they run from any kind of commitment—"

She broke off and, following my gaze, pulled the blanket up around her again.

"I don't mean to make excuses. There are some good men left, I guess. Maybe they're just intimidated by me. Anyway, I really liked Gabe at first. He just seemed so attentive, so helpful...kind of sweet, you know?"

I nodded. "Yes. We all thought that, Kim."

"Well, then he made me start doing...things to him. He said that was part of the deal. Either I serviced him, gave him everything he wanted, just the way he wanted it—*and* got this thing from you—or he'd tell the world about those tapes."

"Did he tell you what this 'thing' was?" I asked.

"He was going to, I think. But then you walked in on us tonight."

"Kim, do you know where Gabe is? Did the two of you leave the cabin together?"

"No. Right after you left, we heard an air horn, and Gabe figured you were calling for everybody to come out to the cabin, that you were going to tell them what you'd seen. Whatever, he took off. You know what he said? 'Cheerio, little darlin'. Don't think it hasn't been fun.'" She grimaced. "I ran, too, but I didn't go the same way he did. I was trying to get away from him."

"Well, you don't have to worry about him anymore," I said, squeezing her hand. "The thing he wanted you to get from me is in a safe place, and there's no way I'm telling anyone where it is. If he comes back, I'll make sure he knows that."

Her eyes widened. "Sarah, you can't do that! You don't know what else he did!"

"What are you talking about?"

"He said...he said he killed some woman because she wouldn't tell him where this thing was. He said he killed her right on this island. I think he must have meant Jane."

I wanted to cry. Not Jane—though he might have killed her, too. It was Angel he'd murdered because she wouldn't tell him where the *Allegra* case was. Angel, who had been loyal to the end.

I leaned forward and rested my head on my bent knees, closing my eyes. I would get Gabe, if it was the last thing I did. And I wouldn't leave it up to the law to punish him. I knew all too well how that worked, in these days of "not enough evidence." Even if he were charged and convicted, there was always that blasted court of appeals.

No...I would settle things with Gabe myself. Scum like that shouldn't be allowed to live.

I didn't realize I'd said it aloud, until Kim said, "I want to help. Whatever you do, I want to help get him, Sarah."

I looked up.

"Me, too," Dana said from behind us. "That filthy son of a bitch."

We turned in surprise.

"Oh, I didn't fall for him or anything like that," Dana said. "But I liked him. What's not to like with somebody that friendly and charming? So one day I told him about my plan—how I was leaving my husband and meeting another man in Vancouver. He asked me all kinds of questions about this other man, and, foolish me, I told him *everything*. What a blabbermouth I've gotten to be. Anyway, he said if I didn't help him get something from you, Sarah, he'd tell my husband where to find us when he got back to the mainland."

"What did you say?" Kim asked.

Dana's chin went up. "I told him to go to hell. I told him my friend and I would be out of the country by then, and Gabe himself would never find us. What's more, I told him if he ever talked to my husband, I'd turn him in to the authorities. I didn't know what he wanted from you, Sarah. But I knew it couldn't be good. I told him to leave you alone, too."

Both women looked at me, a question in their eyes.

"He did leave me alone," I said. "At least, he didn't try to force me into telling him anything. Instead, he tried to seduce me into it."

"That man deserves a dose of his own medicine," Grace said angrily. Only then did we realize she'd come up and was standing several feet beyond the fire's light.

"He needs to feel absolutely vulnerable," she said. "Helpless. Without power. Actually, what he really needs is to die."

I met her angry gaze, and thought about the brother she had lost. I thought about Angel, her life cut short, and my mother, who should never have had to endure the fear she must be feeling now. I thought of Lonnie Mae, who had trusted me to keep her safe, and of Jane—poor Jane—who hadn't lived long enough to see her children again.

"What do you have in mind?" I said.

"I'm not sure yet," Grace answered. "But we're not letting him go. And we're not just turning him over to the law, either. Not yet."

"I agree," I said, standing. It felt good in that moment, having her support my own anger.

Dana stood next to me, and then Kim. We all linked hands around the fire, gazing into the flames as if casting a witch's curse. I don't honestly know what the others were thinking—but for me, it was all about revenge.

After a few moments we squatted by the fire and, putting our heads together, came up with a plan.

It was a hideous plan—one that could only have come out of minds that had been pushed too far and endured too much. But we all agreed to it. We wouldn't really kill him, we told ourselves, much as we might want to. We only wanted to scare him. Teach him a lesson.

The problem was that none of us fully understood our own motives. Or our rage. And that's how it happened...our descent into hell.

# 19

None of us slept much that night. I could hear the others tossing and turning, just as I was. Once, I heard Kim cry out. A soft cry, but to me it seemed there was a world of pain in it.

We left the farmhouse early in the morning, each of us carrying a backpack. Luke was at his cabin using the cell phone to talk to his father. He had told me the night before that our rescue was imminent, and would come about in the next forty-eight hours.

We didn't tell him about our plan. Nor did we tell Timmy and Amelia. They thought we were heading out in search of more wood to build a bonfire, in case a plane or helicopter flew overhead.

Gathering firewood was the perfect excuse for us all to leave together that early in the day. We thought we knew where Gabe might have gone the night before—to the other cabin, the one that stood vacant down the shore from his. He would want a roof over his head, we reasoned, in case of a storm. If, as we suspected, he had killed Angel and knew that we had found her, he might hide out in that cabin overnight. It was nearly a mile from his, more isolated, and a couple of miles from Thornberry. If we got there early enough, we might catch him there before he moved on.

One thing we were certain of—he would not return to Thornberry. Not after I'd walked in on his little rendezvous with Kim.

Dana, Grace and Kim stood at a distance from the cabin, hidden by trees, while I went to the door. If Gabe was there, I was certain I could lure him away, I had told them.

After they saw me enter, they were supposed to go to a spot in the woods we had agreed upon beforehand, a small clearing by the Ghost Tree. Luke and I had hidden the *Allegra* case with the stockings in it the night before, in the hollow of the tree. It would be a perfect spot for our plan.

I knocked, waited, and knocked again. My muscles tensed. What if this did not go the way we all hoped it would?

What if he wasn't there?

After a full minute, the door opened a crack. I felt my breath release. But only a bit. Then the door opened wider, allowing me in.

"Sarah!" Gabe exclaimed, as I entered the small room. "I've been hoping to see you. I wanted to explain about yesterday." His smile was as engaging as ever.

"Drop it, Gabe," I said tiredly. "I know you're not who you say you are."

He looked startled. "What do you mean—"

"Look, let me cut to the chase. I've talked to Kim, and to Dana, too. If you want to keep playing this game, then fine. I'll leave. I just came here to give you what you've been looking for." I threw up my hands. "But if you don't want it..."

I turned toward the door.

"Wait a minute," he said.

I glanced back at him and saw the look of indecision on his face, the need to trust but the inability to do so. It felt good.

He rubbed his chin. "Are you talking about your evidence against the Seattle Five?"

I nodded.

"Why would you want to give it to me now?" he asked suspiciously.

I let my shoulders sag suddenly, and looked at the floor. After a few moments, I said softly, "Because I can't take this anymore. And because I don't want anyone else getting hurt over the mess I've gotten myself into."

I looked up at him then, my eyes pleading. "Please, Gabe. It's got to stop. People have to stop getting hurt. It's not worth it. You can do whatever you want with me. Just leave everyone else alone."

I was certain Kim would have been proud of my performance. In truth, it wasn't that difficult to act out such despair—I had felt just that way, as if I didn't care anymore, after finding J.P. dead. All I had to do was say it out loud.

Gabe appeared to be studying me, weighing what I'd said.

Finally, he held out his hand. "Okay. Let's have it."

I hesitated. "If I give it to you, you won't have any reason to hurt anyone else, right?"

He shrugged. "No reason at all."

I spoke in a hopeful tone. "You'll leave them alone? Even Kim?"

He laughed. "Lady, I couldn't care less about that bimbo. She was just a tool, and not a very good one at that. Soon as I get what I want, I'm making a call from your boyfriend's cell phone and I'm out of here. Nobody will ever hear from me again.''

I nodded and gestured toward the door. "It's outside, then. I've hidden it in a tree. I'll take you to it."

The triumph in his eyes was clear. "It's your show, Sarah. Lead the way."

We walked out of the cabin and down the path to the Ghost Tree.

When we arrived there, I reached into the hollow, pulled out the *Allegra* case and handed it to Gabe.

"Just tell me one thing," I said. "Who are you working for, Gabe? It's pretty obvious you aren't some cop with the Seattle PD that Ian sent to protect me."

Ignoring my question, he opened the case and inspected what was inside. Smiling, he pulled out the bag with the stockings, holding it up to the light. "Sperm? You were going to match DNA?"

I nodded.

"My, my. I thought it must be something like that. And you're wrong about one thing—I am a cop with the Seattle PD. At least, I was. After I get this in the right hands, I may have to leave the area. Lie low for a while."

"You are a cop? Then you're working for the Seattle Five?"

"The Five?" His laugh was scornful. "You think just because there were five cops on that particular shift, that's all there are?"

He put the stockings back into the case, then looked up at me. "Well, that's it, then. You realize, of course, that I can't just leave here with you alive."

"Well, I guess that remains to be seen," I said, folding my arms.

He laughed. "I've got to hand it to you, you've got spunk. But you know, you got off easy. That day when I knocked you out at your cottage? I was planning to take you over and show you Angel's grave. I figured maybe I could break you that way."

The blood rushed to my head when Angel's name slipped so easily off his tongue. Then I realized what he'd said. He hadn't even known I had the *Allegra* case tucked in my shirt when he hit me. When he was dragging me onto the path, he must have been surprised in the act by Luke and Grace and not noticed the case falling out.

"You killed Angel?" I said, trying to sound surprised.

"In point of fact, no. She hit her head—" He broke off, as if irritated at having to even think about it. "It was an accident."

"What do you mean, an accident?"

"Never mind that now. Let's go back to the cabin."

"The cabin?" I asked, wondering what unspeakable things this madman had in mind for me. "I'm not going anywhere until you tell me what happened to Angel."

His smile was cruel, the charm a mere memory. He seemed confident in the power he had over me.

Turning the *Allegra* case over in his hands, he said, "I suppose there's time. The truth is, Angel and I had been seeing each other. I struck up a conversation with her in a bar in Seattle. McCoy's. She was looking, you know? On the prowl." He laughed. "Angel was easy pickings. She'd been alone for a long time, I guess. So long, she'd closed all up. Shit, I couldn't even pry her legs apart at first."

Rage filled me. "So Angel came on to you," I barely managed to say.

"You don't believe it?" Gabe's voice was almost taunting. "She was all over me. Wanted to meet my family, my friends—like we really had something going. Stupid bitch."

I wanted to kill him. My hands were itching to be around his throat and it was all I could do to restrain myself. "How did you know she had something to do with this?" I said.

"She was with you in McCoy's when you told Mike Murty and the others that you had something on them. It would figure you'd tell her more than you told us. It just became a matter, then, of getting it out of her."

"How did that lead to finding me at Thornberry?"

"Think about it. You called Angel's office and left a message and the number for Thornberry with her secretary. When I picked up Angel for lunch that day, I saw the message on her desk. I made up some excuse why I wouldn't be around for a few days, so I could come to the island to find you. When I got here I found a cabin with a For Sale sign on it, and decided it would be a good cover to pretend I had bought it. Not ten minutes after I got here, though, Angel showed up on the doorstep. She had seen through my excuse to be away and had followed me here. Stupid bitch was on to me all the time."

Poor Angel. She'd put her life in this monster's hands, to help me. "What happened? What did you do to her?" I asked softly.

"I decided that since she knew why I was here, I might as well try to make her tell me where the evidence was."

"But you killed her, for God's sake! How could she tell you anything, dead?"

"I told you, it was an accident. She kicked me, and I hit her. I didn't mean to, believe me. I wanted her alive. She'd have told me where that damn evidence was before the night was out. But when I hit her, the chair fell over and she struck her head."

"What do you mean *the chair* fell over?"

"God, you are dumb! I had tied her to a chair to ask her some questions."

"You tied Angel to a chair?" Images of my friend suffering that way burned into my brain. "For how long?"

"I don't know, a few hours. A day, maybe."

"A day. And all this time you were doing *what* to her?"

"Nothing. I told you, just trying to get her—" He shook his head. "Like I said, the woman was a stupid bitch."

"Smart enough to follow you here," I couldn't help saying. "Smart enough to be on to you all the time you thought you were playing her for a fool. But if it hadn't happened that way, you'd have killed her anyway, right? You couldn't set her free to file charges against you back in Seattle. Any more than you can leave me alive now."

He shrugged.

"So you buried her in the woods by your cabin, thinking she'd never be found. But then the quake last night uncovered her."

"So you did find that. I figured as much."

"And Jane? Was she an accident, too?"

"No, but I didn't plan to kill her. I had found the cell phone in Luke's cabin. Since mine had been ruined in the quake, I hadn't been able to call the mainland to check in. I didn't want to tip my hand yet, so I planned to use his phone, then put it back. I took it into the woods to make sure Luke wouldn't catch me using it in his cabin, but Jane came around the bend just as I was dialing out. Man, you should have seen her face when she realized I had a cell phone! That woman freaked—she fought me for it, but since I hadn't found the evidence yet, I couldn't have her calling someone to rescue us.''

"So you killed her.''

"It was more like we had a scuffle.''

He lifted the *Allegra* case up and showed it to me. "And now, my little Sarah, speaking of finding the evidence...I've got things to do, like getting off this shitty island.'' He reached for me.

"I don't think so,'' I said. Stepping back, I said clearly, "It's time.''

Dana and Kim stepped out into the clearing. Gabe turned to look at them, surprise on his face. Grace moved quickly behind him and, using the same walking stick that I'd hit him with the night he'd first appeared at the farmhouse kitchen door, swung without hesitation, connecting to the side of his skull. Dazed, Gabe raised his hands to his head and fell to his knees.

In a second, we were on him.

Grace knelt on his back and pulled his arms above his head, grinding them into the earth. The women had hidden our backpacks in the Ghost Tree, and I reached for mine and dumped it out. Kim pulled a length of garden wire from the pile; she cuffed Gabe's wrists with it. Dana and I took his legs, and the four of us flipped him over onto his back.

Kim sat on him, holding the point of an ice pick at his neck. I dumped the contents of the other two backpacks, and from the pile we picked up wooden garden stakes and two hammers. With the hammers, Grace and I pounded the stakes deep into the ground at three-foot intervals, two above Gabe for his hands, two at his feet. Grace uncuffed his wrists while we all held him down. Then she tied each wrist to a stake, while I tied his ankles to the other two.

It took less than two minutes to have him secured, spread-eagled on the ground.

It had been Grace's idea, but Dana had added the details. An old Indian trick, she said—aloud, now, for Gabe's benefit. "Except that they staked their enemy out on the desert in the hot sun and left him to be feasted on by ants and hawks. It'll be different for you, Gabe. Eventually, hunger will eat away at your insides, and thirst will close up your throat so much, you won't even be able to talk anymore."

She laughed. "Imagine—Gabe without the silver tongue. You might lose that charming grin, too."

"It's supposed to be a nice day, today," Kim said, as if commenting to a friend on the weather. "Sunny and hot. That should help."

Gabe had been too stunned in the first moments to fight us off. That had given us the advantage. Now, as understanding set in, he began to struggle to get free.

"For God's sake, stop this!" he yelled. "Let me up! Have you all gone mad?"

He was probably closer to the truth than he realized.

I, for one, wanted to drive one of those stakes through his heart. And when I looked at Grace, the expression on her face terrified even me. I didn't give Gabe Rossi a snowball's chance in hell of coming out of this alive. And he knew it.

Which was all to the good. We wanted him to suffer fear. A loss of power. The same kinds of torture Angel and Jane must have suffered—and Ramon, Grace's brother.

Beyond that, he had used us. He had played us, conned us into trusting him. We felt foolish and angry. We wanted revenge.

But only a minor revenge. A full day in the woods when he couldn't move in any direction, when he would lie there naked and vulnerable, with time to think about his sins. A day with the turkey vultures overhead.

In the morning we would let him up, then hold him prisoner in Luke's cabin until a rescue team arrived. We'd turn him over to the law.

But we weren't finished with him yet.

Grace began the ritual. Taking a sharp, gleaming pair of kitchen shears from the pile of objects we'd brought with us, she knelt on Gabe's chest again and held them to his face—taunting him with her power to do anything she wanted with them. Then, in a swift sudden motion, she raised them and swung them down toward his chest.

His scream gave me chills, and along with that, a cool, clear sense of satisfaction at seeing his terror. The only problem, for me, was that it didn't last long enough.

When Gabe realized the scissors had paused an inch above his chest, he looked down to see what Grace was doing. She laughed in his face. "You didn't think you'd get off all that easy, did you? Shit, we want you alive.''

She began to cut his shirt away. Dana shoved it aside so that his entire chest was naked. Her face was bland, expressionless, as his skin pumped and jerked with fright beneath her fingers. She looked as she had when playing the drums the other night, as if she'd gone to another plane.

Grace cut the sleeves of Gabe's shirt, and Dana shoved them aside, too. Grace then handed the scissors to me, and I began on his jeans. I stopped when his groin area was uncovered, and handed the scissors to Kim—who held them a moment too long over Gabe's penis. If we all hadn't been there, I had a feeling she might have cut it off.

Gabe thought she was going to. His naked stomach clutched, the muscles cramping. His face turned white. "No, no, please don't! Don't do that," he whimpered.

I took even more satisfaction in the whimper than I had in the scream, wishing only that I'd caused it myself.

Kim laughed. "Funny," she said to him, "that's exactly what I said when you were touching me in the cabin yesterday, remember?" She moved the scissors closer, until the blades were touching him.

"Go ahead," Grace said. "*Do* it."

Kim looked at her. "Should I?"

Grace nodded. "*Do* it! Or I will." She grabbed for the shears.

"No!" Gabe screamed.

Grace laughed. Kim did, too.

By this time every stitch of his clothing had been snipped away. Gabe had little power left, and what he tried to use in his struggles evaporated with one look at his withering manhood.

I wished for the nerve to kill him. I wanted to. But when I really thought about it, he just didn't seem worth it. Instead, I picked up the *Allegra* case from the ground and stuffed it into the belt of my jeans, turning my back on his disgusting face.

We left him there, staked to the ground. We told him to have a "nice night"—provided he survived the night, we added.

Mad witches, we were, over a bubbling cauldron of hate. If I were defending the four of us in court, I thought at one point, I'd probably win hands down with an insanity plea.

# 20

Later that night, I woke and thought I'd heard something—a distant popping noise. I even thought sleepily that it sounded like a gunshot, but since none of us had a gun, or at least that's what I believed at the time, I shrugged it off as a clap of thunder and went back to sleep. Lightning had been streaking the sky all night, and before turning in I had discussed with Grace, Dana and Kim how that might be affecting Gabe. Kim had laughed bitterly and said maybe he'd be struck dead. But none of us believed it. Not in our hearts.

That's the thought I cling to, even now. *We didn't believe it in our hearts.* And though that may not carry much weight with the cold, hard rule of law, it comforted us to think we were doing nothing *really* wrong. That it was just a bit of emotional payback, and we'd release Gabe the next morning, lock him up until the authorities arrived, and all would be well.

It was sometime before dawn that I woke and heard someone open the kitchen door and slip silently into the room. I didn't move, except to pull my blanket down just enough to see who it was.

Grace stood over the woodstove. The embers had partly died down, but there was enough reddish hue left to show that her face was pale and distraught. Her hands, as she held them over the heat, were shaking.

"Grace?" I whispered. "What's wrong?"

She gave me a look through eyes that were wide and black in their sockets, like coals. I asked her again what was wrong, but she didn't answer. Instead she went to her blanket on the other side of the stove and crawled into it, pulling it over her head.

The next morning, when we went to release Gabe, Grace stayed behind. She still hadn't spoken, and in fact had withdrawn from us all. We didn't press her. We told her it was all right, we'd go alone. We understood.

But none of us really understood. Of the four of us, we had thought Grace would be the one to want to taunt Gabe the most. Closure, as Luke had said, for what had happened to her brother.

On the way, we saw helicopters circling overhead. They were looking for the best place for boats to land, we surmised, and with a little luck we'd be out of here and back to Seattle by noon. Luke had left for the shore, hoping to direct the landing to a clearing there. Timmy and Amelia were already packing.

When we got to the place where we had left Gabe, however, we stopped short in our tracks. Shock waves overtook us, every bit as strong as those from the quake.

Gabe was dead, a bullet hole through his head.

After the initial moments of disbelief, we agreed that it was clear Grace had done it. We didn't know how she'd come up with a gun, but, as an ex-cop, she could have had one all along. That decided, we didn't even discuss it further. Instead, we started removing traces of anything that might even remotely have fingerprints or DNA on it. To do this was my idea. But no one objected.

Thus we covered for Grace, of all people. The one woman none of us had liked. We covered for her because we all knew we were just as guilty of Gabe's death. We'd all put him in a position where he'd been unable to defend himself in those final moments.

When the rescuers arrived, we didn't tell them about Gabe, but let them find him like that. The San Juan sheriff's office was called, and the sheriff himself came. He questioned us, but none of us had anything to say.

The investigators searched the crime scene, but didn't find the murder weapon. They did find Jane. And Angel. There was talk of taking us all in, even Timmy and Amelia. Of running tests and taking fingerprints. There would be a thorough investigation of the crime scene. A thorough investigation of all of us—including Dana and Kim, who both had secrets that, if they came out, could destroy their lives.

I couldn't let them go through that. Nor could I let Timmy and Amelia be put through that sort of thing. Not when they had been drawn into all this because of me. So I did what I had to do. I "confessed." I said I'd killed Gabe out of rage when I found out he was in cahoots with the same cops who'd set me up on drug charges, and who then killed both Jane and Angel.

The San Juan sheriff was skeptical. He wondered how I'd managed to take on a man Gabe's size alone.

"I took him by surprise," I said, "and knocked him unconscious. That's what he told me he did to Jane. It seemed fitting."

They couldn't budge me from my story, and every-

one else remained silent, as I'd asked them to. "I'll
work it out," I told them. "Don't worry, I'll be fine."

Whether I would be or not was debatable. But I had
to convince them. I couldn't have anyone else hurt
because of me.

In the end, the sheriff let the other women go, pending further investigation.

Ian had come with the rescuers, and he tried to take
care of me. He talked to the San Juan sheriff and asked
him to go easy on me. He was solicitous, almost like
the old Ian, hovering over me and trying to stand between me and everyone else. He didn't even like me
talking to the other women, once I'd been arrested.
Reminding me of my rights, he said, "Don't talk to
*anyone at all.* You never know who might turn up in
court and testify to something that could make you
look bad."

He was right. I knew that, and I followed his advice.

As the sheriff loaded me into the chopper to take
me to Friday Harbor and the San Juan County jail, I
looked back to see Luke standing with his cell phone
in hand, talking to someone who'd come in with the
rescue team. He hadn't been around much since the
rescue team had arrived. Now, he looked up once as
the chopper lifted into the air. I tried to read his expression, but it was blank. It seemed he pointed to his
cell phone, but I couldn't be sure. I didn't know if he
was sending a message to me, or to someone else.

The women were all there, however—Timmy, Amelia, Dana, Grace and Kim. Holding hands, they had
gathered together to say goodbye. Tears came to my
eyes. To think I'd wanted, at one time, to separate
myself from them, have nothing more to do with them.
Catastrophe had indeed made bedfellows of us all.

# PART IV

# THE ARREST

# 21

SARAH LANSING
*Seattle, WA*
*May 5*

I sit at my father's desk, in my parents' home, tying up loose ends in this journal. They don't come easily, as I'm tired and worn after hours of sweeping broken shards of glass and china from the floors of my parents' home. Some of the larger pieces of furniture are not where they used to be—as if the earthquake had given them feet to choose a new location. But the house is mostly sound. Certain areas of Seattle were hit worse than others, and I was relieved to find that our neighborhood was one of the lucky ones. A generator my father had installed during the Y2K hype provides enough electricity to run the bare necessities, one of which I consider to be my computer.

I still have a book to write—and this account of the happenings at Thornberry to bring to an end.

The words that come foremost to my mind are: *Gather...gathering...gathered.* For my own solace, and largely to sort things out, I write of the way we all came together, of what we did. Every night I obliterate what I've written, in fear of having my work confiscated by the police. Days, my fingers hover over

the keyboard, ever ready to hit the delete key in the
event that what passes for the law should show up
unexpectedly at my door. What we women did at
Thornberry can never come to light.

It has been two weeks since that last day at Thornberry, and we have talked it through and through—
Dana, Kim, Grace and I. We have told ourselves so
many things: We didn't think anything would happen
to Gabe. We only wanted to scare him. Teach him a
lesson. Then we'd turn him over to the law.

We have also admitted that in our hearts, none of
us believed the law would do enough to him. He
would never suffer. Not the way we'd wanted him to.

So we did what we did. We were all guilty of intent, the women kept saying—to which I could only
reply that I was the most to blame. I was the one
who'd spent her life practicing law. Upholding justice. For that reason, more than any other, I insisted
that no one else come forward.

Why open a can of worms and shine the light of
guilt on the others? If nothing else, we had to protect
Timmy and Amelia. They'd had no part in our crime,
but suspicion would surely be cast upon them.

I did ask Grace, yesterday, to tell the truth, just to
me. She insisted over and over that she did not kill
Gabe. She had found him there dead, she said. She
had woken in the night and thought she'd heard a
shot. She didn't want to wake anyone else, so she
went out alone to investigate.

To be honest, she added, she thought I had done
it. *She* was keeping silent for *me*. "I figured it was
the least I could do, since I didn't protect you very
well back there."

Oddly enough, I finally believed her, and that's

when cold hard reality set in: I knew someone else had killed Gabe. But who else had motive and opportunity? Who else on the island had a gun?

Any of the women, possibly. I just didn't really believe it.

Luke, then? I'd only talked with him a few times since the day I got into that chopper. I knew he was staying in Seattle awhile, and that he was still hanging around with Grace. This was something she had told me, while reassuring me that there was nothing intimate between them anymore.

I believed her about that, too. Grace had softened somewhat since Thornberry, but she didn't seem interested in anything now except getting her old job back in New York. She would be going home in a week or so, she said.

Once I believed Grace to be innocent, I started writing down everything that had happened, in my journal, at night, while working on my book during the day. I thought I might be able to reach some logical conclusion if I wrote it out just as I would notes for court.

Amazingly, it worked. Putting all the parts together on paper like that, a lot of things have become clear this past week. Clues rose to the surface that I might not have thought about, otherwise. Clues that had become lost in the worry and anxiety over the quake and everything that followed at Thornberry.

I finally knew—or thought I knew—who killed Gabe.

I was working on this when Ian called last night. Could he come over and talk? he wanted to know. It was important, he said.

I told him yes, but could he wait until tonight because I had a lot of work to do? He reluctantly agreed.

After that I made a few pertinent phone calls.

It is now twenty-four hours later, and Ian is due here at nine tonight. It is 8:40 now, and while I wait I go back to my notes, recalling that before we women left Gabe staked to the ground that day, I had retrieved the *Allegra* case from where he'd dropped it. That night, I'd taken the stockings out of the case and put them, in their plastic bag, in with some dirty laundry I was taking home with me. When I decided to confess the next day, I left them there, and though my luggage was searched for the murder weapon, the stockings must have seemed innocuous to the deputy who did the search. He didn't even take a second look at them. I had some uneasy moments when my possessions were taken from me at the San Juan County jail, but then Ian came to escort me back to Seattle, and my suitcase was returned to me when house arrest was ordered.

Now the stockings are carefully hidden again beneath the corner of carpet where I'd hidden them before going to Thornberry. I have lived with the fear that the Five, who are still uncharged, could come to this house any day with a search warrant, find them and take them from me. The one thing that has reassured me somewhat is that the DNA report is still filed away at the laboratory in the East. Without the stockings themselves, Ivy should still be able to bring charges. *If* she ever brings charges. Lately, I've been thinking she needs a bit of a boost.

I check the clock on the mantel of the fireplace that stands between my father's two mahogany bookcases. It tells me it's 8:50. The ankle cuff rubs against my skin, reminding me of my lack of freedom and how I could lose it forever if things don't work out tonight as I've planned. I take a sip of water and close my eyes briefly, gathering my strength.

The doorbell rings, and I realize ten minutes have passed. Going into the center hallway, I open the door, letting Ian in. I take him into the living room, away from my work, away from the notes, away from Lonnie Mae's evidence. I want nothing tonight to remind him that I'm working things out for myself.

Ian is sharp, however. He glances into my father's study as we pass it, sees the light on at the desk, and guesses at what I've been doing.

"Been working hard?" he asks.

"Oh, just a bit. Still have a book to write, you know." I smile.

"Have you come up with anything about the murder on the island? Any way to clear your name, that is?"

"I've been giving it some thought," I say noncommittally.

"You've been pretty closed-mouthed about what really happened out there in the forest," Ian says, taking a seat on the couch and leaning back, relaxing. "Wouldn't it help you to talk about it?"

"It might," I say, sitting in a chair across from him. "I just don't know where to begin."

"Well, why not begin with how many of you really participated in the crime?" he says.

"Ian, I told you—I told everybody—I was the only one."

He shakes his head. "Sarah, c'mon. Nobody actually believed that. They just didn't have any proof that you'd had help. You did have help, though—

didn't you? You couldn't possibly have done all that on your own.''

''A woman filled with rage can do a lot of things,'' I observe. ''Once the adrenaline starts flowing, an almost superhuman power takes over.''

''There were footprints in the forest grasses,'' he points out. ''More than one set. The San Juan sheriff says he's certain there was more than one of you.''

''I know,'' I say. ''I heard that yesterday. That's why I was pretty sure I'd be hearing from you, Ian. What is it you want from me?''

He sits forward, leaning his arms on his knees. ''Sarah, I've been charged with finding out what really happened on that island and how it relates to the Seattle Five. I need to know if any of the other women know about the Five. If Gabe Rossi told them anything, that is. He might have let something slip that will help us put them away. Also…I understand you have a certain piece of evidence that could be used to incriminate the Five.''

''Did Ivy tell you this?'' I ask.

The small flicker of surprise on his face tells me otherwise. ''Ivy? You mean, Ivy O'Day? No. Why, Sarah? Have you talked to her?''

I wave a hand as if to clear my mind. ''Oh, Ian. There are so many people I've talked to, I can hardly remember them all.''

He looks uneasy. ''You haven't given anyone this evidence, have you? What did you do with it?''

''Given it to anyone? Good lord, no. I hid it inside a tree near where Gabe died,'' I say. ''Don't worry, it's still there.''

''A *tree?* You hid it in a tree?'' He runs his fingers

through his hair. "Dammit, Sarah, there are a hell of a lot of trees near where Gabe died!"

"Not like that one. It's called the Ghost Tree. It's huge and hollow, big enough for a person to sit inside. Big enough for just about anything—including a piece of evidence—to be hidden inside it and not found for hundreds of years."

Ian studies my face as if trying to unveil the lie. "Sarah, are you absolutely sure that's where you hid it?"

"Of course, I'm sure," I say. "I wouldn't forget something that important."

"And you're absolutely sure it's solid evidence? It could convict the Five?"

"Ian, for heaven's sake! It's a piece of Lonnie Mae Brown's clothing. A pair of stockings they didn't bother to remove before they raped her. And it's loaded with the Five's DNA."

With an irritable wave of his arm, he stands. "That settles it, then. I'm going back out to that island."

"Now?"

"Yes, now."

"Why bother?" I say. "Ian, it's late. Let's just call the San Juan sheriff. I'm sure once you explain about it to him, he'll be glad to retrieve it and hold on to it for you till morning. After all, it's not going anywhere."

He hesitates. "True. But we've waited too long for this already. The sooner that evidence is in safe hands, the better off we are."

I decide to end the game. "Who do you mean by *we*, Ian? You and the Seattle Five? Oh, wait, I forgot, with Gabe that makes it the Seattle Six, and then with you... What is it really, Ian, the Seattle Seven? Or are there even more of you in on this?''

He stares at me. ''What are you talking about? I told you, I'm working to put the Five away. I'm one of the good guys—not the bad.''

I laugh slightly. ''You know, old friend, I would love to believe that. But guess what? Luke's cell phone has a feature that shows the last ten numbers dialed from it, and that day the rescue team came to Esme he checked those numbers on a hunch. Your home number was one of the last ten dialed, Ian. Luke told me yesterday that *he* didn't call you. And the only other person who knew about Luke's cell phone, other than me, was Gabe.''

''But that's crazy! For God's sake, if Luke said that he's lying. He's covering for himself, Sarah. Use your head. I never got any calls from Gabe Rossi. I didn't even know the man.''

''Sorry, Ian. Nice try, but it's not going to fly. Luke checked with his cell company, and the time the call was made to you is the same time Gabe admitted using the phone to 'check in,' as he put it. The same time Jane was murdered, in fact. And Luke was with me then.''

''Sarah, a call may have been made to my number, but I certainly didn't talk to anybody. I don't know why Gabe Rossi would have called me.''

I stand and face him, folding my arms. ''Give it up, Ian. It's only a matter of time before they have all the proof they need. See, we're already pretty sure we know what happened on Esme Island. It was you who killed Gabe, wasn't it? He really was your partner—but in crime, not as a cop. You got on the island early somehow, in the middle of the night, and shot him.''

When he starts to protest, I cut in. ''It had to be you, Ian. You were the only one even remotely involved in all this who had a gun—a gun that wasn't even questioned the next morning, because you were a cop. You killed Gabe, and then you met up with the rescue team and acted like it was the first time you'd been on Esme. The only thing I can't figure out is why you shot him. Why did Gabe have to die?''

Ian begins to speak, then pauses. He takes a few steps toward the big living room bay window, which is cracked and being repaired. Parts of it are temporarily covered by brown paper. Ian puts his hands in his pockets, and rocks back and forth on his heels.

''Who else knows about this little theory of yours?'' he says softly.

''Just me and Luke,'' I answer. ''Look, don't make this any harder than it is. Don't make me turn you in.''

He turns toward me and smiles weakly. ''This isn't about me, Sarah. There are other considerations. I wasn't there when they raped that woman, but I've worked with those guys for years. There are…things that might come out if I don't help get them off.''

''I'm sorry,'' I say.

His eyes close briefly. ''So, Sarah. Where's the evidence?''

''I told you where it was.''

He seems almost sad for a moment, then takes a deep breath and walks over to the curtains. He takes a knife from the inside pocket of his jacket, opens it, and begins to cut off a section of draw-cord.

''What are you doing?'' I say.

"I need to go get that evidence—but I can't trust that you told me the truth about where it is. Sorry, Sarah. I've got to make sure you don't talk to anyone, while I go look."

He closes the knife, puts it back in his pocket, and starts toward me with a large section of the cord in his hands.

"You don't have to do that," I argue, backing off. "You could just take me with you."

"I don't think so. That cuff on your ankle would go off the second we walked out the door. Clever of you to think of that, though."

He reaches for me.

"You can't do this," I say, easing back toward the door. "Luke knows about you. He'll figure out what you've done and he'll come after you."

He shakes his head. "Who cares? Nobody will listen. Not when they find the gun that killed Gabe in Luke's hotel room."

My eyes widen. "Are you saying you've done that? You've planted the gun in Luke's room?"

"It seemed fitting," Ian says.

"Fitting. You mean, because it's the same way you planted drugs in my apartment?"

His eyes meet mine. "The same way certain friends of mine, shall we say, planted those drugs in your apartment."

"So it was you who gave the orders to set me up. Funny, I didn't even see it at first. I guess I had to get out of the forest to see the trees."

"You were getting out of hand, Sarah. You never should have gone after good cops like the Five. They were only doing their jobs."

"Doing their jobs! You call rape 'doing their jobs'?

And what about Gabe? Was he only doing his job? Then, why kill him?"

He smiles. "Ah, yes, Gabe. Well, about that you were right, Sarah. I did get onto Esme in the middle of the night. Once I heard they were getting a rescue team together for you, I flew into Orcas and paid a local fisherman to take me over to Esme in his boat and drop me off. I had planned to meet privately with Gabe, but as I walked up onto the shore I heard a man's voice, yelling. I followed it to where you lovely ladies had staked him out like a butterfly on a wall. He sure was a sorry sight—bugs in his ears and up his nose. Actually—" Ian smiles "—it was almost funny."

I smile, too, just to let him know I'm with him.

"Anyway, he admitted he had told you everything, Sarah—everything except my involvement, that is. He said you were coming back in the morning to let him go. I couldn't trust him to keep his mouth shut about me then."

I take a slow step to the side, closer to the door. "So you're telling me you have no problem killing someone just to keep from being found out, and yet you expect me to just stand here while you tie me up?"

"Sarah," he says, his voice tired and strained, "I don't care whether you stand, sit or lay down, but you *are* going to be tied. Go along with this, and I'll try to be gentle. Put up a fuss, and I'll hurt you. Either way, it's the same."

This time he lunges for me, and I spin on my heel and run for the door. It's been my plan to go through it, and I've left the door slightly open, so that when I reach it I can just pull it open and be outside. But halfway across the room my ankle cuff catches on an end table and slows me down. Ian gets to the door before me, slamming it shut, locking it and blocking my path. I know I can't make it around him, so I turn and run back into the living room, my eyes seeking wildly for another escape route. The French doors to the garden, however, are being repaired, and plywood has been nailed over the opening.

Ian is big—big enough to break me in two with one hand, and I realize I am trapped, with no kind of weapon and little ability to fight him off. Only one thing left to do—and I do it. Running full force into the big bay window, I crash through paper and glass, my arms covering my face. Landing on the ground, I feel pain in my elbows, face and knees. I can hear Ian coming through the window behind me, and I scramble up and run across the front lawn.

Before I can get to the street, Ian grabs me from behind with an arm around my waist. With his other hand he wraps the draw-cord around my neck. He begins to pull it taut, cutting off my breathing. My chest heaves as it tries vainly to replenish the oxygen I used up while running.

"Damn you, Sarah," Ian says savagely into my ear. "Now you've done it. The signal from that cuff of yours will have this place crawling with cops in minutes." He yanks harder on the cord. "I guess I won't be tying you up after all, sweetheart. I sure hope that evidence is where you said it was."

As if to emphasize his words, I feel the sharp, thin line pulled even tighter.

Then I see Grace out of the corner of my eye. She's about five feet away, to our left, her legs spread in a stance a little wider than her shoulders, both arms extended toward us with her hands together. In the next instant I see a flash of fire, and hear a loud *snap*. I feel Ian's body jerk violently against me, as the bullet takes him down.

Luke is suddenly at my side, putting his arms around me. "Thank God you're all right," he says. He runs his fingers through my hair and draws me to him. Grace comes over and puts a hand on Ian's throat, feeling for a pulse.

"Still alive," she says.

Police cars begin to arrive. Cops get out, their guns drawn.

When the cops see Ian lying on the ground, I fear they might shoot all of us, right on the spot. But then Joe Pinkowski, Ian's captain, arrives, yelling for them to back off. Joe, I learned yesterday, has been biding his time for months, helping Internal Affairs to gather enough evidence against Ian.

"Did you get it?" I ask Pinkowski.

"We got it all, thanks to you," he says, nodding to a nondescript van down the street. "It's all on tape, and we even had a link to the prosecutor's office. Ivy O'Day and the prosecutor heard him confess. They heard everything."

Luke is picking splinters of glass out of my hair. "Dammit, Sarah, I knew we should have hidden somewhere inside, rather than around the corner. What if we hadn't gotten here in time?"

"It would never have worked," I say, shaking my head. "He'd have known you were there."

"She's right," Pinkowski says. "The van was risky enough."

"Even so…" Luke says, gently wiping blood from my cheek, then my arms, with a handkerchief.

Laughing shakily, I feel my face for cuts. "I guess I never dreamed," I say, "that I'd have to exit through a window."

"There's somebody over there who wants to talk to you," Joe Pinkowski says. He unlocks my ankle cuff and removes it.

I look over at a black sedan that has pulled to the curb. Judge Ford, Luke's father, stands next to it, his thumbs-up reassuring.

Luke puts an arm around my shoulders. "I'll go with you," he says.

We begin to walk toward the car, and a window slides down. My mother sits there, a tremulous smile on her face. "Thank God it's all over," she says, pulling me down for a hug.

# Addendum

SARAH LANSING
*Seattle, WA*
*December 30*

As an addendum to my foregoing notes, I feel sad to have to admit that in the case of the Seattle Five, the real victim—Lonnie Mae Brown—became lost. The media wrote her up as "only" a poor black woman, who made what little money she had as a whore. Women like Lonnie Mae are a dime a dozen on the city streets, the papers implied. They all perform the same services, and are in many ways interchangeable.

That might be true...until you dig down deeper.

I did that. I went looking for Lonnie Mae's children, and I found them, still in foster homes. They had been there for five years. The social services department that had taken them away from her had never been able to find permanent homes for them.

So did they fare better where they were than they would have with their mother? There was no way to know, but they were under a psychiatrist's care. I had a meeting with him, and he told me they hadn't improved much from the first day he'd seen them. They missed their mom, he said.

I told them I'd known their mom, and that she loved them. I don't know how much it helped. But maybe one day they'll remember that, when they need it most.

I've become a CASA in my spare time—a Court Appointed Special Advocate for abused and neglected children. It's a volunteer job, but I managed to get myself assigned to Lonnie Mae's kids, and that makes it worthwhile to put in all those hours without pay. It's my job just to be friends to them, and to stand up for them in court. Tell how much they deserve placement, or to be reunited with a relative. Lonnie Mae's mother showed up one day. She said she'd take them, and she seems to have been a good grandmother, even visiting them in the foster homes, never losing touch. There are some problems, but if I can work them out, I think those kids will be okay.

My "real" job now is working for a commission Judge Ford put together, a group that oversees police conduct. Part of the job is to defend innocent cops. The other part is to see that the guilty ones get put in jail.

Jane's children didn't fare as well as Lonnie Mae's. I looked for them and their father, and learned that the house in Bellevue collapsed and slid down a hill during the quake. Jane's husband's and children's bodies were found in the debris. Jane's body was brought home, and after things settled down I went to the cemetery where all four were buried, and placed Jane's locket on her tombstone. Though my remorse over her death was deep and overwhelming, I could only hope that wherever they were, she and her children were together at last.

I got a postcard from Dana the other day, from

somewhere in Canada. The postmark was smudged so I don't know precisely where she is. She wrote only, "All is well," and added a smile face, which I take to mean that she's with the man she loves and that her husband hasn't been able to find them. Kim Stratton is working on a new film, and in love, according to *Entertainment Tonight.* Now and then we talk, and she told me that the "in love" part is only Hollywood gossip. I doubt she'll ever forget Gabe, or what happened at Thornberry, though she says she's doing her best to move on—as we all are, even though each and every one of us will always live with a certain amount of guilt over our part in Gabe's death.

Timmy and Amelia are building a new writer's colony together on Camano Island, which, though it was closer to Seattle, fared better than the San Juans. The funding, I suspect—though he hasn't talked about it—is coming from Judge Ford. Grace, my old nemesis, has returned to the force in NYC and seems content. Her e-mails to me are snappy and short, but her tone has softened somewhat. She seems to be recovering from the death of her brother, and is working on a special force to weed out bad cops on the NYPD.

As for Ian, he recovered from a bullet in his lung and was honored with a trial of his own. His crimes as head of the renegade cops in Seattle, and especially the murder of Gabe Rossi, were much worse than theirs. He ended up with life—no chance of parole.

Before "the Big One," Seattle had just finished retrofitting all its bridges to withstand as much as a 9.0 quake. The one we had was only a tenth more than that, but a tenth at that level is a lot of power. It had taken most of the bridges down, and the one thing we had to be grateful for was that the *tsunami* generated by the quake had gone to the south, losing most of its power by the time it reached the California coast. Seattle is still recovering, but things are going great. No one can deny the spirit of the people of Seattle, the city leaders, the rescue teams that did such a brave job during those first days after the quake, and yes, the Seattle cops.

Yet we'll never be the same. None of us who went through it will ever go to bed again without wondering if the ground might shake us across the room in the night, nor will some of us ever again take the elevator to the top of the rebuilt Space Needle without wondering if we're taking our lives into our hands. Seeing *Phantom of the Opera* is definitely out. No one wants a chandelier falling on them, real or not.

Ivy O'Day prosecuted the case against the Five, and she did a great job in court. She outlined the DNA, using simplified graphs the jury could understand, and pulled in Barry Scheck to testify about them. He was brilliant. As cofounder of the Innocence Project, he and other lawyers have given much of their personal time to proving, through DNA, that people who've been charged with a crime are innocent. In this case, he was working to help prosecute the guilty. All I had to do was sit there and watch as the net tightened around the Five. Which was a good thing. It hadn't been all that long since I'd taken on a DNA case, but every time a lawyer turns around there's new information. I hadn't exactly had time this past year to keep up.

It helped that the evidence was rock solid. No other five men could have left that sperm on Lonnie Mae's stockings, and her own DNA proved the stockings were hers. When it was clear a conviction was imminent, one of the Five copped a plea and confessed to the Five's hiring an arsonist to torch Lonnie Mae's apartment. He was hoping for a lesser charge, and Ivy promised him one to get him to talk. But the judge who sentenced him wasn't all that lenient. Each of the Seattle Five got life, just like Ian.

It was a tougher sentence than any of them had expected. Not many people are angry enough to go after cops for the rape and murder of a poor black prostitute, who, some might say, "deserved what she got."

I thought of the original words to "Up a Lazy River," the song Gabe had told me about. Seventy years ago when the old jazz clarinetist was writing the words to that tune, defending a murdered black woman—whether she was a prostitute or not—was low on the list of priorities in this country. And while I'll go along with the scholars who say Arodin wasn't a racist, and that it was "normal" to call blacks by the *N* word in those days, I'm glad Hoagy Carmichael came along and rewrote those lyrics. One more epithet bites the dust. I also think it's especially appropriate that Hoagy Carmichael practiced law before he became a full-time songwriter. One day, I'll have to look up some of the cases he handled.

Little by little, drop by drop, things are changing here in America. Maybe there's a whole new slew of bigots out there, who, like the neo-Nazis, want to bring all the ugliness back again. But I'm betting that people who care about freedom in its truest sense won't let them. There are new laws in place every day, and as more and more abuses come to light, the laws will continue to kick in and put the abusers where they belong.

The thing that lifted my spirits most during the trial was that the courtroom was filled to overflowing with Seattle cops. When the jury announced its guilty verdict against the Five, the cops stood up en masse and cheered. No one likes a rotten apple in the barrel, and the Seattle PD had been through a lot in recent years—the World Trade Organization riots, the scandal about the Five, and then the earthquake. Everyone was in a fighting spirit. Everyone wanted to clean things up.

My book came out a few weeks ago, and true to the publisher's predictions, it hit the *New York Times* bestseller list. Now everybody thinks I have answers. I've been invited to go on all the talk shows, tell people how to turn things around.

Hell, I don't have any answers. I just hope my book raises awareness, perhaps inspires conversation among those who are in a position to make changes. I've talked a lot about that with Bill Farley at Seattle Mystery Bookshop. It turned out he was completely innocent of any involvement with the Five, and was simply passing along the invitation Timothea issued to get me to Thornberry.

On a personal note, Luke and I were married a week ago, on Christmas Day. By that time we'd been dating for months, and I couldn't believe I'd ever even questioned his loyalty. Marrying Luke was the only thing, finally, that made good, clear, logical sense. He and I had always looked after each other, first when we were kids, then at Thornberry. I think that to have a man in her life who puts her first, who looks after her at all times—and vice versa—may be the most any woman can ask.

The fact that I love him like crazy—like a seventeen-year-old, in fact—had something to do with my saying yes, as well.

My mother and Judge Ford came as a couple to our wedding. Neither one seems to want to tie the knot a second time, but they've been together a lot since the night Ian was arrested and Mom came home. Luke and I smile at that sometimes, remembering how we had talked about older people losing their husbands or wives and then finding their first loves again, by some quirk of fate. I guess I don't mind too much having been the tool of Fate in this case.

Luke and I have also talked about ourselves. We both know life could get complicated for us. Luke travels a lot for his job, and I'm busy with CASA and my work with the commission. But in this age of tornadoes, hurricanes, quakes, school killings, and who-knows-what's-going-to-happen-next, we have each other, and we intend to keep it that way. Love, after all, is the only lasting thing.

Love, as the poets say, is all there is.

# KAREN HARPER

## SHAKER RUN

Kate Marburn thought she had a new beginning when she found the perfect job as a rose gardener for wealthy widow Sarah Denbigh. When Sarah dies under mysterious circumstances, leaving Kate heir to a fortune in Shaker furniture, the police suspect Kate was involved.

Looking for refuge again, Kate accepts a job at Shaker Run, an historic and once celibate Shaker village. But something strange and dangerous is going on beneath the flawless exterior of the idyllic town. After Kate turns to Jack Kilcourse, a nearby resident, for help, she begins to wonder about his motives.

Kate's dream job could become her worst nightmare....

*Available May 2001 wherever paperbacks are sold!*

# MEG O'BRIEN

66586 SACRED TRUST ___ $5.99 U.S. ___ $6.99 CAN.
66516 CRASHING DOWN ___ $5.99 U.S. ___ $6.99 CAN.

*(limited quantities available)*

| | |
|---|---|
| TOTAL AMOUNT | $_____ |
| POSTAGE & HANDLING | $_____ |
| ($1.00 for one book; 50¢ for each additional) | |
| APPLICABLE TAXES* | $_____ |
| <u>TOTAL PAYABLE</u> | $_____ |

(check or money order—please do not send cash)

---

To order, complete this form and send it, along with a check or money order for the total above, payable to MIRA Books®, to: **In the U.S.:** 3010 Walden Avenue, P.O. Box 9077, Buffalo, NY 14269-9077; **In Canada:** P.O. Box 636, Fort Erie, Ontario, L2A 5X3.

Name:_____

Address:_____ City:_____

State/Prov.:_____ Zip/Postal Code:_____

Account Number (if applicable):_____
075 CSAS

*New York residents remit applicable sales taxes.
Canadian residents remit applicable GST and provincial taxes.

**MIRA®**